From the Moment We Met

A St. Helena Vineyard Novel

Also in Marina Adair's St. Helena Vineyard Series

Kissing Under the Mistletoe
Summer in Napa
Autumn in the Vineyard
Be Mine Forever

From the Moment We Met

A St. Helena Vineyard Novel

MARINA ADAIR

This is a work of fiction. Names, characters, organizations, places, events, and incidents are either products of the author's imagination or are used fictitiously.

Published by Montlake Romance, Seattle

www.apub.com

ISBN-13: 9781477823590
ISBN-10: 147782359X

Cover design by Kerrie Robertson

Library of Congress Control Number: 2014901089

Printed in the United States of America

To Jill Marsal

I hope that every girl is lucky enough to

find an agent and friend like you.

Thank you for your endless support, your willingness to listen to every single one of my ideas—even the bad ones—and cheering me on every step of the way. Without you this series never would have existed.

CHAPTER 1

Most women spend an average of 150 hours fantasizing and dreaming about the perfect wedding. Not Abigail DeLuca. Nope, she'd spent the past seven years planning the perfect divorce, which as of—she glanced at her watch—eight hours ago had finally been granted. And nobody was going to ruin her first day as a happy divorcée.

Nobody, she thought grimly after the doorbell rang and she opened the front door to find a bear of a man in grease-stained coveralls standing on her front porch. The man pulled his Rodney's Recovery, Repossession & Party Rentals trucker hat low on his forehead and flashed a copy of Abby's marriage certificate. "Are you Abigail Moretti, wife of Richard Moretti?"

Abby realized she had to amend her previous statement that nobody could ruin her Divorce Day, because there was one person who could ruin it—her pencil dick of a two-timing ex.

"Ex-wife. As of today," she clarified, pulling her robe tighter. Her new, silky blue robe that did amazing things to her skin—and her cleavage. She'd bought it specifically to wear today, wanting a perky start to her new life. A bold and confident start. None of which included coming face-to-face with Rodney. "And my name is DeLuca. Abigail DeLuca."

She'd stopped going by Moretti the day she discovered that Richard's favorite pastime during intern season was playing hide the salami.

"Abby?" A weathered voice called out from over the picket fence that separated her property from the busiest busybody and gossip in St. Helena, save her Nonna ChiChi. "Is everything all right?"

"Yes, Mrs. Kincaid. Just getting the morning paper."

"Well, you might want to invite your gentleman friend inside before tongues start wagging," Nora chided, peering over the fence. "This is a respectable neighborhood."

Nora was the self-appointed neighborhood watch commissioner of the cul-de-sac and Krug Court, and took her job seriously. She meticulously chronicled her neighbors' comings and goings, being sure to report any odd findings to the community Facebook page. Even issuing citations for infringement of the Good Neighbor Code.

Nora had been looking for a reason to cite Abby ever since the St. Helena *Sentinel* ran an article stating that Abby's dahlias were the best summer bloom in town—a golden stamp of approval that resulted in the upstaging of Mrs. Kincaid's royal crown magnolia tree.

"He's not my gentleman friend," Abby clarified, and because she was raised in a house where being rude to one's elders was considered sacrilege, she refrained from pointing out that spying on thy neighbor was also not a respectable hobby.

"If you say so." Nora sounded unconvinced. "It would be a shame if the neighborhood became a drive-thru for the town's bachelors."

Nora would actually be ecstatic if that happened, because she'd capture each and every transgression on film and post it on Facebook.

Not that there would be any transgressions of the male variety. Abby was finally single, and she meant to keep it that way.

So with a polite smile, she said, "And he was just leaving."

Only Rodney didn't budge.

Raising a brow, Abby reached for the door handle and—as though anticipating her next move, which was to disappear back inside her house, pull the curtains, and toast her D-day with a mimosa—he took a step forward. And wasn't that just like a man: self-centered, domineering, and, even though he was the one who was crapping all over her good morning, determined to be heard.

Abby took in the receding hairline, the frown marks, and the cab of the flatbed tow truck peeking out from behind Nora's enormous manicured shrubs—her gaze landing on the *Repossess* part of his title—and rolled her eyes. "If you're here to repossess Richard's car, you wasted your time, because like I explained only seconds ago, Richard is not here."

Nor was he her problem anymore.

"So if you'll excuse me, I have to get ready for an appointment." Which was not until later that afternoon. But standing on the front porch in her sexy robe, talking to a strange man, where her neighbors idly placed bets on whether he was the first post-D-day walk-of-shamer, was not her idea of easing into respectable singlehood.

"I'll make it quick then. The name's Rodney, of Rodney's Recovery, Repossession & Party Rentals." He pointed to the logo on the front of his hat as though that was all the identification required, and extended a newspaper clipping. "I need to confirm if you are the Abigail Moretti, uh, the Abigail who placed this ad in the local paper."

Abby's face heated as she looked at the full-page ad from the *Sentinel.* It was a copy dating from last summer, boasting a missing persons announcement with a photo of Richard that had been taken on their wedding day. He was dressed in a tux, looking handsome and faithful and like a man in love. Abby nearly snorted.

"Yes, I was trying to locate my estranged husband so that I could"—she paused, her face heating again, but this time with anger—"Wait. Don't tell me that the son of a bitch is trying to sue me for defamation of character? It was an ad. That I had to take out because he refused to show his cheating face so I could serve him with divorce papers."

Richard had successfully managed to elude her, her family, and the law for the past seven years. By Abby placing the ad, which qualified as a divorce by publication, Richard had six months to come forward, otherwise the divorce would be granted.

Richard hadn't come forward, which meant the divorce was granted today.

Rodney raised a brow. "The headline reads, HAVE YOU SEEN MY DICK?"

"It was the question of the hour for women everywhere, I assure you."

"I'll take that as a yes, you are Abigail Moretti, who married Richard Moretti in St. Helena, California, eight years ago."

When Abby only crossed her arms, Rodney gave a decisive nod. Turning around, he waved his hand, signaling—signaling to who, Abby had no idea, but her stomach sank all the same when he hollered, "Bring it on in. This is the right house."

Before Abby could process what was happening, a loud beeping echoed throughout the cul-de-sac, announcing the ginormous truck backing up—right over her lawn, crushing the garden bunny one of her piano students had painted for her, and straight through the center of her dahlia garden. Her beautiful dahlias that she'd planted and nurtured into a masterpiece of horticulture supremeness.

It was the centerpiece of her yard. Hell, it was the centerpiece of the whole damn neighborhood.

"What are you doing?" Abby raced down the steps, waving a signal of her own. "Stop!"

"Sorry, but we only get paid if we make the delivery as per the instructions. And we had some pretty specific instructions on this here delivery."

"But my dahlias!"

Rodney at least had the decency to look apologetic, but the truck didn't stop, not until it had torn up a good half of her lawn and smashed every last bloom in her garden. Then the beeping became more alarming as the open flatbed of the truck lifted—and that was when Abby knew officially, without a doubt, that there couldn't possibly be lower scum on the entire planet than Richard.

Before she could say a word or throw herself in front of the oncoming disaster that was quickly becoming her life, a nude, Adonis-inspired statue slid down the ramp of the truck, landing gracefully on her lawn with a small thud.

"Oh my," Nora sighed with an expression of sheer appreciation. "Isn't that an eyeful?"

Eyeful indeed. Standing well over six feet tall, and except for the embellished bulge and generous amount of hair, the marble statue was a spot-on replica of her ex. Even down to the smarmy smile and trademarked wink.

"Impressive, isn't it?" Rodney asked, and Abby realized she was staring.

"I'll say." Nora fanned herself while a series of impressed grunts came from the two men who exited the delivery truck to take in the sight.

"He wasn't that big," Abby felt the need to point out, then realized how *that* sounded and clarified. "Tall. I meant he wasn't that tall. The man was only five ten. With lifts."

Looking extremely satisfied with himself, Rodney extended a pen and a clipboard. "I need you to sign here, here, and here."

"And I need you to remove that"—Abby waved a hand at the statue—"monstrosity, before I call the cops."

"No can do." Rodney rocked back on his heels. "I got paid for a delivery. It's been delivered."

"Then I'll pay you to deliver it somewhere else."

Mulling over her request, Rodney sized up Abby, then took his time sizing up the statue, finally shaking his head in pure male awe. "You sure? It's a statement maker. Really brings out the character of your yard."

"My yard has plenty of character and *that* is not the kind of statement I want to be making."

"Plus it's in violation of GN Code Twenty-Seven C," Nora said, crossing the lawn and pointing her trimmers at the violation in question. "Garden art can't be more than three feet tall with a base not exceeding half the height, unless it has a water element to it, and then you must get board approval of the fixture."

"Oh, it's got a water feature all right," Rodney explained ever so seriously, raising his hand to rest it on Richard's shoulder. "All Mrs. Moretti's got to do is run a water line to the base and then water shoots out his—"

"There will be no shooting," Abby insisted, her right eye beginning to twitch. "And it's not staying. In fact, I will pay you to deliver it back to where it came from."

She was tired of being manipulated by men. There was no way she'd let Richard weasel his way into her life—not again. She wasn't that lost, heartbroken college student anymore. She was a successful, independent, man-free woman who was in charge of her own destiny and—

Oh. My. God. Abby froze at the sight of a real-life Adonis pounding the pavement—pavement that happened to fall within her neighborhood watch territory. Moving with a confidence and masculine grace that was far too natural to be manufactured, Jack "Hard Hammer" Tanner, as he had been known in the NFL, was 100 percent pure, unadulterated eye candy—no embellishments needed.

At six foot five and 250 pounds of solid muscle, Jack Tanner was a mountain of testosterone and sculpted male perfection. He was sporting a pair of black jogging shorts slung low on his hips, a San Francisco 49ers ball cap, and a matching T-shirt that—*sweet baby Jesus*—dangled from his waistband instead of covering his chest, leaving miles of tan torso that made her mouth dry and her palms wet.

Because in true Abby fashion, it wasn't a sweet engineer or reliable bookkeeper who got her hot and bothered. Nope, after seven years without a single flutter of interest, it was NFL legend, football god, and St. Helena's most lickable and available bachelor who had flicked her switch.

And just like her ex-husband, Jack Tanner was responsible for a good portion of the town's female fuses being blown. Which was why she sagged with relief at the sight of him jogging down the cul-de-sac and past her house.

Her premature celebration ended when, as though her morning wasn't complicated enough, Tanner reappeared, slowly walking backward, retracing his steps, and coming to a stop at the curb of her driveway. He took in Shrine de Richard, then his gaze drifted to Abby, pinning her with an amused look before releasing a lethal smile that left more than just her hands wet.

Another in a long list of reasons to stay away from him.

"Before we can talk terms," Rodney said, and Abby had to strain to understand him over the blood pounding in her ears, "we have to close out this transaction."

"Fine." Abby grabbed the clipboard and scribbled her name.

A here, here, and here later, she was one step closer to eliminating Richard from her life, and it gave her something to do besides gawk at the way Tanner's muscles played as he jogged up the driveway—straight toward her.

Rodney took the clipboard. "I can get your package—"

"It's not my package," she clarified as Tanner strode up. He didn't talk, just silently situated himself way too close for her to ignore. But she tried her damnedest.

"That signature there says it is." Rodney's meaty finger stabbed at her signature scrawled on the delivery slip. Then he flipped the page and wrote up a new delivery form and handed it to her. "Now, if you want to hire me to ship it back, that's going to cost you nineteen-oh-four, with tax."

"Fine. I'll go get my purse."

"We don't take checks."

"I have cash."

"I don't know if I feel comfortable carrying that much money around on my person," Rodney said, running a greasy hand down the front of his coveralls.

At his comment, Abby looked at the total he'd scribbled on the paper and felt her heart plummet straight to her toes. "You meant *that* nineteen-oh-four. You're going to charge me two grand to return a statue that isn't even mine?"

"You signed for it, right there, so legally it's—"

"Mine. Yeah, yeah," Abby mumbled. "But two grand?"

"You see the size of him," Rodney said, his eyes straying back to Richard's package.

"He wasn't that big!"

"Need any help?" Tanner offered sweetly from beside her.

"Nope, I've got it." Abby squared her shoulders and signed the form.

Last year, she'd set out to get herself a divorce and find living arrangements that didn't include her childhood bed or her nonna as a roommate. Check. And check. This year, she was determined to prove to this town—and herself—that she could stand on her own two feet. Starting today.

And that didn't include a man.

"Do you take credit cards?" Abby asked. She had no idea how she would afford two thousand dollars right now. That added up to *a lot* of piano lessons.

"Yup. Let me call the station and make arrangements." Rodney disappeared into the cab of his truck, leaving Abby alone with Tanner.

"I got to hand it to you, if that's your solution to ward off would-be suitors, it's working, darling." The way he said *darling,* low and husky, felt like an intimate caress. Too bad he was staring at Richard's overembellished ego. "It's enough to give most guys a complex."

"You intimidated, Jack?" she asked, pulling her robe even tighter.

"Nope."

Of course he wasn't. The man was far too capable and accomplished to give in to anything as silly as intimidation. Most people admired that about Tanner. Abby just found it annoying.

Almost as annoying as the way her heart picked up as his gaze took a lazy journey down her body. She revisited the urge to smooth down her hair, just like she resisted the urge to kick him in the shin, when his gaze reached her feet and he chuckled. She didn't need to look down to realize that she was wearing her Godzilla slippers—they were big, green, badass, and growled every time she walked.

"And I'm not just any guy," he said, leaning in until she could smell the clean sweat and male perfection wafting off him. "I'm a Hall of Famer."

Abby glanced at the big Super Bowl ring on his right hand and rolled her eyes. "For most pass receptions in the NFL."

"Yup, I'm in that Hall of Fame too." His lips twitched and so did her thighs.

"What are you doing here?" Because this could not be happening. Today was supposed to be the start of her new life. And she didn't want to begin it with an eerily lifelike replica of the man who had broken her heart, her confidence, and the bank when he'd absconded with twelve million of the town's dollars. Not to mention staring down the man who'd taken her virginity and something so much more valuable—her ability to trust.

"Darling, half the town is here." He pointed to the curb, and sure enough, all her neighbors were on their lawns—or hers. "When Richard here came up Main Street it was as though he was Jesus, walking on water, and people just started following him. I saw the senior center loading up their bus and heading this way, headlights on, I'm assuming to be part of the procession. They'll be here any minute."

Great.

"So you came to watch the show?"

"Nope." He tucked a piece of hair behind her ear and heat curled low in her stomach. "I came to see if you wanted to go grab a bite to eat. The show's just a bonus."

"You already asked me out on a date. I said no." Although she'd wanted to say yes. Not to the date part. She'd always hated dating. But to the good-night kiss part that usually followed said date. And maybe even to what naturally followed the kiss. Tanner excelled at both.

"You said you were still a married woman, so I backed off." He smiled. "You're single now, so the question is back on the table."

"I'm divorced," Abby exclaimed, perhaps a tad shrilly. "And I'm not interested."

"You're not divorced," Rodney hollered over the hood of the car, informing everyone in a three-block radius.

Nora pulled out her phone and began filming.

Abby felt everything inside of her still. "Excuse me?"

"That there isn't just a piece of masterful art carved from a rare marble found only in remote parts of Italy. It's a vessel," Rodney said, pointing to the vase in the statue's hand and taking a moment of silence. "I'm sorry to inform you, Mrs. Moretti, but your husband, Richard Moretti, passed away, long before that there divorce decree was signed. And according to his lawyer, as his widow you are the sole heir to all of his assets."

"The hell, I am!"

Jack Tanner watched Abby tear across her lawn, arms swinging and robe flapping at the bottom like some superhero cape. She had her pissed-off female vibe dialed to *castrate*. "I am a divorced woman. Not a widow. This is just another one of Richard's stupid scams! Probably a way to elude the police or my lawyer."

In any other situation, Tanner might laugh. Here he was, watching the DeLuca Darling standing in her front yard in that slinky new robe—yeah, he noticed—staring down a man three times her size with a statue of her naked husband behind her. And the shit of it was, she still managed to turn him inside out every single time he saw her.

"So you're saying you're not his widow," Rodney ventured carefully, as though struggling to understand. "And that you don't want the statue?"

"Yes, and for the last time *yes*!" Abby pressed, and damn if Rodney didn't flinch a little. Abby might be small, but she packed lethal doses of attitude.

"If you aren't his wife, then you don't lay claim to his beautiful statue."

"Which means?"

"You don't decide its fate, moving it or otherwise."

"The 'beautiful' statue that is on *my* private property?"

"Well, there is that." Rodney looked at his truck as though contemplating locking himself inside. Tanner felt for the guy. "I can call the lawyer who hired me, but even if I get his approval, I can't move your husband today."

"Ex-husband, and why not?"

"I don't have the manpower or equipment to handle getting someone"—Rodney's gaze fell to Richard's boys—"his size back on the truck. So, I gotta come back with my other truck. Maybe Sunday."

"Sunday?" Nora and Abby said in unison. Rodney looked skyward.

"As in almost a week from now?" Abby's voice wavered a little as she took in the swelling crowd. Living in St. Helena was like living in a giant fishbowl, and right now Abby was the fish of the hour. "That doesn't work for me."

"Me either," Nora said. "I got the Historical Preservation Council coming by to do their yearly inspection for the Memory Lane Manor Walk. We can't have visual pornography marring up the neighborhood."

Krug Court was home to some of the oldest residential buildings in all of St. Helena. With a dozen or more houses dating back as far as 1864, it was always a highlight on the Founder's Day Memory Lane Manor Walk, which was to be held the first weekend in September.

"She's gotta get a permit from the board if she wants to keep that thing here all week," Nora said to the crowd, who uh-huhed and nodded their allegiance.

"I don't want to keep it!" Abby defended, not a hint of darling in her voice. Oh no, the woman was 100 percent DeLuca. "He's not even mine anymore. So why don't you," she slid the cell phone from Rodney's belt clip and slapped it against his chest, "get Richard on the phone and tell him to come get his stupid statue?"

Rodney took off his hat. "I'm sorry, ma'am, but your husband is deceased."

"Did you see Richard's body?"

Rodney looked at the statue.

"Before it was placed in the *vessel*?" Abby clarified.

"No, ma'am. I was hired by his lawyer."

"Then he isn't dead."

"If you say so." Rodney looked at his phone. "So who do you want me to call?"

And that was Tanner's cue to step in. Abby was a pint-sized bomb of frustrated and emotional female who was one redundant question away from an explosion of epic proportions.

Normally he would steer clear of a woman on the verge. But if he took that approach with Abby, he'd never see her. She tended to act all pissy and put out every time their paths crossed, which was often. Tanner made sure of it because he liked her, almost as much as he liked to drive her crazy. She was hot when she was in a mood. Hell, she was hot period, which was part of the problem.

To everyone else Abigail was sweet and accommodating, a real people pleaser. The DeLuca freaking Darling. With him, though, she was all spit and fire, a real *look but don't touch* number who worked hard at appearing unaffected, distant, as though he hadn't seen her naked once upon a time. Which only made him want to look and touch his fill until she was clawing mindlessly at his back and there wasn't even a breath of space between them.

Scratch that. Until she was clawing mindlessly at his back—while naked—and there wasn't even a breath of space between them—in his bed. Or hers. He wasn't choosy.

But today he was a man on a mission. A mission to help Abby secure an important client for her budding interior design firm, which would get Tanner one step closer to landing that date he'd been dreaming about. Not to mention securing a talented designer would make his overstressed business partner's life a whole lot easier. And Tanner was all about easy.

Abby being frazzled right now wouldn't help his cause. She'd refuse his help to land a client then hide in her house to avoid a confrontation. So he did what any man in his shoes would do.

He stepped up, placed his hand on her shoulder in a sign of support, and whispered in her ear, "In case you forgot, I have the manpower and more than enough equipment to handle all of your needs, Abs. Just say the word."

She turned and looked at him, her lips pursed, her eyes narrowed into two irritated slits of rage, and he could tell she had just the word for him. Several, in fact.

"Would I be stupid in assuming you're just being neighborly and offering to haul that statue away?"

He rocked back on his heels. "Depends on what kind of agreement we can reach." Slowly, he took in the slippers, tan legs, and silky robe. "I've got a few ideas."

Like clockwork Abby's chest rose, followed by her shoulders and that bristly pride that made him smile.

She was gearing up to control her temper, which was a whole hell of a lot better than falling apart.

"Thanks, Tanner." She patted him—a little too hard—on the shoulder and turned to Rodney. "You need a tool? I've got the biggest one in St. Helena, maybe even California, right here at your disposal."

"Biggest one?" Tanner gave a low whistle. "Wow. I mean, I've always received compliments, but biggest? Really?"

Abby's eyes narrowed in on him and, he couldn't help it, his lips lifted into a big-ass grin. Hers, however, pressed into a stern line of disapproval that demanded his best behavior and made him feel like one of her exasperating piano students—which he was. He'd been on the receiving end of that look many times during their lessons over the past year.

But before he could prove he was immune to *the look*, she was back to ignoring him.

"Rodney, I'm giving you two minutes to figure out how to get this thing off my property or I'll call the sheriff."

Rodney, smart man that he was, locked himself in the cab of his truck. Then, satisfied with the big guy's level of fear, Abby turned those big brown eyes on Tanner. "You only get two seconds, so go."

"To show my gratitude for that moving endorsement, I'd like to return the favor. Say," he looked at his watch, "lunch in an hour?"

She gave a big exasperated huff and crossed her arms, sending that teeny-tiny little robe of hers on a trip due north and leaving him to wonder what color panties she had on—because it was clear she wasn't wearing much else under there.

"I'm not going on a date with you," she said sternly.

"Who said anything about a date?" Her face flushed and, *ah, yeah*, she wanted to say yes. Stubborn pride was the only thing between him and a second chance to prove he was good enough for the DeLuca Darling. "This is strictly a professional proposition. To talk about a design job I referred you for."

She blinked. Twice. He, on the other hand, moved closer, crowding her body until he saw proof of just how affected he made her. "Although now that you mention a date, I'm flattered. And the answer is yes. Does this mean you pick up the tab or me? I'm game either way."

She ignored that, but didn't back away. "Why would you recommend me for a job?"

Why wouldn't he? She was one of the best designers he'd ever worked with.

"You do clean work, and I know you're reliable. And your designs make people want to sit down and stay for a while, which is exactly what the client needs. Bottom line, you'd be perfect for the project."

He watched her face soften, flush a little—only this time from his praise. He liked the riled Abby, but he loved the shy one even more. It reminded him of the girl he'd met and fallen in love with back in high school. The sweet teenager with the big, trusting eyes who, no matter how hard he tried, he couldn't shake.

"Well, I'm no longer doing closet redesigns or nurseries, so if that's what this job is, better look elsewhere," she said with a self-conscious laugh that hurt his heart. "I'm only doing full renovations and rehabs now, not a coat of paint and shelves."

Then she sobered, her face going coolly blank.

Without warning, she grabbed him by the arm and—whoa, Bossy Abby sent his body humming—dragged him to the front porch—which was one creak and groan away from being condemned—and away from prying eyes. "Did my brothers bully you into recommending me for the job?"

"Sweetheart, I've got at least thirty pounds and three inches on your brothers."

She snorted. "Yeah, but there are four of them. And they don't fight fair."

"Neither do I, not when I want something." And he wanted her. More than he'd ever wanted a woman. And she wanted him too. It was right there in the way she swayed closer, the way she didn't let go of his arm, and in the way her eyes kept darting to his lips.

Oh, she had it bad for him. She was just too Italian to admit it.

"They didn't bully me into anything. I'm asking because I know that"—he leaned in and whispered—"the Hamptons are secretly in the market for a new designer."

She leaned in, her voice mimicking his, although hers held a note of smugness. "I know. I'm meeting with Babs Hampton for a late lunch. It appears I am the front-runner to become their new, *secret* designer."

Tanner inwardly cringed, because he knew what she said wasn't actually correct. She was one of three on the list. And the least qualified. When Ferris Hampton had called Tanner yesterday, begging for the name of a local designer who could work with his mother and didn't scare easily, Tanner had immediately thought of Abby. She was tough, talented, and would deliver—regardless of what Babs Hampton, whose indecisiveness and complete 180s in vision for her premiere wine and cheese shop had managed to scare off the last six designers, threw at her. Babs's flightiness was something that drove her son, Ferris, to distraction. A distracted Ferris meant trouble for Tanner and his business partner, who were trying to land a major deal with the Hampton Group.

"Look, I know how the Hamptons work. They are particular and demanding, especially Babs, and I know what she is looking for in a presentation," he explained. "With her it's about the way you present your ideas."

"And let me guess," she laughed. This time *at* him. "You want to come with me to lunch and hold my hand so I don't screw this up?"

"I was talking about lunch, with me, to prep. And darling," he tucked one of her curls behind her ear, pleased when she gave a little gasp, "your designs speak for themselves. If they pass, it's their loss, not yours."

She looked shocked at his comment, then immediately suspicious. "If you think I have this in the bag, then why should I have lunch with you?"

"This is a Hampton project, and there is no way that you are the only candidate. The other firms are big, flashy, and they have a solid foundation behind them. What they don't have is insight into the customer. I do. And I think that with what I know about the project, you can fine-tune your pitch and create a customized proposal to match their expectations."

Her eyes were big and dreamy, and he wanted to pull her into his arms and kiss her. Only instead he said, "And Abby, I've wanted to hold your hand in public since the day I met you."

"Hey, Tanner," Libby Alistair hollered from her front porch. Libby was blonde, stacked, smoking hot, and always up for a fun time. She also had a horrible sense of timing, and was apparently Abby's neighbor. "Niners' preseason starts Sunday. You think they'll take it all the way this time?"

And even from across the street, no one could miss the way her expression lit up in blatant invitation. An invitation that a few days ago Tanner would have gladly accepted. But now that Abby was back in play, there was only one invitation he was interested in gaining. Too bad her expression was dialed to *eat shit and choke on it.*

"Funny," Abby said, not an ounce of funny to her tone. "I promised never to give you the time of day when you broke my heart." *Right. That.* "And unlike you, DeLucas never go back on their word."

"So is that a no on lunch then?"

Without answering him, she tugged her robe tightly around her and brushed right past him into her house, those ridiculous slippers of hers growling with every step. The best part was that her hips were moving at such a velocity that the bottom of her robe kicked up, flashing him a hint of peach silk that went a long way toward making his morning even brighter.

"Was it the 'who pays' part?" he hollered after her. "Because I'm okay with going dutch."

The door slammed in response. Followed by the dead bolt clicking loudly, and Tanner had to smile. Abby was running, which was fine with him. He'd known her long enough to understand she only ran when she was scared. And she was scared, all right.

Scared she wanted to go back on her word.

CHAPTER 2

Abby needed this job. *Badly*, she thought, scooting to the far end of Babs Hampton's couch, the moleskin cushions shedding on her black skirt.

After spending the past four years designing grand wineries for her family and not-so-grand closets for everyone else, she needed a break. That one person who would believe in her designs enough to take a chance on a newcomer.

She had the vision, the drive, and the talent. What she didn't have was a stellar portfolio with clients whose last names were not DeLuca.

Minus the recent string of nurseries she'd designed for the Wine Valley's Mommy Troop and the men's station at Stan's Soup and Service Station, there wasn't a single job in Abby's portfolio that wasn't a direct result of her smothering brothers or family name. Which was why she had to land the Hampton job.

Her family was friendly with the Hamptons, but they didn't have a long history with them. Which meant it was all up to her. Something that felt exhilarating and liberating and a little bit foreign.

"It isn't polite to stare," Abby said to the four-legged dust mop whose lips were peeled back, exposing a set of very large, very pointy teeth. She scooted as close to the far edge of Babs's couch as possible and stated, as calmly and rationally as one could when facing down a growling dog, "In fact, I'd appreciate it if you'd move back a little, your breath is invading my personal space and your paws are leaving prints on my presentation."

To her surprise the dog moved—just enough to situate all four feet on her superglossy 8½-by-11 presentation, which she'd spent all day perfecting. Then he sat, making sure to slide his butt and all of his apricot-colored tail over her cover page, crinkling it.

Not willing to let another overbearing male ruin her chance at happiness, Abby reached out to snatch it back.

The dog growled. Low and lethal. His diamond-studded collar flashing in the afternoon sun.

"You may think you're scary, but you're not," Abby whispered, snatching her hand back—right as Babs Hampton peeked her head out from the kitchen doorway.

"How is everything going, dear?"

Abby eyed the dog, who was still showing his teeth, and smoothed her palms over her skirt. "Great."

"Oh, lovely, I hope The Duke was being a good host," the older woman said, beaming with delight, her kitten heels clicking the marble floor as she strode across the foyer and into the sitting room.

The woman was notorious for wearing leisure suits with coordinating robes and eye shadow. Today the suit was teal, the robe pooled to the floor, and she had on a stunning diamond choker. With her birdlike face, frail limbs, and halo of out-of-the-bottle apricot curls, she looked just like her dog.

"Did I misunderstand our meeting time?" Abby asked, because

she'd been sitting with The Duke for over an hour while Babs busied herself elsewhere.

"Oh. No, dear." She sent Abby a sly wink and gracefully reclined in the wingback chair next to the dog. "I was preparing lunch. And giving you two some privacy to, you know"—she reached over and patted Abby's knee—"bond."

No. Abby didn't know. But Babs was opening an exciting new shop on Main Street. And Abby wanted to be a part of that moment.

The Pungent Barrel, when complete, was rumored to be set to become wine country's premiere destination for wine and cheese connoisseurs. The innovative reimagining required to turn a historical bottling plant into a world-class tasting room would allow Abby the chance to showcase her knowledge of wine culture and spatial transformation.

Not to mention being a Hampton project lent it the kind of prestige that would look stellar on her resume and, more importantly, if Abby could create a wine and cheese experience that appealed to all the senses while managing to gain the Babs stamp of approval, which she would, it would be the kind of in she desperately needed—where getting hired for other, more exclusive projects would be a snap.

So if it took bonding with Fang over there to get this deal, then she'd start packing doggie bones laced with mood stabilizers.

"I brought these for you. Just a few samples of my work." Abby pointed to her portfolio and The Duke snapped his jaws. "Why don't you take a look, see the range of projects I have designed, and then we can discuss . . ."

Abby stopped because, what was she doing? She wasn't a hard sales kind of girl. She was a people pleaser and she wanted to please Babs. But she also wanted to be honest. "I know that your last designer left and you are anxious to resume construction, so I want to assure you that I am able to move fast, adapt efficiently, and, if you decide to use my firm, I am ready to begin work immediately."

"Oh, that's just lovely," Babs said excitedly.

Lovely.

Abby felt her lips curl up into a triumphant smile. She was going to land this job without Tanner's referral, without her family's influence, and without the glossy sales pitch Tanner had gone on about. She was going to land this job on her portfolio, talent, heart, and good old-fashioned communication—and she couldn't wait to rub it in Tanner's face.

Confidence bubbling, Abby went on. "I have to admit, I called around and discovered that you use Valley Textiles, and they were nice enough to send me some samples of what you had already picked out. Very elegant and modern. I was impressed."

"Thank you." The older woman preened at the compliment, and Abby had meant it. For a woman who usually favored over-the-top, the color scheme was sleek and innovative.

"Since you are looking for a historical rehab with a modern twist, I think you'll love what I did with the master suite at the villa in Italy." She grabbed her portfolio and flipped to the section showcasing her family's destination getaway. "If you look here, you can see how I merged old-world details original to the farmhouse with—"

"Hydrants," Babs provided and smiled as though that made perfect sense.

"Pardon?"

"Fire hydrants. The Duke loves fire hydrants. And fire engines and fire hats and his favorite color is, oh my, it is, uh . . ." The woman's lips pursed in concentration as she snapped her fingers.

"Red," Abby offered.

"Yes." She clapped her hands and the dog barked. "The Duke just loves fire-engine red. With yellow accents and little bones everywhere. That will be nice, don't you think?"

"Um." Abby's cheeks were beginning to hurt from the weight of keeping her smile in place. This woman was as crazy as her dog. No wonder she had scared off six other designers. "I've never considered fire-engine red as a soothing color. But maybe if you showed me the space, explained what you envisioned, I could better understand—"

"You saw the space when you came in." Babs looked as confused as Abby felt, and suddenly that bad feeling—the one that had formed in the pit of her stomach when Richard showed up on her lawn that morning and gotten worse when she'd learned she was stuck with him for a week—turned into a painful ache that swelled up into her chest until she was afraid she might pass out.

"Right," Abby ventured. "The old Jackson Bottlery downtown, the one at the end of Main Street. I passed it on my way here."

"No, the bottlery is for my cheese shop," Babs explained slowly, her brows furrowing even more. "I was talking about my late husband's old den. I pointed it out when you arrived. It's the perfect place for The Duke's new doggie habitat."

Which explained the "bonding" hour. And why Babs had set out a bowl of kibble on the coffee table next to the nuts. She was setting the scene for Abby to meet her new client. "But I don't do doghouses."

"Habitat, dear. They're all the rage," she said, steepling her fingers beneath her chin. "The Duke and I saw a lovely alpaca habitat last week on our morning walk, and it got us thinking, 'Now, wouldn't that be nice?'"

Yes, lovely and nice, lovely and nice, lovely and nice. They were the only adjectives the woman knew. *Oh my God*, Abby was going to lose it right there. On Mrs. Hampton's settee. With The Duke playing witness.

"Then I ran into your brother, Nathaniel, at the market, such a nice boy." She gave that smile that every woman between newborn and not quite embalmed gave when they encountered Abby's older brother. "I was buying some prime rib for The Duke's dinner and Nathaniel told me that you helped him design the alpaca habitat. Invited me over for a tour, even gave me a bottle of that fancy wine of his wife's, and I have to say I was impressed."

"With the wine?"

"With the habitat. Although, that I acquired a bottle of Red Steel was all the talk at the Garden Society's Friday tea."

"I bet." Abby was going to be sick.

"But the real star was that habitat. What a serene, playful, and perfect space you created, Abigail." She patted the dog's head. "Only we want ours red and with bones. Maybe even a little siren he can ring." The Duke looked up at his mistress and barked, and Babs clapped once with excitement. "Or maybe a palace-themed habitat. I see royal, regal, elegantly fit for a duke. But with hydrants. Gold ones."

"I only directed Nate to a site that sold habitat blueprints. I didn't actually design it."

"He said you helped add on the reading room and exercise corral as their wedding present."

"Yes, I did."

Screw sick, she was furious. Not only had Nate butted into her life, something that all of her brothers had spent a lifetime mastering, he also felt as though he had to bribe an old lady with fancy wine in order for Abby to book an interview—for a freaking habitat.

Closing her eyes, she let her head drop back against the couch, wondering how she could have been so stupid.

Her husband was naked on her lawn and the entire town was flocking to get a look. Her family thought she was as good as her last closet. She was considering taking a job building a doghouse for a four-legged duke. And, *oh God*, the worst part of all—Tanner had all but told her so.

Her life was a mess. She was a mess. A talentless, jobless, pathetic mess.

Your designs speak for themselves. If they pass, it's their loss.

Tanner had been wrong on both counts. Her designs wouldn't be seen, let alone heard, and if Babs passed, it would be Abby who lost out. And she didn't know if she'd bounce back. Because after her hellish day, she stood to lose a whole lot more than a stupid job.

Tears burned her throat, so she reminded herself that her designs were incredible.

So what if she was called here to pitch a glorified doghouse? She had designed million-dollar wineries. Completely renovated an Italian farmhouse, making it one of the most exclusive destination rentals on the Mediterranean. Who cared if the property belonged to her family? They hadn't done the work, she had.

Every grueling and inspired inch of it.

"I'm sorry, Mrs. Hampton." Abby sat up and snatched the proposal right out from under The Duke's paws. "My firm no longer specializes in nurseries or habitats. I came here to help you turn that old bottling plant into a wine and cheese shop that will be the envy of the vine and curd community. I want to make your dream a reality and ensure that your shop shines."

Babs took the offered package and flipped through it, her eyes scanning with practiced precision, her fingers running down the length of the pages. Abby could see it, the way her face lit with excitement, how her hands shook as she saw the potential of what Abby's Designs could bring to her shop.

"This is impressive," Babs said, professional appreciation lacing her voice.

Then she reached the proposed budget Abby had put together and her eyes dimmed. Not a lot, but enough that the back of Abby's throat began to burn. "But I think that the habitat is more in line with your . . . comfort zone."

"If it is the size of the project, I assure you that I am more than qualified to handle it," Abby clarified, tired of people underestimating what she could handle. "If you'll turn the page, you will see that I have handled budgets three times this size."

Babs closed the folder and placed it on her lap. "Yes, dear, but that was with your family's money."

It was as though time stopped, rewound, and lodged itself right through Abby's chest. She knew the look on Babs's face, knew it well. It was the same look the paramedic had given her when she'd asked if her parents were going to be okay. The same look she'd received from the investors when she'd explained that Richard, and their money, had disappeared. It was the same look her family was going to give her when they discovered that Richard had returned—albeit in statue form—and was somehow her problem once again.

"Are you afraid I won't be able to handle a project this complex?" As the words left her mouth, a sick sense of dread made it difficult to speak. "Or are you afraid I'll have a hard time keeping the money from disappearing into my pocket?"

"Oh, no," Babs said, her hand clutching her chest in genuine horror. "I would never think you could steal. From me or anyone. You're not that kind of girl. Never have been."

Abby felt herself relax a little. Sometimes, when she was too tired to pretend everything was all right, she wondered if what happened with Richard was part of the reason people in town always went with other designers. She was relieved to know, whether she got this job or not, that wasn't the case here.

"No, dear, my concern would be that someone would sweet-talk you into gaining access to the account. Plus, my son would never allow it. Ferris was one of Richard's original investors."

Tanner rested his arms on the top of the steering wheel to get a better view of the deserted parking lot as though he were a detective on a stakeout when, in fact, he felt more like a Peeping Tom.

He had no idea how he'd managed to get stuck on Abby duty. Except, oh right, he'd lost big at last week's poker game and the guys had called in their marker. Guys who happened to be named DeLuca.

Not that it was a hardship, he thought, watching Abby roll on her toes to peer inside the abandoned bottling plant. Nope, not when her shirt shifted *way* up, emphasizing the sweetest ass in the history of the world and two very toned, very sexy legs.

He reached for his thermos and took a pull of coffee, wondering A) what she was doing creeping around a dark construction site at night with her face pressed firmly against the window, and B) if she bent over just a little farther what color silk would he find peeking back. His brain already knew the answer to the first. Too bad his dick couldn't stop thinking about the second.

For a girl who'd spent the past few minutes diving behind an overgrown shrub every time a car drove by, she sure picked the wrong outfit to lie low. Her tight cream skirt and matching sweater set was like a freaking homing beacon, radiating under the parking lot lights.

Drawing him in.

He pressed speed dial, calling Abby's brother Marco. Having a wife and new baby daughter to worry about should have calmed Marco down a bit when it came to his kid sister. It hadn't.

"Did you find her?" Marc's voice filled the cab of his truck.

"Yup."

"That's it? Yup?"

"Yup."

They'd had this argument less than an hour ago, when he'd made it clear that playing spy for a group of domineering brothers wasn't going to happen. Tanner had only agreed to find Abby because they'd been worried sick since she'd decided to go radio-silent after the naked Dick appeared on her lawn. Then, there was the botched interview with Babs earlier—he should have known her brothers wouldn't be able to help themselves. Which was why he figured she'd been avoiding them to begin with.

"I said I'd make sure she was all right. She is."

"At least tell me if she's crying. She doesn't do well with this kind of stuff. Never has," Marc said, but Tanner wasn't listening. He was too busy watching Abby pull a flashlight out of that ridiculously gigantic bag she always carted around, kick off her shoes, and step up on a raised flowerbed to shine the beam through the widow. "God, I'm going to kill Nate if she's crying."

Tanner wanted to kill all of her brothers. It was an urge he fought on a weekly basis. This week it was stronger.

When would they figure out Abby didn't need a keeper—never had?

Something Tanner knew firsthand.

"She's not crying." *She's tougher than that.* "Although Nate will be when she kicks his ass. What was he thinking? Abby could have landed the Pungent Barrel account if you guys hadn't undersold her as a doghouse designer."

He could almost hear Marc flipping him the bird through the phone because he knew Tanner was right. They'd screwed up. Big-time. And Abby had lost out.

"We're considering calling Gabe, asking him to come home early and help deal with this whole Richard shitstorm," Marc said, referring to the eldest DeLuca brother, who was currently vacationing in Italy with his wife and three daughters.

"We as in you, Nate, and Trey?" Were they serious? "Because I guarantee you, there is no way Abby would agree to that. Bringing Gabe and his family back just in time for little Holly to see a naked statue of her father sounds like a complication Abby would want to avoid."

Richard hadn't just slept with his interns—he'd gotten one pregnant, then abandoned her. By some weird twist of fate, Richard's mistress, Regan, was now married to Gabe, making Richard's love child Abby's niece. And the rest of them one big, happy family.

"Dick is still in her yard?"

"Until Sunday."

"Sunday! That's a long time to keep this from my nonna. Because if he's still here when she gets home from her bachelorette party, all hell will break loose."

ChiChi had recently ended a sixty-year feud with their family's biggest rival, Charles Baudouin, and the two were now planning a wedding, an event that ChiChi and her geriatric brigade were currently celebrating in Vegas—at a strip club, according to the updates on Facebook. And Marc was right to be concerned. ChiChi was so unpredictable Tanner had no idea what she'd do when she learned that the most notorious Dick in the valley was once again stinking up her granddaughter's life—only that it wouldn't make the situation any easier for Abby.

Marc sighed like he was all put out, then went on. "You think you can still get her to the Sweet and Savory by seven?"

Abby took that moment to see just how secure the locks on the windows were. When the first one didn't slide up, she stomped her foot, nearly falling off the flowerbed, and huffed her way toward another window on the far side of the building. "Not looking good, bro."

"Christ," Marc mumbled. "Lexi will be crushed if she doesn't show. She's been planning this party for months. Got the whole bistro looking like some kind of twisted bachelorette party, only in reverse."

Right, because, again, what Abby really needed right then was a surprise divorce party?

"I'll try my best to get her there," he said, smiling when she dug through one of the half dozen pockets and flaps on her purse and pulled out a screwdriver, which she wedged between the window and the sill and—if his eyes didn't deceive him—started jimmying. Here her brothers were worried she was sobbing her eyes out in some dark alley, and Abby was getting ready to add breaking and entering to her resume. "But I wouldn't hold my breath."

Worst. Day. Ever.

Okay, not worst, since she'd had quite a few of those in her lifetime. *But easily top ten,* Abby thought as she wiggled the window to see if she'd loosened it enough to—

"Yes!" she squealed when it slid open, and she did a silent happy dance that included several fist pumps and a lot of booty shaking.

Feeling pretty darn proud of herself, she scanned the dim lot once more to make sure she was alone—not that she was breaking in so much as taking a peek around.

Walking away from the Pungent Barrel project wasn't an option. Not anymore. She had been living a half-life since the day Richard left. And just when she thought she'd been given a break, had finally let her guard down enough to allow for something amazing, something more, Richard had once again crapped all over her plans. Then her brothers and their insistent meddling had smeared it all around.

Well, she was done allowing people to mess with her life, even when it was done lovingly and with her best interests at heart. If the Hamptons wanted a resourceful, savvy, take-charge person to head this project, then Abby was going to give it to them.

Starting tonight.

Step one: gather inside information.

In order to get Babs in her corner, Abby needed to walk the space, measure the layout, see what had been done by the previous designers so she could come up with accurate blueprints, an exact budget, and a complete design package to present.

Which meant she had to get inside.

Flashlight between her teeth, she stuck her head through the window and wrinkled her nose. The heavy scent of damp cork and fermented air blasted her as she leaned farther inside to glance at the floor. It wasn't very far down. Then again she wasn't very tall, a fact that ticked her off—especially tonight.

Dropping her purse inside first, she looked over her shoulder and did a thorough sweep of the area for any bypassers. When the coast was clear, she tugged her skirt up around her waist and slipped one leg through the opening, then the other, until she was sitting on the sill. Turning around, she shimmied her way down, clutching the ledge with her arms. Unable to shimmy any more, she took a final breath and dropped to the floor—with a loud thud.

Her flashlight flew across the room, her tailbone smarted from the nasty collision with the concrete floor, and she was pretty sure she was going to be sick from the jarring impact.

"Do you know how many nights I fell asleep dreaming about how you'd look sneaking out your window, only to wake up with a woody?" a smug, annoyingly male voice said from somewhere inside the building. Somewhere close enough that she could smell his cologne. "Never once, in all those years, did I picture it like that."

Yup, definitely going to be sick.

"What are you doing here, Jack?" Because really, Tanner catching her sprawled out on the floor, with her skirt to her ears, easily catapulted this day into the top five. Scrambling to her feet, the cool air whooshing past her southern region, she yanked her skirt down and tried to glare at him—only it was too dark to see where he was.

"You mean besides getting a glimpse of the sexiest panties in town?"

"Says the man who's seen everyone's panties in town," she mumbled, squinting harder. "Plus, it's too dark to see."

Just to be safe, she tugged at the bottom of her skirt again and, since she was already there, batted away what felt like wet clumps of sawdust. She also batted away Tanner's hands, which were giving a valiant effort of dusting off her backside.

"Just trying to help," he laughed, but didn't move his hands, except to slide them up to gently grip her hips. "And I have excellent night vision. It comes from years of playing night games."

"The NFL uses stadium lights, Jack." She tried to back up, get some distance between them, because he was so close she could smell him. Feel her brain cloud over and her hormones kick in.

"Did you know that, besides my mom, you're the only one who ever called me Jack?"

Something she'd started doing shortly after they'd met the summer before her senior year. Tanner, it seemed, belonged to everyone, but Jack was just hers—or so she'd thought. He'd walked into her life at a time when she'd desperately needed something new—something that didn't remind her of what she'd lost.

Because he lived two towns over, he didn't know her family or parents or the happy, carefree girl she'd been before the accident—the one who everyone obviously missed and would do anything to get back. Only *that* girl was never coming back. The easy-to-love Abby died in the car with her parents, and with Tanner there was no pretending, no apologizing—she could just be.

In the end, though, that girl hadn't been enough for Tanner, either. A fact that her body seemed to have forgotten, since it was straining to get closer.

"What are you doing here?"

"Wanted to make sure you were all right."

"I'm fine." When he didn't move, she reluctantly admitted, "It's just a little sore."

"I wasn't talking about your butt, although, if you think my night vision is impressive, you should check out my massaging skills."

She felt the air shift around her as though he was moving closer, moving into position to give her a hands-on demonstration of those skills. The mere idea of his big hands on her jump-started every suppressed urge she'd been ignoring since Richard walked out.

"I'm fine." She shoved at his chest, not wanting any of his skills, massaging or otherwise, near her. He was so refreshingly male that, just like most women in town, she didn't think she'd be able to resist, even on her best days.

"Are you, Abs? Because if not, I'm here to help you," he whispered, sliding an arm around her waist and proving her point. Desire and something much more vulnerable rushed through her body and settled in a part of her chest that she'd long ago designated off-limits to the dicks of the world.

And in true Jack Tanner fashion, his hands slipped even lower, proving that the kind of help she needed and the kind he was offering didn't match up. The only reason her body heated up, she convinced herself, was that seven years with only a vibrator for company could do that to a girl.

Nope, taking him up on his kind of help was a bad decision. It wasn't the guaranteed hot night she was worried about. It was the cold bed and even lonelier morning after that were sure to follow.

CHAPTER 3

Really, Jack?" She took a big step back and reached down for her purse and—*whoa*, what was up with the *don't touch me asshole* glare? "The last time you used a line like that on me, you managed to help me right out of my kick pants, only to take off with some blonde afterward."

"What line?"

She raised a brow and, okay, so maybe putting his hands on Abby had been a serious lack of judgment. Sure, she'd looked lost and disappointed and in desperate need of a hug. But the second his hands slid down her back and she snuggled closer, all of his good intentions went to shit. And all he could focus on was that his fingers were inches from her ass, and her breasts—the ones he'd been dreaming about since he was seventeen—were crushed up against his chest. And that she needed him.

The DeLuca Darling, who didn't need anyone, needed him. Then she gave a horrified expression, as though realizing who she was talking to, and it became "I don't want to talk" and "hands off."

Which worked for him, since listening to her talk about the dickwad she'd been married to always managed to make him mad. Although the "hands off" part he'd like to change.

"And I was only going to take Kendra Abrahams to homecoming because she'd already asked."

"You had sex with me the week before."

"I couldn't cancel. I had her corsage ordered and everything," he explained. "Not that it mattered, since *your* school's mascot mysteriously ended up in *my* truck for a joyride," he said, smiling when her only response was a long, weighted silence. Guilt did that to a person—especially Abby. "But if I hadn't been banned from the dance, I would have wanted to go with you."

At that she looked up, and the expression she shot Tanner about singed his soul. He wasn't joking about his night vision. Lit only by the faint glow of the moonlight, he could make out that her big brown eyes were slit into a glare that was too frosty for his taste, and her lips twitched slightly as though trying not to laugh in his face. A task at which she failed miserably.

"And we were in high school," he added as though that made up for the fact that he had taken her virginity in a wine cave.

He'd gone there with good intentions; she'd called him crying and upset and needing a friend. What happened after he'd arrived, after she'd started kissing him . . . well, he hadn't been thinking like a friend. Worse, he'd behaved exactly like people expected him to.

"I was actually talking about junior year of college, after the UC All-Star Bowl," she said.

Now, there was an image. "Well, you were wearing red kick pants, I thought it was a go."

"My whole cheer team was wearing red kick pants," she said, fumbling around in her purse and coming up with a tape measure and a little notebook. "But with that lovely reminder, you can help me out by leaving."

Not waiting for him to respond, she turned her back on him and, hands out in front of her, blindly searched for her flashlight. He watched her for a good minute, especially focused when she dropped to all fours, shaking that heart-stopping ass for his viewing pleasure, then started back toward him, giving him something else entirely to focus on. The moonlight cast a faint glow across her face and the generous shot of cleavage she had going on.

"And leave you here to fend for yourself? Nah." He took one step, bent over, and picked up the flashlight, clicking it on. "Looking for this?" When she just stared up at him, irritated and a little confused, he added, "Night vision, remember?"

There went that glare again. It should have been scary as shit to be hit with that look, but considering she was on her knees and her overall adorableness, it only managed to turn him on and make him smile.

With a huff, she stood and he lost his view—and the flashlight. "Thank you. Now you can go."

Instead of heading out the back door like he should have, he followed her to the front part of the warehouse and braced a hip against an entry-wall arch she was sizing up.

She ignored him, scribbled a few notes in that notebook of hers, then, flashlight stuck between those pursed lips, reached up to measure the height from the top of the arch to the floor. Only she was too short.

She tried again, giving a little hop that did nothing but make him grin, then kicked the wall—twice—and mumbled something about the male gender that was way too dirty to be darling.

Smart man that he was, he silently took one end of the measuring tape from her clutches and pulled it all the way up until it touched the highest point of the archway—being six five had its benefits.

Abby paused for a moment, as though deciding if she wanted to kick him or just write down the measurement so she could get away from him faster. Amazingly, she took option two, and they worked their way around to the back part of the room, him reaching the tall parts and her making detailed notes.

If she was thankful for the help, she didn't say. In fact she didn't speak at all. So when they moved into the main part of the warehouse, he was surprised when she opened her mouth.

"I guess Babs was one of the investors in Richard's winery." She looked over her shoulder and snapped the measuring tape, and he flinched. "But I assume you already knew that, considering you're Ferris's new go-to guy and all."

"Yeah." He knew. Although Ferris wasn't his anything—other than another potential client. Tanner wasn't even sure he liked the guy.

After his mom had walked out, Tanner was too young to stay at home and had spent his summers swinging hammers with his old man for college money. He'd worked on a few Hampton projects in high school, but hadn't officially met the developer until they both lost big on a local start-up winery gone bad. Richard's.

"Wait. You didn't know?"

Abby shook her head and, *holy Christ*, he didn't know how it was possible she hadn't known. Not that he should be so surprised; Abby was so damn trusting she was the last one in town to figure out she'd married a lying, cheating sack of shit.

"Nope, and I am tired of being left in the dark. Tired of being screwed with. Which is why I went to see Judge Pricket after meeting with Babs today about getting my divorce."

"What did he say?"

"That it's too late. Richard is, um . . . three years ago he was in a car accident in Budapest and he and the passenger both, um . . ."

He heard her swallow, and a bad feeling settled in his gut. "Rodney was telling the truth."

Ah, hell. He hated the SOB for what he put Abby through, but for it to end this way was probably tearing her apart. Especially since he'd bet everything that Richard's passenger was a very young, very attractive woman. "I'm really sorry, Abs."

"Me too." She cleared the rawness from her throat. "Since the divorce wasn't filed until this year, I am legally his widow."

"Abby." He moved in to hug her, but was met with a tape measure instead.

"Can you tell me the measurements of the windows on the wall behind you?"

He looked at her for a long moment, and when he saw that she needed a minute, he eyeballed the top of the window and said, "Eleven by four."

She shrugged and wrote it down.

"Are you going to fight for a divorce?" he asked gently. Richard was the last person he wanted to talk about, but if she had just been hit with that news, she probably hadn't talked about it with anyone yet.

"I don't think so." She dropped her head to look at—well, he didn't know, except that it wasn't at her sketch. And that she didn't do it fast enough to hide the way her eyes shimmered, or the way she worried her lower lip—something she did when she was lying. All signs Richard had won, and he hated that. Hated that Abby had worked so hard to open her firm, get her life back on track, only to have that son of a bitch weasel his way back in and derail everything.

"Is that what you want?" he asked, measuring the width. And, yup, four feet exactly.

"No." She stood, and even though she had that chin-up, shoulders-back thing going on, she still only came to his chest. "The last thing

I want to be is Richard Moretti's widow. And I sure as hell don't want to go down as the woman stupid enough to stay married to a man who slept with half the town. But I want to move on . . . *need* to move on, and before I can, the town has to."

"You think a legal battle will bring it all back up again?"

"No, but if I get the divorce, I don't get Richard's estate, which is still quite large, according to his lawyer, and the courts will divide it. If I'm his widow, I get the estate, and it would be enough to cover a lot of what was stolen from outside investors. Including you."

Last year, Abby had freaked out when she'd discovered Tanner had lost a million dollars in Richard's scam.

"Abby, if there is money to get, the investors will get theirs." This he knew for a fact. His voice mail was filled with several messages from different investors, already asking him to help create a united front. "The minute that statue showed up, people got their lawyers working."

"Did you?"

"No." He stepped closer. "I'm a big boy, Abs. I understood the risks that came with investing in a start-up. This one didn't work out. Most of them don't. It's not your fault." When she looked up to argue, he cocked a brow. "They'll get the money regardless of what you decide to do."

"That could take years and they've already waited a long time. I don't want them to wait any longer."

Such a textbook Abby move. She was going to stay married to appease a group of people who'd turned on her during one of the hardest moments of her life. Not that it would matter. A good half of the people in town still believed Abby had covered for Richard, giving him enough of a lead to disappear. The other half just thought she was too stupid to notice that her husband spent more time training interns than he did getting the vineyard up and running.

Tanner knew the truth. Abby was loyal and smart, and when it came to love she went all-in. She wasn't stupid and she wasn't gullible, Richard was just a master of deception. He'd fooled the entire town and several surrounding communities. How Tanner saw it, Abby had been played the same as everyone else—except her loss was staggering in comparison.

"I want my life back, want to make my firm a success, and I can't do that if I'm always wondering how Richard factors into things. I need to make this right so we can all move on, have a clean slate."

"You know the slate was always clean with me, right?" He prayed to God she did. They had enough history to wade through without her husband wedging his way back between them.

"Does that mean I don't owe you a lifetime of piano lessons?" After discovering Tanner's investment, Abby had vowed to pay him back in monthly installments.

"No way. A deal is a deal."

He didn't want her money, let alone another reason for Abby to avoid him. He wanted time with her—a safe place for her to come to terms with the chemistry that was between them. So they struck a deal: payment in piano lessons. Which meant that every Tuesday and Thursday evening, Tanner got to be bossed around by the one woman who drove him absolutely crazy.

"Plus, you made me do that embarrassing as shit recital at Vintner's Hall with all those eight-year-olds. Well, guess what? I'm in the next grade, which means I get to do right by *my* ten-year-old self at the next stupid as shit recital and play the theme to *Star Wars*."

"*Star Wars?*" She laughed, and it sounded a hell of a lot better than her in near tears. So Tanner dropped the topic of Richard and everything that *that* must have brought up for her and went with light. He was good at light.

"Yeah, the Imperial March. I already bought the sheet music." Actually, he'd bought it when he was a kid. Only he'd never actually learned how to play it.

"I see." She crossed her arms in an attempt to appear intimidating, but on her it just looked cute. "Well, I don't allow students to play that piece until they are grade four or five. You're a grade three, which is more of The Sugar Plum Fairies or The Entertainer."

Hell, no. The guys on the crew were already giving him a hard time over cramming his body onto the same bench as most of their kids. "What do I have to do to get to a grade four before the next recital?"

"Besides practice at home, and not just when you're at my house?"

"Yeah. Besides that?" He hated practicing. His body was too damn big for that tiny little bench, which was why, after a year of lessons, he was only a grade three.

"How about another trade?"

"As in a barter?" He liked the sound of that.

"I'm meeting with my lawyer tomorrow to start the paperwork for a transfer of Richard's funds. I want to pay the Hamptons and everyone else back by the end of the week, if that is even possible. If not, I'll call Babs and explain my plans, then resubmit my ideas for the Pungent Barrel. I need to know that if she says no, it is because my work isn't what they're looking for, not because of something that happened in the past."

Tanner smiled. This was the Abby he knew lurked beneath the DeLuca Darling facade. "So what do you need from me?" he asked.

"What I need is for you to hold this." She smacked the measuring tape to his chest. "No recommendations, no favors, just help me measure the length of the room and tell me exactly what the

Hamptons expect in a proposal, so I can resubmit my plans and prove to Babs that I am the best person for this job."

Tanner crossed his arms. "All right, two extra practices a week, plus the promise that I get to play the Imperial March at the next recital, and I will make sure you get that job."

"Won't that cut into your dating life?" she said.

"Darling, my dating life is nonexistent since the girl I keep asking out keeps shooting me down."

She rolled her eyes. "One extra lesson a week, and not starting until *after* I meet with Babs." She went up on her toes, trying to look like she meant business, which was ridiculous. She was so petite he could pick her up and stick her in his pocket. "I had to cancel all my lessons this week to focus on landing that job."

"Deal." He took the tab of the measuring tape and started walking the length of the room.

"Oh, and Jack," she said in an unsure voice that was like a punch straight to the chest. "If the offer still stands, an extra set of eyes on the final designs would be great."

"Abby, anything you need, you know I'm just a call away."

She nodded. "It's just I want to make sure I meet her expectations when it comes to proper submission."

"Deal. As long as you tell me one thing."

"What?"

"Is that whole clean slate thing a general all-encompassing deal, say, covering all of the crap between us? Because I want to know when you're going to stop being stubborn and just admit you want to go out with me."

"What makes you think I want to go out with you?"

"All I'm saying is that, in my experience, when a lady wears a guy's color, she's making a declaration," Tanner said.

"And what color would that be?" Abby held her arms out to display her outfit in a challenge.

"Those Niners-red panties you're wearing."

"Declaration my ass," Abby mumbled after Tanner helped her into the cab of his truck, then slammed the door. She buckled herself in and watched Tanner make his way around the front of the truck. He slid in behind the steering wheel, started the engine, and flashed her one of those crooked grins of his that always made her stomach flip.

"Are you claiming that every woman who walks around town in a red top is issuing you your own personal invitation?"

"Just the ones wearing matching underthingies," he said, maneuvering through the parking lot.

"You mean underwear?"

"Oh, I already know those are rooting for the home team. I just wasn't sure if you had on a matching set." He stopped at the exit, the truck idling while his eyes took a slow trip down her neck to the deep V of her top, and damn if her cheeks didn't heat up to the perfect Niners red.

Knowing better than to go there with him, especially after he'd spent the past hour crawling around a dusty bottling plant with her, she said, "Thanks for helping me out tonight. And for offering to drive me to my car, even though, like I said, I could have walked. I'm only parked a few blocks up, near the Sweet and Savory."

"In those shoes? I'd give you three storefronts until you started hobbling. Five before you went barefoot." He shook his head and reached for the gearshift, then paused. His face scrunched a bit, then he released a weighted sigh. "I can take you to your car or I can take you home. Trust me, I think you should take door number two."

"And miss my surprise D-day party?" Trying hard not to let the truth show—that she'd rather pose naked with Richard and let Nora take pictures than go to that party—she forced a causal shrug. "Lexi would be crushed."

"You knew?"

He pulled out onto a sleepy Main Street. St. Helena rolled up its welcome mats early, so it wasn't surprising that the central section of town was nearly empty.

"Lexi sucks at keeping secrets."

Tanner pulled in behind Lexi's minivan and put the car in park. She reached for the door handle, but at the last minute looked back over her shoulder. "Thanks for the ride. And . . ." *Go on, Abby, say it.* "Thanks for helping out tonight, Jack."

"That wasn't so hard, was it?" Before she could answer or even roll her eyes, he was out of the truck and opening her door. Ignoring his smug smile, she slipped past him, reaching for her purse. Only he was quicker, grabbing it and refusing to let go.

"Abby," Deputy Jonah Baudouin said, stepping out of his cruiser and sending her a warm smile. Tanner frowned. "I've been trying to get a hold of you."

"Oh, I forgot I had my phone on silent." To avoid her family's seven hundred calls.

"Everything okay?" Tanner asked, shaking the man's hand and puffing out his chest. Abby wanted to roll her eyes. Jonah's sister was married to Nate, so in a way that made him family. Nothing more.

"Remember that missing person report you filed last year? It seems your missing"—he looked at the sky, then back to her, shifting on his feet a little—"uh, husband is no longer missing. Phone's been ringing all day with people reporting sightings around town.

Apparently there was a parade, then someone claims to have spotted him skinny dipping in the fountain at the community park and, well, Nora Kincaid has called 911 three times already to report a naked Peeping Tom on your lawn. She's claiming he's a dead ringer for Richard Moretti, and that he's staring at her through the windows while she tries to dress."

"About that. Richard's not . . . uh, well," Abby mumbled, toeing at the curb. "He's, um . . ." Her throat closed as though her body refused to say the word.

"Dead," Tanner explained, scooting his body a little closer to Abby's. "Richard is dead."

And there it was. The word she'd been avoiding all day. Tossed out there with so much authority that it ended all speculation and cut through the awkward sidestepping that was about to begin.

"I'm sorry to hear that," Jonah said gently, taking off his hat.

"Me too," Abby said again, because there weren't enough words in all the languages in the world to express what she was feeling or just how sorry she was. There were a lot of things that Richard deserved, like a complete ass kicking from her, but dying young wasn't one of them. "His remains were delivered to my house in a lifelike statue. But the movers are coming back on Sunday to take it away, so the Richard sightings should calm down after that."

"That would explain why," Jonah opened his notebook, flipped to a page of scribbled notes and read, "Shirley Bale from the senior center requested a license to hold her weekly art class on your lawn." Jonah pocketed his notebook and gave her an uncomfortable pat on the shoulder. "Let me know if there's anything I can do to help."

After a quick thanks and a series of good-byes, the deputy climbed into his cruiser, leaving Tanner and Abby alone.

"You sure you're okay?" Tanner asked. "Because I'm here if you want to talk, I'll even promise to keep my hands to myself."

Abby shook her head, because what she wanted was some time alone to process. She'd pushed through earlier, using the bottlery as a distraction so she wouldn't have to admit the truth—Richard was dead, and she'd never know why he left.

But now it was out there, and in a few hours everyone would know. And Abby didn't know how she was supposed to act, how she was supposed to respond to questions that she had no answers for. She was angry and sad and embarrassingly relieved, and that made her feel guilty. "I'm good, but thanks." She tugged her purse from Tanner's hand and headed toward the bistro. Only, the stubborn man followed.

She picked up the pace, passing the Paws and Claws Day Spa before reaching the Sweet and Savory. Like the rest of Main Street, the two-story brick-faced building looked as pristine as the day it was built back in the late 1800s. Tonight it had little twinkle lights outlining the red-and-white-striped awning and two beautifully sculpted potted cypresses next to the door that had—*Lord help her*—little dildo wineglasses hanging from each branch.

Bracing herself for the party of the decade, Abby peeked in the window, and even through the glass she could smell the vanilla, cinnamon, and crushed unicorn horns that went into every Lexi-inspired pastry. She could also see that, based on the empty tables inside, she was early. And that every horrifying nightmare she'd had about tonight was going to come true—only worse.

A million times worse.

The Sweet and Savory, the locals' favorite bistro, was covered in D-day streamers, helium-filled condoms, and whatever else was considered divorcée chic these days. What woman would want to be the honoree of *that*?

Especially when in about fifteen minutes the entire display was going to be witnessed by her closest friends, family, half the town, and anyone else who her sisters-in-law invited to come celebrate a divorce that never happened.

"The tree that keeps on giving," Tanner said, touching a branch, the glasses sounding like wind chimes. When she didn't laugh, he took her hand. It was a gentle brushing of his fingers, really, but it packed enough heat to create a small spark.

Abby pulled back and his smile faded. "It's not too late to change your mind. Taster's is still open. We can drive on over and share a burger and fries. No questions, no pressure. Then after, I can drive you home."

For a brief second Abby considered saying yes, considered what it would be like to take him up on his offer and not have to pretend. Not have to hide or fake how she was feeling and just allow herself to feel—whatever it was she needed to feel to get through the shock of today.

Maybe grabbing a burger and fries at their old spot would help her forget for a few hours. And maybe, like in the past, it would lead to making out in the back of his truck. Lead to *more*, period.

She'd entertained quite a few fantasies lately that started with Tanner and a simple piano lesson and ended with them having sex right there on the bench.

When she was around him and his big, strong man-sized arms, it was easy to get lost. Easy to forget, well, everything. Forget about her fears, their past, Richard, and the fact that if she couldn't make it work with the one guy everyone, including herself, had considered the sure thing, then there was no way she'd be able to make it work with a guy who had more offers now than when he was a free agent after winning a Super Bowl.

Nope, forgetting wasn't in her best interest, and neither was letting a man like Tanner in. She wasn't looking for a soul mate, but she also wasn't looking to be one of many. Been there, done that, bought and returned the shirt.

Well, tried to. Only the owner of said shirt was still naked on her lawn.

"Thanks for the offer, Jack." She wiggled one of the wine glasses. "But I have enough dicks in my life to worry about."

Tanner took a step back. "Whoa, there. You're calling me a dick?"

"Huh," Abby said, then smiled sweetly. "I guess I am."

"You! Get out. Out out out," her best-friend-turned-sister-in-law, Lexi, yelled the second Abby walked through the door.

Standing on a ladder with a party banner dangling from her fingers, Lexi wore a slinky black dress, pink mile-high heels with a matching boa, and what looked like a glob of chocolate ganache on her butt that matched the Death by Chocolate cake on the food table.

"Fine by me," Abby said, already backing up toward freedom. She'd take her piece of cake to go and wallow in her crappy day alone. Thank you very much.

"No, wait," Lexi said, coming down the last rung and setting the banner on a table. "I'm sorry, it's just that you being here really takes the surprise right out of surprise party. Which is why I told Marc to have you here at eight"—she looked at her watch and frowned—"not seven. Why would he drop you off at seven?"

"Long story," Abby said, not wanting to go into the fact that it wasn't her brother who dropped her off, but the one and only Jack Tanner.

"Were you naked when you told him?" her other sister-in-law, Frankie, asked Lexi, pushing through the swinging kitchen doors, a cluster of condom balloons in hand. "Because if you told him the time while you were naked, then it doesn't count."

Lexi's face went red, but her expression stayed neutral. "I was wearing my apron."

"But were the girls visible?" Frankie went on as though a little piece of Abby's soul wasn't dying with every question. "Because it's best to put them away when talking about important things. Boobs are like some kind of magical earmuffs for men." Now she was making hand gestures, the remaining condoms jerking with every circle of her hand. "They can't hear a thing when they're out."

"Oh. My. God," Abby snapped, making some earmuffs of her own. "Can we not? I mean, I'm standing right here while you two talk about nakedness, boobs, and my brothers. A trifecta of gross." Abby gagged a little, shoving aside some festive D-day streamers, and collapsed into an empty booth. Her entire body felt heavy, and her heart—well, she didn't want to go there. Didn't know how. "My day was scarring enough."

"Oh, boy," Lexi said, shooting Frankie a look. "I think we need chocolate."

"Lots of chocolate," Abby clarified, because hearing about her brothers' sex lives didn't even make the list today. And if she was going to get through her rapidly spiraling life, she'd need more than a pat on the back and a bouquet of helium-filled condoms.

Everyone crammed into the booth, and over a piece of Death by Chocolate cake, which came with three forks, a mountain of whipped cream, and hot fudge, Abby explained everything about the day from the statue to the doggie habitat, and when she was done, collapsed back against the bench, emotionally spent.

"Three years?" Frankie asked, forking off a bite. "How the hell did it take you three years to find out he's dead?"

Abby shrugged. "He was using a different name."

"Wow." Lexi put her bite down and pulled Abby into her arms. "I don't know what to say."

"That makes two of us," Abby said, frustrated that a little tear escaped. "I think I'm angrier at him now than I was when he left. I mean, who commissions a statue to be delivered to his estranged wife just in case he dies first?"

Lexi pulled back, her eyes wide as an owl's. "He meant for it to arrive today?"

Abby nodded. "If Richard was no longer alive, his lawyers were instructed to have it delivered on the day the divorce became official. And that was today. Lucky me."

"And what would have happened if you'd never filed for divorce?"

"Then it would have arrived on our twenty-fifth anniversary." Such a Richard move. He had always tried to control her life, always had to have the final word, and for years she had allowed him to. But she was done with a capital D.

"Isn't that kind of morbid?" Frankie asked. "Planning how to stick it to you even after he died? He wasn't even that old."

Nope, but he was that egotistical. "Richard always needed to make sure he won, and he did, so point to him, because technically I'm his widow."

Information that would make her Nonna ChiChi extremely pleased. A widowed Catholic was far more respectable than a divorced one. Even if her husband had broken every marital vow known to man—and a few against nature.

"Does that mean I can lose the hat?" Frankie asked, yanking the DIVORCÉES DO IT BETTER tiara off her head. "It clashes with my dress." Which was leather, black, and as badass as the owner.

Lexi shot Frankie a look, then sent a very different kind of look Abby's way. One that left Abby squirming in her seat. "Well, of course you are. The accident would have happened before you filed."

"Yeah, well, about that." Abby let out a breath, but it didn't help. She had broken a promise to her best friend, then lied about it. Not intentionally, but in the end that was what it would look like. Because, last summer, tired of being played by cheating bastards who posed as husbands, Abby and Lexi both set out to take back their lives and made a binding pact. Lexi vowed she wouldn't let her messy divorce stop her from opening her dream eatery, and Abby promised to file for divorce. Which she had.

She also may have, in a Tony Robbins–inspired moment, promised to go out on a date—with one sexy hammer for hire. But she didn't want to think about that. Not when she was still married to her deceased husband and having more-than-inspiring fantasies about Jack Tanner and his tool belt.

God, what a mess.

"Remember how I filed last October?"

"I do. I went down to the courthouse with you," Lexi said in a tone that had Abby studying the wood grain in the tabletop.

Abby didn't do disappointment well, which was why she'd rather flee town than let someone down. Especially when that someone was family.

"Well, I got a notice back in November that there was some kind of mix-up. So, I, uh—"

Panicked. Freaked out. Took it as some sign I was making a colossal mistake.

"—waited to refile."

Lexi's eyes went wide. "You waited?"

"Until right before I left for Italy." Which was in February, right after Valentine's Day, and right after she'd realized there was someone she actually wanted to spend the most romantic night of the year with—but couldn't because she was still married. Not that it would have mattered. According to Facebook, Tanner had shown up with a pretty blonde on his arm.

"I was wondering what was taking so long, but didn't want to bug you." Lexi went so quiet Abby felt it in her bones. "Why did you wait?"

Now it was Abby's turn to go quiet. She didn't want to lie, but she was too afraid to admit that a husband, no matter how estranged, was a great deterrent from playboys who had the power to break her heart all over again.

"Holy shit." Frankie's eyes went big with shock, then narrowed into two very scary slits. "Don't tell me you're still in love with the A-hole?"

"What? No." She wasn't. A part of her would always love Richard, but that was the naive young girl who had hoped he was the answer to the aching loneliness that had taken up residence in her chest since the night her parents died.

In the end, he'd left her brokenhearted too. Which was why Abby was content to go it alone for a while. She couldn't lose what she didn't have.

"Why didn't you tell me?" Lexi whispered, and it took everything Abby had to crush down the panic threatening to take her under.

"She chose to stay married to the Dickless Wonder," Frankie explained, waving a corresponding gesture in the air. Another pointed look from Lexi, which Frankie returned—only pointier. "What? Would you admit to that shit?"

Abby ignored this. "It was just that between pregnancies and weddings"—*and all the marital bliss that's been floating around these days*—"there never seemed to be a good time to bring it up."

Or a good time to admit that this was it. That once she filed that paper, she'd be the only one in her family who was truly alone.

CHAPTER 4

"Like I said the last two times you begged me, it's not going to happen," Tanner clarified. He couldn't believe that his best friend was starting this shit with him. "Ever."

"You have to help me out here," Colin Palmer said, signaling the waitress for another beer.

Since it was Wine Down Wednesday at the Spigot and the San Francisco Giants were playing baseball on the big screen, there wasn't a spare seat in the joint. Otherwise, Tanner would have taken his beer and found somewhere that didn't stink of desperation and whine. Preferably someplace quiet. And romantic. With Abby, who he hadn't seen in two days and was realizing that was far too long.

But that would have to wait, since she was avoiding him and because he was expecting Ferris Hampton, the world's top golf course and luxury resort developer, to arrive any minute. They were set to discuss the final details of the proposed new PGA golf course and luxury estates Ferris wanted to build—right here in St. Helena, with Tanner Construction as his partner.

Tanner owned the land. Ferris had the capital to develop. It seemed like a perfect partnership. Only Ferris wasn't 100 percent sold yet. There was another piece of property in Santa Barbara he was considering—and it was up to Tanner to get him to commit to the Napa Valley.

"I did help," Tanner said. "I recommended Abby. She would have smoothed out the problem with Babs before the last contractor even considered walking."

"And like I said the last time you brought up Abby, not going to happen."

Tanner shrugged. Not his problem then. He'd recommended a great designer. It wasn't his fault Colin couldn't get over this ridiculous man-trum he was throwing. So Richard had pulled one over on him? Tanner had lost some money too. So had half the town. Time to move on.

"Come on, we're partners. You have to say yes," Colin continued.

"You sound like my ex-girlfriend. And no."

"Babs says she doesn't need a designer anymore since she's convinced she can handle the job on her own, which is why Brandon walked, leaving me short a general contractor for the cheese shop. No sane person is going to step into the middle of a project this screwed up, especially with Babs Hampton giving the orders," Colin pleaded.

"Thank God I'm sane." Man, the guy was relaying every reason to say no. "We're about to start construction on the DeLucas' new wine cave, and we're a week or two out from getting the certificate of occupancy on your house. Which means you can finally move out of mine." He sent Colin a look, which the guy ignored. "There is no way I can also oversee Babs and her ever-changing ideas." Tanner let out a breath. "Then there's my dad . . ." he added almost as an afterthought.

Three months ago, Gus Tanner suffered a minor stroke. Instead of listening to his doctor and taking it easy, good old Dad decided to take on a framing job up the valley, found himself in a nasty altercation with a wood lathe, and lost. Meaning Gus had spent the past eight weeks sporting a knee-to-ankle cast, and Tanner had gained another roommate. The cast was gone, though his dad was still monopolizing Tanner's television.

"I'm asking you, as my best friend and business partner, to do me a favor," Colin continued. "This Hampton project with Ferris is almost in the bag. Helping his mom out would go far in sealing the deal."

"Col, I know just how huge this could be." The golf course was the kind of project they had been working toward since founding Tanner Construction. "But we don't do these cheese shop kinds of jobs for a reason. They're a lot of headache for very little return. And I want to give Ferris every reason to say yes, I do, but not at the risk of messing up the legit jobs we have on the line."

"We haven't even gotten all the permits for the DeLuca cave," Colin went on as though Tanner wasn't up on every detail of their company already. "And the Pungent Barrel will take, what? A few hours a week for maybe two weeks to get it ready for opening?"

"Do I even need to call bullshit? That *two-week* remodel has already taken over four months."

"That's because she keeps scaring off the help. With you it would take a month. Tops."

"We both know that even if this were a simple renovation, which it's not, since the building is old as dirt and falls under the Historical Preservation Council's jurisdiction, not to mention fixing all the loose ends the last contractor probably left," Tanner shook his head, "we're talking two months of me on the site, busting my ass all day long."

"Shitshitshit." Colin thunked his head against the back of the booth a few times before looking at the ceiling as though asking for divine intervention. Tanner was right and he knew it.

"Babs has scared off every reputable contractor in the county," Colin continued. "No general contractor means the project will never end. Ever. Why would a guy like Ferris want to spend the next two years here, building his next project with his mom breathing down his neck, driving him crazy with chasing off crews?" Colin rested his arms on the table and leaned in—way in. "If you sign on for Babs's project, then I know it will get done and the crew won't walk and everyone will be happy. If you don't, then I guarantee the Pungent Barrel will become the Winchester Mystery House of cheese and wine shops, and break some record for the longest renovation project in the history of the world. Every day that her project goes unfinished, Santa Barbara gets better looking for Ferris, man."

Colin sat back and sighed. "Hell, if it were me, I'd choose Santa Barbara just because it was six hours away from her."

"Maybe you should have thought about that before you wrote off Abby," a threatening voice said from behind. Tanner didn't have to turn to see who it was.

Trey DeLuca, the youngest and the biggest hothead of the brothers—and that was saying a lot—sank down onto a bench on the other side of Tanner.

"How can I write her off? This isn't even my project," Colin lied.

"Tanner Construction might not be the builder, but everyone in town knows you are managing the subcontracting as a favor to Ferris," Trey challenged. "And you told Babs that Abby wasn't a solid choice."

"Wait, you told Babs what?" Tanner demanded to know.

"Exactly what I told you last week. She asked if Abby was a good choice, and I said I didn't think she was the right fit," Colin said casually, sending Tanner a look that was anything but casual. It was the same pissy glare that summed up every conversation they'd ever had about Abby.

Tanner glared right back.

"How would you know? You didn't even look at her ideas," another voice challenged. Marc, shoulders shoving and elbows jabbing, took up residence next to Colin, making sure to get up in his personal space.

"Babs wasn't impressed."

"Babs has a chartreuse-green urinal in her sitting room that she calls art," a third voice added. Nate pulled up a chair at the head of the table, strategically blocking Colin in.

Colin wasn't a small guy by any means. He was six one, in good shape, and could handle himself in a bar fight—something Tanner knew firsthand. Only in this bar, smashed between a herd of DeLucas, his buddy didn't stand a chance. Nope, one-on-one, Abby's brothers were beyond intimidating; as a collective force they were scary as shit. And when it came to the women in their lives, a wise man would give them a wide berth.

Colin wasn't a wise man. "Look, can we cut the crap? You're here because I didn't recommend your sister. And no matter how much you threaten and whine, I'm not going to recommend your sister. End of story."

The look on Nate's face said the story was far from over as he slid a folder of very official-looking documents across the table to Colin. "The money that Richard took from you and Ferris will be repaid in full. Tomorrow. With ten percent interest. All I need from you is the account you want your money wired to, where Ferris wants his, and in twenty-four hours, as far as this whole Richard BS is concerned, we're square."

Jesus, Tanner thought as Colin picked up the bank instructions. They were more meddlesome than a bunch of old ladies. And

Tanner couldn't help but grin because, man, Abby was going to kick their collective asses when she found out they had gone behind her back to distribute the funds to the investors.

"Huh." Colin flipped slowly through the documents, only to close the folder and say, "I guess that whole adage 'Better late than never' is a crock, since I don't feel any better and it doesn't change the fact that I am never hiring your sister since she isn't the right fit for this job."

"Well, then maybe Tanner Construction isn't the right fit for us anymore," Trey said, standing.

Yeah, moron, Tanner wanted to say when Colin shot him a panicked look. Tanner Construction was the exclusive builder for DeLuca Wines. In fact, Tanner had cut a deal with them that would help make their company the newest giant in the wine cave business, a business built on constructing subterranean facilities for the aging and storing of wine. It was a cave they'd spent the past year planning for. A cave that, if Colin didn't screw this up, they were weeks out from breaking ground on.

"Actually, Abby's the perfect person," Tanner said casually, not even bothering to see if Trey would take his seat—which he did with maximum grumbling. "She is talented, easy to work with, and most importantly, she is available. Plus, after having dealt with these idiots for thirty years, I know Babs and her sporadic whims won't even faze her."

That earned him a hard look from all of the brothers. He just shrugged. It was true. But Colin wasn't convinced, which was obvious from the *are you fucking kidding me* look he was shooting Tanner's way.

"Your hiring Abby would go far where the community is concerned. It could really open up doors for her and end this boycott," Nate explained.

"So, what will it take for her to get a fresh start with you and the Hamptons?" Marc asked, and if Tanner didn't know any better, he'd think Abby's brother had just offered to bribe Colin in order to get Abby the job.

Colin looked shocked. Then he looked right at Tanner and calmly set the contract on the table. A sinking feeling started way down low in Tanner's gut, because he knew how this was going to play out. And it wasn't going to be good for anyone involved. Colin only got that calm when he was about to tell someone to go fuck themselves, which was why Tanner leveled him with a hard look. "Everyone deserves a fresh start, right, Colin?"

Colin leveled Tanner with a look of his own, then shrugged. His partner was stubborn as hell, but he knew when to back down. And right now was that time.

"You know what, Tanner? You're right. Everyone deserves a fresh start." He looked at the rest of the table. "But as for Babs's shop, seems she has chased off another contractor. So she's too busy looking for a GC to talk about designers right now. Tell Abby I'm sorry," he finished, not sorry at all.

"Tanner can do it," Trey said. And just like that Colin's plan backfired. "He liked working with Abby. They did a bang-up job with Lexi's bistro."

Marc turned to lance Tanner with a glare that packed enough warning to send most men scurrying. Tanner wasn't most men, and he didn't scurry. Instead, he feigned confusion, as though he didn't know that Marc was the only brother who suspected "like" didn't begin to cover how Tanner felt about working with Abby. Doing that remodel with her had been the best part of last year.

Problem was, if he agreed to this, made some ridiculous deal to secure her a job that her talent should have been enough to get to begin with, he would be no better than her brothers.

"Like I was telling Colin a second ago. I don't have time. I don't do small retail renovations. And I don't feel comfortable managing Abby's career behind her back."

"We're not managing her career," Nate defended. "We are simply—"

"Managing her career," Tanner interrupted. "She is a grown woman who doesn't need her brothers underselling her abilities."

His phone buzzed. He fished it from his pocket and stared at the screen in surprise, then he smiled. He couldn't help it. It was big and stupid, and he didn't care.

"I gotta take this," he said to the table and, ignoring the irritated glares shooting his direction, hit talk. "Well, hello there."

Nothing but silence. And maybe some heavy breathing. He pressed the phone closer to his ear and, nope, not heavy breathing so much as huffing. Loud, irritated huffing.

"Hello?" he prompted again. Clearly, Abby was considering her options: one, hang up and hope he didn't have her number stored in his phone—which he most certainly did. Or, two, pretend she'd misdialed. He went for option three. "I can hear you breathing."

A frazzled sigh came through the earpiece before she finally said, in a tone that told him frazzled didn't even begin to cover her state of being, "Hey, Jack, it's Abby."

"I know, I recognize your huff." He leaned back in the booth and his smile became a full-on grin. "Yup, that one right there."

"Remember how you said that if I ever needed anything, that I could call?"

"I remember everything we have ever talked about."

"Right. Well, I'm calling."

He'd almost forgotten. "Do you want me to swing by and take a look at the desi—"

"Oh my God, don't say it out loud," she whispered, loudly. "Especially if you're with my brothers . . . are you with my brothers?"

He eyed the men in question, who were all eyeing him back. "Yup."

"Don't let them know I'm on the phone."

Tanner sighed. "Give me a good reason and I'll consider it."

Again with the huffs. "My asking isn't enough?"

"Nope."

She hesitated long enough to make Tanner worry he'd blown it. That he'd pushed too far and she was going to hang up, and then he would never know what kind of call this was, and what kind of help she needed. Which would suck, because he had several scenarios playing out in his head. Some involved wine, others lace and silk, but all of them ended with breakfast in Abby's bed. Naked.

"Fine." She sounded tired. "When I bought this house, Marc said it was a dump. Gabe swore the only reason it hadn't been condemned was because it was historically protected. Nate went on and on about how I wouldn't buy a used car without having a mechanic look under the hood, so why would I buy a house without seeking professional advice."

"Ah, darling, I'm a professional who happens to do house calls, especially ones that involve under-the-hood inspections."

She ignored him and went on, "I agreed, the house needs work and figuring out just how much I'd be committing to would be smart and, even though I would have bought it regardless, I called a contractor."

Not him, he noted.

"But Trey had to be a jerk and add that there was no way he'd let his sister be the one stupid enough to fall for the charming porch and bay windows packaging, because the roof was leaky, the foundation cracked, and the pipes were one winter away from bursting. So I pointed out he wasn't a contractor or professional, and I bought the house."

"They burst, didn't they?" he said, careful to keep his face neutral.

"How did you know?"

Tanner slid out of the booth and, ignoring the heated barbs tossed at him from the table, walked toward the back of the bar. He leaned back against the wall and knew he was going to cave.

Why?

Because the thought of walking away from her made him sick. He'd done it before and it had nearly destroyed him.

"It was either that or you were calling me from the bathtub. Either way, I would be more than happy to lend a hand. Or both, as the project requires. Although, I have to tell you that I am partial to bath salts, but I can deal with the standard bubbles."

He could practically hear her rolling her eyes through the phone. "The leak is in the garage."

Leak my ass. He could hear the steady stream of water pooling on the floor. It sounded like a set of sprinklers blasting the inside of her garage. "First thing, you need to turn the water off—"

"I'm not a complete idiot, Jack," she defended.

"At the main?" There was silence, then he heard sloshing through the water, the garage door open and shut, and a couple of rusty squeaks. "Good girl, now can you see where the leak is?"

"Hang on." More sloshing. "Yeah, it's right above the new washing machine."

"Who installed it?"

"I did." *Oh boy.* "Followed the directions to a tee." He dropped his head back against the wall so hard it vibrated, because Abby and directions never mixed well. "Anyway, I called three plumbers, but no one is answering and there is so much water I'm afraid my car is going to float away." Her voice shook a little and damn if that didn't make his chest pinch. "I don't want to eat crow on this with my brothers, and I only have today and tomorrow to finish my designs so I can submit them to Babs on Friday. I'm already looking at pulling an all-nighter and well . . . you're my last hope."

Ignoring the odd feeling in his chest at being the last pick for Team Abby, which was incredibly difficult to do, he pushed off the wall and headed back toward the table to grab his keys. "Make sure that the water valve is completely shut off, and I will be there in a few minutes."

"What? No! I didn't mean *you*. I was just calling to stealthily get the number of a plumber you've worked with before. One who might be able to squeeze me in and keep his mouth shut."

"I know the perfect guy, and all-nighters are his specialties. He'll be there in ten minutes."

Tanner ended the call before she could argue and—dropping a few bills down to cover his beer—really looked at the group of men who were starting to piss him off. Too bad they didn't know the Abby he knew, the real Abby. Because if they did, they never would have thought she would be okay with getting a job she didn't earn—career changing or not.

"I gotta go." He picked up his keys and headed for the door.

"Go?" Colin barked. "What the hell, man? Ferris should be here any minute."

"Tell him something urgent came up. He'll understand." Tanner got as far as the next table when he turned back around. "And since you all seemed to have forgotten, let me remind you—Abby is one of the most talented designers in the area. Period. Her work speaks for itself." He leveled Colin with a glare. "If you pass on her, that's your problem. Either way, I don't do renovations, and I don't," he looked at the whole table, "sell my friends short."

CHAPTER 5

Ten minutes later, Abby was considering building herself an ark. The water had risen high enough to make galoshes a necessity. And even though she was standing on the dryer, she still couldn't reach the cracked pipe, which was leaking in a steady stream.

Still, she had a more pressing problem. She'd called Tanner. The same Tanner who had invaded her dreams as of late. Something she blamed on hormones and a depressing lack of orgasms that didn't require batteries.

Her fault, of course. After Richard, she hadn't had the heart to put herself out there, so she'd used her marriage as a dividing line between her and, well, everyone else. Especially men. Only Jack Tanner, male incarnate and man who went the distance daily, made his fortune breaking through even the toughest defensive lines.

And if she wasn't careful, she'd let him break through hers. And then break her heart all over again.

A determined pounding sounded over the loud gushing of water, and Abby headed for the front door. She trudged across the garage, through the kitchen, and into the front room, muttering a few choice words when she saw the forest of lingerie. Afraid that using her dryer would be like dropping a hair dryer into a full bathtub, not to mention she'd installed that too, Abby had opted to hang dry her laundry—down the banister.

Not the smartest choice, seeing as she was expecting company and it looked like an orchard of panties and bras, their straps swaying in the wind of the ceiling fan.

Before Abby could dispose of them, the doorbell went off. Clipped and impatient. She tiptoed toward the front window, pulled the shades open a tad, and peered through—to find Tanner on the other side of the glass.

Not at the front door, but at the window, as though he'd anticipated she'd chicken out. Their gazes met and she felt herself tingle. He stood there, toolbox in hand, looking cool, collected, and oh so capable.

Damn him.

His dark blond hair was tousled, as though he'd had on a hat earlier and decided at the last minute to leave it in the truck. He was dressed in a pair of dusty work boots, well-worn jeans, and a soft gray T-shirt that was stretched to capacity, leaving no doubt as to just how many two-by-fours he lifted a day.

The part that had her going all breathy was the tool belt riding low on his lean hips, which read, SATISFACTION GUARANTEED. The OR I'LL DO IT AGAIN UNTIL YOU'RE SMILING was merely implied.

Yup, Jack Tanner looked like your basic sexy contractor for hire—and she wanted him for more than just his pipe work.

"You going to let me in?" he asked, holding up a business card between his fingers. "I brought you the card of a good plumber."

She squinted through the glass. "That's your card."

"Yup, best in the county. I can provide references."

She just bet he could. Hard Hammer Tanner was the contractor of choice for the women of wine country. One look at his SATISFACTION GUARANTEED belt and generously endowed work boots, and anyone with double-X chromosomes would be lining up to talk about his tools. And Abby had had enough experience with tools, specifically his, to know that letting him inside would be a bad move.

Her banister of panties was already waving in surrender, which was why she said, "Never mind, I got it handled."

"We can do this all night long, darling. Although . . ." He looked toward her driveway, then back to her, and let out a smile that was 100 percent trouble. "I can already see the water coming out the bottom of the garage door. And last I heard, you had to have approval for a water feature to be in Good Neighbor Code compliance." She didn't budge, except to check that the lock was bolted. "You can either unlock the door or I'll pick it. Either way, I'm coming in."

"You do and Nora will have the sheriff here in no time. She's got him on speed dial."

With that she crossed her arms in her most intimidating stance and waited for him to open his tool box and try to pick her lock. Instead, he flashed her a killer smile, pulled her spare key out from under the flowerpot, opened the door, and stepped into her house.

"I like what you've done with the place," he said, taking in the new décor. Then he turned to face her, taking her in, and his lips curved up at the corners. "Colorful."

"I'm not hiring you, Jack," she clarified, because the last thing she needed right then was more time alone with him.

Tanner was charming and funny, and made her feel things she shouldn't. Not for him. The only thing they ever managed to successfully accomplish was disappointing each other. In fact, they were two for two in that department, and she was older now, wiser, and knew that giving in to the heat between them would be a mistake.

She was done with mistakes.

"You said you needed a look under your hood, here I am," he said casually, making himself right at home, sifting through the sketches and samples she had collected for the Pungent Barrel proposal, which she'd forgotten to hide.

"They're not done yet," she said, wanting to smack herself for how desperate she sounded.

He looked up at her through his brows. "You want to keep the existing conveyer belts?" he asked right as something large and solid got caught in the ever-growing current in her garage and slammed into what sounded like her car.

"You want to talk about my designs? Right now?" Another loud thunk echoed down the hallway. "Maybe we should call that plumber."

"In a minute," was his only reply, then he turned the sketch sideways. "It looks like you want to turn the conveyer belts into counters."

"Well, use them as the foundation," she said, looking over her shoulder toward the garage. No sign of water above the door's threshold—thank God. "They'll have to be lifted and resurfaced, but I think that utilizing as much of the original structure as possible will make the space unique, attract a different clientele than just your average cheese and wine connoisseurs."

It would also add an edginess to the normal cheese and wine tasting experience that no one else in the valley had.

"The other designers had it scheduled to be ripped out," Tanner said, talking over the low and steady rush of water.

She glanced toward the garage door again. "Jack, should we . . . ?"

Mr. Contractor didn't so much as bat an eye, just kept studying her designs, so Abby sighed and figured, what was another few hundred gallons? "The other designers didn't take the time to understand the space as a whole, which is a shame if you ask me. See the way the conveyer belt snakes its way through the space? At first glance it seems random. But if they had really looked at it they'd see that the design was purposeful. Exact. It is the perfect way to divide such a large space and make it approachable. It also maintains the historical integrity of the building."

When he didn't say a word, just kept staring at her, she felt a rush of insecurity come back. Whenever she'd pushed for restoration over demolition, Richard had warned that, while unique seemed romantic on paper, it often came across as naïveté disguised as taste. So she felt compelled to add, "New isn't always better. Sometimes it's just new."

"Huh," was all he said, continuing to flip through until he got to the preliminary drawing, where he stopped—right along with her heart as she watched him pick it up, his intense blue gaze meeting hers over the papers before it returned to meticulously study the designs.

To everyone else, they would look like a jumble of ideas and fabric swatches, but she had put her heart into this job. That proposal was her on paper, right there for anyone to see if they knew what to look for. And Tanner was looking, all right. Taking in every sleek line, every bold design choice, even the bit of whimsy hidden beneath the sophistication. And suddenly she was terrified of what he'd see.

Despite the panic bubbling inside, Abby straightened, bracing herself for his reaction. She'd been dying to get a second opinion, a fresh set of eyes to make sure she wasn't missing something, that her ideas were as amazing as her gut told her they were. That Richard was wrong and she had a knack for finding beauty in the forgotten.

But a small part of her feared that Richard was right. Tanner was shrewd, knew the client, had a natural eye for spotting talent. He also had a natural eye for sifting out crap. And that scared her because his approval would mean everything. More than everything. His rejection would crush her. Which was why she hadn't taken him up on his offer and called earlier.

But he was here now and apparently had seen enough, because he gave a definitive nod with some kind of grunt that, damn him, was impossible to translate.

"Well?" she asked when he just stared at her. "What do you think?"

"I think we should go outside so I can carefully inspect each and every one of your pipes." Although his eyes weren't looking at her busted pipes—they were too busy studying her bare legs.

Wishing like hell she had on something other than ladybug galoshes, a pair of ratty old cutoffs, and a white T-shirt that was thin enough to advertise that *all* of her bras were currently drying, Abby weighed her options, then gave in.

Sort of.

She needed a plumber and Tanner had a black book that rivaled Donald Trump's when it came to the construction professionals. Maybe he could patch it enough to last until Friday—after her meeting with Babs.

Plus, needing his opinion was pathetic enough. His knowing it was not going to happen.

"Fine, you can look at my pipes, give me an idea of what I'm looking at," she said, snatching her papers back. "Then you can recommend someone I can call to fix it."

"I thought you'd never ask."

"That someone being not you."

Without another word, she strode toward the garage and trudged to the washer, not bothering to see if he'd follow.

Never one to be rushed for anything, Tanner took his sweet time, coming to a stop at the threshold of the garage and eyeing the pool of water. With a grimace he stepped down, the water line coming midway up his work boots. Unaffected and swagger in full effect, he moseyed over, pulled out the washer, and inspected Abby's snazzy install job.

Abby leaned over the machine to have a look-see, only the movement caused her shirt to gape at the neckline, and Tanner gave her a look so innately male her nipples perked up at the attention.

"I'll just give you some space," she took a small step—in the opposite direction, "and stand over here."

But Tanner wasn't listening. He was too busy hopping that fine ass of his up on the washer to look at the damage.

What he was looking for, Abby had no idea, but based on the fierce concentration going on she figured he didn't like what he found. Not to mention the low whistle he gave sounded way too expensive for her checkbook. Between keeping her design firm afloat and buying this house a few months ago, the closet remodels and piano lessons weren't cutting it.

Bottom line, Abby was strapped for cash. And going to her family was not an option.

Unable to help herself, she walked back over, careful to give him enough space to work, and assessed the damage. Since she had no idea what to look for, she resigned herself to assessing the squeeze factor of his butt. It came in at a tantalizing ten. "Is it bad?"

"Not sure yet."

Eyes firmly on the pipe, he grabbed a wrench and fiddled with the joint. Two twists later and a loud creak echoed throughout the garage, followed by a geyser of water that hit Tanner straight in the chest.

"Oh my God." Abby jumped back, hands shielding her face. "I don't know why it did that. I turned it off like you said. Well, I turned it as far as I could. It was kind of rusted in place."

Tanner didn't say a word, didn't even try to lecture her about how she should have hired a professional. He just quickly retightened the joint and hopped down with the grace of the former football stud he was, all that yummy Capable Man oozing from his pores.

"Do you think it's a one-pipe-being-a-jerk kind of thing or more of a major project?"

"I have a replacement pipe in the truck that should do the trick," he said, and she could tell he was trying really hard to look her in the eye. A fact that became obvious when his gaze slipped to her chest and he cleared his throat. Which was fair, since her gaze was doing some gawking of its own. Needless to say, it wouldn't have escaped anyone's attention that they both looked like candidates for a wet-T-shirt contest.

He finally peeled his gaze back to her eyes and held up a silencing hand. "And before you remind me that I'm not on your approved list of plumbers, know that you can either let me get to work or start fluffing up the guest pillows, because I'm not leaving until you have water. So, what's it going to be, Abs? Should I grab my overnight bag from the car?"

She knew from his tone that he wasn't backing down. He would dig in deep, fight her on this, and in the end he'd win. Because she needed running water, and he was her only hope. Plus, Tanner, for all of his laid-back charm, was one of the most determined people Abby knew. Stubborn too. And sexy as hell when he was shoving all of that protective swagger her way.

She threw her hands up in defeat. "Fine. Just give me a rough estimate. What are we looking at?"

His eyes softened, but nothing else did as he stepped into her space. He was all hard lines and stubborn attitude. He stood so close that all she'd have to do was raise up on her toes and they'd be kissing.

"I don't want your money, Abs."

"If you do the work, you get paid. It's only fair."

"We're friends," he said very softly. "That's what friends do. They help each other out."

"You're friends with my brothers and you charge them."

"I charge your brothers because they bug the shit out of me." Tanner smiled wickedly, his gaze skating over her like a caress. "And your brothers aren't nearly as much fun to look at."

They both took in her current state of dress and she laughed. "You mean funny looking."

He flashed a single, devastating dimple her way. "Sexy is sexy, darling. You could be in cleats, a jersey, and full football pads and you'd turn heads. In fact, that sounds like one of my fantasies." He winked. "You got a jersey? If not, I have one I can lend you. It even has authentic Super Bowl dirt on it."

"How do I know it's Super Bowl dirt?"

"Matches the ring." He held up his hand and flashed the giant nugget of athletic domination her way.

She shrugged. "I already have a jersey."

"Really?"

"Yup." Abby hid a smile when his eyes went all hot. "It's navy and bright green and has a cute little Seahawk on it. Right here," she lied, tracing a circle over her chest.

"You wouldn't." A cute crinkle creased his brow. "Anything but a Seahawk."

"A Seahawk," Abby confirmed with a nod.

"Yeah, well, bet it doesn't have authentic Super Bowl dirt on it." When she neither confirmed nor denied it, just held his gaze, his cute crease turned to a full-on frown.

She smiled. Then the pipe started groaning like Old Faithful ready to blow.

Tanner looked up at the labyrinth of exposed pipes and let out a long breath. "Look, best guess is the pipes can't handle the water pressure from the new washing machine and they need to be replaced. If you want, I can patch the leak and give you the number of a guy on my crew. He's reliable, smart, married, great with plumbing issues, and won't rip you off."

"Married? Is that a requirement for a plumber these days?"

"For me it is. He'll give you a fair price, but it will still cost you a few grand."

"A few grand?" Did her heart just stop?

"Or you let me stay and we fix it tonight, problem solved. I have enough spare pipes, valves, fittings, whatever you need left over from the last project I did."

For the first time in a long time, "we" didn't sound so terrifying. The idea of having someone to help out, someone who would treat her like an equal, was refreshing.

Abby looked at her flooded garage and back to the big ox, wanting to be sure they were on the same page. "I'm not looking for some superhero to come in and save the day."

"I've always considered myself the handy but handsome sidekick." He shrugged. "You can wear the cape, that's cool with me."

She laughed. "Fine. But I want to repay you. This isn't a favor." He waggled a brow and she jabbed a finger in the middle of his chest. Not that he even felt it. The big, handy, handsome, badass sidekick. "I meant piano lessons or something."

"Already used that trade. I want something else."

"I'm not sleeping with you," she clarified sharply, although the thought of his big hands on her body made her girly parts sing.

"I'm the sidekick, which makes you my boss, and I'm not that kind of guy." There went both dimples. "I was thinking a night with you that ends in a kiss."

"That's it?"

"Nope." And here it came, she thought sadly. The moment when he'd turn into every guy she'd ever met because he had the upper hand. "Also a slice of that wine cake you used to bake. The one with the powdered sugar sprinkled over the top."

"We hang out, I feed you a slice of cake, and we're square?"

"Don't forget the kiss. Oh, and make it a whole cake so I can take some home to my dad."

"You live with your dad?"

"Yup." Tanner sighed, and she knew that sigh well. Had sighed it herself a few times.

She'd lived with her Nonna ChiChi for the past few years, and even though they were close, and she loved her nonna, it was challenging, to say the least. Tanner and his dad, well, they gave the hard-love thing a whole new spin.

"A few months ago my dad had a minor stroke, then hurt his leg. I didn't want to put him in assisted living while he was recovering, so I moved him into my place. Getting him to do anything, let alone come to the table and eat with me, has been a constant battle. Probably because most of what I attempt to make isn't edible. Or maybe because he is as stubborn as I am. Either way, I need to get him up and moving, doctor's orders."

Abby placed a hand on his chest. "I'm sorry, Jack. I didn't know."

"Yeah, well, we're still figuring things out, but I think a nice home-baked cake could give him incentive enough to get up off his ass and turn off the television."

"Wine cake it is." She looked at her hand, which was now covered by his bigger one, and she could feel his pulse vibrate through her.

"And Abby." Tanner smiled and patted her hand in a way that sent warm currents fluttering. "Your designs are inspired."

It took everything she had not to cry a little, because after today she needed that. "Inspired enough to stand up against big firms with big portfolios and big names?" She could hear the hope in her voice. "Because I guess Babs has a few outside firms submitting. Schmitt and Warner is even sending someone out from New York."

Not that Abby blamed the woman. After scaring off all of the local talent, her only hope to get a crew back to work quickly was to attach a big name to the project. A name Abby didn't have.

"How do I even compete with Schmitt and Warner? They designed half of Manhattan."

"Don't compete," he said as if it were that simple. "The other designers will give Babs their flashy title along with their flashy ideas."

"Babs likes flash," she murmured.

"But she *loves* this town. She loves the history, the tradition, the story hiding behind every crack. Babs wants a connection to something real, something with depth that inspires conversation, which is why she chose a hundred-year-old headache instead of a storefront in that new strip mall in Napa." He took in her shoddy foundation, the busted pipes, and smiled. "You said it earlier, sometimes new is just new. Flash fades and Babs knows that, she just needs to be reminded that real is better. Real lasts."

Then his smile faded, and so did hers, because she was aware of just how close they stood, and how badly she wanted him to lean down and—

Kiss me.

Tanner's eyes seemed to be saying yes, so she rose up, just slightly, but enough to change the game. The tips of her nipples brushed against his wet chest, and Abby knew she was going to do the most spectacularly stupidest thing possible. They'd been here before, and she'd promised herself she'd never go there again.

Yet here she was.

"You sure?" he whispered, lifting his hand from hers only to slide it through her hair and gently cup her face.

No. She wasn't sure of anything except that if she said as much, he would back off. Immediately. Which was what she should do.

Instead, she slid her palms slowly down his wet chest, tracing each and every ridge of his stomach, loving how the muscles flexed under her touch, until finally resting one hand on the top of his tool belt, the other wrapped around to his lower back to pull him against her.

He tilted his head down, way down, so that their noses were brushing, their breaths mingling, and damn if a needy little moan didn't slip out.

Always the gentleman, he gave her one last chance to take the sane route, to change her mind, only there was nothing sane about the way her body was buzzing or the way her mind had stopped working the second his shirt went translucent.

She closed the last inch and, look at that, Tanner was making some noises of his own, so raw it made her body heat up to inferno.

"I do owe you a kiss," she whispered. "As payment. And a deal is a deal."

His mouth was suddenly on hers, hot and sure and so damn confident she felt her toes curl up right in her rubber galoshes.

"Holy Christ," he whispered and hauled her up against him, deepening the connection.

Abby had to agree, kissing Jack Tanner was like a religious experience. One taste was all it took and Abby was reborn. Somehow transported back to that first night, when Tanner had kissed her in the darkened cab of his old, beat-up Chevy, when he'd made her forget that her world was falling apart, made her feel as though she could put it back together.

That with him she would be okay.

And right now she felt okay. More than okay. She felt amazing and alive and like she wasn't a thirty-year-old widow who hadn't had sex in the better part of a decade. And then she felt his hand slip down her back to cup her butt, and suddenly she was sitting on top of the dryer, Tanner between her legs, her fingers under his shirt, and it got her thinking—if this was his idea of spending time together, she was on board. For as long as that ship would sail.

Warning bells buzzed loudly. Too bad her brain was so busy having a meltdown from all of the nerve endings firing at once to listen. What started out as settling a debt turned into a heated frenzy that officially blew her mind.

Tanner had been good back in college, but he was even better now—which should have scared her, but somehow only managed to make her hotter. Then he slanted his mouth over hers, taking it to that next level in a way that only Tanner could do, kissing her harder, again and then again, his hands running up her thighs to cup her ass, his body pressing against hers in all the right places, caging her between that amazing chest and the back of the dryer—and the warning bells got louder. More persistent.

Buzz buzz buzz.

Tanner abruptly pulled back and swore. The sudden emptiness in her chest told her that it wasn't just physically. He was going to stop, be the gentleman, and give her time to process, and she didn't want him to. She wasn't open to the complete Jack Tanner experience, but she was hoping for another few moments to really get reacquainted with his body. And that mouth.

Abby struggled to take in a breath and, as though he'd heard the same warning bells as she had, explained, "It's just the dryer."

Tanner was doing some struggling of his own, and way too much thinking. He ran a thumb over her lips, and even that sent a zing south of the equator. Then, with one last look at her very wet, very see-through shirt, he turned and disappeared out the side door.

Abby leaned back against the dryer and closed her eyes. What was she doing?

Nothing good, that's what.

Tanner was dangerous. A menace. A big, sexy hazard to her well-being. No matter how much she'd hoped that time would have done its job and diminished everything she'd felt for him, it hadn't. And that kiss had just proved it.

The only way Abby was ever going to move forward with her life was to stop revisiting her past. And Tanner was a part of her past that she most definitely needed to steer clear of.

Which was going to be a little tricky since that one kiss had catapulted him into something much more recent. Something that felt a whole hell of a lot like her present.

CHAPTER 6

To-go bags in hand, Tanner walked up the front steps of his house, frowning when he saw Colin's Mercedes parked out back. The game should have still been in full swing at the Spigot—just like Colin's meeting with Ferris.

He opened the front door, and for the first time since acquiring roommates he didn't seem to mind the piles of crap or muddy paw prints all over his handcrafted stone floor. He was too busy thinking about Abby in her thin, wet shirt, no bra, and itty-bitty shorts. The galoshes had been an adorable bonus, coming up well past her knees as though she were trudging through the swamplands.

And those lips, man, he'd renovate her entire dump of a house from top to bottom if it meant spending more time with her mouth fused to his.

Tanner shut the door behind him, and the sound of claws on the floor was the only warning before a warm body plowed into his legs.

Part wolfhound, part bigfoot, and a complete pain in Tanner's ass, Wrecking Ball, his dad's dumb-as-dirt mutt, was so excited Tanner was home that he wagged himself all over Tanner's entryway, leaving a yellow happy trail three feet long.

"Outside," Tanner scolded, pointing. When Wreck only panted joyfully, Tanner dropped a pile of paper towels over the puddle, which he left by the door for just such an occasion. "You do your business outside, got it?"

Wreck barked. Tanner cut him a hard glare, then, shucking his wet boots, made his way to the kitchen—the dog followed, his nails tapping the slate floor and his big, wiry tail wagging so hard he knocked over everything he passed. Including a wadded-up receipt that sat on the entry table, which he promptly ate.

Tanner dropped the Chinese food on the counter and poked his head into the family room to find Gus and Colin drinking beer and watching the game.

Gus was in his ratty old recliner, socked feet kicked up on the footrest and his silver hair sticking up in the back as though he'd slept right there all day and hadn't budged. Which he probably hadn't. Gus had arrived with a suitcase, his dog, a bad attitude, and that damn chair. The only thing that had budged since move-in day was the dog.

Colin, on the other hand, was sprawled out on the couch, his cold beer sweating on the leather armrest, his work boots scuffing up the coffee table. Wreck jumped up beside him, licked himself a few times, then curled up in Tanner's spot, tongue hanging out.

"Dinner's in the kitchen." Tanner met his dad's gaze. His wiry brows puckered, making it clear that he was in a mood. "So eat it in the kitchen and save some for me. I'll be down in a minute."

"Is that Chinese I smell?" Gus asked, not even pretending he was going to head into the kitchen. "I hate Chinese."

"We had Chinese last week."

"Hated it then too."

Tanner looked at his dad and wondered why he was busting his balls this time. "You had three helpings. Asked me to order Mongolian beef."

"Didn't want to be rude, seeing as I'm a guest here," his cranky voice snapped.

And here we go. Tanner took a calming breath and waited to speak until his blood pressure wasn't bordering on unnecessary roughness. "You're not a guest, Dad. This is your home. I want you to feel comfortable here."

"Good, cuz comfortable is me eating my dinner, right here from the comfort of my chair." He waved a hand at Colin. "Now turn up the volume, I can't hear the score over all the chatter."

Tanner gave up. Living with his dad was like living with a two-year-old. Gus had spent most of his first thirty-five years alone, so when Tanner had come into the world, the man was already set in his ways. Ways that didn't have much room for a wife or a son. So it wasn't surprising that Tanner's mom went out for a drive one day and never came back.

"Did you get extra noodles?" Colin asked. "You know how much I love noodles."

"No. Don't remember inviting you to dinner and don't want to give you a reason to stay."

"You can eat Jack's," Gus offered. "Serves him right for not taking me to the bar to watch the game."

"You said you didn't want to go."

Gus shrugged, eyes fixed on the flat screen.

"Dad, next time if you want to go, just say yes when I ask you."

"I wasn't ready to go yet," Gus said, a fluster of hands and huffs, gearing up to one of his tirades. "I was still watching my Jeopardy and you took off. That's what's wrong with your generation, you have no patience."

Something he would love to argue another time when he wasn't wet and starving. Eight weeks into sharing space and Gus was still alive: proof that Tanner was the most patient man on the freaking planet.

"Don't answer your phone neither," Gus added, sounding a little winded. In fact, when Tanner looked closer, his dad seemed pale and clammy. And old. Really old. "Figures that the only time you don't answer that ball and chain is when I'm calling."

"You called?" Tanner checked his phone and sure enough, there were two missed calls from his dad.

"No matter," he said in a tone that said it mattered—a whole hell of a lot. "Colin here entertained me. Let me join the party. Even bought me a draft while we watched the game with that Ferris fella."

Tanner paced to the window, looked out, and—*ah, Jesus*—felt his entire chest drop. His dad's three-hundred-year-old truck was gone, meaning Colin must have driven Gus back. "You aren't cleared to drive."

"According to that doctor, I'm not cleared to go to the john by myself neither, but I didn't see you offering to hold my hand then."

"Dad, you behind a wheel is not an option. Ever. Dr. Johnson said that—"

"Dr. Johnson's got as much sense as a stump. I've had turds older than that boy."

That boy was older than Tanner, and Ivy League certified.

"Funny, since the Department of Motor Vehicles agreed." Tanner ran a hand down his face. "Maybe we should reconsider hiring someone part-time. I still have that list of nurses who—"

"No way," Gus said shaking his head. "And don't you even think about hiring one behind my back, I'll chase her away before she even gets settled. Remember when Clive Evans threw out his hip last year? He hired himself a nurse, and all she did was rob him blind and give him a woody. Poor guy's homeless now."

"Clive's wife took care of him. And Helen got the house when he admitted he was sleeping with that lady from their canasta club."

He waved that bit of info off. "I don't need some hot young thing throwing herself at me and trying to sleep with me for my money. Between you and Colin and me, we can handle this."

It was Tanner's money, and he didn't want Colin hanging out here any more than he already was, especially when he finally had a chance with Abby.

"Well, your staying here alone obviously isn't working out. Jesus, Dad, you could have hit someone." And wasn't that an awful image. "That's it. I'm serious, no more driving." Then he pictured his dad and his dog, hobbling their way down the highway. "And no more leaving the house unless someone is with you."

And if there was one way to make sure Gus did something, it was to tell him the opposite. Which meant Tanner had just guaranteed that Gus would be zipping around town in his truck every time Tanner left the house, most likely doing drive-bys of Dr. Johnson's office, flipping him off with his cane.

"Everything's fine," Colin said carefully. "No one was hurt. Gus and I tossed back a beer, caught up a little, and I drove him home so we could watch the game without all of the noise of the bar."

Which meant Gus had been tired. And probably in pain. And Colin had to cut his meeting with Ferris short.

Shit.

"So why don't you go put on clothes that aren't soaking wet and I'll get dinner?"

"Thanks," Tanner mumbled, suddenly feeling exhausted. The high he'd been riding since kissing Abby was gone. Five minutes with his dad and—*poof*—the excited giddiness of knowing she wanted him was all replaced by an overwhelming heaviness that went bone deep. "I'll be back down in a few. To eat my chow fun. In the kitchen. Which is where you will all be eating."

Tanner headed toward his bedroom. Wreck hopped down and loped behind him, licking the floor as he went.

When he'd bought this house he may have indulged himself a bit. To say his hilltop estate was sprawling would be an understatement. His Tuscan villa was big and badass, and had plasma, Sub-Zero, and state-of-the-art bling up the wazoo. It was everything a broke kid living in wine country dreamed of owning when he made it big.

And Jack "Hard Hammer" Tanner had made it more than big. First in the NFL, then in construction. He had more money, more toys, and more respect than he knew what to do with. The only thing he didn't have was the one person he'd worked so hard to impress.

Abby DeLuca.

And tonight while sitting in that lemon of a fixer-upper with her, he realized that no matter how big his house was, how many toys he filled it with, it still felt empty.

By the time he took a quick shower and threw on a pair of workout shorts and a tee and made his way to the kitchen, it was light on people and to-go boxes.

With a frown, he grabbed a beer from the fridge, took a long pull, and made his way to the family room, where an empty noodle box and Colin sat. Gus was gone.

"He went to bed." Colin handed Tanner a half-eaten box of Mongolian beef. "Seemed pretty tired, so I made up some lame excuse about how I had to talk to you in private about business and helped him to his bedroom."

"Thanks," Tanner said, looking at his friend, who was looking back and about as worried as Tanner was. "Just thinking of what could have gone wrong makes me sick."

"Well, if it helps, I think he scared the shit out of himself driving to the bar. Must have been hard working the clutch and the brakes down the mountain and through town with one good leg."

Tanner sat back and shoveled some food into his mouth. Good, but not noodles.

"I have no idea what to do. He refuses to do his physical therapy. He canceled his last two appointments without telling me. The other day I found him facedown on the bathroom floor." That had been a wake-up call. "I guess he got tired and sat there so long that his legs buckled when he tried to stand. He said he'd only been there for a few minutes, but I'm guessing it was more like a few hours."

"Jesus, I had no idea it was so bad."

"Yeah. Pride or not, I'm going to have to get him a nurse. Or at least someone who will stay with him while I'm at work. I just don't know who I can hire that he wouldn't scare off."

"Then don't hire anyone, just bring him to work with you," Colin said. "Put him in charge of something simple, something that doesn't require power tools or his feet leaving the ground."

"You don't think that would be a problem?" Tanner asked, and it was like someone had just lifted the three-hundred-pound lineman he'd been carting around for eight weeks right off his chest. "You think I could get away with bringing Dad to the worksite?"

"To the DeLuca cave site, no. There is too much going on there, it would be a huge liability." Colin at least had the decency to look apologetic. "But to the Pungent Barrel, you bet. It's a remodel, so no demolition. Plus, it will be a smaller crew. Not to mention it would give Babs someone to dote on."

Babs loved to dote. Another in a long list of reasons she had a hard time keeping crews around for long—she was more interested in feeding them lunch than making a concrete decision. Plus, Gus needed a little doting. Maybe being smothered by Betty Crocker would be just what the doctor ordered.

"This might work," Tanner said.

"Yup, and with you there to watch out for him," Colin added and took a chopstick full from Tanner's box. "Everyone wins."

"Oh, no." No longer hungry, Tanner handed his food to Colin, who went to town. "Don't do this to me."

Because everyone involved would win except for him. And Abby. God, it would look like he'd been in on this from the beginning and had something to do with her not getting hired. Worse, it would look like he was one more overimportant male inserting himself into her life. And he wouldn't blame her.

"Think about it," Colin went on as though Tanner's life wasn't rapidly spiraling. "Babs is busy on her project, Ferris is happy, your dad is out of the house and in a safe environment feeling useful and alive, and we get to focus on blowing up the side of a mountain and building a state-of-the-art golf club."

"You," Tanner slid him a look. "*You* get to focus on blowing up the side of a mountain. *I* get to babysit the elderly while building a wine and cheese shop. Which, in case you forgot, I hate wine." He left out the part that lactose tore him up, because that was just too pussy to admit.

"I'll handle the preliminary inspections, getting bids for supplies, and the remaining permits, all the crap you hate anyway. So when the shop is done, you get to jump right into the good part. Blowing stuff up and driving bulldozers around."

Tanner knew from experience that gutting a mountain to build a wine cave took a lot of preparation and a whole hell of a lot of skill.

Between Gus, Colin's house being unlivable, and the DeLuca project, Tanner already felt there were so many balls in the air that one more could send them all crashing down.

Now Colin was talking about him taking on two more projects. His head hurt just thinking about it. "How did it go with Ferris?"

Just like that, Colin's face went hard. "Good at first. I explained you had an urgent family emergency, which worked until your dad showed up. I didn't know you were walking out on the biggest meeting of this whole goddamned thing to get all hot and heavy with Abby."

"How do you know I was with Abby?"

"How the fuck do you think I know? Nora Kincaid took a picture of you two all wet and looking mighty cozy on Abby's porch and posted it on Facebook."

That was not what he wanted to hear. He was finally making progress; he didn't need Nosy Nora giving Abby one more reason to back off. She already had a boatload of reasons stored up. "She had some plumbing issues."

"Yeah, well, tell that to Brandi, who showed up looking for you. Seems you had a date."

"Shit."

Brandi Thomas was a bombshell who spent her days teaching Zumba at the gym and her nights training to be this season's newest Gold Rush Girl for the Niners. They'd met several months back at a Niners benefit dinner in San Francisco, shared a few laughs, then breakfast—at her place. They'd exchanged some pretty steamy texts and she'd mentioned she might be up his way in the next few weeks. They may have even set a date, he couldn't remember. But he was guessing it was tonight.

"Yeah, she came over all pissed, flashing her cell phone, asking if you were dating Abby. In front of her brothers, who went ballistic, by the way, when they saw the photo. Turns out their loyalty to Tanner Construction doesn't go as deeply as you originally thought."

They both knew Colin was talking about a whole lot more than Tanner Construction. The DeLucas were more than just his biggest clients; Tanner considered them friends. But being good enough to watch a game with and good enough for their sister were two distinctly different things. He hoped they thought he was fit for both positions.

He guessed that over the next few weeks he'd find out just how far their relationship went. Because he wasn't backing off with Abby. He'd waited long enough to see where they could go, and finally their timing had lined up.

Something he was more than determined to take advantage of.

This definitely was not how Abby saw her Friday morning going.

When Mrs. Hampton had finally returned her call late last night, agreeing to meet at the bottling plant, Abby had nearly fainted with relief. She put everything she had into the new designs. Using the architecture of the original plant as a foundation, she took the fabric swatches from Valley Textiles and built around those, being conscious to make sure Babs's taste meshed organically with the architectural integrity of the building.

The end result was stunning, the perfect solution for the unique space. She knew it.

Only there she was, in the back of the bottlery, sitting across a long wooden table from the gatekeeper and her devil dog—who was showing Abby just how big his teeth were. Her designs were spread out between them like a dividing line, one that could only be surpassed by her brothers, who were still managing to screw her out of a fresh start with their overwhelming *famiglia* love. Or at least the kind of fresh start that Abby had envisioned.

"What kind of 'arrangement' did my brothers offer?" Abby asked, shoving down a ball of frustration.

"Well, I was already more than impressed when the funds you wired landed in my account yesterday morning. Not everyone would have righted a wrong that costly when the law isn't forcing them to. It made me look at you a little harder, rethink my stance and wonder just what other strengths you're hiding."

The Duke's ears perked up at her last word and, tail wagging, eyes alert, he ducked under the table.

"Like I explained when you called—"

Hot breath singed her knees and Abby pulled her legs up under her and went on as though the dog wasn't contemplating gnawing her kneecap off. "I wish I could have paid you back in full, but I wanted to make sure all of the investors got the pro-rata share of repayment, and there just wasn't enough to pay back everyone completely."

There had been enough money in Richard's estate to pay back 90 percent of each shareholder's original investment. Not including her family's. That would take her a lifetime.

"But I am working on a plan with my accountant to make sure every penny invested is returned. It might take me a few years, but I promise you it will happen."

"Which was why I was confused." Babs folded her hands on the table, and her gold bangle bracelets clanked against the metal top. The hot breath under the table stopped, only to be replaced by a wet nose pushing at her foot. "A transfer in the sum of the entire amount plus ten percent landed in my account this morning."

Abby felt all of the blood leave her head and the oxygen whoosh out of her lungs. "Who wired it?"

She already knew the answer, already knew her brothers hadn't trusted her enough to handle her mess. But that didn't mean the pain was any less debilitating when Babs said, "It seems you did. The money came from a DeLuca Wines account."

She was going to be sick. Her brothers had paid back Babs with the family's money. Money she had been more than clear would not be used to right her wrongs. And they had done it behind her back, without even consulting her.

Granted, her brothers wouldn't have liked her suggestion of exactly where they could stick their money and their unwanted help. But still. It was her marriage, her mess, her problem—so why couldn't they let it be her solution?

Plus, they'd recently sunk an enormous amount of the family's money into the Italian villa she'd refurbished earlier that year. They couldn't afford to keep bailing her out.

"I take it by the look on your face you didn't know." Babs reached across the table and patted Abby's hand.

"No, I didn't, and," *oh God, this is going to suck*, "I'm afraid I am going to have to ask you to return the money."

"I see."

Teeth. She felt the distinct sensation of very sharp, very pointy teeth slowly sinking into her right shoe. Which hurt almost as much as the sharp pain shooting through her chest.

She shook her foot, but the dog wouldn't let go. So she shook harder and heard a muffled snap. "I understand if this ends our interview." Especially since they hadn't even arrived at the presentation portion of the morning.

"I see," the older woman repeated.

That was it. That was all she said. Babs didn't try to comfort her, didn't apologize that it wouldn't work out. She didn't even look through the designs on the table. Designs Abby had poured her entire heart into. She just looked at Abby, as though this were some test and she'd just had a big red *F* Sharpied onto her forehead.

"Yes, well thank you for your time," Abby said, proud her hands didn't shake too badly when she gathered up her things. "And thank you for agreeing to meet with me. Again. I hope you find the right designer and that maybe in the future we can work together."

"I have already found my designer." Babs stroked The Duke's head—who was suddenly by her side, a familiar black heel dangling from his jowls. "I only hope you can start right away."

Abby struggled to read the woman's lips, because with all of the blood pumping through her ears, she must have misunderstood. "Are you saying I'm hired?"

Babs smiled. "If you can start in a timely fashion."

"Absolutely," Abby said, her hands shaking from excitement this time. And her grin was so big she could barely contain it. "I can start today, if that works. Right now, even."

"That's wonderful," Babs said, not an ounce of wonder in her tone. And her smile was more reluctant than real. "Because I am afraid we are also short a general contractor. The inspector warned me last time that if we don't have one here by Wednesday for the sign-off on plumbing and electrical, he will have to reschedule, and that means postponing our Historical Preservation Council application. Again."

"Again?" Abby asked, because the woman had practically whispered the last part. "Are you saying we haven't submitted to the HPC yet?"

Babs gave a guilty shrug. "Between all the turnover, we haven't even gotten on the waitlist to submit our application."

Not what Abby wanted to hear. The Historical Preservation Council of St. Helena was a town-appointed council enlisted with the responsibility of preserving the historical integrity of the community. They took the responsibility seriously and, as such, adopted a zero-tolerance stance on big business, fast food franchises, and palm trees. They also took their sweet-ass time making decisions.

The waitlist to present to the HPC's board was booked out months in advance—time Abby didn't have if she hoped to make the grand opening happen before her nieces went off to college. The Jackson Bottlery was originally part of the Jackson Olive Plantation built in 1898, well before the town's official hundred-year marker. It was a historically protected building, meaning all renovations, cosmetic or otherwise, fell under the intense scrutiny and jurisdiction of the HPC.

No stamp of HPC approval meant no cheese shop. Period.

They were so screwed.

"How close is the plumbing and electrical to being complete?"

With the few minor additions she had in mind for turning the basement into a drinking cellar, and given how long the project had already been in progress, Abby didn't imagine Wednesday being a problem for the inspection.

Except, Babs looked as though it was going to be a problem. A big problem. The Duke, however, just looked smug, using the heel of her pump as a toothpick.

"You know, I don't know, dear. When Brandon left, I forgot to ask."

"Brandon from DuPont Developers?"

"Yes, nice boy, but no vision. Said he didn't want to be steering the ship when it hit the iceberg. Such pessimism these days."

Abby's stomach plummeted. Brandon was on her short list of general contractors to call. They had gone to school together and he was the contractor Abby had hired when building her first big project, Ryo Wines.

"We-can attitudes are so much more exciting to work with."

We-can attitude in full effect, Abby slid a copy of her designs across the table. "Why don't you take home my preliminary mock-ups and see what you like, what you don't, so we can get to work and have all of the structural changes, including fixtures and appliances, finalized by Monday."

"By Monday?"

"I'll go down to the planning department and see if we can get them to move the inspection to Friday. But that still puts us on a tight schedule, so every day matters. We have to have the new blueprints ready to go for the crew as soon as they show up for work."

The older woman clapped her hands, practically tittering with excitement. "I knew you were the perfect person for this job. Such drive and ambition. Just draws people in, makes them want to believe! I can see why Richard married you."

Choosing to focus on the "drive and ambition" portion of her statement, Abby gathered her things and stood, a burst of confidence humming through her veins. "If you could send over a list of who you have already worked with, I will compare it to mine and come up with a group of vetted general contractors by Monday. The Historical Preservation Council meets every second Tuesday of the month, which gives us a little over a week to prepare, and I want to be ready. To get on the waitlist, we have to pass that inspection first." A difficult task with a building built before electricity and indoor plumbing were invented, but not impossible.

It would mean being on the site at all times, getting dirty with the crew, pulling all-nighters, and working side by side with the GC. But Abby was willing to do all that and more. She was even willing to move into the bottlery if it meant making this a reality.

This was her big chance, her way to turn things around—for everyone. All of Babs's indecision and 180s and those sporadic whims, which changed with The Duke's mood, had turned into

Abby's opportunity. Now all she had to do was remain patient and see this through.

"I think it would be easier if I just gave you a list of who I haven't worked with yet," Babs said quietly, and The Duke whimpered. If Abby didn't know better, she'd say the woman looked embarrassed.

"All right," Abby said, a little of her earlier confidence fading. "Why don't you e-mail it to me at your earliest convenience?"

The woman smiled big and bold and Abby allowed herself to breathe. "Well, that's easy," Babs said. "There's only one left. It's Jack Tanner."

CHAPTER 7

A few hours later, Abby crossed the foyer and opened the front door as the late-afternoon breeze swept through the house, bringing with it the tart smell of tannins and wildflowers and all of the things that made summer in wine country wonderful. Yet instead of spinning around like Julie Andrews in a garden of dahlias for landing her dream job, Abby found herself glaring at Richard, with his chiseled abs and rock-hard buns, sporting the biggest lie ever told to mankind.

"This was on your lawn." Lexi held up a plush teddy bear holding a rose. "Please tell me you have a secret admirer."

"Nope, it's for Richard." And didn't that just make her day so much crappier. "Yesterday there was a bundle of Mylar balloons tied to his arm, on Wednesday someone set a basket of lilies at his feet like some kind of offering. And don't even get me started on whoever is placing the lit Jesus candles around the statue."

"I hate to say it, but I kind of see why," Lexi said, staring at the statue in awe. "I loathe Richard as much as the next person, probably more, but look at the lines on that statue, the symmetry. It really is a work of art."

So she'd been told.

Abby took the bear and threw it on the sofa, then took a long swig of wine. Straight from the bottle.

"Isn't it a little early for that?" Lexi eyed the bottle.

Dressed in a cute pair of capris, a bright red top with matching ballet flats, and a disposition sunny enough to give Abby a headache, Lexi looked more like a preppy co-ed than the mother of a two-month-old. She also looked like she had an agenda—one that most likely had to do with Abby's brothers—or Tanner. Two topics that were off-limits.

"Yeah, well, I thought I would be able to come home from my meeting and be rid of irritating males." Abby glared at Richard, then took another swig. A long one. "But instead I come home to my husband still naked and my front yard looking like Graceland. Penny from the Paws and Claws Day Spa is even telling people that one of my dahlias dried in the form of Jesus's face, so his homecoming must be the sign of a miracle. I think that deserves a drink or two."

"Want me to grab some straws and tissue paper? We could spit wad him to death," Lexi offered, and although that sounded like a fun way to blow off steam, Abby didn't really feel up to it.

She considered pulling out her old slingshot from the attic and knocking that God's-gift-to-all-women smirk right off his face—then aiming lower. "Nah, I'd have to clean it up."

"Good point." Lexi grabbed the wine and breezed into the house. "But if you drink all this, you won't have enough to make an extra cake."

Blowing out a breath, Abby closed the door and found Lexi already comfy at the kitchen counter helping herself to a fingerful of batter. "How did you know I was making cake?"

"You didn't call after your meeting. So you were either here with your spatula, mixing away and making a plan—"

When Abby was stressed, Abby baked. And since there were only two things in the world she could rock in the kitchen, wine cake and Rice Krispies treats, she hadn't even bothered to change out of her suit before pulling out the sherry and mixing bowls. Plus, if she ended up having to grovel to Tanner, she'd better have his cake.

"—or you were at the Spigot. Drunk," Lexi said, grabbing the bowl after Abby poured the batter in the pan. "I went by the bar first since I was sure Babs told you about the money."

"You knew they were going to bribe her?" Lexi's silence was proof enough. "Of course you knew. You're sleeping with one of my meathead brothers."

Lexi laughed at that—hard. "You do remember we have a two-month-old, right? There is no sleeping. Of any kind. And yes, I knew because I told him that couples who have secrets don't have sex." Lexi waggled a brow. "I made sure when I said it that I had on nothing but an apron, heels, and a plate of cream puffs. He caved in three seconds and the cream puffs ended up all over our—"

That was all Abby heard. Hands firmly over her ears, she said, "Again, my soul dying with every word you speak. Plus, my day is bad enough without adding that lovely image. You could have at least warned me."

Wow, for a woman constantly smothered by her family, Abby sure felt alone. Completely and utterly alone. A direct result, she was sure, of what happened when one chose to stand stagnant while everyone around moved on, fell in love, paired up.

"I didn't know until you had already left for your meeting or I would have told you." Lexi gave up on using her finger and stuck her head in the bowl. "And don't be too hard on them. Your brothers are fixers, Abby. They can't help themselves, especially when it comes to the people they love."

"Oh. My. God." Abby snatched the bowl away from Lexi and smacked at her hand when she refused to let go. "It finally happened. You're actually siding with my idiot brothers."

"Just one idiot brother. And I'm not siding, merely pointing out that his heart was in the right place, even if he might have overstepped a little."

"Overstepped?" She dropped the bowl into the sink and put soapy water in it, just in case the traitor tried to snatch it back. "Last I heard, bribing someone into giving their sister a job is a tactic the mafia uses. They paid the woman ten times what I even stand to make on the project."

"Wait. Stand to make? Are you saying you got the job?"

Abby grimaced. "Kind of. We still need the Historical Preservation Council's approval before we can start any real demolition. I want to submit our plans at the next meeting."

Lexi blinked long and slow. "Abby, the next meeting isn't until next month."

"September? But they meet every second Tuesday."

"Not in the weeks leading up to Founder's Day, they don't," Lexi said, and Abby felt her chest tighten with a familiar sense of dread that always managed to precede impending doom. "They're too busy screening Memory Lane Manor entries."

Thousands of tourists flooded the valley during the Founder's Day celebrations to partake in the annual Memory Lane Manor Walk, where they explored some of the most historic and beautiful homes in St. Helena. Each residence offered gourmet nibbles and bottomless wine tastings, which attracted foodies and historians from all over the world. Hundreds of houses entered and five were selected by the Historical Preservation Council as finalists, but only one got to wear the exclusive plaque of Memory Lane Manor of the Year. It was the only thing the HPC would be focused on.

"I'm cursed." Abby dropped her head to the counter.

God, how had she overlooked that? There were posters plastered around town. Her neighbors were preparing for the Memory Lane Manor Walk, which went right through her neighborhood.

"This is karma coming back to bite me for marrying a moron then speaking ill of the dead."

"You're not cursed," Lexi said, and Abby lifted her head and raised one challenging brow. "And Richard was a moron. That's not speaking ill, that's the truth and . . . wait." Lexi placed a finger to her lips and tapped it three times—a sure sign she was scheming. "Unless," Lexi said, doing a little dance in her chair. "You have Babs nominate the Jackson Bottlery for a Memory Lane Manor Walk hopeful."

"The bottlery isn't a residence, therefore doesn't qualify. There is no way it would win."

"Babs is always going on and on about some couple who fell in love and lived there for a whole sinful summer." Lexi flapped a dismissive hand. "But the point is, you don't have to qualify. You just have to nominate the building. Every nominee has to have their floor plan examined and the historical accuracy of their renovations approved as part of the process."

"But we haven't even renovated yet."

"Exactly, but you're going to as soon as you get the go-ahead. The first phase is a simple on-paper screening, which I'm betting is nowhere near as detailed as what you put together for Babs. And if the board approves your proposed plan as historically sound and up to code, then it would be the equivalent of getting a two thumbs up. Abby, you could start on the restoration as early as next week."

"The building isn't up to code, and I don't know if getting it done in time is a realistic goal. The electrical isn't even started, the plumbing needs to be redone, and don't even get me started on Babs's idea of timetables."

Lexi reached out and took Abby's hand. "You can do this, Abs. The final panel for presenting is a week from Tuesday. I know because Sweet and Savory was hired to cater all the events."

Lexi was right. If Abby could get her plans reviewed by the board, then she could apply for the permits to start construction. The Pungent Barrel could be open for business as early as next month.

"Abby, this year, the winner will be highlighted in a four-page spread in *Architectural Digest*." That got her attention. "And *Martha Stewart Living* is sending out a team to cover the event from the hearth and homemaking point of view."

Which was why Lexi had agreed to cater the event for free, Abby remembered. That, and the proceeds of the evening went toward restoring the old firehouse into a much-needed community center and performing arts building.

"This could be huge," Abby said, getting swept up in the possibilities of what-if.

"This could change your career, Abby."

The truth was, it could change her life. It would take her from laughingstock to respectable designer in one project. It would give her the kind of credibility that ten years of busting her ass designing closets never could.

"I need to hire a general contractor by Monday if I want to be ready for the inspector."

"Then hire a contractor."

"I've spent all morning on the phone calling nearly every contractor I have ever met, even a few I haven't. They are all either in the middle of a project, starting one, or if they were interested, it evaporated when they discovered exactly *which* project. No one wants to sign on to a project that is guaranteed to be 'the *Titanic* of the foodie world.'"

"They said that?"

"And worse." Abby sighed. "I still have a few left on my list and am waiting to hear back from some messages I left, but it doesn't look hopeful."

"I don't see what the big deal is, since according to Facebook you've been getting pretty cozy with a certain sexy hired hammer."

"I wasn't getting cozy with Jack." At least not in the picture. All of said electrical jolts happened well before Nosy Nora had slipped out from the bushes and snapped that shot.

"Uh-huh." Lexi was so not buying it. "Well, Facebook has a poll going. There are four-to-one odds that Tanner's already gotten you properly wired and up to code."

"You handle your business like a man?" Tanner asked the wolfhound through the screen. "Because if you're lying and your business ends up on my newly mopped floor again, I'll call that animal rescue in town."

Wreck didn't seem overly concerned with the empty threat or Tanner's newly mopped floor, he just lifted his lips in a smile and barked.

"Uh-huh." Tanner wasn't falling for the big-doggie-eyes trick. That's how he'd wound up mopping his kitchen at the crack of dawn on Sunday in the first place. "Humor me and make another round or two. Take a whiz on Colin's Mercedes while you're at it. Maybe it will encourage him to move out."

What had started as his buddy crashing in his guesthouse for a few months until his place was livable had turned into an eighteen-month unwanted houseguest who ate his food, drank his beer, and left a never-ending supply of dirty socks scattered around the house. Most of which Wreck ate.

"Can't blame the dog," Gus said, hobbling into the kitchen and grabbing a mug from the drying rack. It was red, chipped, and had 49ERS CAN SUCK IT scrawled across the front. It was the only mug he'd brought from home. Tanner had a dozen unchipped, unconfrontational mugs, but the old man refused to use them. "Wrecking Ball was just showing you what it feels like to have another man mess all over your plans."

Gus sat at the counter and shoved the mug forward, his way of asking for coffee. Tanner obliged.

"And what plans are we talking about? Him wanting to use my work boots to sharpen his teeth or use my house as some kind of upscale litter box for dogs?"

From somewhere outside, an offended bark sounded. Tanner just hoped it came from the vicinity of Colin's tires.

"No, the sex party you're throwing here tonight."

"There's no sex party. I just told Colin he could invite a few of the guys over for the game." A few guys meaning Ferris, because Colin swore that a game at Hard Hammer Tanner's house was the only way to make up for running out on their meeting to rescue Abby.

Gus snorted, his eyes straying out the back window toward the pool. "Tell that to the two ladies swimming in their birthday suits as we speak. The blonde one with the Dolly Parton flotation devices was on the phone, inviting all her friends, saying it's a bikini-optional kind of event." Gus shook his head in disgust. "Bikini-optional kind of girls have perfumed purse dogs, and I don't want that kind of lady sniffing up to Wrecking Ball. No man would."

If Dolly and her devices were anything like the women Colin usually spent time with, any man would. Including Tanner. Normally. But not today.

Nope, he had two former playmates naked in his pool, and instead of inviting them in for a little breakfast and get-to-know-you, he poured himself a second cup of the morning and scavenged the pantry for something that didn't have preservatives, saturated fats, or alcohol. A testament to just how sad his life had become was that he couldn't even muster up the interest to talk up a beautiful naked lady.

Well, he could. It was just the beautiful naked lady he wanted to talk up wasn't interested in anything he had to say.

"I'll talk to Colin." Because suddenly the last thing he wanted was a big party at his place.

"Good, because you said I could host poker night here and if I call the guys and cancel, I'll look like a heel."

Tanner had never actually said his dad could host poker night. He had offered to drive Gus to poker night last week and pick him up. Which Gus had responded to with a heartfelt, "Do I look like I need a chauffeur?"

Not that Tanner wasn't happy his dad was feeling comfortable enough to invite his buddies over. He just wished it had been for another day. Because bikini-optional or not, Colin was going to lose it if Tanner told him he had to cancel.

"Why don't you tell the guys it's game day? We can all watch some ball then you can disappear after and play poker."

Tanner opened the refrigerator and pulled out some eggs, onion, and cheese. An omelet was healthy and one of the few things he could cook that his dad would eat. Except the cheese was looking a little fuzzy and the onion was sprouting.

Eggs and toast it was.

"With knockers like that girl's got?" Gus shook his head. "The guys would be too busy staring to pay attention, plus Sal's got an appointment to get his pacemaker checked. Until that happens, I don't think his heart could handle all that stimulation."

"They're not going to be parading around naked." If Tanner had anything to say about it, and since it was still technically his house, he did. So no parade. Period. This Sunday was going to be about beer, ball, and bros. Especially when the Niners were playing and it was the first preseason game of the year.

Tanner cracked a few eggs into the skillet and dropped four pieces of bread into the toaster. "Wait. How do you know the size of her . . . flotation devices?"

Gus had the worst eyesight on the planet, and since he refused to wear his glasses he was like Mr. Magoo in a china shop. So if he had gotten a good look at Colin's latest pillow fight, then Gus must have gotten pretty damn close. Or he was using his binoculars.

"I went out for my morning walk, doctor's orders, when my leg started giving me trouble, so I pulled up a lounge chair and took a little rest. Not my fault she forgot her bathing suit."

Gus hadn't followed a single one of his doctor's orders, especially taking daily walks. But Tanner kept that to himself and flipped some pretty perfect eggs onto two separate plates and lightly buttered the toast.

Breakfast ready, he slid one across the counter toward Gus and dug into his own. He finally had his dad in the kitchen and was about to feed him a meal that didn't consist of caffeine or hot wings. He wasn't about to piss the old guy off.

"Don't worry, Dad, we'll stick to the TV room. You and the guys can take the game room since it has the poker table, but you'll have to share the kitchen. Colin and I are just trying to finalize some business with these guys, that's all."

"If you'd gotten a degree you'd be running your own business, not finalizing other people's and trying to impress a bunch of starched loafers."

"I did get a degree, one I use daily when running my own business," Tanner informed him like he had a thousand times before and resisted the urge to point out that if he'd gotten a business degree instead of one in construction management, he'd be one of those starched loafers.

"Yeah, well, just because you have a fancy ring and slap a logo on the side of your truck doesn't mean you don't swing hammers for a living. Don't need a big school education for that now, do ya?"

Gus had seen football as a means to an education. Tanner had opted out of grad school to play in the NFL. Something most dads would have been proud of.

Not Tanner's dad. And now that he'd said his piece, Gus stood and palmed his mug before walking his cantankerous ass right out of the kitchen.

"What about breakfast?" Tanner hollered. And the fact that his fancy ring afforded them both the opportunity to move out from over a dry cleaner into the kind of house his dad used to build for those starched loafers?

"Dr. Johnson said I need to watch my cholesterol," Gus hollered back. "Those eggs have enough in them to kill a man half my age."

Taking a bite, he tried to shrug off his dad's words and get back to his relaxing morning, but he'd barely had time to recover from one temperamental roommate when the screen door flew open and in came the other.

"You want some eggs? I hear there's enough cholesterol in them to kill you." Tanner pushed the plate forward. "Have a seat and eat up."

From the look on his face, Colin didn't want the eggs and he didn't want a seat. He wanted a fight. And all Tanner wanted to do was enjoy his nice, leisurely Sunday breakfast in peace.

"Want to explain to me how Abby DeLuca landed the design job for the Pungent Barrel?"

Abby got the job? Tanner wanted to smile, wanted to call her and tell her how proud of her he was. But that would have to wait. Colin was just getting revved up, so Tanner shrugged and said, "Talent."

"And what talent would that be? Her designs or her ability to make you think you stand a chance? Because last I heard, Babs had passed. Then Abby lets you play with her pipes, and oh, look at that, she shows up to the interview with designs that are way too spatially exact to be guesswork and a proposal that already looks Hampton-approved."

Appetite gone, patience gone, breakfast over, Tanner picked up his plate and scraped the eggs into the sink. "I helped her take some measurements, gave her a few pointers. Not the end of the world."

"Tell that to Ferris. You know, the guy who made it clear he did not want Abby DeLuca anywhere near his mother or a Hampton project. The same guy we are trying to convince to take a chance on us. What were you thinking?"

"That Abby was the best person for the job."

"Is that your professional opinion or your dick talking?" Colin misread Tanner's frustrated silence for a green light to continue. "My guess is your dick, because that's the only way you'd be stupid enough to take on the general contractor position, when you know it could screw up everything."

Tanner ran water over the plate and slammed it in the bottom of the sink. "Two nights ago, *two*, you were begging me to take the job."

"Things change," Colin snapped.

"Not here. I already told you that I don't do small retail renovations and I'm not doing this one."

"Then why did Babs tell me that Abby's first official decision was to hire you?"

That had Tanner going silent. Abby wanted to work with him on this project? He would have thought she'd rather work with, well, anyone but him. Not that he had the time, but maybe it meant she was coming around.

"She didn't ask me to submit a bid," he said truthfully, wondering what he would say if she did ask him to sign on as GC.

Colin released a pent-up breath and slumped down in the chair. "Good, that's good," he mumbled, piling Gus's eggs on the toast before taking a bite. "I was afraid I'd have to explain how playing grab-ass with the DeLuca Darling wouldn't sit well with Ferris."

"You don't and it wouldn't, but even if I agreed to be the GC, my choices are no one's business but mine." Because he'd heard enough about his bad life choices from his dad, he didn't need it from his buddy or some uptight developer—no matter how badly he wanted that job.

Colin stopped midbite and sent Tanner a scathing *are you fucking kidding me* look. "We get jobs based on our reputation, and that's not going to happen when you're messing around with a girl who stole money from half this town. The half who can afford to drop a couple hundred mil on a golf course."

"Abby didn't steal it. Her husband did," Tanner argued in a tone that told Colin he was on the line, about to step over it, and get a face full of Tanner's fist.

"I don't get it, man. You're willing to risk everything we've worked for over a few weeks of fun. What is it about you and this girl?"

That was the question of the hour. One Tanner didn't have an answer for. Abby was difficult and stubborn, and she drove him bat-shit crazy. But she was also genuine and determined, so real he couldn't seem to stay away. Looking back, his relationship with Abby was the most real one he'd ever had with a woman—how pathetic was that?

Abby didn't care about his big-ass house or that on any given weekend he could take her to a dozen celebrity-filled events. If anything, that only seemed to piss her off further. Something that made Tanner smile.

"She's real," he said simply.

"Real?" Colin said, a boatload of sarcasm weighing down his words.

"Yeah, real."

"What's real is she got you benched from the biggest game of your high school career," Colin said as though Tanner hadn't lived the entire frustrating event.

"She had just lost her mom and was a scared kid. Plus, I was leaving for school." Or he would have been if Abby's shenanigans hadn't gotten him benched. "Just bad timing all around."

"So, what? The timing is finally right? She's single and desperate and, oh yeah, broke. You're not. Perfect timing if you ask me."

"Back the fuck off, Col," Tanner threatened, leaning across the island and throwing his size behind his words.

"Jesus, Tan, you ended up throwing ball at the junior college instead of University of Alabama. You considered giving up playing for Buffalo because you saw her again."

He'd done a hell of a lot more than see her that weekend. He'd *seen* who she was deep down, the amazing woman who hid beneath the darling facade. That made moving to New York hard as hell, but in the end he'd left—and she'd married Dickwad.

"I'm wearing a Super Bowl ring, so I don't think my career suffered all that much."

"Yeah, well, everything I have is wrapped up in this deal," Colin said in a tone that had Tanner going on the defensive and feeling like he was a screw-up of a kid all over again. "You might be okay with living off your name and no real merit behind it, but I don't have that luxury, because if the golf course goes south, I don't have a Super Bowl ring to fall back on."

"Sure you do." Tanner didn't take his eyes off Colin. "Seems you have mine."

Colin froze, and that's when Tanner knew he'd pushed too far. Colin might not have a ring or some fancy-ass degree, as Gus had so amply called it. He'd never had the chance to leave the valley like Tanner had. But he was smart, damn good at what he did, and had worked his ass off to get Tanner Construction to where it was today.

So yeah, his name might not be on the magnet—door or otherwise—but he'd earned every percent of the fifty he owned. And Tanner was completely out of line.

"Shit, Col." Tanner pinched the bridge of his nose. "I'm sorry. I woke up to Wreck messing all over the floor, then Gus was pushing every button I—"

Colin held up a hand. "You know what? I don't care. You're a big boy. If you want to go there again with her, fine. Just don't let it affect the company."

"You make it sound like we're picking out baby names. We haven't even gone out on a date."

"No, but you've spent the past year hanging out in the wings, waiting for her to be single, waiting for her to say she made a mistake. Waiting for her to . . . hell, I don't know. You just wait."

"I haven't been waiting," Tanner argued.

Sure, he'd gone out of his way to be around her as much as possible.

But that was because riling her up was fun, not because he was some loser following the homecoming queen around waiting for her attention. Right? "I've dated dozens of women over the past year."

"Yeah, whose collective IQ is lower than their bra size. Hell, Tanner, there isn't a single woman you've paraded around town who had any potential other than to piss off Abby. So you know what, let's cut the shit, speed this along. You sign on as GC—"

"I'm not taking on this project."

"Yeah. You are. And we both know it. You'll spend all night thinking about it and by tomorrow you'll have guilted yourself into it. You're a sucker when it comes to helping people out, plus you know the only way Abby will ever get that job done on time and on budget is if you step up. So yeah, you'll do it, regardless of what it could cost us."

A silent staring contest ensued, followed by a standoff so tense it had Wreck whimpering at the back door.

"She's one of the best at what she does," Tanner finally said, working hard to push down his anger.

Colin didn't know Abby the way he did. All Colin saw of their relationship was the aftermath.

"Doesn't matter. I don't trust her. Never did. Not with our company or our business partners. And I especially don't trust her with you."

Colin shoved his stool under the counter and headed for the back door. He stopped at the threshold and looked back. Wreck took the opportunity to nudge his way inside.

"If she didn't want you back then, man, she sure as hell doesn't deserve you now," Colin said smoothly. "How's that for real?"

The door slammed and Tanner rested back against the counter.

A warm nose pressed against his thigh. Tanner looked down to see Wreck at his feet, all drool and support. Then the dog crouched down in the squat position, his ears back in concentration and—

"No! You do not get to crap all over what is left of my weekend," Tanner yelled, shooing the dog out the door. Not that it made a lick of difference. Wreck had been heard and Tanner went to look for the mop.

CHAPTER 8

"Good luck with that."

Abby paused in surprise at the finality in Brandon's voice. She hadn't expected him to flat-out turn her down.

She shifted her phone to the other ear, paced the front room of her house once more, and forced a smile. "I don't need luck. It's a solid plan of action."

"You do know there are only so many Memory Lane Manor entries accepted each year." She did now. "Last I heard, they were full. So unless you have a marker to call in, getting them to look at your entry will be impossible this late in the game."

"I'm already on the list," she lied. She had no idea how she was going to get into that meeting, but she was going to make it happen. Even if it meant going as Lexi's assistant. "Come on, Brandon, I need you if I am going to get the place up to code by the inspection. Plus, it'll be fun!"

"You need a new boss if you're going to make that happen. And nothing about being crammed in that bottlery with Babs for any amount of time sounds like fun. Not after these past few months."

Neither was listening to another rejection while still in her robe and Godzilla slippers. But he didn't hear her complaining.

"When Colin told me about the job, it was supposed to be a simple retail remodel, minimal crew, five weeks max. That was more than two months and the Taj Mahal ago. And I was the third GC to be hired. At least she isn't under the delusion anymore that she doesn't need a designer."

Abby ran a finger down her list of prospective contractors and—

Gulp.

—It was official. She'd exhausted her entire list. Well, except for one name. And that was *not* going to happen if she could help it. Getting Brandon back was a must.

"I'm willing to make it worth your while if you come back to the job."

Heck, if it meant she didn't have to work beside Jack Tanner and could still bring this job in on time, she was open to splitting her earnings with him.

"I like working with you, and I bet your designs are amazing, but I already had to bump three other projects because that woman changes her mind every two seconds. Amazing designs or not, I can't spend any more time on the town's *Titanic*."

Yeah, that was what the other eight contractors had called it.

"It's already a half a million over budget, weeks behind, and with no crew. I have to admit, I am a little surprised you'd be willing to risk taking it on after . . ." *Richard turned up naked on your front lawn* went unsaid, but she got the point. Her life was in total chaos and everyone was already watching.

"I can make this work," she heard herself say.

Brandon's pause said he thought differently. "I hope so, because I think you're really talented. There is already so much buzz circulating around this place that if you get it considered as a Memory Lane

Manor Walk entry, everyone will be watching. And I'm not just talking about the Napa Valley. If it is a half-ass finish job, which is a huge possibility, that's what people will remember, that's what will go under your name."

"I was thinking the same thing," she said. "Only that when I pull it off, everyone will take notice."

Brandon was silent for a moment, probably wondering what to say since he was too polite to tell her she was delusional. "I could send you over a list of guys who do clean work."

"Thanks, Brandon, that would be great." Although she already knew who he'd send and she'd already called them.

"But I got to be honest, most of the guys I know are like me, they run a small crew and are usually pretty booked up this time of year. Your best bet would be to go after a bigger company, one that has a roster of guys to pull from. Hang on, I got a guy."

She could hear Brandon scrolling through his phone, even knew the precise moment he found his "guy," because her body went wonky, especially her breathing, so it was no surprise when he said, "Jack Tanner. Not sure if this is his kind of project, because if it were, he'd have signed on when Colin did, but it's worth a try."

And wasn't that the story of her life? She was minutes away from finally, *finally*, ridding herself of Richard. And now it seemed the only way to repair the damage done by that relationship was to jump into business with another man from her past.

"I still have a few more people to call," she lied. "But I'll keep him in mind."

"I wouldn't waste too much time calling around, because in my professional opinion he's your best bet." Something she was slowly coming to understand. "This town loves their local celebrities, and Tanner isn't just famous, he was homegrown. Hell, his name on a project always helps grease some wheels when it comes to working with the planning department. And trust me, with this project, you need all the greasing you can get. Throw in an autographed ball and some free tickets, and you're golden as far as gaining permits and approval."

And wasn't that a sad statement.

"Thanks, Brandon. And let Tommy know I am sorry about canceling piano lessons again. But next week we'll start back up." After a few more pleasantries, she disconnected.

Admitting defeat, she sank down on a barstool, her slippers growling, but even that didn't make her feel tough. She rested her forehead against the counter with a loud thunk.

The tiles felt cool against her face, and if she closed her eyes long enough she could almost see the iceberg in front of her, could hear everyone screaming for her to change direction, to get out of the way of the gigantic glacier of professional doom that was going to sink what was left of her reputation in one deadly crash.

"Over my dead body," an elderly and very angry voice came from the front yard, followed by some shouting—and was that a police siren?

Abby was on her feet and, because it was *that* kind of shouting, grabbed the baseball bat that sat by the front door—a housewarming present from her sister-in-law Frankie—before walking out to the porch. The early August heat was sweltering and carried a sweetness from the nearby vineyards.

Growling with every step, Abby reached the edge of the porch, raised her hand, and squinted into the sun—and into the red and blue flashing lights speeding down the cul-de-sac right toward her house—swearing when she saw the only person who could stand between Abby and her freedom.

"Nonna?" she shouted. At least she tried to, but she didn't think her voice could be heard over the revving of the tow truck or the blaring siren that died when the patrol car slowed to a stop. "What are you doing here?"

She raced down the steps, and then dropped the bat when she saw Deputy Baudouin climbing out of the cruiser. The last thing she needed was to involve herself in a brutality. That was when three frosted heads turned to look at her in surprise.

On the lawn, dressed in mourning black and the most elaborate bonnets known to man, stood Nonna ChiChi and her posse of two, Pricilla Moreau and Lucinda Baudouin. Mesh netting pulled low over their eyes, they were holding hands in what could only be called the ring-around-the-rosy position, looking ready to start belting out hymns.

"Got a call about an assault in progress," Jonah said, hand firmly on his sidearm. Then he saw the three grannies holding hands around Richard and looked heavenward.

"Assault?" Rodney asked, sounding startled in the back of his tow truck. He had a greasy RODNEY'S RECOVERY, REPOSSESSION & PARTY RENTALS T-shirt stretched thin over his spare tire and a thick metal chain dangling from his hand. "I was minding my own business, trying to load up Richard like Mrs. Moretti . . . um, the lady who owns this statue, now asked me to, when that one," he pointed to ChiChi, "said I was desecrating sacred ground. Then the one with the bad attitude assaulted me with her purse."

All eyes went to Lucinda.

"He was trying to goose me," Lucinda accused, her face looking as though she wasn't as opposed to the idea as she was pretending. "I was just acting within my rights. Defending my temple."

"Is that true?" Jonah asked, slowly moseying his way over, almost looking sorry for the guy. "Did you try to goose my aunt?"

"No, sir." Rodney took off his hat, showing everyone his sincerity and big bald patch. "That was an accident. One that could have been avoided if she hadn't cuffed herself to her lady friends and the statue."

Abby stepped closer and sure enough, fuzzy pink handcuffs adorned all of their wrists—including Richard's. "Are those real?"

"According to the nice young man who gave me a lap dance, they are," Pricilla said, holding up her wrist. "See, it says one hundred percent certified Anaconda Steel, right here on the chain."

"I think that's the strip club's motto," ChiChi explained.

Pricilla's round face puckered in confusion, then, as though understanding suddenly dawned, a bright red tint lit up her apple cheeks. "Oh, that's what he meant."

Jonah picked up her wrist and inspected the cuffs. "You got the key?"

All three ladies smiled, then shook their heads. Here Abby had been so sure her day couldn't get any worse.

Jonah nodded, looking resigned, as though this was a normal day in his small-town life as a St. Helena deputy. "Well, then it looks like I'm going to have to cut them off."

"What if we refuse?" Lucinda asked in a tone that had everyone taking a step back—except for the deputy. "You going to arrest us?"

Eyes on the cuffs, not the least bit intimidated, he said, "No, Aunt Luce, I'll bring out the riot gear and hose you all down."

Abby didn't know if he was joking or serious, but either way it did the trick. The ladies actually looked nervous.

Jonah looked at Abby. "You want me to arrest them for trespassing?"

Abby felt a surge of guilt because that was exactly what she wanted. For Jonah to load up the grannies, then back over Richard with his squad car and make them all disappear so she could go back inside, eat the entire wine cake while watching highbrow reality television, and forget that today ever happened—that the past eight years had ever happened.

Then she realized that was what the old Abby would do, the old Abby who was a pushover and let people run her life, and gave in when things got hard. The new Abby, the one who was going to figure out a way to get a top-notch contractor and make Babs's cheese shop a celebrated piece of modern design, looked ChiChi in the eye and said, "You know what? I'll give you ladies five minutes to find those keys or I will let the deputy make that call."

"Abigail Amelia DeLuca," ChiChi chided, going heavy on the guilt, "what has gotten into you? Threatening to have your elders, your *grandmother*, arrested for spending quality time with her grandson-in-law."

"It's not a threat, Nonna. So I suggest you start looking for those keys and explain to me why you are here, cuffed to Richard, when you are supposed to be whipped creaming it up in Vegas."

ChiChi tried to cross her arms sternly, which didn't work so well since she was tethered to her coconspirators.

Jonah pressed his shoulder radio and asked for backup, and ChiChi decided to start talking.

"Last night we were at Anaconda, making some new friends, when Father Giuseppe called, asking if I knew my grandson-in-law was back, God rest his soul," ChiChi said, somehow managing to make the sign of the cross, her friends' arms being yanked in all directions. "So we caught the next flight home."

"You came, you saw, now move aside, Chiara," Nora said from over the fence. "Rodney is here to remove the illegal garden art, and time's a wasting."

"This is not an illegal anything," ChiChi snapped. "And it is a fabulous rendering. A very, um," ChiChi cleared her throat, "larger-than-life take on things."

"Fabulous?" Abby had to ask, because her nonna had used many adjectives beginning with the letter F to describe Richard, and none of them had come anywhere near the word *fabulous*. "You refused to acknowledge Richard even on our wedding day, so you want to tell me what this is really about?"

Nora appeared from behind the fence, inching closer, camera poised, wanting to hear the truth from the source herself.

"It's that Father Giuseppe," ChiChi hissed, and Abby suddenly felt a thousand years old and fifteen again all at the same time. "He called last night saying we should respect Richard's dying wish about the statue, that it's the godly thing to do."

Father Giuseppe had been running the local parish since before St. Helena got indoor plumbing. He was built like a mule, smelled like guilt, and, to ChiChi's dismay, was half Italian and half Sicilian—which was why ChiChi claimed his word was only good when it was Italian, meaning every other day of the week and rotating Sundays.

"But yesterday was Saturday," Abby pointed out, because if ChiChi was siding with a man of the cloth over the removal of Richard, Abby didn't stand a chance. "You never listen to him on Saturday."

"Which is why he waited until a minute past midnight to call, knowing it was his Italian day and I couldn't say no. If you ask me, that was his Sicilian side calling. No God-fearing Italian would call a woman on her bachelorette party and interrupt a stage production of *Magic Mike: The Musical*."

"Nonna," Abby whispered, her heart so far up in her throat it made talking difficult, "I can't keep him here."

"Not forever, child," ChiChi whispered, leaning in even closer, which had all of the neighbors, who were drawn to drama like flies to shit, pressing closer to catch what bit of gossip they could. "Just until Richard's grandmother comes to pay her respects. She wants to see him in his chosen resting place."

"Richard has a grandmother?" According to him, after his parents died, he had no family. Something that had resonated deeply with Abby, had drawn her to him. And right then she didn't know what made her angrier—that he'd lied to her from the start or that she might just be stuck looking at his face for longer.

"I guess the Morettis are very devout." ChiChi rubbed her thumb over her fingertips in the universal sign for big tithers. "She had her priest call Father Giuseppe, asking for a few weeks to put things in order and come pay respects to her grandson. She even showed her devoutness to Deidra Potter, offering her all kinds of payment if she'd lay flowers at his feet daily."

Oh boy. Deidra Potter was not only the owner of Petal Pushers: Buds and Vines, the local bouquet goddess of wine country. She was also ChiChi's sworn enemy, which meant that if she was involved, Abby was screwed.

"I offered to call Richard's grandmother and tell her just what kinds of things other women did at his feet when he was married to you," Lucinda said loud enough to carry three towns over.

"Lucinda," Pricilla chided, then just as loudly turned back to Abby and picked up the earlier thread, "Only, that Deidra beat us to it. She knows ChiChi is thinking about running for the Garden Society Chair this year, and the only way she can win is to make your grandmother look bad."

"She knew having him in your yard like this," again with the sign of the cross, "showing off his wayward boys to the town, would get my blood boiling, so she hijacked the Garden Society, held a secret meeting, and they voted."

"Voted on what?" Abby asked, not sure she wanted to hear the answer.

"Project Primrose," Lucinda said.

Abby waited for them to continue, but when they didn't, she motioned that she needed more information, because she had no idea what they were talking about.

"The St. Helena Garden Society will now bring sunshine and support to the grieving families of St. Helena, one petal at a time," Pricilla explained.

Abby let this sink in, then she understood. "And their first recipient is Richard," she finished. That explained the mountain of flowers at the statue's feet.

"Yes, siree," Lucinda said, her eyes going hard. "And Deidra's planning on announcing her candidacy on your front lawn with the media here at the unveiling of Project Primrose."

Abby didn't point out that St. Helena's only "media" was a single photographer for the *Sentinel.* "So if I get rid of the statue, Deidra will make it look like ChiChi wasn't thinking in the best interest of the society?"

"Oh, child, I don't care about what those old biddies think," ChiChi lied. If there was one thing ChiChi cared about, it was her reputation in the community. The other was beating out Deidra.

Abby eyed the cuffs and the public dramatics on display and knew Deidra was in for one tough campaign cycle. ChiChi was poised to hijack Project Primrose and turn it into a spectacular, raving success, more than Deidra could ever dream. She wasn't going to fight Deidra—she was going to join her—and in the end, Deidra would rue the day she ever thought she could beat ChiChi.

Then it would start all over again between them.

"I was thinking about his grandmother," ChiChi whispered, blinking a little too much for it to be part of the show. "Thinking of what she must be going through. Knowing her grandson was a rotten SOB, but wanting to do right by his will and visit his statue while it sat in its resting place. Trey was a pain in my backside before he met Sara, and between him and Marco, I am sure there are a hundred women who would love to take a chisel to certain parts of their anatomy. But, former Casanovas or not, I would hope I'd get the chance to say good-bye, in my own way."

And there it was. The only thing that could have Abby wavering. She knew all too well what it was like to wish for one last moment with someone. After being trapped in a car with her dying parents while emergency workers struggled to get them out, wondering if her mother heard her whispering just how much she loved her, how much she needed her to live. Even begging her, when it got grim, to take her with them . . .

No, Abby could never deny another person the chance to get closure.

With a sigh she felt all the way to her bones, she whispered, "All right, I can give his grandmother until the end of the month. But then Richard has to go. For me and for Regan and Holly."

The last thing Abby wanted was for her niece to come home from her family vacation and find out her dad was dead by seeing his ashes—and other parts—on her front lawn. Richard had created enough heartache for this family to last a lifetime.

"I know it wasn't the easy decision, *mia piccola bambina*." ChiChi leaned in and gave Abby a kiss on the cheek. When she pulled back, the pride in her gaze had Abby squirming in her shoes. "So much compassion and heart. A grandmother could wish for nothing else from her favorite granddaughter."

Abby smiled at the familiar statement. "I'm your only granddaughter."

"Yes, well, favorite all the same. Now, if you'll take a small step back, I have to make sure Deidra doesn't win this one," ChiChi whispered.

Abby wasn't sure what her nonna was going to do, but she could tell by the giddy flutters of her lashes that it was going to be epic.

And embarrassing. And most likely come back to bite Abby in the butt. Because when it came to getting her way, ChiChi was a ninja.

At that, Abby smiled. Maybe she could harness ChiChi's antics for good. "I'll step back, but only if you'll get me into the Memory Lane Manor meeting with the HPC next Tuesday."

All three women gasped. "You're asking for a miracle."

Didn't she know it. "And you're asking me to live with Richard for another three weeks *and* take the fall so you can beat out Deidra Potter."

All three women looked at Richard's boys then back to Abby. Lucinda gave a curt nod. "My cousin Perkins sits on the board. I gave him one of my kidneys back in sixty-seven. He owes me."

"Then make the call," Abby said and took a huge step back right as ChiChi faced her adoring crowd.

"So by the power vested in me, as the official presidential candidate for the St. Helena's Garden Society, devoted member to Project Primrose, and this young man's grandmother-in-law, I hereby proclaim that Richard stays, God rest his soul," ChiChi declared, and with a quick sign of the cross, the three ladies rallied, pulling the circle in closer until they were pressed against the statue. "Cheating bastard or not, family is family. And we're Italian." She sent a sly wink Abby's way. "Put that on Facebook, Nora. And make sure you tag that sneaky Deidra Potter."

One hour and a nice chat with her girlfriends later, Abby pushed through the doors of the Spigot. It was still early into the first quarter of the game, but the sports bar was already packed, a sea of red-and-gold-clad fans taking up every booth and stool. Pitchers littered the tables, shot glasses lined the bar, and the giant red-and-gold San Francisco 49ers light flashed boldly.

Game face on, Abby scanned the bar for her brothers, her mental war paint cracking a little when she spotted them sitting on the far side, taking up an entire booth and shouting at the flat screen hanging from the ceiling. She patted her briefcase, which held the one thing she needed to ensure her plan would work, but it didn't help.

Even the sight of the blow-up doll in a Seahawks jersey and a green thong hanging from the ceiling by a noose—just in case a tourist wandered in and wasn't sure exactly whose territory they'd entered—wasn't enough to calm the anxious feeling in her stomach that she always got when walking into a confrontation.

"Hey, Abby," Marc said, standing and pulling her into his arms for the best big-brother hug she'd had in a while. "I didn't know you were coming."

She looked up, way up since she only came to his chest, and he flashed her that trademark DeLuca smile, which was so contagious even she wasn't immune. Which was how she found herself smiling back, damn it. "Kind of a last-minute thing."

She was passed to Trey and finally Nate, and with each hug it became progressively harder to let go—and progressively harder to stay angry. Especially when all three brothers remained standing, waiting for her to sit—because they were good guys. Good, loving, respectful, Italian men who—

"Want to tell me why the hell Nora Kincaid just posted on Facebook that she is heading up the Occupy Krug Court in protest of the"—Trey picked up his phone, scrolled and swiped, then read from the screen—"Illegal Placement of Dick? I thought you said he'd be gone today."

—Men who were overprotective, bossy, and knew just how to push her buttons.

Frustration burned up her spine, and a kink started in her neck. "Will you all stop looming over me and just sit!" When they didn't move except to gesture for her to take a seat first, she waved off the gentlemanly offer. "I'm not staying long."

Not to mention even in her take-charge stilettoes they had well over a foot on her. Sitting next to them at a table was like being Alice after she'd taken the shrinking pill. And with the conversation they were about to engage in, Abby needed all the height she could get. She wanted to be looking them in the eye when she told them to butt the hell out, not looking up to them.

Something she was fast learning was part of the problem.

Abby loved her brothers, admired and respected them, tried really hard to live up to the kind of capable and successful people they had each become—and somehow always managed to come up short. It had been easy in the past, when things got messy and hard, to step back and let them handle it, because they were so damn good at fixing her life.

But Abby was ready to fix her own life. Ready to stand on her own two feet and see how she fared—success or failure, it wouldn't matter as long as it was all hers.

"I can handle Nora. I can handle the Richard mess. And I can most definitely handle securing a job without my big, scary brothers bribing my clients." They didn't even have the decency to look ashamed. Nope, they looked proud and stubborn and as though they were in the right.

"We're not scary." Marc smiled. "It's called charm."

"I'm going to say this once, so listen up. I married Richard, I messed up, and I am going to fix this . . . my way. And that includes me handling his remains and the investors."

Ignoring the worried looks flying around the table, Abby pulled out the spreadsheets and detailed plan of action she and her accountant had drawn up. It showed who had received what and her aggressive plan for paying back the remaining balances. It relied on her firm becoming a success, depleted what was left of her savings account, and would leave her with very little money to live on. It also meant selling her shares in Ryo Wines, which broke her heart because it was the company she and ChiChi had started, but that money would mean finally being able to right the wrong.

Finally being able to move on.

When Nate looked at her over the top of the paper, she swallowed—hard. "I didn't include our family on the list, but I plan to pay you guys back as well. It will just take me a little more time."

"We don't care about the money, Abby." Nate dropped the paper and looked up at her with those soft, caring eyes—no judgment, no blame, just concern. And she felt her eyes sting.

"We just want this to be over. For you and for us," Marc said softly. "We just want to help."

"Good, then you can help me by butting out." To make her point, she sent them her most intimidating look. It was one that scared her piano students into a practicing frenzy and got results no matter the age.

Not a single one of them looked concerned in the least. To her utter frustration, they actually appeared amused. Then they shrugged in unison and she knew they were merely placating her.

"I know this is hard, and that meddling is what you guys do."

"We don't meddle." Trey looked so offended she would have laughed if she hadn't felt like strangling him.

"Yes. You do. You are like a bunch of little old ladies, sticking your noses in everyone else's business."

"We're just trying to make this whole mess a little easier," Nate, the ever-rational brother, explained as though she were the slow one.

Unbelievable. Abby looked at them and shook her head. "I don't want easier. I don't want to be coddled. And I sure as hell don't want you guys treating me like a child," she shouted, very childlike. "I'm not that same scared person I was when Richard left or when Mom and Dad died, so stop treating me like I am." That got their attention. And then she brought out the big guns. "So as of today you will no longer manipulate my life."

Abby reached into her briefcase and pulled three envelopes out and slid them across the table. Inside were personalized contracts ensuring they would butt the hell out. But what had Abby smiling were the three swirly signatures at the bottom, which from the looks on her brothers' faces were more terrifying than the actual contracts, titled THE BUTT OUT AND PUT OUT RESOLUTION. Because they were handcrafted and signed by the women who shared their respective beds.

"What the hell is this?" Trey asked, pointing to the third clause on his resolution, a thin sheen of sweat breaking out on his forehead. "No dance skirts after seven p.m.?"

"If you participate in a level three meddling violation, then Sara will only wear her dance skirts during studio hours." Something Trey's fiancée had so creatively devised. "If you think that's bad, then check out the 'No Tent Making' clause."

"Jesus, if I commit a level two or higher meddling violation, no sampling the cream puffs for a week." Marc flipped through the contract frantically. "What the hell is a level two MV?"

For the first time since Abby moved into her new house and was given the Good Neighbor Code handbook, she decided rules were beneficial. Inspired, even.

Effective.

"Mine has one sentence," Nate said, shifting in his seat. "How can it have one sentence?" He flipped the page over a few times, then read, "Because meddling is a pussy word for saying you don't believe in someone, any meddling violation of any kind ranks as a level one violation, which results in your wife going for your nuts." Nate pointed to his one-page, one-line resolution and finished, "And not in a good way."

"It's simple, fellas." Abby clapped her hands, feeling mighty proud of herself. "I need time to fix this mess without you guys making it harder. So the women have chosen sides, and it seems they are tired of your constant meddling too, because they took a firm Team Abby stance. In fact, we're getting shirts made. So if you want any action, then stop meddling in my life because if I'm pissy, then they're pissy. Which means your lives will be miserable."

Marc's face went pale. Trey choked on his beer, and Nate looked at her in utter horror.

With a smile so big her cheeks hurt, she patted each shocked face and kissed each puckered forehead. "Now, can someone tell me where I can find Jack?"

"*Jack?*" Marc asked, his voice going all authoritative. "Why do you need to find him?"

"Since I need a contractor and Jack happens to be one. And," she leaned over and pointed to the top of the page, "according to Lexi, an MV involving my career is an MV of the second degree. She told me how much you love her cream puffs."

Marc narrowed his gaze on her. "I wasn't talking about your job, I was talking about the way Tanner stares at your ass every time you wear those jeans." He pointed to the offensive jeans in question and Abby smiled, because really? He stared? "I should have kicked his ass the second I saw that picture Nora put up, the one of him on your porch. Who looks at his buddy's sister like that?"

"You married your best friend's ex-wife," Abby challenged, resisting the urge to ask exactly how Tanner was looking at her, but only because it probably wouldn't help the situation. Marc looked ready to follow through on his threat, and Trey and Nate were on board to join in the fight.

"Ex–best friend, and Jeff is a total tool. Not to be trusted. Just like Tanner."

"Well, it's my call and I trust him." About as much as she trusted herself around him. Which wasn't saying much. "Oh, and Marco, be careful, according to Lexi, an MV involving my love life would be a level one violation."

Marc scanned his contract, and she knew the minute he found the punishment per Lexi's specifications. The whole bar knew because he stood, knocking over his beer in the process. "The apron! She burns her apron?"

"Not just any apron, the lavender one, I believe." Abby ran a finger down and stopped at the detailed list Lexi had put together. "Yup. See, right there."

"This is bullshit," Marc shouted, his charm and easy smile gone.

"I'll be sure to tell your wife that," Abby said, eyeing the Seahawks jersey hanging from the ceiling. "Now, where is everybody's favorite hammer for hire tonight?"

CHAPTER 9

The Seattle Seahawks jersey, Abby admitted, was probably a mistake.

Almost as big as her decision to come right here after confronting her brothers. One step inside Tanner's house and it was obvious she was overdressed and apparently didn't meet the height requirement for such an event. Even in her five-inch heels, all she could see was a crowd of pecs and shoulders—all adorned in Niners red.

"Did you bring some legs with the wings?" an older man with bushy brows and spiky silver hair asked, eyeing the tinfoil-covered plate in her hand. Even though he hunched a little, relying heavily on a cane to stand, he still came in at a whopping six two. "I can't let you in unless you show me the wings *and* the legs." He waved an impatient hand.

Not sure if it was a reference to her mascot of choice or some kind of come-on, Abby clutched her wine cake to her chest. "No wings. No peeks. Just here to see Jack. Is he around?"

"Jack, huh?" The old man patted down every one of his pockets, and since he was wearing a pair of faded contractor pants with a dozen pockets and a couple of tool loops, it gave Abby a chance to sneak a peek inside the house.

She couldn't help it. She'd moved back to St. Helena nearly two years ago, yet this was the closest she'd come to stepping foot inside Tanner's house.

The overembellished foyer with its vaulted ceilings, dual staircases, and elaborate chandelier was not what she'd expected. In fact, she tried to reconcile the laid-back, no-nonsense guy she knew with the flashy surroundings and came up short. More than short. She was baffled.

Until what looked like a linebacker in a home-team jersey, dusty jeans, and oddly bare feet walked by, one hand curled around his beer and flashing a Super Bowl ring, the other around a stacked blonde with mile-long legs, a red miniskirt, and matching bikini top. And Abby got it. Tanner had built himself his very own Playboy mansion.

The guy looked at her jersey. "Is this a joke?"

"Obviously not a good one," she said, wishing she had just stuck to her jeans and blouse. "I'm looking for Jack. Do you know where he is?" she asked again, because Mr. Show Me Your Legs was still fumbling around in his pockets.

"He's around." He gestured vaguely over his shoulder toward a set of veranda doors, or maybe he meant the pair of circular stairs.

Suddenly, an explosion of angry shouts erupted from the back of the house, and Abby hoped he meant the stairs, especially when he added, "Although I wouldn't recommend going through the house dressed like that."

"I can handle myself," Abby assured him.

The guy shrugged. "Your life. Oh, and leave your shoes by the door."

Abby faltered midstep. She didn't wear heels for the fashion of it, although she loved how her navy peek-a-boos matched her new jersey. Nope, she wore them because at five one, it was almost impossible to be taken seriously when people were literally looking down at her. And since she was about to face the biggest man she knew, she was counting on her extra five inches of courage.

"Sorry, house rules." He didn't look sorry at all, even wiggled his bare toes for effect, then disappeared into what she assumed was the entertainment room.

"Don't mind Meat Grinder," the old man said. "Always been a bit of a kiss-ass if you ask me—aha!" The patting stopped and he extracted a pair of glasses from his shirtfront pocket. Sliding them on, he looked directly at her jersey and a big, bright smile took over his face, shedding ten years and exposing a very handsome man. "Not your fault Tanner picked the wrong team."

That's when Abby saw the resemblance. Beneath the nooks and crannies sat the most intense blue eyes and a familiar crooked smile.

Abby stuck out her hand. "You must be Mr. Tanner. I'm Abigail DeLuca."

"Call me Gus. And is that wings in there?"

"No, it's a cake."

"Huh." The old man took a closer look and licked his lips. Maybe the cake was her ticket in. She lifted the Tupperware lid and let some of the aroma of sherry and nutmeg seep out.

Gus took a step closer just as a big ball of wiry silver hair with enormous paws and a deadly tail ambled between them, his wet nose immediately going for Abby's crotch in a big doggie hello.

She gave his buttery-soft ears a little scratch, which must have translated into a green light for a kiss, because he went up on his hind legs and licked her from chin to forehead.

"This here is Wrecking Ball. Sit, boy." And the dog sat, but his eyes stayed locked on Abby's crotch. "He wants the cake. Why don't you let me take this off your hands. It'll be safer."

"I made it for Jack," she explained as he put the cake to his nose and took a whiff.

"He's watching his figure, always harping on and on about sodium and saturated fats. Don't want to tempt him."

"That's very nice of you." Abby would bet the strict diet was more for Gus than Tanner, but if Gus stealing Tanner's cake got her inside, then Tanner would just have to deal with it.

"Yeah, well, I do what I can." He looked at Abby again and his brow raised in surprise. "Well, now, you're that girl who stole St. Helena High's mascot and hid it in my backyard."

Oh boy. She could kiss her invite in good-bye.

"Actually, I put it in the cab of Jack's truck, in the passenger side, wearing his Napa High jersey." That was after she broke into her school and stole it—only to hold it hostage for the week leading up to the biggest game of the year. "It was supposed to be a prank." Actually, it was supposed to be her way of letting Tanner know she was mad—that he'd hurt her.

He'd used her, broken her heart, then just walked away like he hadn't shattered her world.

The day after the most amazing night of Abby's young life, Tanner hadn't called. He hadn't called the next day either, and come Sunday, Abby had convinced herself he hadn't called because he was as shaken by their night as she'd been. That he needed time to process what had happened between them.

Only come Monday, Abby's biggest competition for homecoming queen, Kendra Abrahams, announced to the entire student body that she and her overspirited pom-poms were taking Tanner to homecoming. Abby had been devastated. Even worse, she had been played. Tanner was the first person she'd let in after her parents died, the only one who made her feel like she wasn't so alone, and in the end she'd fallen—hard.

Only Tanner hadn't fallen. Nope, he'd taken her virginity, then taken off for perkier pastures.

So Abby did what any sane teen girl would do. She got even. Since Tanner went to the rival school, Napa High, Abby pulled the greatest mascot prank in the history of wine country—placing the kidnapped mascot in his truck after a series of random notes ignited a citywide hunt for the Saint statue—praying it would get him banned from her school's dance.

Mission accomplished. He'd been banned. And brought into the sheriff's station for questioning. What she hadn't counted on was that it would cost him a full ride to Alabama University.

"Got him benched from the biggest game of his high school career. Ended up playing at the community college for a while before he had a chance to impress the big guys again."

A choice Abby never fully understood. Tanner had proof she'd done it, took a picture of her breaking into his truck with the golden statue, which if he'd handed it over would have exonerated him, yet he hadn't said a word. Not until after homecoming weekend—not until after the scouts had left and Abby was crowned homecoming queen.

"I don't know if you read it, but I sent your family a letter of apology. I was too embarrassed"—*and heartbroken*—"to say it in person. But I truly was and am sorry."

"Sorry?" Gus's laugh sounded rusty. "Best thing that could have happened to him. He gained two inches, twenty pounds, and shaved two-tenths off his forty that year at the JC. Not that it kept him from wearing those pussy colors."

That was when Abby noticed Gus wasn't wearing Niners' pride—he was sporting an Oakland Raiders shirt.

"If you ask me, that year was the reason he beat out a slew of upperclassmen and played first string when he transferred to USC. That season of swinging hammers and playing ball taught him a lot, and it got him in the NFL."

"I don't know if he'd see it that way."

"Everything comes easy to my son, especially ball. The kid needed something to work for, something that would challenge him, get him riled up. Still does." Gus took in her shirt once more and there went that Tanner smile—equal parts charm and trouble. "I think you'll be good for him."

Before Abby could clarify she was here in a strictly professional capacity, Gus added, "Anyway, he's out on that back patio of his, disappeared in there a little while ago, grumbling about too many damn people in his house leaving water marks on the table or some nonsense. Make sure you tell him the pizza and wings never came, and we're getting hungry. Oh, and ditch the shoes, he's like a damn woman when it comes to scuffing up his floor."

Gus and her cake hobbled down the hallway, scuffing his big work boots—that were not by the door but on his feet—the entire way. Wrecking Ball looked at Abby's crotch longingly, then barked and tore off after his master, knocking over a few empty bottles and a potted plant on the way.

Determination set, Abby slipped off her shoes and waltzed into the house, right through the middle of the red sea, when the blonde in the bikini top gasped at her jersey, and the party—well, that came to a standstill.

Shouting halted, television watching stopped. It was as though the game ceased to exist.

Good Lord, the place was packed with bikinis and bulging pecs. But what had Abby surprised was, while a good portion of the party-goers most likely worked at Hooters, an equal percentage would qualify for a senior snip at the Prune and Clip. Even more surprising was that everyone was silently staring—*glaring*—in her direction. All over a little bird's head on her shirt.

She hesitated slightly, even considered turning around, returning home, and calling Babs. Considered explaining that she couldn't find a contractor, that she was afraid she wouldn't be able to pull this off. In order to keep the *Titanic* from sinking, she needed Tanner, which meant she'd have to beg him to take the job. That was the only way he'd agree. And begging the man who had ripped out her heart would be almost as difficult as working side by side with him and not giving in to the chemistry.

Then she remembered how Richard was still on her lawn, how her brothers had believed they needed to bribe an old lady to get her a job designing a doghouse, and how tired she was of people underestimating her ability to get things done.

Inner resolve in full effect, she offered up an energetic, "Go Seahawks!" with a coordinating fist pump, then gave a small little wave and just kept walking toward the back of the house, making sure she stood at her full five foot one. Because wrong jersey or not, Abby was determined to get a win today—just one.

Tanner didn't have to open his eyes to see who was hovering over him. He'd heard her huffing and mumbling even before she'd stepped out onto the patio off his office. He also had a pretty good idea of why she was here—Colin's words echoed that Abby had already committed

Tanner to be the GC—and for the first time in this whole situation, Tanner felt as though he actually had the upper hand.

He just wasn't certain he wanted to use it.

"You here to pick me up for our date?"

"Date?" Abby said crisply, then laughed. "I can see how you might get confused with all of the half-naked party girls on display, but I think you have the wrong girl."

Huh. Maybe instead of killing Colin for inviting the Stanford cheerleading team, he'd actually thank the guy, because if he didn't know any better, he'd guess Little Miss Not Interested was a wee bit jealous.

"You sure?" He cracked open one eye and bit back a smile. Wrong girl his ass.

The only reason Abby would wear that god-awful jersey was if she was into him. Not that it mattered. The jersey obviously wasn't hers. It was probably borrowed, because it was at least a size too small for her chest, showing off those tight curves. And her skinny jeans—*hot damn*—they fit like a glove, hugging her toned legs and, he'd bet, hugging her ass to perfection.

Impatient and stubborn as ever, she tapped her bare feet . . . and, well, look at that, shiny red toenails.

"Yup. Right girl." He leaned his head back and closed his eyes. "Wrong jersey, though."

"I like my jersey and I don't remember agreeing to a date with you."

"You didn't agree, darling. You offered. I fix your pipes, we go out. Remember?"

"Actually, you said you'd fix them in exchange for a night that ended in a kiss."

Was she serious?

He opened his eyes and, *yup*, dead serious. "We were changing a broken pipe in your garage—"

"And there was a kiss." She smiled, thinking she'd won.

"A very hot kiss," he agreed softly and found Abby staring at his mouth. He smiled to let her know he was thinking about that kiss too.

She glared at him some, then crossed her arms. "One that isn't happening again. We're all square."

"Your toes say differently." A dramatic roll of the eyes was all he got out of her before she leveled him with what he'd come to know as her *get down to business* look.

She glanced around the secluded patio. It was Tanner's favorite place in the house for its lack of people, party fanfare, and, more importantly, lack of flash. It was private, comfortable, and the only place in all of the eight thousand square feet of mansion that Tanner had built for himself—without the thought of resale value.

A small frown creased her brow. A frown he found incredibly adorable. Man, Abby managed to be stubborn and adorable all at the same time.

Tanner had a real weakness for adorable. The stubborn part just turned him on.

"Why are you out here?" she asked.

"Because everyone else is in there." And he needed space that wasn't filled with people wanting a piece of him. Already today he'd been asked to introduce some guy he'd never met to his old coach, play in a celebrity golf tournament, and MC the upcoming Vintner's Association conference. Even Colin, who had promised him a small get-together, which wound up being the exact kind of situation Tanner had moved back to St. Helena to avoid, had been in his face to talk up Ferris.

So he had the ability to run really fast while holding a ball, big deal. Which was why it always felt weird when people clamored, and it felt even worse when all they seemed to need was his name, money, or face on a box of jock itch cream.

"Oh," Abby said gently, then looked at the door as though considering bolting.

"And why are you here?" he asked.

"To tell you that I got the job with Babs."

"Well done, DeLuca." He smiled because she looked so happy and he was so damn proud of her. "You deserve it."

Her cheeks turned the cutest shade of pink. "Thanks. It's going to be a challenge." Understatement of the year, and they both knew it. "In fact, my first assignment is to hire a new GC."

"Do you need a list of guys?" he asked cautiously, since Colin's words were beating around in his head. "I think Dave over in Yountville just finished up a job and might be free."

"I already called Dave." She shook her head and all of those pretty curls spilled over her shoulders. "Nope, what I need is . . ." She looked up at the sky as though asking for a divine intervention—or maybe courage—then back down at his beer. "A drink. You got another one of those?"

Offering up his beer, he scooted over and patted the seat next to him, surprised when she plopped down on the lounge chair and took a long pull. With a heavy sigh, she kicked up her feet and, resting the beer on her flat belly, let her head fall back to rest against the towel he'd folded up like a pillow.

The chair was narrow, or maybe it was that he was a giant. Either way, she was close. Temptingly close. He could feel the warmth from her small body and, when the warm breeze kicked up, he caught a whiff of her perfume. Or maybe it was whatever she washed her hair with. Either way, it was sweet and spicy and reminded him of—

"Do I smell wine cake?"

Abby took a whiff of her jersey. "Yup. Delivered as promised. Although you might have to fight your dad for it."

"Oh well, you can just make me another one."

"The deal was for one." She took a sip of the beer and he could see her throat working.

"I guess I'll just have to smell my fill." He leaned in closer, sure to nuzzle her neck a little with the tip of his nose, and accidently brushed her throat with his lips and—God, she had the softest skin. She also had on a jersey with an extremely low V in the front, which when he shifted closer gave him a great view of creamy cleavage disappearing into bright yellow lace.

"You're tickling me," she whispered.

"You're not moving," he pointed out and flashed her a grin—one she returned before handing him the half-empty beer and going back to watching the clouds glide by. It was a telltale sign Abby was deciding if she was going to step up and explain why she was here or pretend her world was peachy and go home.

Tanner thought it could still go either way.

He didn't know how long they lay there, and didn't care. All he knew was they were side by side, silently staring at the sky, passing the same beer back and forth. Something they'd spent an entire summer doing when they were teenagers. The only thing missing was his arm around her and her fingers gently stroking his chest.

God, he'd missed this. He'd missed her.

"I'm going to nominate the bottlery for the Memory Lane Manor Walk," she finally said. "It's the only way to guarantee the Pungent Barrel can open before next year. All nominees have to get the Historical Preservation Council to sign off on their designs."

"And if you nominate it, you skip the waitlist." *Smart and beautiful.* "But I didn't know the bottlery was a residence."

"I didn't either, but . . ." She rolled on her side to face him. He could see the little flecks of green in her big brown eyes and the little smattering of freckles that were normally hidden by her olive skin. He could also see that with a slight tilt of the head, he'd be kissing her. But her face was so serious he held back.

"But?"

"Babs said when her husband bought the bottlery, he received a packet of papers on its history. And you know the little building off the back of the loading dock? The storage room? Well, before Prohibition it was a carriage house."

"And during Prohibition?" Drawn to her like a magnet, he rolled on his side too. And man, was it worth it, because she let loose a smile that made breathing hard. Hell, it made him hard, period.

"Back then, Randal Jackson's oldest son was in love with Susette, the daughter of a migrant picker who came through every year for the olive harvest. His parents were adamantly against the match, so Randal Jackson Jr. converted the carriage house into an apartment under the guise he was supervising the building of the bottlery. When in reality he had a secret summer-long affair with Susette."

"Smart man," Tanner said, seeing the parallels to Abby's family. They hadn't even gone on a date yet and already her brothers were all up in his shit, making things difficult.

"Babs said they only lived there a little while, but long enough to fall in love and get pregnant. He even went against his parents' wishes and married her."

"He knew what he wanted and went for it." Something Tanner admired. He wasn't sure he was ready for marriage and kids right now, but someday he wanted a full house of mini linebackers. And maybe a cheerleader or two who had curly brown hair and whisky-colored eyes.

"And Tanner," she said so quietly his eyes went to her lips.

"Yeah?"

"About earlier, what I said." She moved even closer, her breath brushing his lips, her gaze boring into his with that intense DeLuca determination, and he felt something in his chest catch, then shift.

He didn't know what "earlier" she was referring to. He was too busy thinking about later when he found a carriage house of his own to bring Abby to.

"What I need is you."

What a statement. One he'd waited his entire adult life to hear. Scratch that. It was almost the statement he'd been waiting to hear. With one simple word, Abby suddenly became just like everyone in his life—*needing* something from him. For a minute he could almost give in and pretend it was enough, but not this time.

Not now. Not here. Not with this girl. And not anymore.

"There is a strict timeline on things I must have in order to get the nomination heard by the council, one of which is having a new general contractor by Monday."

"I know a bunch of guys who might be able to do it."

She shook her head and everything inside of him stilled.

"I doubt there is anyone on your list who would be willing."

Yeah, well, he would have been willing, had even convinced himself last night that if she actually asked him to help, it would be a *hell yes*. That was when he thought she considered him first string. Now, he wasn't so sure.

"Sorry, I don't do small remodels or retail renovations."

"I know. I wouldn't even be here except that . . ." She faded off and so did her gaze, which was now focused on anywhere but at him. That's when Tanner really got it. When his chest stopped working and head actually began to throb with disappointment.

"I'm it, right? You called everyone else on your little list, a list I guarantee didn't include my name, which makes me your"—how did she put it last week?—"last hope?"

She gave a small, tired nod. "If I don't have you signed on as the GC by Monday, there is no way we will be ready for the electrical and plumbing inspection, and we'll have to wait to submit our plans until after Founder's Day, and by then the waitlist could be months long."

Even her candid honesty didn't lessen the tightening in his gut. He'd had a feeling that was why she was here, but he'd been stupid enough to hope he was wrong.

"What's in it for me?" he said.

Her eyes went wide with disbelief.

Welcome to it, darling. Two could play at this.

"A job."

"Already got one. It pays a lot more than what you're offering and it doesn't come with the headache of dealing with Babs, the HPC"—he looked her in the eye—"or you."

"Oh."

Yeah, oh. For a woman who claimed to hate being trampled over, she sure knew how to lay a few footprints of her own. And with him they always managed to plant themselves in the same spot in his chest.

"Fine," he said, suddenly tired. Tired of favors and always being the one to give while getting zilch. Tired of waiting for the woman who he was pretty sure he was half in love with to pull her head out of her ass and admit there was something between them. To give him a chance. "You want something from me? Well, darling, I want something from you. And I'm not talking about a cake or small talk while fixing your pipes. I want the real deal."

"I already told you, I'm not having sex with you."

"Wow." He raised a brow. "I like that your mind went there, but that's not what I'm talking about." He leaned up on his elbow, moving in closer, until her lids went heavy and her breath caught. "Though I am more convinced now than ever it will happen, Abs," he whispered, running his thumb over her lips. "But I'll leave the time and place up to you."

"It's not going to happen, Jack."

Oh, it was going to happen. That was a fact. That she sounded so offended while struggling to keep her gaze off his mouth only solidified his belief. Yup, he and Abby were going to spend an entire night blowing off some of the pent-up steam between them. And, *hot damn*, it was going to happen sooner than he'd originally thought.

"You sure about that?" he said. "Because I know how much you hate being wrong."

She opened her mouth to argue, so he took the opportunity to stop her before she made some other ridiculous vow she'd never keep.

Tanner felt his mouth brush hers and, *oh baby*, just like that, one touch and there it was. That sweet blast of fire followed by pure, staggering heat.

Abby held back at first, trying to prove her point, but he knew the moment she gave in. Her hand raised, hovering in the air for a moment, then both were fisted in his hair and she was pressing herself up against him, holding him to her, taking over. It was the most arousing sensation. The rush of triumph actually had his heart going instantly soft and everything else instantly hard.

He let her lead, because why the hell not? This was Abby, the girl of his dreams, kissing him like she'd been starved for it—and something about that thought should have had him slowing down, taking a step back, and acknowledging she most likely hadn't been with anyone since Richard.

But he was male, and she was abso-fucking-lutely female—soft and curvy and when he moved down her neck to the hollow of her throat, nibbling and sucking, she started making those breathy little moans he'd forgotten about, and there was no way he could bring himself to back off when—

Wait, how the hell had he forgotten what she sounded like when she was turned on? They were the most erotic little gasps he'd ever heard, and yet somehow they managed to get lost behind all of the frustration and anger. Well, he wasn't frustrated or angry anymore—he was in heaven, and this kiss was worth the wait.

Her hand slid down, stopping on his chest, pressing to encourage him to lie back so she could climb on top. He always had worked well with encouragement, so he relaxed and let her take charge. Then her fingers were on the move, heading downfield, past his stomach, showing no signs of slowing down, and—bingo—she wasn't going to stop at the line of scrimmage. Nope, she was bypassing the zipper and going straight for the end zone, encouraging him all the way to an ill-timed, but more than welcome, touchdown.

Only there was a flag on the play in the form of a big, hairy face nudging its way between their bodies, weaseling them apart. Panting and grunting, Wreck was a dog on a mission, and Tanner was terrified this interference was going to be a game changer.

"Wreck. Off." He shoved the dog, but it didn't deter the furry beast from jumping right back up on the lounger, his tail smacking Abby in the face and his wet nose going right for her—

"Whoa, back off there, pal," he said while Abby desperately tried to ward off all of the unwanted doggie high fives to the crotch.

Tanner had to wrestle the dog off. With a final tug, the dog was on the ground, his big eyes blinking up at Abby, who was already standing and straightening her clothes, ready to bolt. He skewered Wreck with a look.

The dog panted happily.

"Sorry about that," Tanner said, walking around the chair and brushing Abby's wild curls out of her face and, *man oh man*, she was beautiful. Messy hair, swollen lips, do-me eyes. Yeah, she wanted him, and he absolutely knew if the mutt hadn't interrupted, the DeLuca Darling would have had her hands down his pants in no time flat.

He glared at Wreck. "Bad dog."

"Don't blame him," she laughed, and what a great laugh she had. That was one sound so imprinted in his brain he knew he'd never forget it. "It's the cake. The smell drives him crazy."

"Me too." It wasn't the cake. It was the woman herself. In fact, he wanted to take another sniff, and maybe a lick, but Abby was already stepping back.

She pressed a hand to her lips as though testing to see if the kiss was as mind-blowing as it felt. He wanted to tell her she could touch her lips all day long, but that zing wasn't going away anytime soon. Neither was the Tanner-sized hickey on her neck.

He had to smile because she was going to be pissed when she saw that. Pissy and irritated and huffing up a storm.

"So about the job?" she said.

Right. Back to that. "Let's talk terms."

"The terms are I hire you, you say yes, we get it done on time, we both win."

"I saw it going a little differently. Want to hear how?"

"No." Gaze locked and loaded, she stood silently, trying to outstare him. Running backs, though, had all the patience in the world if it meant catching the pass. So he crossed his arms and decided to wait her out.

Three seconds in, she started fidgeting on her feet, toeing at the floor, dusting off imaginary fuzz from her pants. Then finally she broke.

"Fine. Terms. What do you want?"

"You." *Plain and simple.* "You. Me. More of this." He reached out and ran a hand down her arm until their fingers tangled, satisfied when he felt a small tremor run through her body. Or maybe it was his. Didn't know, didn't care. All that mattered was when he was with Abby, he could just be. No pretense, no posturing, nothing but being Jack Tanner. And that felt good.

She eyed the lounger suspiciously. "You need to be more specific. *This* could mean a lot of different things."

All of which he was open to. Then she broke eye contact and looked out over the pool. He watched as a mix of uncertainty and confusion washed over her, and his heart did a double kick right to the gut. The only thing he was certain about was walking away from whatever *this* was would be the smart thing. The easy thing.

But Tanner was tired of taking the easy way out of everything.

"How about we start with hanging out, holding hands, sharing a meal or two, and watching football on the couch."

"I hate football," she said, and he laughed.

"Darling, we can watch competitive piano for all I care. I just want it to be real, no stress, and no BS."

Abby looked into his eyes as though trying to figure out his angle. And for the first time in a long time, Tanner didn't have one.

"I have to think about it."

"Well, then think fast. My offer expires at midnight tomorrow."

He didn't mention it expired because he had already decided to take the job and they couldn't waste any more time. And if she said no to his terms, there was no way he could pass up four weeks working side by side with Abby.

Four weeks of doing whatever it took to get the DeLuca Darling to change *need* to *want.*

CHAPTER 10

At exactly seven minutes to eight on Monday morning, Abby turned onto Main Street. Narrowly missing a group of tourists meandering across the street to catch the Napa Valley Wine Train, she pulled into the cobblestone-and-brick driveway belonging to the community park.

Wear a skirt and bring éclairs, had been Tanner's advice. *And don't be late.*

Epic fail, she thought as she finished her third tour of the parking lot, which was also packed full of tourists, tourists, and more tourists. Clock ticking, she decided to jump the curb and snag a spot in front of Stan's Soup and Service Station.

Okay, so maybe it wasn't a spot so much as a gas pump, but it would have to do. August was the height of tourist season in St. Helena, which meant parking was at a premium. One more turn of the lot and Main Street would be so congested that driving would be impossible.

She was due at town hall any moment and *still* had to pick up her order from the Sweet and Savory.

According to Tanner, Eddie Floor, the town's only building inspector, was a by-the-book hard-ass who liked his morning coffee with a lot of sugar and leg.

Abby looked down at her short legs and sighed. There was nothing she could do about giving Eddie his leg quota for the day, so she was overcompensating with a lot of sugar to make up for being late to a meeting she had begged for.

Another thing she blamed on Tanner. She'd spent last night staring at the ceiling and touching her lips. Which still somehow managed to taste like him. And over an hour this morning trying to cover up the annoying hickey on her neck that was the exact shape of Tanner's mouth. When that didn't work, she opted for a cap-sleeved shirt with a high collar she'd buttoned up tight to her neck.

"It was just a kiss." She rested her head against the car window and groaned.

No matter how many times she said it, it didn't stop her lips from throbbing. Because it wasn't just a kiss. It was the kiss to end all kisses.

The kiss that had undeniably rocked her widowed world so hard she had been taken right out of herself.

And that hickey . . .

Abby took a deep, calming breath, which only managed to make the collar of her shirt droop and the hickey on her neck more visible—damn the man—and hopped out of the car. She had four minutes to grab a box of Lexi's famous éclairs and get to town hall for her meeting. What she didn't have time for were thoughts of Tanner's lips, of Tanner naked, or how the morning heat had her skirt shrink-wrapping itself to her thighs.

Sticking the nozzle into her gas tank, she pretended to run her credit card through the pump's reader and gave Stan a casual I-got-this wave through the window. He waved back, then disappeared behind the counter, and that's when Abby ran for it.

Grabbing her purse, she ditched the car at the pump and, sure to look both ways, sprinted across the street and pushed breathlessly through the front door of the Sweet and Savory. A warm blast of cinnamon and oven-sweet air greeted her.

The bistro was already at standing-room-only capacity, with the line for the to-go pastries and specialty coffees winding back through the restaurant to the window display, which showcased an array of decadent cakes and tarts.

Lexi came out from the kitchen wearing a NO SAMPLING THE CREAM PUFFS apron, a tray of cream cheese croissants in one hand and a rolling pin in the other. Both baker and apron were covered with a light dusting of what Abby assumed was flour.

Lexi caught Abby's eye and waved her up to the front. Being BFFs with the owner of the most popular bistro in the valley had its perks.

"Hey, you gotta wait your turn like everyone else," Nora Kincaid said, whacking at Abby's ankles with her cane when she leaned over the counter to check the morning's specials. "This here is the line and you are a cutter."

"She's not cutting," Lexi explained, serene smile in place. "She called ahead and I have her order ready."

"I called ahead," Nora challenged loudly enough for everyone in the bistro to hear. "And I had to wait in that line. If you ask me, your cream puffs are good, but not that good."

"My husband would disagree." Lexi pointed Abby to the end of the counter, away from Nora and her sharp cane. "But feel free to go someplace else if you feel like it."

Nora mumbled something about cheaters and the neighborhood going to hell before ordering Brooke, Lexi's part-time counter-girl-slash-barista, to get her a lavender latte and pucker-up lemon tart to go.

"Thanks," Abby said when they were out of earshot. "I'm bribing a city official with a half dozen of your éclairs and a few of those chocolate croissants everyone loves. The ones with sea salt sprinkled over the top. And I don't need Nosy Nora poking around. Oh, and I need them ASAP."

"Okay." Lexi smiled, but she didn't move. Except for her eyes, which were narrowed in on Abby's shirt.

"As in, if I don't make this meeting, I won't be able to enter Jackson Bottlery in the Memory Lane Manor Walk, so could you scoot your butt over to the pastry section and bag up my order?"

Lexi just rocked on her heels. "Kind of hot for a turtleneck, isn't it?"

"It's not a turtleneck. It's just a high collar." Abby fingered the collar of her cap-sleeved blouse. "And I picked it because it said professional, trustworthy, 'Yes, Mr. Inspector, you can make an exception for me just this once.'"

"Uh-huh," Lexi mumbled. Her BS meter was flipping Abby the bird, which was the number one reason Abby had considered skipping the sugary bribe and relying on her charm. But since Eddie was a leg man, she'd decided to risk facing Lexi. Bad decision. "You hate high collars. They make your boobs look enormous and take three inches off your height. Even in heels you come off more Oompa Loompa than grown woman." Too bad Eddie wasn't a boob guy. "So try again."

Keeping a secret from her friend had always been hard. When that secret happened to be a huge hickey covering half her neck, it was downright impossible. And since *that hickey* was special delivery via the very fine lips of one Jack Tanner—a topic she'd rather not talk about *ever*—Abby had done her best to steer clear of her friend. And the man in question.

Not that either one was an option anymore. She needed this project to be a win, and in order to do that she needed Hickey Master to bring his grade-A tool belt to the site tomorrow morning. Which meant she needed her friend's perspective.

Lexi knew their history. Knew how badly he'd crushed her. And obviously knew something was up.

"Fine," Abby said, leaning in and lowering her voice. Nora was still within earshot and had the fastest texting fingers in town. "Jack and I may have shared a kiss or two."

"I knew it." Lexi actually had the nerve to start clapping. "I knew you still had a thing for him."

"It's not a thing, it just happened."

"Says the girl wearing a high collar in the middle of August." She reached out to pull the collar down.

"Can you yell that a little louder?" Abby hissed, batting her hand away and holding her palm to her throat just in case. "I don't think Marc heard you next door."

"Did you two, um . . ." Lexi made a little swivel motion with her hips.

"No!"

"But you want to," she practically sang. "I know you do."

Abby did. So badly. But that wasn't up for discussion. Or consideration. Although, if she were being honest, she'd considered herself into quite a state last night. Just thinking about it had tingles starting low in her belly and spreading out in all directions.

"Back to whispering," she warned with a stern look. Lexi was not intimidated in the slightest. She was too busy making kissy noises. "And before you start plotting my love life, you need to tell me it can't happen again. The kissing," she corrected. "The kissing can't happen again."

"Sure it can." Not what she wanted to hear. "You need something fun and shiny to distract you from everything going on."

"What part about bribing a city official, entering the Pungent Barrel in the Memory Lane Manor Walk, and Richard's statue did you miss? The last thing I need is a distraction. I'm going to have a hard enough time staying focused as it is."

And working with Tanner, remembering what he looked like naked, was going to be hard enough. Seeing him naked—as a full grown man—then expecting to work side by side with him, all those long nights holed up together in that bottlery?

Impossible.

"Focused on what? How big his tool belt is?"

"Not appropriate, Lexi. I just became single. I mean, a widow." God, that sounded weird.

"Right. I guess we should google the appropriate mourning time first, then add in the fact you've gone seven years without sex and . . ."

Lexi whipped out her smart phone, started fiddling with the Google app, and instead of googling sex etiquette for widowed thirty-year-olds, held up a photo of Hard Hammer Tanner.

In nothing but a creatively placed football.

Abby swallowed.

"Hello?" Still waving the phone. "Do you think you are expected to wait another seven? I say jump his bones and get it over with."

"Again, not appropriate." Abby grabbed the phone and, taking one last look—maybe two—shoved it in Lexi's apron pocket. "Neither is my dating. I'm single for the first time since college and I finally have my life back. You're supposed to tell me to lie low, get my act together, prove to this town I am not a woman to be taken lightly. And jumping into a relationship wouldn't help. Especially with someone I am bound to work on projects with."

If not the Pungent Barrel, then another project. It was only a matter of time before they would be stuck working together. St. Helena was too small for their paths not to cross. And often, if Abby pulled this job off. *When* she did—it was no longer an if—her design firm would take on bigger, more exclusive projects. And that was Tanner's specialty. Along with kissing. Jack Tanner was a world-class kisser.

Not to mention a world-class playboy.

Lexi pulled out a pink box and started filling it with pastries. "You've been lying low for so long, I think you deserve to treat yourself a little. Although, from what I've seen lately, nothing about Tanner is little."

Nope, Tanner was big, built, and so gentle, Abby knew sex with him would be like finishing a one-course meal and wishing she'd ordered the buffet. She was sure women everywhere agreed.

"Last time I slept with someone I worked on a project with, he was also sleeping with everyone else, then stole twelve million dollars and left me a widow. I think I am done with workplace affairs."

Lexi set the box on the counter. "Honey, Richard was a jerk."

"And Tanner has more women frequent his house than Hugh Hefner."

"Maybe because the woman he wants keeps telling him to go suck it." Lexi placed a hand on Abby's and her voice went soft. "I know Richard's death is affecting you more than you're letting on. His showing up right when you were ready to start living again is like having one more person leaving before you get your answers."

Abby had never voiced that fear to anyone before, but she shouldn't have been surprised her best friend had figured it out. For years after her parents had died, Abby would stay up all night playing the what-if game. What if she hadn't gone to that recital? What if she had won instead of coming in fifth and they stayed for the finals? What if Richard had never loved her and their marriage had all been some sick game?

And what if she were missing that one elusive piece of herself that made people want to stay?

Her confidence wasn't unraveling because Richard had gotten the last word. She was scared to move on and start dating because all the words she wanted to hear him say were sitting in an urn in her front yard, reminding her that all of the unanswered questions her heart needed to understand would never be explained.

"What if I put myself out there and get hurt again?"

"And what if you take your sweet time and he moves on?" Lexi pulled out the phone and flashed the photo of Tanner for emphasis. "You don't get to turn a man like him down over and over, then hold it against him that he's dating other women."

That's not the problem, Abby thought, looking at his rippling abs and gorgeous pecs. She was afraid she'd say yes, they'd go out, she'd fall hard, then find out he wanted to keep dating—other women. Other hot women with mile-long legs, twentysomething's boobs, and no-strings capabilities. "I think Jack is more of the all-you-can-eat buffet type."

Just like Richard was.

"Or what if he just needs to find the right woman?" Lexi leaned forward, getting as close as she could to being in Abby's face with a giant pastry box and a counter between them. Then she fluttered her lashes and Abby knew she was in trouble. "Something you can find out when you finally settle our little pact."

"You can't hold me to that!"

"I can and I will. And before you pull some 'friends don't let friends date jocks' speech, just be honest and tell me he doesn't get to you. Because if you look me in the eye and say he doesn't, then I will drop it."

Abby met her friend's eyes, and when she went to open her mouth and deny it, *oh God*, she couldn't.

Jack "Hard Hammer" Tanner got to her. Even worse, he *got* her. Like nobody else in her world.

And damn if that didn't piss her off.

"You know what, Lexi? You're right. Friends don't let friends date jocks. And since people having sex don't keep secrets and the last person I want to know about my business is my brother, you'll just have to wonder."

Not giving Lexi a chance to respond, Abby grabbed her box and headed out the door, thankful Stan hadn't towed her car. She crossed Main Street and made her way up the wide front steps of town hall, her breath catching when she saw the banner advertising the Founder's Day festivities flapping between the white columns.

ST. HELENA'S ANNUAL FOUNDER'S DAY MEMORY LANE MANOR WALK: WHERE PRESERVATION AND INGENUITY MEET AT THE CORNER OF MEMORY LANE AND THE ROAD TO TOMORROW.

Collar in place, Abby tugged her skirt a tad higher than midthigh and pushed through the doors, not stopping until she reached the welcome desk. Setting the unmistakable pink box of sweets on the counter, she smiled at the welcoming committee of one, who didn't smile back. "Good morning, Roz."

Roz Kale was about four thousand years old, friendly as a porcupine, and her bright red lips were pressed into a thin line, making it more than obvious that today Abby took the good right out of her morning.

"Éclair?" Abby offered.

Roz looked down at her elastic-covered waistline and glared. "Do I look like I need an éclair?"

Not going there. Abby smiled and said, "I'm here to see Eddie Floor. Could you ring him and tell him Abigail DeLuca is here?" When the woman didn't move, she added, "He's expecting me."

Not taking her eyes off Abby, Roz picked up the phone and punched a series of buttons and mumbled something unpleasant into the mouthpiece. Two seconds later she shot Abby an *Are you satisfied?* glare and hung up. "He'll be out in a minute. You can wait," she pointed to the chair on the opposite end of the lobby, "over there."

With a defeated sigh, Abby hazarded to venture. "Let me guess, you invested in Richard's vineyard?"

"Nope." There went the condemning lips again.

"You or someone you know slept with Richard?"

"Nope. My granddaughter, Sidney, is supposed to go to a Niners game next week with that nice Jack Tanner. She's interested in being a sportscaster." Abby would bet that wasn't all she was interested in. "Only now I'm hearing on Facebook that you poached him and he's going to cancel."

"I haven't poached him and Jack's always been the kind of person who does what he wants," Abby said, surprised at just how badly that statement hurt, and irritated she let it get to her.

The woman finally smiled. "Well then, my Sidney will be happy to hear that. She's got what they call the X factor, and has the face for television too. Plus, she's a big football fan, and an even bigger Hard Hammer Tanner fan."

Join the club, Abby thought, looking at the picture of the blonde pinup girl with impressive cleavage and porn star lips on Roz's desk.

She doubted there was a single lady in town who wouldn't let Hard Hammer Tanner put a ring on it. Well, except for Abby.

Although he didn't want to put a ring on it. Nope, St. Helena's resident stud muffin wanted to hang out. Hold hands. Be real. Kiss a little. All the things she and Tanner did best together. And all Abby had to do to make it official was stop playing the what-if game and smooch the hometown hero who looked amazing in nothing but a football and day-old stubble.

A small giggle escaped her lips at the thought, then another. And Abby had to bite her lips to keep from laughing. Not that it helped. She looked at her reflection in the city clerk's window and had to do a double take. She was smiling, big and dreamy. In fact, she was glowing.

Holy cow. Abigail DeLuca, town martyr and woman scorned, was glowing. No ifs about it.

She touched her lips and felt them tingle and couldn't help but wonder, could it really be so easy? Just say yes, pucker up, and all of the BS that had become her life as of late would disappear?

It would, her mind said. Although her heart added the, "At least for a little while." Because their problem had never been connection or getting lost in each other. It had been Tanner's ability to pick up and move on without her.

But he wasn't going anywhere. His roots were firmly planted here in St. Helena. And she wasn't naive enough to think forever was in her future.

But temporary? That she could do.

Sex. She could so do that. At least she hoped she could. It had been a while.

Excitement and something else, something distantly familiar and much more dangerous to her well-being, slid through her body.

Because she was going to get Eddie Floor to give them an extension and then she was going to call Tanner and tell him he was hired—for whatever position he felt himself qualified.

Widow or not, Abby was single and needed a little fun in her life. And fun was never as exciting as when it was had with Jack Tanner.

"Actually, Roz, you might want to have Sidney check with Jack before she dusts off her Niners jersey. I think he's going to be a little busy for the next few weeks. Oh, and . . ." Abby opened the pink box and snagged an éclair, not concerned her collar sagged a little. Around a mouthful of custard she added, "If you could buzz me through, that would be great. It seems Mr. Floor is waving me in."

Roz didn't answer. She just hit the buzzer and glowered.

With a murmured thanks, Abby shoved the last bite of éclair in her mouth and, licking her fingers clean, grabbed the box and headed down the hallway.

It was midafternoon by the time Tanner made it to the site of the new DeLuca wine cave. He pulled down the gravel road, around the hundred or so acres of cabernet vines and, ignoring the wiry tail smacking him in the arm every three seconds, parked under the gnarled branches of a massive oak tree.

It had been a hell of a day so far, and the only thing that could have made it better was a call from a woman.

A testy, stubborn, five foot nothing of a woman who'd starred in a few very steamy dreams he'd had last night.

Smiling, Tanner checked his cell for the tenth time that day. Nothing. No text. No missed calls. No message with Abby huffing into his phone about her meeting with Eddie Floor. More irritating still, no message telling him if she'd considered his offer and had come to a decision.

He'd been tempted to give her a call and hurry that decision along, but had to remind himself he'd given her until midnight.

Swearing, Tanner reached for the car door handle and paused to look at his copilot. "I'm going to open that door and you're going to sit right there until I'm out, and then you're going to stay by my side. Got it?"

"Woof."

"Sit," Tanner clarified.

Wreck sat—right on top of Tanner's favorite hat. Then put on his best obedient doggie face.

When Tanner opened the door, Wreck made a run for it, leaping over Tanner's lap, not even touching ground until he was outside the truck. Too bad for the dog, Tanner had already leashed him, which meant his escape lasted about zero point three seconds, then the four feet of lead pulled taut and Wreck indeed sat—with a thud in the dirt.

Tanner stepped out of the car. "I told you to sit. Now we have to do it the hard way. Heel." He gave a gentle tug on the leash to let Wreck know exactly who was in charge, and headed toward the pack of burly, pissed-off-looking Italians standing by the side of the hill.

One look at Wingman, Marc's bear of a dog, and Wreck did some tugging of his own, ripping the leash right out of Tanner's hand, bulldozing through the field and three rows of grapevines, leaving a happy trail in his wake. "Wreck, stop!"

Wreck didn't stop until he made contact, even bypassing Wingman altogether so he could greet everyone with a wet nose to the crotch. A few sniffs later, he realized there were no ladies in the group and plopped down in the grass with a sigh.

Tanner actually felt for the mutt.

"Hey guys, sorry I'm late," Tanner said to the group. "I got held up at the planning department."

The group didn't seem to care. Maybe they were too busy trying to look tough and intimidating to respond. In fact, the only one who wasn't sending him an *eat shit and choke on it* glare was little Cooper Reed, who was holding Trey's hand and smiling like it was the best day of his life.

Tanner understood. Blowing up shit, or even talking about it, was fun. So he had no idea what had crawled up the other guys' asses.

"Is that your dog? Is he friendly? Can I pet him?" Cooper Reed asked, getting low to the ground, his hand already stroking Wreck's head.

Cooper took piano from Abby every Tuesday and Thursday before Tanner, so he was used to seeing the kid dressed in a little button-up shirt and dress shoes, but today he was sporting a pair of rugged work boots, carpenter's pants with a mini hammer hanging off the loop, and a shirt that read TEAM BROS. It matched Trey's ball cap, which was fitting, since Trey was marrying Cooper's mom in the fall.

"This is Wrecking Ball, but you can call him Wreck. And he's my dad's." Tanner didn't have to answer the friendly part, since Wreck was already on his back, legs up in the air, begging for a belly rub. "But today he's hanging with me since my dad has a doctor's appointment."

And because in the two hours it took to get everything handled at the planning department, Wreck had eaten through one of the couch cushions, a pair of socks, and half a roll of toilet paper. The other half was strewn around the downstairs.

"Plus, Trey said you're building a man cave," Cooper added. "Which is why me and Wingman got to come. You know, for some quality bro time. Little Bella is just here cuz she fell asleep on her daddy. I got some juice boxes and string cheese in the car for after. Enough to share."

Wingman barked his bro support. Wreck stood and started giving puppy-dog eyes at the "cheese for all" statement. And the only part of Bella visible from the pastel-striped hammock, which hung around Cooper's daddy's neck, was her little hand.

Tanner considered fist-bumping the baby for the hell of it, but he was afraid Marc would fist-bump Tanner right back—in the face. And he didn't think hugging it out would help any, so he settled for ruffling Cooper's hair. "That sounds great. How about you go grab the snacks while I talk to the guys about this wine cave?"

"Man cave," the kid corrected. "And can I bring Wreck?"

Tanner eyed all three and a half feet of Cooper, then Wreck, who was staring at the kid's boots like they were what was for dinner.

"Sorry, buddy. But Wreck needs to learn how to follow directions."

Tanner took the leash and tied it to a tree that cast a nice patch of shade.

"Are you putting him in time-out?" Cooper asked, his eyes staring at the dog with sympathy.

"Afraid so."

Wreck sighed. So did Cooper, who looked as though he was going to sit next to the mutt in protest, but in the end thirst won out and he scampered off to get the juice boxes and cheese sticks.

Tanner turned to the brothers. Who had yet to say even a word. "So the soil reports and geological survey came back approved. All I'm waiting on is to hear back from Colin, who's meeting with the cave engineer now about the where the interior design specifications stand. As soon as he calls with an update, I'll file for the permits and then we are good to go, though I wanted to do one last walk-through of the site to make sure you're all comfortable with where I want to put the mobile office and equipment staging area."

Tanner Construction had done a small wine cave for the DeLucas' personal collection last winter, but this cave was different. This one, when finished, was going to be the largest underground wine storage facility in the valley. It was also going to be the largest build and, with room set aside for storage, tasting rooms, and entertainment areas, the most complex underground project Tanner Construction had ever done.

And with the DeLuca family estate just off the other side of the vineyard, Tanner wanted to make sure the brothers understood just how invasive this build was going to be. Especially since ChiChi still lived in the house.

"Are you thinking right over there, behind the small rise, like we originally talked about?" Marc asked, gently swaying even though the bundle inside the hammock was already asleep.

"Yeah." Tanner started walking toward the pasture Marc had pointed out. "Unless you guys had a better place in mind, because once the permits come in and we get going, the cave will take at least two months to drill and another four to build out. And that's with no problems and two crews working week-round."

Nate let out a low whistle, picking up the pace. "That's a lot of traffic and a lot of equipment. I don't want it to affect harvest."

"Which is why Gabe and I picked out this location," Tanner said as they rounded the curve of the hill. "We'll put in a new entrance that will let the crews access this part of the property from the road, bypassing the house and most of the vines. The separate entrance and concrete pad we lay now will make a perfect parking lot for tourists when the cave is open. Sure, it will be a tight fit this harvest, but if all goes well, we should be out of your hair when planting season comes around."

Nate, the expert on all things wine making, gave a short nod. "And what happens if Ferris decides to develop your land? Will the Oakwood project affect our timeline?"

So that's what was up with all the attitude. "When have I ever come up short on a deal with you guys?"

They exchanged a look, and Tanner felt himself relax a little because the guys were relaxing.

Colin's words had really messed with his head. Tanner had worked his ass off to be the kind of man Abby deserved, so it would hurt if her brothers didn't think he was enough. Not that Tanner would walk away from a chance with Abby if it presented itself just because they took issue with him as a man.

God, he hoped that chance presented itself—he checked his phone—tonight would be nice.

But her brothers had become more than just his clients. They were some of his closest friends. They were also on a very short list of people who Tanner could just be himself around.

Sure, he had the guys on his crew, but his name being on the side of the work trucks always seemed to complicate matters. His old teammates were either still playing or scattered across the country. And lately Colin had been so focused on growing the business that it seemed any conversation always managed to lead right back to work.

With the DeLuca crew Tanner could just hang out, laugh, shoot the shit. With them he felt a part of something special, and he didn't want to lose that.

"Even if Ferris bites, it will take at least a year of prep before we can actually break ground on Oakwood."

"And if Ferris doesn't bite?" Trey ventured.

Tanner shrugged. "If Ferris goes with the other property in Santa Barbara, who knows? Maybe I'll develop it myself."

A bold statement, but one Tanner was considering.

When he'd purchased that land as a foreclosure several years back, it was with the intention of turning it into a gated community. But at the time a project that size was way out of his comfort zone. So when Ferris had stepped up, offering to shoulder the financial risk while giving Tanner a front-row seat to the mechanics of a large-scale, high-end development, it was too great an opportunity to pass up. Lately, though, Tanner had been wondering if he'd made the wrong choice.

"Either way, it won't distract from the project here. You have my word."

"And what about the cheese shop? Do I have your word it also won't affect things?" Marc asked, and there was a hard edge to his voice that took the bro right out of bro time.

"Abby went looking for you last night. Told us she was going to offer you the GC position," Trey added, and Tanner began to wonder just what else she had told her brothers.

He refused to lie to them, but he also didn't want to say more than he needed to, especially since he had pretty much bribed Abby into dating him. So he was careful in choosing his next words. "If Abby and I can come to terms, I will take the job. And no, I don't think anything that happens there will affect our project here."

At least he hoped it wouldn't, but from the looks on her brothers' faces, he wasn't so sure.

Nate rocked back on his heels, then squirmed a little in his shoes. "So, do you know how everything is going with Babs and Abby?"

Jesus, what the hell was going on? "You'll have to ask Abby that."

At this the guys exchanged a cryptic look that had every one of Tanner's senses going on high alert. But when Nate took a big breath and mumbled, "We're not allowed," Tanner burst out laughing.

Holy shit. He didn't know how Abby had done it, but she had finally shut down her brothers' meddling. And they were not happy about it. Not one bit.

His phone buzzed and, thinking it was Colin calling with news, he hit talk. "It's a go for Tanner."

"Okay, before you say anything, I have to get this out," Abby's voice came through the phone and he wished like hell he'd picked it up instead of hitting speaker.

"Abby, hang on, let me call you back from the truck."

"No. Don't call me back. Don't move. In fact, don't even talk or I'll lose my nerve." *Oh shit.* "I thought about what you said last night and . . ."

She took a big breath and so did Tanner because all three of her brothers were closing in and they did not look happy.

"I agree to your terms, but I have a few of my own." Again with the "oh shit," because Tanner didn't want to risk her losing her nerve, but he sure as hell didn't want to have this discussion with her brothers staring him down. "I want more than holding hands and watching football and hanging out. I want sex. With you. And you were right, it is going to happen and I don't really know the when or the where, but I hope it's soon."

Then she stopped and so did Tanner's heart. It stopped right there, standing in the middle of a vineyard with his dad's dog tied to a tree and his soon-to-be sex partner's brothers listening.

To. Every. Fucking. Word.

"Tanner? Did you hear what I said?"

"Jesus," Marc said, putting his hands over his ears. "We all heard what you said, and my ears are bleeding."

"Those are your terms?" Trey yelled, and yup, Tanner was pretty sure this conversation would come to blows before it was over.

"Oh my God," Abby whispered through the phone. And yeah, she waited until after that info dump to start whispering. "Is that my brother? Am I on speaker phone? God, please tell me he didn't hear everything."

Tanner flipped it to handset and put the phone to his ear. "*Brothers.* As in all of them but Gabe. Not on speaker anymore. And I am so sorry. I was expecting Colin with news and you called and I didn't check the phone and . . ."

Jesus. He ran a hand down his face. He may have screwed up his one shot with Abby—a shot she was hoping would be "soon"—and his relationship with three of his best friends, all in one ill-thought-out push of the button.

"What are they saying?" she asked, and he could tell she was freaking out. "I can't hear anything."

Tanner cautiously took in the scene. Trey looked ready to beat the shit out of him, Marc was swaying the baby a little faster now and trying to incinerate Tanner with a single glare, and Nate, the only brother known for his calm and cool persona, was visibly fighting the urge to take the first swing.

"Not much. They're just sorting through all the new info." *And plotting my death.*

"They're threatening to kick your ass, aren't they?" she asked. "Because they do that. A lot. It's their twisted way of helping. But I don't want you to get hurt."

"Ah, darling, saying things like that can make a guy think you care." Because in the end, that was what this came down to. That Abby cared. About him. It shouldn't matter, but it did.

Too fucking much.

"Really, Jack? This is what you want to discuss right now? Your man feelings?"

Yeah, he did. But he saw her point.

"Don't worry about anything here, we're all good," he lied, because under normal circumstances they would be. Tanner would explain he hadn't used their sister's desperation to extort sex from her, the guys would grumble a lot, but in the end they'd toss back a beer and work it out. Because they were friends and that's what friends did.

But he didn't think the bro bond was going to cut it. Not this time. There was something different about the looks they were sending him. It went beyond anger, bordering closer to Italian Mafioso and betrayal. And how could he blame them?

If Tanner had a sister and some jackass had bribed her to have sex—not that that was what had happened, but it sure as hell had sounded like it—then the guy would already be fitted for a pair of concrete boots.

"We're all good," Abby said, "is man speak for 'It's about to get real.' I have four meathead brothers. Remember?"

How could he forget?

"So, put me on speaker."

"Abby, I don't think that—"

"Speaker, Jack."

With a sigh he hit the button. "I hope you are all listening, because I wanted to remind you that kicking my—um, well I'm not sure just what he is yet—but if he agrees to the rest of my terms, he's mine." Tanner could live with that title. And if it meant sex with Abby, he'd agree to just about anything. "Let's just say anything happens to him and it is a level one MV, and I have my girls on speed dial."

Tanner had no idea what a level one MV meant or what girls she was referring to, but it sure got her brothers nervous.

"Am I being understood?" she asked with enough authority to have her big, bad-ass brothers mumbling like obedient toddlers, and

Tanner smiling. "Now, I am going to hang up and you guys are going to finish your meeting. Then Jack will get in his truck and drive home—unharmed. Or I call the girls. Tanner, take me off speaker."

He did.

"Do they still look dangerous?"

Tanner sized up the situation.

The situation sized him up right back. To the average passerby they appeared cool, calm, a group of guys shooting the breeze. But there was enough testosterone in the air that one spark and the whole thing would explode.

"Nope. I think we're all good." Tanner smiled. The guys did not. "We're good, right fellas?"

Nate was clenching his jaw so hard Tanner wouldn't be surprised if it broke. "Let's just say it's your lucky day, Tanner, because although there is nothing more I want to do right now than kick your ass, I happen to like my nuts right where they are."

"What did he say?" Abby asked.

"Just wishing us well on our new relationship." And for the first time since he'd arrived, Tanner shot them a look of his own. Friends or not, he needed them to know he wasn't going to back down when it came to Abby.

"We can't be in a relationship because I haven't finished listing my terms yet."

Who knew the word *terms* could be so damn hot?

"Darling, I don't think I can handle hearing any more of your terms right now." Then, holding up a finger, he turned his back on the brooding trio. "Although you name the time and place to finish this discussion, and I'll be there. But I don't want to press my luck with your family."

After a long pause, during which she took a bunch of breaths and even huffed a few times, she whispered, "I'm really sorry if I embarrassed you or made things awkward with my brothers."

"You could never embarrass me, and don't worry about them."

"Okay." She gave a relieved sigh. "Why don't you meet me at the bottlery tomorrow morning and we'll finish talking terms?" *Yup, his new favorite word.* "Oh, and make sure you bring your tool belt."

"Darling, I always come equipped."

CHAPTER 11

Temperamental, my ass.

Flashlight in hand, Abby stared up at the electrical schematics on the wall of the bottlery, then at the electrical panel to her immediate right, and felt a bead of sweat roll down her back. After making sure every switch was in the correct position, every wire was properly connected, she sent up a heartfelt prayer to the electricity fairies and, putting some weight into it, yanked down on the huge lever marked MAIN FLOOR LIGHTS.

Not a single thing happened.

Swallowing down a growl of frustration, she glared at the detailed notes in her hand, trying to see what she was doing wrong. Perkins Baudouin, owner of the St. Helena Corkery, whose electrical was installed by the same madman back in 1933, had kindly given her a list of ways to troubleshoot issues as they arose. Apparently, troubleshooting was not her strong suit.

She looked at her list, checked it twice, and pulled down on the switch again.

"Dang it!" She drew back her foot and kicked it. Hard. Which did nothing for the lights, but managed to scuff the toe of her favorite leather boots.

No matter how long she stood there or how many times she flipped the stupid switch, she couldn't seem to get the warehouse lights to work. It seemed that after four years of interior design school and another six spent in the field, Abigail DeLuca, founder and owner of Abby's Designs, couldn't manage to turn on a light.

Something that would have been hilarious if she wasn't expecting Tanner any minute. On the off chance he brought his crew ready to work, Abby wanted to at least have the lights working so they could see what needed to be done. Not to mention she'd already had two cups of coffee and really needed to use the bathroom—something that was not going to happen if she couldn't see what else was using the facilities. The cobwebs on the door were enough to let her know she wouldn't be alone.

At that thought, she yanked on the lever one more time. "Shit!"

"Darling, all the yanking in the world won't accomplish what a little finesse can."

"That hasn't worked out so well for me in the past."

Not bothering to face him, Abby reached for the lever, but before she could pull it again, he placed his big, warm hand over hers. And if that wasn't enough to render her immobile, he scooted closer, until she could feel all of that six and a half feet of solid muscle and sculpted male perfection pressing up against her back. "Maybe you've been finessing the wrong people," he said.

Before she could comment, his hand moved to a little unassuming switch off to the right, flipped it, and—bingo—the lights came on.

Abby looked up and smiled. "How did you do that?"

"I know which switch to flip."

With a roll of the eyes, Abby turned around and—good Lord—the man was big, bad, and equipped to flip every female switch she owned.

Not only was he in a pair of low-slung tan cargo shorts, which had a thousand little pockets and flaps inspiring a thousand different fantasies and adventures, but he had on a tool belt that said everything there was to be said—and more.

Even worse, he unleashed those dimples her way and leaned a shoulder against the wall, making the soft gray HARD HAMMER CREW shirt he wore stretch and pull over his impressive chest, barely containing all that was Jack Tanner. And something entirely inappropriate began to pulse below her belly button. As if she didn't already have enough to deal with.

"But that switch isn't on the schematics," she explained.

"I installed it yesterday after our call. I wanted to know what I was signing on for so I called Babs, asked her if I could get in and assess the project, see if getting this done on time and budget was a possibility. The last electrician left the panel a complete disaster, so I did a quick patch so you wouldn't be in the dark, but I'll have my guy start on the rewiring right away."

"Right away?" She swallowed. Did that mean the sexy part of the bargain would start right away too?

"Depends on two things. How did it go with Eddie?"

"Besides the fact the town's inspector is not a leg man? It seems he likes boobs," she said.

Tanner's gaze cut to Abby's chest and he smiled. "I know."

"Then why did you tell me to wear a skirt?"

"Because I didn't want him looking at your boobs." Why that sent little warm fuzzies racing down her spine, she had no idea. Abby didn't do possessive or overbearing in her men. But on Tanner it worked. "Plus, you have great legs."

She looked down, taking in her pencil skirt and knee-high boots. "So you're okay with him looking at my legs, but not my boobs? Is that why you gave me a hickey?"

At that a big, cocky smile covered his face. "I was enjoying myself and got caught up. The hickey was just a bonus."

Abby didn't even bother rolling her eyes. "Yeah, well, now he isn't sure if he can move the inspection to Friday. He said appointments are made to be kept." She used her best Eddie voice. "And that the proper procedure when one can't make the scheduled date and time is to reapply. Then *I* explained *I* just came on board and could he please make an exception since we are on a time crunch."

"And?"

"And he said he'd have to call me back. But he sounded all put out."

Abby looked at the exposed pipes running the length of the room, the wires sticking every which way out of the fuse box, and knew that even with wine country's fastest hammer and his super-crew on the case, there was no way they would be ready by tomorrow.

Damn. She should have worn a V-neck shirt. Tanner's eyes were saying he wouldn't mind if she'd worn one today.

"Did you tell him I was the new GC?" he asked, tearing his gaze off her chest to poke around in the fuse box, trying to locate the source of the suspicious-looking puff of smoke drifting from the right side of the panel. "Eddie's a huge football fan."

"Fan? The man had a life-sized poster of you hanging on his door. And no, I didn't."

Calm and unruffled, as though he wasn't holding enough live volts to scramble his brain, he pulled out a handful of old wires that were spliced and frayed, studying them intently. "Why not?"

Tanner sounded casual, like her answer didn't matter, but the way he was leaning against the wall, head down, still studying the already capped-off wires in his hands, told her differently. "Because if he can reschedule he should just reschedule, and having Hard Hammer Tanner as the GC shouldn't make any difference."

"But you know it does," he said, looking at her, and suddenly Abby had the urge to hug him.

"I also know what it's like to have everyone looking at you a certain way, with certain expectations," Abby said gently.

The second she had seen Eddie's GO GOLD OR GO HOME Niners mug, it was clear that dropping Tanner's name would—what had Brandon said?—oh, yeah, grease the wheels.

"It gets old. Really fast," she continued. "And I wasn't going to leverage your fame."

"Even if it means we don't get the extension?"

"Even then." Abby was beginning to understand something about the town's easiest going celebrity and toughest running back in the NFL. The easygoing was a front, and the big, bad giant of a man wasn't built as tough as everyone thought. "So if I don't hear from Eddie by lunch, then I guess I'll pull out the big guns and go back wearing my tightest tank top."

Whoa, and there went the dimples. "Which brings us to the second point in the morning's agenda. Your terms."

Dropping the wires, he stalked toward her until their bodies brushed.

"Right. Terms." Telling him over the phone exactly what she wanted was one thing. Telling him while he was standing so close that she could smell the body wash on his skin was another.

"And then after you lay out your list, which I am sure is lengthy, I get to add a few of my own," he said, his gaze taking a leisurely journey down her body and back, causing the big guns to take off their safeties.

Then he stepped even closer, his hands went to her hips, and her mind went from thinking about terms to thinking about sex. With Tanner. Right here.

Which would be in direct violation of rule number one.

"No touching in the workplace. I don't want people thinking I got this job because of my," she looked up at him, way up, "pipe work skills."

"All right, no touching at work," he said, skimming his palms down her thighs and breaking the first rule on so many levels. "But as soon as it hits five o'clock you have free rein of my pipe."

She shoved at his chest, which did nothing except to have him pull her closer, hard proof his pipe was in excellent working order. "I'm being serious."

"So am I." And so were his thumbs, which were now running under the hem of her skirt and along the patch of skin on the back of her thigh. "Anything else?"

"Yeah, no kissing at . . . oh, God," she moaned, her head falling back when his mouth brushed her neck. She told herself to ignore how sexy he smelled or how good his mouth felt on her throat, nipping and sucking, but her hormones weren't listening. "Definitely no kissing at work."

"I'm not kissing, I'm nibbling," he whispered against her neck, and that's when the reality of exactly what she had gotten herself into settled. Terms, rules, guidelines, or not. There was no way she could keep it platonic at work. Not if they were doing this at home.

But she had to try, she reminded herself, while tilting her head to give him better access.

There was no sense in busting her butt to prove to the town her talent was enough to carry her, only to get a reputation for getting frisky with the contractor.

"And no one else," she said, closing her eyes. "I mean not forever, but for as long as we're doing, um, *this*, I need to know I'll be the only one you're doing *this* with."

Tanner froze. Hands on her ass, lips on her throat, body shrink-wrapped to hers in a way that had her brain short-circuiting—all of it went stock-still. She felt him pull back and knew he was looking at her. Just like she knew that mere minutes into whatever they were calling this, she'd managed to disappoint him. Which was why she kept her eyes closed.

"Abby," he said, his voice so serious she squeezed her lids tighter.

He didn't speak again, instead sliding his fingers through her hair, tipping her face up, and she knew he was waiting for her to open her eyes. Never one to do well in contests of patience, she finally did and, *oh boy*, Tanner looked a little dazed, a whole lot turned on, and completely pissed off.

"I know we're not in high school anymore," she started, "and I'm not asking to wear your jacket or anything, but this is all new to me and . . ." Lord help her, her lips wouldn't stop moving. "Mature affair or not, I just don't think I could handle being one of many. So if that isn't okay, I get it, but I spent most of the last ten years not telling people what I want, and with you I want to be honest," she swallowed, "about what I want."

"Are you done?" he said. She nodded. "Good. Then let me tell you what I want." His big blue eyes, so intense and sincere, locked on hers. "You. That's it. No one else. I don't need or want anything else from this but time with you. So no pressure, no games, just us . . . being real. Starting tonight. Got it?"

Again with the nod. The man had just said the most romantic thing in the world, and all she could do was move her head.

"Good." He gave her a hard smack on the lips. "Now, I agree to your terms, but I have a few of my own."

Abby didn't know if she should be thrilled he'd thought about this enough to have his own conditions, or terrified. Because how the hell would a woman who hadn't had sex even once in the better part of the last decade measure up to his terms?

"Okay, first one, and this is nonnegotiable." Tanner took in a deep breath and looked at the ceiling for a minute, as though considering if he even wanted to go there. "If this is going to work, I need you to let me have the final say on the project."

Abby took a step back. "As in, your word is all-powerful because you don't believe in my judgment?"

"No." He frowned, then ran a hand down his face. "No, I meant in terms of the crew. I need to bring a crew of my choosing, no questions asked, even though I know not all the choices will seem logical." He expelled a long breath. "Okay, only my dad will seem illogical, but I don't know what else to do. The doctor said he shouldn't be left home alone anymore. Dad won't even consider letting me hire outside help. And if he finds out this job is just my answer to babysitting he'll walk."

"We'll make it work," Abby said, slipping her arms around his middle. "And we'll do it in a way that saves his pride."

She felt his body sag with relief. Had he really thought she'd tell him Gus couldn't work on the project? She knew he was being pulled between work and taking care of his dad. And she knew it was wearing on him.

"Anything else?"

"Yup." This time when he looked at her, his face was more relaxed, more Tanner. "I also need piano lessons to resume. ASAP. Because sitting next to you while you wear those little tops of yours is the best part of my week."

"Easy enough. I already called my students and have resumed lessons." Canceling lessons for an entire week when her students' next recital was scheduled for the beginning of October had been pushing it. Regardless of how many hours she put in at the Pungent Barrel, Abby couldn't let her students down.

"I didn't get a call. And I'm one of your students."

"I did call you, only you put me on speaker." Which, had she known lessons were the best part of his week, she might have risked her brothers' tempers and booked him immediately.

"And I'll have you know I already ordered another phone. It doesn't have speaker capabilities. Because the next time you call me with an offer like that, I'll be damned if I don't get to hear the whole thing. Uninterrupted." He winked and her heart gave a hard pump to the ribs. "As for lessons, I'll bring my sheet music. The Imperial March." Of course the fate of her world came down to *Star Wars* sheet music. "Tonight. Oh, and make sure mine is the last lesson of the evening so we can share coffee and dessert afterward."

"Seven o'clock, then." This was really happening. "I'll make another wine cake."

And with that, his smile went full-blown. "Yeah, that sounds good too."

"Is that all?" she asked, giving him a little "yeah, right" shove to the pecs. But she knew one more lesson sitting next to his hard, sculpted body on that way-too-small bench and he'd have her saying "Yeah, right."

Yeah. Right there!

"Nope. One last thing." This was the one he'd been gearing up for. She could tell because his smile turned wicked—and hot. "Since I don't want to rush you, but I also need you to give this a real chance, you have to promise me we have until the end of this project. Think of it as half up front and half on delivery."

"What half do you want first?"

Six hours later at a meeting Tanner had called to see where everyone stood, he was still hard-pressed to choose which half of Abby he wanted first. Maybe it was the high-collar shirt, but he'd always considered himself a breast man, and Abby was beyond impressive in that department. Hell, the way her snug blouse hugged her every curve as she studied the electrical plans in front of her was more than inspiring. But when she rested her hand on the table, lifting one of those sleek black boots, which had her even sleeker black skirt tugging across that perfect handful, he was having a change of heart.

Not that Abby didn't have a pair of perfect tens. But her ass was the kind locker room legends were made from.

"The good news is I can start on the main runs and conduits as soon as the stock arrives, which should be tomorrow," Ben Burns said. Tanner tore his gaze off Abby and back to the meeting at hand.

"Don't you know you should always lead with the bad news? That way you end on a high note," Abby said, studying the impressive electrical plans Ben had thrown together in the past few hours.

"Yeah, well, since the good news pretty much blows in comparison, I didn't think it would matter, because unless I can find a new electrical panel that will work, none of the rest will matter." Dressed in a black graphic tee and pair of black skinny jeans, floppy hair hanging in his face, Ben looked more like a basement-dwelling gamer than an electrician. Despite being only in his early twenties and preferring wires to people, he was one of the best electricians Tanner had ever worked with. Fast, creative, a perfectionist—and staring right at Abby's cleavage.

"I called every supplier I know, and a panel running the kind of power we need doesn't exist. At least not one made after Roosevelt took office," Tanner said, shooting Ben his most threatening look over Abby's head.

Wisely, Ben focused on the bundles of wires scattered through the warehouse, which ran the length of the exposed brick walls. Tanner knew without him having to say, they were too outdated to run a laptop and hairdryer at the same time without starting a fire, let alone do what Tanner needed them to *and* pass inspection. Which meant they would all have to be ripped out and replaced.

"I know a guy who makes custom boxes," Gus said. "He takes the old panel then rebuilds it with all the new bells and whistles. I already gave him the specs on that old dinosaur over there." He pointed with his cane, his posture a little straighter than it had been as of late. "He's had some experience with that particular model. And he's done a few projects for me over the years, so I know he does clean work and will charge a fair price."

"That's great, Gus," Abby said and—*Jesus*—was his old man preening? Then she aimed that four thousand watts of joy his way, and it appeared it was an affliction that affected all Tanner males. "Is he available to come down today?"

"Yup." Gus rocked back on his heels.

He looked healthier than Tanner had seen him look in months too, which made Tanner feel better about his decision to bring Gus on. Originally, he'd done it to get his dad out of the house, let him feel useful again—in a place Tanner could keep tabs on him. But maybe this would work out after all. His dad was smiling, flushed with excitement, and, more shocking, they had been in the same space for most of the day and hadn't argued even once.

"Melvin said he can be here anytime after seven, but he'll need help getting some stuff from his car."

"Melvin from your poker group? As in Melvin Schwartz?"

Gus shrugged a thin shoulder.

"Dad, Melvin doesn't have a car, and his electrical skills as of, oh, the last decade, consist of building engines for his model plane collection."

"Which is why I lent him my truck. And before he retired, he wired things for Uncle Sam," Gus said, and Tanner realized the only reason they hadn't argued was because they'd been too busy working on different projects. "Before that he was in the CBs during Nam. And if he could figure out how to pipe in electricity to a jungle in the middle of a damn war zone, I think he can figure out how to keep cheese cold. Now, you hired me as your foreman. You going to let me do my job or keep nagging like an old hen?"

Tanner wanted to point out Melvin was practically blind, hence the lack of a car, and he was only available after seven because that was when he could sneak out unseen by the nurses at his assisted living complex, but he kept his mouth shut. Because that could be construed as nagging—and Tanner was not a nagger.

Then he started thinking about how he'd been since Gus moved into his place, and sighed. Shit, he was a nagger. He was also man enough to admit that, sight impaired or not, Melvin had a way with wires and could save their collective asses. Except for one glaring issue.

"Melvin's state license expired when I was in high school."

Gus obviously didn't see a problem with that, since he started harrumphing and huffing as though gearing up for an argument, which Tanner knew would be epic. Well, too bad. Tantrum or not, Tanner was the GC, his word was final, and his dad would do best to remember that.

Something Tanner opened his mouth to relay when Abby shot him a look, then placing a hand on his dad's shoulder, she said, all smiles, "Gus, that is a great idea about going custom. And you're right, it would answer all of our problems."

And wouldn't you know it, the man was back to preening. Abby, with all of her five foot nothing of sweetness, was acknowledging his old man while taking a firm stance. Something Tanner hadn't managed to accomplish in a really long time.

Eyes still on Gus, as though genuinely interested in his opinion, she said, "I worked with this guy who finished installing all of the coolers for Ryo Wines last year. He actually retrofitted the old storage facility that came with the building with solar. Do you think he could handle customizing the electrical panel?"

Gus scratched his head and Tanner found himself doing the same thing. "How old was the original building?" Gus asked.

"Built in the twenties."

"Sounds pretty creative to me. I say he'd be a fit."

"If I got you his number, would you want to give him a call and feel him out before you pass it along to Tanner?"

"I can do that," Gus said, man with a mission.

"Great." Abby turned and smiled sweetly up at Tanner, and he felt all of his earlier frustration fade. She wasn't just giving his dad a way to salvage his pride, she was giving Tanner an out.

He wanted to lean down and kiss her, or at least say thank you. But everyone was watching, so he asked, "Any word from Eddie?"

"Nothing." She shrugged, and a few of those curls she tried so hard to manage slipped free from her clip and framed her pretty face. "I'll call him while you guys finish up. And thanks, Gus, for thinking of going custom."

Abby rummaged through her purse, grabbed her phone, and—bingo—like a moth to the flame, Tanner zeroed in on her ass until she disappeared into what was to become the new office. So did Ben—until Tanner punched him in the arm.

"What was that for?" Ben said. "You were looking too." Tanner leveled Ben with a look that had his eyes bulging. "Oh . . ."

"Right, oh." When he was good and convinced Ben got the point, he turned to Gus, who was already heading toward the electrical panel, taking measurements and making notes.

Two seconds later, the office door swung open and out walked Abby. She handed Gus a piece of paper. "His name is Carlos. Just tell him I sent you. If you need me, call my cell. I've got to see a guy about a cheese shop."

Frown firmly in place, she bent over to grab her purse and, *look at that*, Tanner had his answer. Ass, boobs, legs. Didn't matter. Tanner was a confirmed Abby man.

Which was why when he saw her heading toward the parking lot, Mary Poppins bag in hand, hips swishing with purpose well before the quitting time, he turned to Gus. "Ray should almost be done pressure testing the plumbing system. When he's finished, can you call Carlos?"

To that Gus only raised a brow and Tanner went for casual, as though Abby wasn't already halfway to the door. "If he can come out tonight, that would be great. If not, we need him here as soon as—" out the door she went, "Jesus, can you handle it or not?"

"Yup. Was just waiting for you to finish flapping your gums."

"Be back in two." According to Abby's rules, Tanner couldn't officially blow her whistle until five, which meant he needed to make sure she was coming back. He saw her walk past the window, fiddling with her top, and he knew exactly where she was going. Despite Eddie not answering, it seemed she was planning a pop-in.

"Make that an hour," he said over his shoulder, already fishing his phone out of his pocket and dialing Eddie. Halfway through the first ring the guy answered.

"What a surprise, I was just getting ready to call you," Eddie said, his tone dialed to kiss ass, and Tanner had to suppress the urge to hang up. He knew Eddie had just sent Abby to voice mail. "I was in the office when your paperwork for the cave you're putting in on the DeLuca property came in. I pulled a few strings and had them push it through for you, so you can come by the planning department anytime after tomorrow and pick up the permits to start drilling."

"You didn't have to do that," Tanner said. He wasn't going to be able to start drilling until the equipment was delivered. And before that could happen they needed to pour the foundation for the staging area.

"Hey, no problem," Eddie went on as Tanner cut through the bottlery, taking the rear entrance to make up time. "That was some game last week. I still can't believe the Seahawks won. I was telling my brother-in-law, who's up with his wife visiting from Wisconsin, that if you were still playing we'd have had that in the bag. I mean, the fumble that happened at the end of the fourth would have never happened with you playing."

"It was just a preseason game," Tanner felt the need to point out. "They're still feeling each other out, but they'll come back."

"That's what I told my brother-in-law you'd say."

He could hear the man self-fiving himself through the phone. Tanner would bet he told his brother-in-law a hell of a lot more than he was letting on. Most of it was probably BS. Which was why Tanner had no problem doing what he did next.

"Well, thanks, man. And for having my back I have two seats for next week's game against the Packers. Fifty yard line. They're yours if you want."

"Are you serious?" Eddie's voice exploded through the phone.

"Yeah, I can't use them. Plus, you can take your brother-in-law if he's still in town, show him what the Niners are all about. Have a few drinks on me." He pushed through the door and scanned the lot. He didn't see Abby or her car. He doubled back to check the front lot. "I can give them to you when you do the plumbing and electrical inspection on the Hampton project out at the old bottlery."

"You're working on the cheese shop for Babs?"

"Just signed on." When he was absolutely sure he'd missed Abby, he kicked the curb. "I can give them to you—oh, wait, I have to have them Express Mailed to me. When do you come out for the inspection?"

"Tomorrow," Eddie said. "But I was thinking of moving it to Friday, if that works better for you."

What worked for Tanner was not having to talk to the tool while his date sped off.

"You know what, that's a great idea, Eddie. Pencil me in for Friday so I can give you the tickets."

For five freaking minutes Tanner fielded questions about who he thought had a shot at the Super Bowl, what he would have done differently if that had been him last week, and if the Niners were going to pull out a win this weekend against the Packers. And if Tanner wasn't already sitting on the curb, he would have asked the guy if he wanted him to bend over so Eddie could apply his lips directly to Tanner's ass.

Then finally, *finally*, when Tanner ended the call, he felt that familiar sense of frustration rise. Sure, he'd missed out on seeing Abby off and sure, he'd just bribed a city official with his name—two things that pissed him off. But what had his head pounding and his chest struggling to relax was that maybe Colin had been right.

Maybe all of his success in town had more to do with his being a celebrity than his being good at what he did. Tanner had always assumed it had a little to do with both, but that in the end, it was about the relationships he'd made and the hard work he'd put in.

"Thanks, you saved me a trip," Abby said, taking a seat next to him. "I figured he was avoiding my calls so I was going to stop by. Surprise him."

He sent her a sidelong look. "He would have just had Roz tell you he was out."

"But you knew he'd answer if you called?"

Tanner shrugged.

"You didn't have to do that."

"I thought you left."

"I did, then I realized I forgot my swatches for my meeting with Babs later. But I heard you laughing and it was the same kind of laugh you gave when my brothers were threatening to kick your ass, so I wanted to make sure they weren't paying you another visit."

At that he laughed, and this time it was real. "I don't know if you've noticed, but I'm a pretty big guy." To prove it he held his hand out, palm down. "Your brothers aren't even tall enough to reach my face."

Marc was, but Tanner could totally take him.

Then Abby did something that had his chest tightening even further. She laced her tiny fingers through his and squeezed. "I wasn't afraid for your face, Jack. I was afraid they'd say something to hurt your feelings."

"Don't worry about me, Abs. My delicate man feelings are intact."

Although he was afraid his heart no longer was. Not after that one sentence. Not after the way she'd said it—as if he was important to her. As if his happiness was important to her. Not because she needed something from him, but because she wanted to make sure he was okay. Make sure he knew that he meant something to her.

Tanner was on the cusp of having everything he'd always wanted, and while that had something catching high in his chest, it also scared the shit out of him.

CHAPTER 12

An hour and a half later, Abby stood in the back room of Valley Textiles, staring at the gold-leafed tile sample Babs placed on the counter and hoping to God the woman was joking. Out of the thousands of tiles to choose from, the woman had picked the most expensive and obnoxious tile available. Not to mention it was a special order—which meant extra ship time.

"It's just so bright and happy," Babs said, flipping through the fabric catalogue as though they hadn't already exhausted it an hour ago. "Everyone needs more happy in their day, right? Happy people make happy customers."

Normally Abby would entertain the idea, try to figure out a way to incorporate a tile more fitted toward Her Royal Highness's loo than a cheese and wine tasting room with the already agreed-upon rustic earthy pallet. But today her patience was in limited supply.

Maybe it had something to do with Babs's suggestion to paint over the nineteenth-century handcrafted bricks that covered the Roman cross-vault ceiling. Or how their ten-minute "finalize the order" meeting had turned into Babs selecting a whole new creative direction based on the excitement level in The Duke's eyes.

Either way, Abby needed to get this design train back on track before they ended up with a Liberace-inspired cheese shop.

"I really think we should stick with the reclaimed limestone in the original designs," Abby said, keeping a watchful eye on the way The Duke inched closer every time she shot down one of Babs's ridiculous suggestions. When she explained that replacing the factory windows with stained glass ones altered the historical integrity of the building, Abby thought she was going to lose a hand. "It pairs so beautifully with the distressed brick walls and the hammered steel countertops Tanner is making out of the old steel doors."

Babs flapped her hand as though unconcerned with how changing direction this far into the game could affect the timeline. "We can always change the countertops. In fact, I love the idea of maybe using dark wood, like the whole counter is one big cutting board. Very Western style, so it could match the barstools, which I think will be the pièce de résistance of the room."

Only if that room were a saloon in the Wild West, Abby thought as she looked at the picture of barstools Babs had been clutching to her chest all afternoon.

"Is that goat hide?"

"Yes, aren't they lovely? I found them on this website last night and just knew they'd be perfect. You know, cheese shop . . . goat hide . . . get it?"

Oh, Abby got it. Just like she got that, if left to Babs's whims, the Pungent Barrel would be boycotted by every animal activist group on the planet. Because they weren't just goat-hide-covered seats; the feet of the barstools looked to be made of hooves. "You don't think eating on the carcass of the animal that provided the food might ruin people's appetite?"

Babs actually had the gall to look horrified, as though Abby were the insensitive one. The Duke just bared his teeth.

"I think people will find it a fun play on cheese shop couture."

"Well," Abby said, relieved to see the fine print. "It says here all stools are handcrafted at time of order, and due to flux in herd size"—*gross*—"to expect four to six months delivery."

"What's a few more months when the goal is perfection?" Babs said with dramatic flair.

Abby took a breath. If she could get Babs to stick with the original plan, they could be open next month. She was sure of it.

"It's a goal we can accomplish in a fraction of the time by sticking to the original designs. But I like this idea of the goatskin," she added.

Babs blanched a little. "You do?"

No, not really. And suddenly, Abby wasn't so sure Babs did either. Which made no sense.

"What if we ordered one for the shop office?" Abby ventured. "We could even get a few of the gold tiles and use them as the top for the shop desk. Maybe even go a little flashier with the hardware. That way you get everything you want and we still stay on schedule. Because in the end, that's why you hired me, right? To keep this project on budget and on schedule?"

Babs nodded, but didn't look convinced. Her eyes scanned all of the tiles and swatches and yards and yards of fabric bolts. Then she picked up the packet of samples Abby had compiled for the proposal and thumbed through them—yet again. It was as if the woman would rather stand there for the next year exploring possibilities than make a decision.

"You want this to be an elegant shop that people come from all over to visit, then talk about. And I want to give that to you," Abby said with so much confidence even she believed herself. "With these designs, I can."

"I don't know," Babs said, her eyes big with uncertainty and maybe a little touch of sadness. And for the first time since she'd taken this job, Abby noticed how lost the woman appeared. "Maybe we should wait until Ferris sees these. I took pictures of the samples and your preliminary designs, even figured out how to send them to him via that interweb, but he hasn't gotten back to me yet."

A small knot of panic settled low in her belly at the word *preliminary*. As far as Abby was concerned, those designs were final. "Does Ferris usually weigh in on these kinds of things?"

"No," Babs said, her apricot halo bouncing with each shake of the head. "But my Leroy used to sit for hours with me, making sure every decision was right. This is the first project I'm doing without him."

A familiar ache settled in Abby's chest for the woman. She understood better than most how hard it was to go from being a partner to going it solo. For Abby, it wasn't success or failure, or that it was her decision she'd have to live with. It was that success or failure, in the end she would still be alone.

"Wow, I just realized I didn't eat lunch," Abby said, looking at her watch and noting she had less than two hours before her first student would arrive at her house for their lesson. She looked at Babs's expression and noted how she shifted on her feet, her normal we-can attitude vanishing completely at the idea of Abby leaving.

Yup, Babs was stalling.

"How about we head over to the Sweet and Savory for a little afternoon snack? And maybe over a pastry and cup of coffee you can explain to me what you like about each component of my design and what concerns you might have. If you want, we can even talk about what Leroy would've thought."

"Oh." Babs brought her clasped fingers to her lips and let loose a delighted laugh. The Duke even wagged his tail. "That sounds lovely. I adore Lexi's tarts, and her King Kamehameha Mocha always brings a smile to my day."

That's because her King Kamehameha Mocha was one part Kona coffee, two parts coffee liqueur, and enough kick to bring a smile to even Nora's normally puckered face.

"That is, if you have time?" Babs added, and the feet shuffling ensued.

"Of course I have time," Abby lied, because even though she had a to-do list a mile long, which included making a wine cake and dropping by the Boulder Holder to pick up something lace and silk for dessert—just in case—she was starting to understand Babs wasn't the most difficult customer in wine country. She was just lonely. And that was something Abby could relate to on every level.

If listening to Babs rehash her choices would make her confident in moving forward, then Abby was game.

With just enough time to change her clothes before her first student arrived, Abby pulled into her driveway exhausted and exhilarated. Exhausted from spending most of the afternoon with Babs, which forced Abby to cram two hours of errands into twenty minutes. Exhilarated because in less than two hours the sexy contractor who had yet to decide which half of her he wanted to start with was set to show up for his piano lesson.

A lesson he'd said was the highlight of his week.

Abby felt her skin heat. Had she really asked him where he wanted to start? The real question was, when Tanner made up his mind, would she follow through?

The answer to both was a resounding yes. Something that terrified her as much as it excited her. Abby wasn't just dipping her toes into the sex pool. Nope, she was doing a swan dive into the deep end—naked, with no lifeguard on duty.

Pink pastry box in one hand and a gold bag from the Boulder Holder in the other, Abby bumped the door closed with her hip and hoped the cream puffs made up for the lack of wine cake on the menu. Then she remembered how itty bitty the red silk panties and matching bra she'd bought were and figured Tanner would be too busy trying to see what was under her top to even care about cake.

Smiling, she stepped around the car and nearly dropped the cream puffs and panties. Hand firmly clutching her chest, the Boulder Holder bag swinging wildly from her fingers, she saw twelve sets of eyes move from Richard's body to Abby's bag.

"This is private property!" Abby said.

Shirley Bale poked her head out from behind an easel, a smudge of charcoal marring her rosy cheek. Dressed in a stained smock, bright red Crocs, a matching visor, and a face full of wrinkles, Shirley set her charcoal next to a mason jar, filled with what Abby prayed was iced tea and not homemade Angelica, and clapped her hands excitedly.

"You made it!"

"I didn't know I was invited."

"Of course you were." Shirley widened her smile, which only managed to make her look guilty. And standing behind her, the group of gray-haired ladies, all dressed in matching smocks, looked around nervously. "Now, go change. We're just getting started, so you haven't missed much, but the rules state that five more minutes and you are officially a no-show, then I have to start calling the waitlist, and I have a dozen ladies on speed dial who are dying to take your easel."

"My easel?"

"For our life art class." Shirley walked over to the statue, who was wearing a painter's tarp around his waist, and gave herself a little fan of the hand. "Haven't seen a specimen this impressive since my days sketching in Italy. They breed stallions over there, so mere mortal men can't compare. But him? Well, we sure got us a real treat today, right ladies?"

With a single flick of her frail wrist, Shirley yanked the loincloth away and a series of *Uh-huhs* and *Oh mys* filled the air, followed by Mrs. Rose, current wine commissioner and head of the Hunting Club, who held the county record for most kills at less than two hundred yards, giving a heartfelt, "Stallion indeed."

Abby looked heavenward. This was not happening. Richard, God's gift to women, was being ogled and admired by a group of women—like he was a god. Granted, they were wrinkly and smelled of turpentine, but they were women all the same. And they were capturing his essence on canvas.

The worst part was Deidra Potter and her Project Primrose were in full effect, because the statue was surrounded by blue hydrangeas, which gave him the look of walking on water. Combined with his smarmy wink and smile, it was as though the prodigal Casanova had returned and somehow reached sainthood.

"Sure puts that Stan to shame," one of the silvered sketchers said.

"Stan O'Malley?" Abby choked out, then gagged a little because Stan was the local mechanic, owner of Stan's Soup and Service Station, and wore lifts in his shoes like Tom Cruise. And that was where the similarities ended, since he was old as dirt, missing a few teeth, and like any good mechanic, carried around his spare tire everywhere he went.

"Yup. He was the first nude model we brought in."

"I had to take one of them blue pills just to keep myself awake during that class." Mrs. Rose laughed, which sounded odd since she usually had a carry-and-conceal kind of attitude. Even odder to see her in a smock with a tray of pastels in reach.

"Didn't know you sketched, Mrs. Rose," Abby said.

"Don't," the older woman said. "But when I heard they were bringing in nude men and it was legal, I signed up. After Stan, we went back to sketching fruit bowls."

"How can you get excited about painting a bowl?" Shirley said quietly. "If you've sketched one banana, you've sketched them all."

"Only now it seems we found someone worth sketching." Mrs. Rose gave Richard a thorough once-over. "He is a no-pill-required banana if you ask me."

Blue pills were never Richard's problem, Abby thought, looking at the statue and back to the group, surprised when the sharp pain, the one that usually started behind her shoulder blade and felt like it went straight through her chest, never came. In fact she felt nothing other than a slight annoyance that Richard was invading her plans. "You know it's not real, right?"

"Honey, I was married fifty-one years, been a widow for nine. I've forgotten what real even looks like."

Abby had only been married to Richard for a year and a widow for eight whole days, and she wasn't sure she even knew what real was. Which was why she'd taken Tanner up on his offer. He said he wanted to be real—with her.

Starting tonight.

Abby looked down at the bag of lingerie and blew out a breath. Somehow she didn't think Tanner envisioned getting his dessert with the Senior Center's art club acting as chaperones. Not to mention having an unsanctioned art class on her front lawn was the last thing Abby needed. That Nora had already given her one GN violation for illegal art was bad enough. Two violations wasn't going to happen.

"You'll have to get a permit to hold a class here," Abby said apologetically.

The ladies exchanged glances, but it was Shirley who spoke up. "We were told Richard was supposed to be moved. But yesterday I was in the neighborhood and saw he was still here. So I figured it was a sign the universe had sent me something other than a fruit bowl, something to challenge and stir my creativity, so I called the ladies."

"And we went guerilla-style on art," Mrs. Rose said, her eyes lit with excitement. "You know, no permits, no watercolors, no blending brushes, just our easels, charcoal, and the naked form."

"It was either him or another fruit bowl," Shirley explained, and Abby wondered if fruit bowls were the sketcher's equivalent to nurseries or doggie habitats. "And I'm ready to sketch a new kind of plums and banana."

"No permit means you don't have approval of the GN," Abby said, then cringed because—*listen to that*—she sounded just like Know It All Nora.

She held up her hand in apology. "You know what? Never mind. Have fun painting, ladies."

"You're going to let us stay?" Shirley asked, her black-penciled brows disappearing into her hairline.

Abby just shrugged. "I know what it's like to draw the same fruit bowl. As long as you are gone by sunset, I say paint away."

By the time Abby made it into her house, she'd had enough hugs and cheek pinches to last her a decade. Dropping the cream puffs in the refrigerator and her gold bag on the bed, she searched through her closet for one of "those little shirts" Tanner seemed to like so much.

Pressed for time, she settled on a deep scoop-neck tank top and her new bra—the panties would have to wait until next time, since she wasn't sure if she was that bold—and went downstairs to prepare for her first student of the night.

She was just setting out the sheet music when her five o'clock knocked at the door. When she opened it, instead of greeting a four-foot-tall kid with freckles and a Kool-Aid mustache, she found herself staring up at six and a half feet of the best dessert ever.

Fully equipped and licensed to rock her foundation, Tanner rested a hip against her porch rail, that easy smile of his ready to demolish any last hesitations she harbored.

"Well, no wonder you didn't want to paint with us," Mrs. Rose hollered from the grass. "Seems you got a live one there."

"They told me I couldn't pass until I showed a little skin," Tanner explained, and Abby laughed.

"Well, did you?"

"No, I outran them," he explained. "Although there was a moment where I thought Mrs. Rose was going to bring out her guns."

"I still might unless you give us a little shimmy. I've got a hundred bucks riding on you being the real deal, Hard Hammer Tanner," Mrs. Rose said, and the tips of Tanner's ears went pink. "Peg here thinks those pictures of you in your birthday suit were enhanced."

Abby crossed her arms. "Seems like a pretty serious allegation to me. I think you better take care of it."

"Is that right?" And boom, a smile that said he was more than up to the challenge spread across his face and both of those dimples came into play. "Tell me. What did you have in mind?"

Oh, Abby had many things in mind. Some ranked higher on her list than others, but unfortunately, none of them included an audience, so she tapped a finger to her chin, taking her sweet time to make him sweat a little. Only Tanner never sweat, he just stood there perfectly at ease.

"All right, take off the shirt and show us the goods," she said and gestured for him to turn around and—*oh my*—the show was just beginning.

Eyes locked on hers, Tanner grabbed the back of his shirt with one hand and pulled it up and over his head, exposing yards and yards of tan skin, sculpted muscles, and enough testosterone to have Abby sweating. With a cocky wink that said *Got ya*, he turned around to face the ladies, then gave a little shimmy when his back was once again to the crowd.

The ladies gave an elated clap and a few dreamy sighs before fanning themselves. Abby was doing a little fanning of her own when Tanner flashed the most self-conscious smile she'd ever seen him wear.

Huh, between the ladies making his ears go pink and this smile, it seemed the man wasn't totally unflappable.

"I'm sorry, Peg, but I think Mrs. Rose won this one. Tanner is one hundred percent real," Abby said, and she wasn't just talking about his fine-tuned and carefully honed body. Tanner might be a little too charming, a little too flirty, and a whole lot too tempting for Abby's well-being, but the more time she spent with him, the more Abby began to realize there wasn't anything fake about Jack Tanner.

"Tightest tush in the NFL," Mrs. Rose declared. "Now, pay up!"

While the women argued about who owed what, Tanner walked to the doormat, and instead of tugging his shirt on, he tucked it in his back pocket.

"Aren't you going to put your shirt back on?" Abby asked his chest. The well-muscled, too-impressive-not-to-stare chest that was gloriously tan and slick with summer heat.

"Nope. You going to take yours off?" His eyes took a slow journey all the way south, which meant he still hadn't made up his mind where to start. Or maybe he had and he wanted a little reminder to make sure he'd chosen well. Either way, his blatantly male appreciation caused every cell in her body to go into party mode. Even her nipples popped their corks. His grin said he noticed. "Or you want to talk about the little shopping spree you did earlier today?"

"Shopping?" Her face heated. Did he know she bought a pair of home team panties? And if so, would he be disappointed she hadn't put them on?

"I was talking about getting Babs to finally sign off on the hardware, flooring, and counter." Tanner held up an order slip from Valley Textiles. "But judging by the look on your face, it seems you had a different kind of shopping in mind."

Abby skipped right over that one, and in one smooth move, she grabbed the shirt from his back pocket and pressed it to his chest. Then focused really hard on the order slip, and even harder on not watching him get dressed.

"Great, Valley Textiles got the order placed. I was afraid we'd missed the cutoff for today."

"They even put a rush on it. Free of charge. Tom doesn't even do rush orders for me, extra cost or not."

Abby shrugged. "Tom's son, Kyle, takes piano from me."

Tanner stepped forward, resting his palms on the top of the doorframe, not coming in the house but invading her space all the same. "I know, I remember him from the last recital. He's one of your favorites."

He was also one of the first students she'd taken on when she'd moved back to St. Helena. And over the last two years he had gone from a shy little boy who cried at the thought of playing in front of a crowd to a proficient pianist who played every Sunday at church.

"I don't have favorites." She smiled. "I love all of my students the same."

He leaned in even farther, the movement causing his arm muscles to bunch and his shirt to pull taut across his chest. He tilted his head until she could smell the sawdust on his clothes and feel his lips brush her cheek. "Liar."

"Why are you here"—she gave his stomach a little shove and, after he flexed for her gripping pleasure, moved back enough so she could breathe without her body going into meltdown—"a whole two hours early?"

"To tell you your guy Carlos is perfect for the job and, more importantly, he can start right away." That was exactly the kind of news she needed to hear. "He's meeting me at the shop in an hour to look at the electrical panel in person so he can figure out what he needs to order."

"That's great. Does he think he'll be done in time for you guys to finish the wiring?"

"We're going to run all of the wires and take care of the outlets this week while he refits the panel. He thinks he can be done by Thursday, so we have Friday morning to get the chillers in and finish up. He won't know for sure until he gets here, but he sounded optimistic."

Tanner's smile faded and a weird feeling started in the pit of Abby's belly.

"Why do I feel like there is a big *but* coming?"

"Because he said he'd need at least three or four hours tonight to get a feel for the project and understand the way the original electrician wired the place, which means—"

"You have to cancel our lesson," Abby said, not bothering to hide her disappointment.

"Date," Tanner clarified, sounding disappointed himself. "And not cancel, postpone. I was thinking Saturday. That way the inspection is over."

"Saturday? That's four days away." Her body couldn't last four whole days. Especially not when those days would be spent working in close proximity while he hauled two-by-fours, lifted pipes with those big arms, and handled everything in the factory—but her.

"I know, trust me," Tanner said, his eyes dropping to her strategically selected top. "But with everything left to do, just getting the place ready by Friday will be crazy." His gaze locked on hers, hot and hungry, and suddenly she wasn't so sure she could wait. "You drive me crazy."

"You came here to tell me I drive you crazy?"

God, she hoped not. She drove her brothers crazy, her grandmother crazy, her neighbors crazy. The last person she wanted to drive crazy was the first potential date she'd had since college.

"No, I came here to tell you it's five o'clock." He stepped into her, his good parts crowding all hers, forcing her into the house. He kicked the door shut, and before she could register what was happening, his hands were in her hair and his mouth, oh God, that mouth, was on hers. And Abby knew she was in trouble.

Serious trouble.

Because Tanner was wrong—this wasn't crazy. It was beyond all reason. The heat generated by a single kiss was damn near combustible. Because just like that, with one taste, her brain clocked out.

She didn't move, except to run her palms up under his shirt to explore those abs for herself. She felt him shiver under her touch and there was something so sexy about that. About the way his body wrapped tighter around hers, about how his hands spanned the width of her back to pull her closer.

Closer was good. Closer made her feel treasured and sexy and safe, three things she hadn't felt in a long time. Three things she didn't want to stop feeling. Ever.

When a knock sounded at the door, he reluctantly pulled back. They were both still breathing heavy when he said, "Screw Saturday. Let's make it Thursday. That's only two days. We can make it two days, right?"

"I think so," she whispered, although after that kiss she wasn't feeling so sure.

"Good. I'll pick you up at six."

"What if Carlos doesn't finish in time?" she asked, hoping two days was enough time to get up the courage to put on the red panties.

"He'll be done." His gaze dropped to her neckline and he smiled. "I'll leave dessert up to you."

CHAPTER 13

"I didn't know this much raw land existed in St. Helena," Abby said, standing near Tanner's truck, staring out at the hundreds of acres of gently rolling fields covered in bright orange poppies and giant oak trees. The scent of dry grass and grapes from a few wild vines growing nearby permeated the air as their purple fruit swayed gently in the early evening breeze.

It was beautifully serene and she should have felt calm, at peace even, but after two torturous days of waiting for this moment, her body was vibrating with anticipation. She inhaled deeply and eyed Tanner out of the corner of her eye, trying to force herself to stay here, in the present with him.

"Technically we're just outside the city limits, but it is still zoned for St. Helena schools and utilities."

Which would be an important selling point if Tanner Construction built homes up here. St. Helena wasn't just known for its wine, but also its education system.

The top selling point, Abby thought as she walked around the front of the truck to look over the edge of the mountain, *would be the view*. That alone was worth whatever millions he'd paid for this land.

"I can see the entire valley from up here," Abby said, not surprised by the awe in her voice. They were so high above the valley floor it looked like one huge vineyard of bright green vines and yellow mustard weed spanning for miles.

"Over there is Calistoga." Before she could turn to look, Tanner slid one arm around her waist, effortlessly pulling her back to his front. She'd been dying to touch him since he'd pulled up in his truck looking delicious in a pair of butt-loving jeans and a blue button-up rolled to the elbows. He also had on a ball cap, red, well-loved, and pulled low. "On a clear day you can see all the way to Napa."

Abby couldn't see anything past his big, bulging arm, which was flexed and rippled as he pointed toward the towns he was naming. She also had a hard time focusing on what he was saying because his fingers, the ever-so-capable fingers of his other arm, were sliding back and forth across her stomach, reminding her of just how gentle her giant could be.

"In the summer, I come up here in the early morning to watch the sunrise and hot air balloons take off, but man," he said, and she could hear the love in his voice for this land. "During the winter we're so high up I can see the storms rolling in from the north."

"How long have you owned this property?"

She felt him shrug, then he leaned back against the grill of his truck, pulling her with him until all she felt was heat. Heat from the grill of this truck, heat from the sweltering summer day, both of which had nothing on the heat from being encased by that much solid man. "I bought it with my first signing bonus."

Abby craned her head to look up at him. "You made enough with one signing bonus to buy all of this?" He nodded. "Huh. I should have gone into football."

Smiling, he laced their fingers. "Nah, your hands are too small. Plus, all the guys would spend the whole game trying to tackle you just so they could cop a feel." She elbowed him and may have snorted. "What? I spend all day waiting for you to walk by in those heels, swishing your hips, and hoping you'll have to climb a ladder for some reason so I'll have an excuse to touch you." He leaned in, just a little, and his lips brushed her ear. "Your rules are very difficult to follow."

She hated her rules. At least a dozen times a day she considered doing away with them completely.

Between the sexy winks and "coincidentally" sharing the same two square feet of space every time she needed to measure something, Tanner had managed to keep her hormones in a constant frenzy. But just when she was about ready to give in, she'd watch him lift a heavy copper pipe over his head, watch the play of his muscles bunch and tense, and know without the rules they'd end up naked—in the bottlery.

A state her body was hoping to get to sooner rather than later since he hadn't so much as kissed her since that five o'clock whistle blew two days ago.

"Show me what you're going to do with the property," she asked, taking his hand and leading him farther into the field. Maybe her sundress and strappy sandals hadn't been the wisest choice, she thought as the dandelions brushed her bare legs and she nearly broke her ankle navigating the gopher holes in five-inch heels.

Always the gentleman, Tanner slowed his pace and wrapped her hand around his forearm for balance. "What do you want to know?"

"Like where are you going to build your house?"

"The residential development will cover the entire north side, from that row of oak trees all the way back to the pine trees."

"That's a lot of land."

"Ferris wants to build a lot of houses. About three hundred semicustom when all is said and done."

Abby wondered how many homes Tanner wanted to build, and how the guy who'd started his company on the grounds of handcrafted luxury felt about the term *semicustom*, but he was already moving on.

"Up on the bluff over there is where the clubhouse and pro shop will go. And right here, where we're standing"—he bounced on the balls of his feet a few times for effect—"this will be the eighteenth hole."

"Huh." Abby looked around at what he'd just explained, then back to him. "Where would you have put the clubhouse?"

"Nestled in the pine trees to give it more of a rustic, natural feel so it works with the landscape and surroundings instead of against it."

No hesitation, no second guesses. Why would he agree to build it somewhere else?

"But Ferris says the clubhouse should overlook the entire course." *Ah, Ferris.* "It should make a statement about the design of the course and community. So the bluff it is."

Abby had a statement in her front yard. It was intrusive, pretentious, and nothing more than a sculpted stroke to the ego. She imagined Ferris's clubhouse would have the same effect here.

Before Abby could ask if Tanner had mentioned his ideas to Ferris, his phone buzzed. He looked at the screen and smiled. It was real and warm and so boyishly sweet, it was adorable—and in complete contrast to the smile he'd worn when talking about the three hundred semicustom homes.

"Come here." Taking her hand, he led her back to the truck and dropped the tailgate. Hands firmly around her waist, his fingers taking a little detour over her bottom, he set her up on the lift, giving one last look before he disappeared into the cab.

When he reemerged, he was holding two tumblers and a bottle of wine.

"What's that for?"

"We're celebrating."

"But you don't like wine." Tanner was a beer guy, straight up. If you couldn't hold it by the neck and take a swig in public without breaking any social codes, then he wasn't into it.

"But you do." He set the glasses on the tailgate and, after popping the cork, poured each glass a quarter full. "Ben just texted and we are all set to pass inspection tomorrow."

He handed her a glass, then held up his own in salute.

"It's really happening," she said quietly. It was actually coming together, and Abby couldn't believe it.

That she'd landed the job had been a miracle on its own. That they'd managed to get the entire factory rewired and fitted with all new plumbing in just under sixty hours was incredible. And a testament to just how hard Tanner had worked, and just how good he was at his job.

Now, she was going to work on a project that could change everything for her. A project that would say something about the kind of designer she was. The kind of person she was.

Tapping his glass, she took a sip of wine, her heart racing with excitement and something that felt oddly like pride. An emotion she hadn't experienced in a long time. An emotion Tanner had helped facilitate.

"Thank you, Jack. I know how hard you and your crew worked to get ready in time, and I couldn't have done this without you."

"It worked out." He gave a self-conscious tug at the brim of his hat, turning it around, and Abby found her heart racing for a whole different reason. Tanner could wear a hat like nobody's business. But when he tugged it backward so she could see the faint hint of vulnerability tinting his cheeks, she was surprised a guy like that could get so undone by a simple compliment.

Almost as surprising as the realization they were drinking Ryo wine. Abby and ChiChi's wine was presold years in advance to high-end restaurants and specialty wine shops around the country, making it expensive and extremely hard to come by. That he had a bottle was sweet, and flattering.

"So your plan was to bring me up here and charm me with the beautiful views and my own wine?"

"Nope." Without another word, he just flashed her that fantasy-inducing grin of his, the one that was kind of crooked and promised everything Abby was too scared to ask for, and moved in.

Two strides and he was wedged between her legs. But instead of touching her, he rested his hands on the tailgate, effectively caging her in, the smell of his aftershave mingling with that sexy rugged man thing he had going on.

"I brought you here to show you my favorite place on earth and get you drunk. And since I know jack shit about wine, I went with yours, since I know you would never put your name on something you didn't love." His eyes dropped to her lips. "Plus you get handsy when you're drunk. So bottoms up."

He tipped his hand in silent gesture.

With a helpless laugh, she tipped her glass back and emptied it. The deep liquid warmed her throat as it went down, and the way Tanner stared at her mouth, watching her drink every last drop, warmed . . . well, everything else.

"Too bad you don't like wine." She licked her lips. "This is great."

"Maybe I've been too harsh in my assessment." But instead of taking his glass, he took her mouth in one hell of a searing kiss. His hands stayed on the tailgate and the only part of them touching was their lips—which was beyond erotic.

"What do you think?" she asked.

"Sweet, bold, definitely full-bodied." He pulled back slightly and waggled a brow. "And sexy."

"You mean, spicy?"

"Let me have another taste." And taste he did. He tasted her until she had no other choice but to taste him right back and—*sweet baby Jesus*—he tasted incredible. And had her body flushing hotter than if she'd downed the entire bottle of wine.

When they came up for air, his cap was on the ground, her legs were tight around his waist, and she was leaning back on the bed of the truck with 250 pounds of badassed male pressed against her, running his big hands everywhere he felt bare skin. "Nope, sexy."

With a final smack to her lips, Tanner straightened, collected his hat, and sat next to her, the truck sagging a little under his weight.

"Are we stopping?" she asked, still leaning back on her elbows.

"Just slowing down," he said, his eyes glued to her lips. "Savoring."

Abby sat up, her feet dangling by the license plate, and smoothed down her hair. Picking off a stray metal washer that had stuck to her elbow, she tossed it in the air and caught it. Balancing it between her thumb and forefinger, she looked at her empty tumbler between them, judged the perfect distance, and bounced it off the bed of the truck—

Ping.

—right into the tumbler landing with a solid clink.

Tanner looked her way and smiled. "You've still got it."

"Yes, I do." Abby eyed the washer sitting in the bottom of the tumbler and smiled back.

In high school they used to hide in her parents' wine cave and play Bullshit with beer he'd sneak from his dad's fridge, a game of quarters meets truth or dare, where every sink in the glass earned the shooter a question of their choosing.

She pulled back the washer and launched it again.

Ping.

Clink.

Her smile hurt it was so big, and Tanner let out a laugh. "Darling, Bullshit requires me to slam a beer every time you think I'm lying. And since I'm driving home, that isn't happening."

And if Abby called bullshit on his answer, and it was indeed the truth, she'd be the one to have to chug.

"Then I guess there won't be any lying." Abby was not backing down. There were answers to questions she'd been waiting since senior year to hear, and she wasn't letting this moment slip by. But she'd start with an easy one.

She picked up the washer and dried it off on her leg. "Tell me why a guy who hates wine wants to be the go-to guy for wine caves in the valley."

"Because I like to blow stuff up." Tanner sat up and snatched the washer. Concentration had him closing one eye as he weighed the washer. "Plus, I fell in love with a girl in a wine cave, so I have a good association with them."

Abby's heart stopped—so fast she couldn't breathe. When she and Tanner had made love for the first time in that wine cave, she'd felt a connection unlike anything she'd ever known. Like she'd somehow managed to find a safe haven in the aftermath of her parents' death. And she'd been sure Tanner had felt it too, that his entire world had changed with hers. Only he'd never called. Never given her any indication what happened that night was mutual.

Until now.

"Jack, about that—"

Ping.

Clink.

"Ah, one question per sink. And since I just sunk it . . . that makes it my turn."

Oh boy. Asking him questions was one thing. His turning the tables on her? This could get real. And fast.

As though wanting to make her sweat—which she already was—Tanner leaned back against the wall opposite her, taking his time to get comfortable, his long legs stretched out in front and crossed at the ankle. He scooted the tumbler to the middle of the truck bed, then leaned back and crossed his arms.

"Where would you build my house?"

That was not the question Abby expected. And from the look on his face, it was not the one he'd intended to ask. But she was happy he had.

"Right here. Where Ferris plans to put the eighteenth hole."

He didn't move, didn't give anything away, but Abby knew her answer had fazed him.

"Why do you say that?"

It was a second question, but she answered it anyway.

"Because you showed me this spot first. And when you talked about watching the sunrise it was right over there." She let her gaze fall to the view beyond the truck, where she could see him sitting on his big back porch, staring out at the sunset while drinking a beer. "This is where you stood when you decided to buy the land, right?"

Tanner stared at her for a long, tense moment, and that's when she saw it. Something between them shifted, went from real to raw.

Tanner felt it too, because when he spoke his voice was husky. "I stood right there and looked out on the valley and it felt like . . ." He cleared his throat and gave a small laugh. "I don't know, but it was enough for me to dump every penny I had in my pocket on this land."

Abby had a pretty good idea what he felt. It was what she'd felt all those years ago when she was with him.

Needing to lighten the mood, she grabbed the washer.

Ping.

Clink.

"Full disclosure, Jack. I want to know. Was that *Sports Illustrated* photo doctored?"

Tanner let out a laugh, then sat forward. "You can't say a word, but yes, it was."

He crooked one finger at her, asking her to lean in. She did. How could she not? Hard Hammer Tanner photoshopped?

When they were nose to nose, he said, "They had to make the ball bigger," then sat back with a smug-ass grin on his face.

"Bullshit!" She poked at his chest. "I call bullshit!"

Tanner grabbed her finger and did a little in-your-face action of his own, bringing their mouths a breath apart. "Prove it."

Suddenly, Abby didn't want to play the game. She didn't want to bounce the stupid washer. She wanted *him* to prove it. She wanted him to take her in his arms and not stop until everything was okay again. She wanted him to—

"Tell me the truth," she whispered past the lump in her throat. She picked up the washer and, eyes on him, sank it. "Why didn't you turn me in?" When his forehead creased in confusion, she went on, surprised at how much talking about that time in her life still hurt. "You knew I put the mascot in your car, you had a picture, but you waited until after the game to turn me in. Why?"

Because once upon a time Abby had thought she'd spend the rest of her life with this man. Actually, twice. In high school she'd chalked it up to being young and inexperienced. But in college, after the most intense weekend of her life, she was convinced. Two incredible days and nights spent in his arms, talking about the future, their hopes and dreams, was enough for Abby to know, enough to allow herself to fall. Allow herself to stop being so afraid and believe that maybe she had found a happy ending to all of the sadness in her life.

She had been ready to tell him that she loved him—only before she could, he dropped the bomb that he was moving to New York. Buffalo had chosen him as their first-round draft pick, and he chose to move on without much more than a good-bye.

Tanner cupped her cheek, and when he spoke he looked her in the eyes. *No bullshit*, he was saying.

"You told me how you had found your mom's dress and how you were going to alter and wear it for homecoming. I figured I'd pretty much messed up any chance of being with you, but I wanted you to wear that dress."

It hadn't been just any dress. It was the dress her mom had worn when she'd been crowned homecoming queen. It was also the dress her mom was wearing when she told Abby's dad she loved him.

"But not telling cost you the University of Alabama," she whispered.

His thumb slid across her lower lip, and he gave a small smile. "I have no regrets, Abby."

Abby had a hard time believing somebody would give up an opportunity that huge for her. A chance to live out his dream for a stupid high school dance and a stupid dress.

"Most guys wouldn't see it that way."

Tanner was quiet for a moment, just watching her. He didn't budge, didn't lose his smile, but the earlier lightness in his expression was gone. Abby could feel the frustration spark and grow in its place, until it filled the narrow space between them. They were face-to-face, and yet she suddenly felt like she was on the other side of the mountain.

"When are you going to see I'm not most guys, Abs? Not with you, I'm not."

A mixture of understanding and sadness—sadness for her—flicked across his face, and Abby had the sudden urge to just give in, tell him she believed him. Believed he was different and that this time it could work out for her. Because when he looked at her like that, as though making a silent promise to never let go, Abby wanted to believe.

But no matter how hard she tried, she just couldn't. Life didn't work out that way for her. Never had.

So to protect herself from the heartache, she did what she always did when confronted with something that would only lead to disappointment. She pulled back until it didn't hurt to breathe.

Resting on her knees, she held out the washer. "You didn't shoot."

Tanner picked the washer out of her hand, his fingers rough against her skin. Holding out the shot, he paused, his blue eyes so intense, yet so gentle she found herself holding her breath.

"And Abs, seeing you in that dress was worth losing ten scholarships."

"You saw me in my mom's dress?" she asked around the knot forming in her throat. "You came?"

His answer was to hold up the washer. "My shot. My question."

Ping.

Clink.

"You ready?" he whispered gently.

She nodded, then shook her head, then felt like crying. She didn't know if she'd ever be ready.

"I need to know the truth. This is important. Are you really a damn Seahawks fan?"

There went that grin of his, double-barreled dimpled and so damn reassuring she felt herself start to laugh. Felt all of the disappointment and sadness fade into something lighter. Something hotter. Something fun and flirty.

Tanner had that effect on her. Always had. Even when they were kids he'd had a way of easing the hurt, making her laugh instead of cry. He used to say his job was to make her smile.

And Tanner always took his job seriously. And so did Abby. And it was time to get down to business.

Stepping to the ground, she stretched her hands behind her to grab the zipper of her dress, slowly tugging it lower until she was pretty sure one roll of the shoulder was all that stood between her and the night air.

Tanner knew it too. All humor gone, he stared at her with a quiet intensity, his eyes glued to her chest as though willing her to drop the dress.

Desire poured over her, and with a quirk of the lips she asked, "Want to see?"

Want to see what? Confirmation he was the luckiest son of a bitch on the planet?

Fuck yeah, he did. Tanner had waited ten years for this chance again. Ten long years, and he wasn't going to let his dick run the show this time. Giving in to the desire had cost him Abby twice, and Tanner didn't want to repeat history. Almost as much as he wanted her to lose the dress.

He'd wanted her to lose the dress the second she'd walked out on her front porch and the breeze caught the bottom of the skirt. The dress was a soft yellow, outlining her every curve, and had little straps and a deep neckline showing way too much and not nearly enough. Then there were her shoes—Jesus, her shoes were tall and slinky and when worn with that dress, it was a design to mess with a man's mind.

And being that Tanner was a man, and Abby was one hundred percent woman, his mind had decided to take up residence in his pants. He opened his mouth to do the right thing—which was not taking her in the cab of his truck—and ended up holding out the tumbler and saying, "Darling, 'want to see?' is a question. And according to *your* rules, a question requires a sink."

Challenge flashed in her eyes and Tanner found himself smiling. Nothing was sexier than Abby when she was feeling competitive. When he was the prize, she was damn near irresistible.

Without warning, Abby gave a circle with one shoulder, so small it had Tanner sitting up straight and holding his breath, praying it was enough. And—*ah, man*, he was toast—it was.

The strap slid down her arm, inch by inch, and when it hit her elbow it came down to a simple matter of mathematics.

Mass plus velocity meant Tanner was about to see, once and for all, if the kick pants matched the pom-poms.

And thank God math skills did translate to the real world because, like clockwork, the dress slid to the grass in one glorious swoop, leaving her in those mile-high heels, tan skin, and enough hometown pride to make his heart swell.

He'd had his share of fantasies over the years involving Abby and her pom-poms, but watching her finger trace the scalloped edge of red lace on her bra, while she walked toward him in what he could only call do-me pumps, ranked right up there with playing mud football with her—naked.

Then she gave a little turn, showcasing the merchandise, and holy hell, the lacy panties she had on might be boy cut in the front, but they were all thong in the back and, when standing in the setting sun, incredibly and miraculously sheer.

Man, she was gorgeous. The biggest brown eyes he'd ever seen, full lush lips, a body that was compact but curvy in all the right places—and headed his way.

She smiled as she joined him on the tailgate, not stopping until she was straddling his lap with her bare backside firmly planted on his thighs. With a smile that had him about to blow right out of his jeans, she plucked the washer out of the glass, held it over the rim and—

Oh, hell.

She just dropped it in. No bounce, no rebound, no more games. She just sank the washer right in the tumbler with that sexy smile that pretty much said, *Fuck the rules.*

Tanner was on board immediately.

"Last question, so listen up." A hard task when her breasts were right there, demanding all of his attention. "Which half do you want first?"

"Well," he said, his hands exploring the edge of her panties until he felt smooth skin—skin that was so damn soft.

He didn't stop until he had two palmfuls of the sweetest ass he'd ever held. Tightening his grip, he spun them around until she was trapped between the truck bed and his body, looking up at him a little shocked, a whole lot turned on. "I think I need to do some research before I can make a decision this important."

He let his hand slide up and over her stomach, loving how her muscles quivered. "Some up close and personal research."

"I was a research assistant in college." Her hands fisted in his hair. "Maybe I can help?"

"Maybe," he said against her lips, then kissed her, and he'd bet his land she'd gotten straight A's as an assistant. She helped him right out of his shirt, tossing it over the side of the truck, then went to work on his pants, which he hoped led to the kind of assistance he really needed.

In fact, he was seriously considering asking Abby to be his assistant, so they could do this five or six times a day—ten on the weekends. And all the assisting would be done naked. And outdoors.

Yeah, naked and outdoors would be amazing.

She was amazing. Amazing and smart and stubborn and sexy and funny and—*Hello*—she was going for his zipper.

He may have groaned, maybe even said some nonsense aloud, but he sure as hell felt his eyes roll to the back of his head when her fingers brushed against the hard ridge of him. Before he could unscramble his brain, her elegant fingers, the ones he'd watched twice a week for the past year stroke the keys of her piano, made their way under the fabric of his briefs, running lightly over the tip, then shyly stroking him before giving a gentle squeeze.

"Abby," he groaned, taking her mouth again.

There was nothing shy about the way she made him feel. And he was feeling a hell of a lot. Which was the only excuse he had for pushing farther into her hand, letting her know just what she did to him, and damn if she didn't meet him halfway.

He nibbled down her neck, to her shoulder, loving the little breathy noises she made when he paused to suck her skin into his mouth and how she arched up into him, as though as hungry for his touch as he was for her taste.

"I forgot how . . . oh, my . . ." Her breath caught and she trailed off as he traced her nipple through the fabric with his tongue.

"You forgot what?" he asked against the wet lace.

"How much I like it when you do that." She arched up.

He looked up at her and smiled. "I didn't."

He remembered every damn thing about her. How she liked to be touched, how she liked to be teased, and how, when she was in his arms, moaning his name, his whole world felt right.

"Do it again."

"Yes, ma'am." And he did. Using his teeth, he gave the fabric a gentle tug and, *would ya look at that?* She spilled right out over the top. So he did it to the other side and, *man oh man*, she was about the sexiest thing he'd ever encountered.

She was also special. A thought that made him stop—midtease. Here she was pretty much naked, lying on the cold bed of his truck in the middle of a field, and once again—he was *that* guy.

"Abby," he said, pulling slightly back.

"Are we savoring again?" She wrapped her legs around him. "Because I'm done with the savoring part. We can savor next time."

Well, at least she was thinking about a next time. Problem was, he was thinking about the time after that and, well, a whole summer of next times and maybe even stretching into the fall and winter. But *this* time—*this* time was different. Special.

Deserving of her.

Something he should have realized the first time, but was too young, too stupid, and way too horny to understand.

"I want this to be special," he admitted, and when she smiled up at him like that, like he was everything she needed, he realized he wanted to be the guy who made her every moment special. "I want to take you out to a nice dinner, then take you home and lay you out on my big, soft bed and explore every inch of you, then wake up holding you and do it all over again."

"I don't want a fancy dinner, and I don't want to wait until we're in your bed, Jack. I want you." Her legs tightened. "Right here, in the middle of this field you obviously love."

Tanner actually felt his entire world stop. Felt something between them warm, become softer. Oh, the heat and the passion and the need were all still there, so intense that one spark and—boom. It would always be like that with them. If a decade couldn't take the edge off, this sexual intensity would be a forever kind of thing.

"But," she said, and there it was.

Tanner's heart gave a final, painful pump to the chest and waited for her to finish. For her to point out the buts and exceptions and conditions he'd heard his entire life.

She leaned up and crushed her mouth to his. "We need to get you out of these clothes."

How was a man to argue with that? Out of all the scenarios he'd run in his head the past few days, he'd never imagined this evening would end in the back of his truck with her naked—taking off *his* clothes.

Always a team player, he went to work on his boots and, after pulling out a condom from his back pocket and setting it on the tailgate, together they made short order of his pants, although her hands were doing more copping than helping, but he was okay with that. More than okay. He was so okay with the turn of events that he was smiling like a damn idiot.

Oddly enough, he was okay with that too. In fact, he was still smiling when she kissed him again. Considered giving her an enthusiastic high five when she gently pushed his shoulders until he was completely on his back and—best day ever—her panties joined his pants on the grass.

But she left the bra on.

Not that it was doing much more than acting as a tray for his viewing pleasure, since he'd managed to tug the cups all the way down.

God, she was a sight. Straddling him with the orange sky behind her made her skin glow and highlighted her brown hair as it tumbled over her shoulders and around her face, making her features appear even more delicate.

"Um, Tanner." She held out the condom. Her hands were shaking. "Do you want me to . . . ?"

While he was staring his fill, he'd neglected to remember it had been a long time for her. And she was beyond nervous.

"Come here." Sitting up, he took the condom from her and wrapped his arms around her, his hands going immediately to her ass. After a gentle squeeze, he scooted her toward him, and when she was so close they were sharing the same heat, he whispered, "I wanted to see if you still love it when I do this."

Tanner lifted her slightly, then let her slide back down, all of her soft parts rubbing against his hard ones. The breathy sigh she gave told him she more than liked it. So he did it again, taking his time to make sure she was too turned on to be nervous.

She arched her back at the first contact, pushing against his massive erection, taking the friction from hot to holy fuck.

"Tanner," she whispered against his neck. "Now. I want you inside of—"

He had the condom opened and on and was sliding home before she could even finish her sentence. But instead of moving, he just held her, fitting her perfectly against him while rubbing his hands up and down her back as they both took a moment to remember how amazing this felt.

Abby pulled back and looked up at him. "It's better than I remember."

"It's exactly how I remember it." Perfect.

Tanner lifted her slightly then let her slide back down. She wrapped her arms around his neck, holding on so tight her breasts were crushed to his chest.

She began moving incredibly slowly at first, and he could feel every part of their bodies rub and grind against each other. It took everything he had to hold on.

The pace picked up, their skin slick with the summer air, and the sensations were so sensual they blew right past mind-blowing and were quickly approaching life-altering when her gasps came closer and closer. Her eyes slid half-closed with pleasure as her arms hugged him tighter and tighter, and he knew, *knew*, she was there. She was one flex of the hip away from—

"Perfect. You feel perfect," she said on a gasp, throwing her head all the way back, and that was it. That was all it took.

He called out her name as her body tensed around him and they both fell together. Tanner held her tightly to him, refusing to let go until they rode out every last wave.

They were still both breathing heavily when she opened her eyes and smiled shyly up at him. That's when Tanner knew he was in serious trouble. With that one smile, Abby turned what was supposed to be a simple first and goal into something more complicated.

Somewhere between playing Bullshit together and a blitz attack from the DeLuca Darling, Tanner ended up fumbling his heart.

CHAPTER 14

It was a perfect day in wine country, Abby thought as she made her way up the steps of town hall and between the two massive columns, her blueprints clutched to her chest and her Certificate of Inspection slip in hand. The mustard weed was in full bloom, painting the valley a brilliant yellow. Early-morning tourists made their way up and down Main Street, window shopping and sipping their morning pick-me-ups. Even the weather was perfect, bringing a gentle breeze to combat the warm August sun and rustle the bright purple lavender that lined the streets and scented the air.

Proud they'd passed inspection with flying colors and exhilarated to get this project rolling, Abby pushed through the ornate wooden doors, loving how the raw silk of her little Jackie O–inspired dress swished as she walked. It was dusty blue, sleek, and sophisticated, with an inspired little bow in the back adding a bit of romantic to the professional. Matched with her favorite vintage heels, it made the perfect statement.

Designer on a mission.

A mission she was about to put into action. The Pungent Barrel was the first order of business of the morning, and the board was expected to make its ruling by the end of the work day. Which meant Tanner could finally start installing the materials and retrofitting the old conveyer belt.

Just thinking about Tanner made her stomach flip. Not only had he given her the best sex of her life, he'd brought her to his favorite spot, shared a piece of himself with her. Something he'd never done before.

In the past, Abby had been the one to share, and Tanner would listen, but he'd always kept big parts of his life to himself. On their date, he'd opened up to her and offered to let her be a part of something important to him.

"Morning, Roz," Abby said with a smile so big it hurt her cheeks. When Roz's greeting was to keep clicking away on her computer, Abby pulled out the bright orange application form and held it up. "I'm here for the Historical Preservation Council's meeting. I am nominating one of our town's most historical and unique buildings for the Memory Lane Manor Walk."

"Well, how exciting for you," Roz mumbled, but hit the buzzer all the same.

The door buzzed, and with a little wave, which went unreturned, Abby made her way through the glass doors.

Confidence bubbling, Abby strode down the long hallway, smiling as she passed photograph after photograph of over a hundred years of the town's architectural history, knowing someday soon her name would be added to that small but prestigious club. She was going to walk into that meeting, wow them with her preservation-conscious designs, and by the end of her speech, have the full support of the HPC behind the project.

"You got this," she said quietly, pushing through the antique gothic door salvaged from one of the original wineries in the valley, waltzing right into that room, and—

She so did not have this. Not even close. In fact, she wondered just how unlucky one person could be. Because no one's karma could be this bad. No one's.

"Abigail." Nora Kincaid stood from behind the conference table, her eyes glued to the nomination application in Abby's hand. "Perkins was just explaining your situation. Said you asked if we could make an exception and allow you to nominate a residence so late into the selection process. Imagine that."

Yeah. Imagine that.

"Why do I have to always be so stubborn?" Abby asked, fiddling with the label on her beer bottle as she sat between Tanner's legs on the lounger. Her head rested against his chest as she stared past his patio to the setting sun. "They're never going to approve the plans now."

"You don't know that." Tanner tightened his arms around her, wishing there was something he could do to make this all better.

"I have a naked statue on my front lawn, Jack." She gave him a look. "A naked statue that stares into the windows of the most honored Memory Lane Manor of the Year Award recipient, who happens to sit on the council deciding who gets approved and who doesn't. I can already tell you what group we'll be in."

Tanner wanted to point out her decision to leave the statue in her yard was selfless, and if anyone had the right to complain, it was her. Learning to manage people's expectations while still maintaining a healthy balance of personal happiness was something Abby struggled with. Bottom line: Abby hated confrontation almost as much as she hated disappointing others, so she tended to let her people-pleasing side dominate.

"Darling, they accepted your nomination application, so now it is just a matter of reviewing your plans. And trust me," he said gently, tilting his head down so she had to look at him. "Your designs are more powerful than an angry neighbor."

That got a small smile out of her, so he stole the beer and took a swallow. Only when he handed it back, she was frowning again. "Then why haven't they called? Perkins said end of the business day."

"It's not quite five, you've still got a few minutes."

"He said end of the day *Monday*. It's Tuesday," she clarified, as though Tanner wasn't well aware they'd been at a standstill for two days while the HPC took their sweet-ass time making a decision that, if you asked him, should have been a slam dunk. But instead they lost another twenty-four hours from their proposed project plan, which would create all kinds of scheduling issues.

Sure, they'd managed to finish stripping the walls down to the original brick and his crew had prepped the floors for the limestone. But they couldn't alter anything original to the building until they received the okay. So retrofitting and covering the conveyor belts was pushed, bumping the metalsmith to Thursday. Except the metalsmith had another job on the books that day, but could possibly squeeze them in on Saturday. The same day Tanner had planned on taking Abby to an antique festival in Santa Rosa. Followed by a nice dinner in the city and dessert in his hot tub.

Setting the beer on the patio table, he ran his hands down her arm, linking their fingers and giving a reassuring squeeze. "Maybe they were so impressed that he wants to tell you in person."

"Or maybe Nora sunk me." She turned around to face him and, as though unable to meet his gaze, lay down with her cheek right over his heart. "I should have let you haul the statue away that first day when you offered."

He tucked a finger under her chin and nudged her until she met his gaze. "You weren't ready."

He could see in her eyes he was right. And he wasn't sure how he felt about that.

It was hard enough when she was married to the douche bag, but now Richard was gone yet somehow still here, and Tanner wasn't sure where that left him and Abby. Competing with Richard wouldn't be hard. Competing with the wreckage he left behind, though?

Abby still needed closure. And that was the one thing Tanner couldn't give her.

"Does that make me pathetic?" she asked quietly.

"No." He cupped her face and brought it up to his. "It makes you human." He gave her a gentle kiss. "You're letting his grandmother come and pay her respects when it would be easier to take a sledgehammer to it. That makes you special, Abs."

Then he gave her a not-so-gentle kiss, and when he pulled back, her hands were shoved up his shirt, his were on her ass, and Wreck was sitting on the end of the lounger watching.

"Come on, man," Tanner said. He pointed to the floor. "Down."

Wreck lay down—on the edge of the lounger.

"Off."

"Woof." Wreck wagged his tail and panted some. Tanner rolled his eyes and went back to kissing Abby.

"I think he likes you," she said between kisses.

"I think he is checking out your ass."

"That would be you."

Yeah, that was him all right. His hands were plastered to her butt, partly to scoot her higher so kissing her would be easier, but mostly because she had an amazing ass. That was buzzing.

"Oh!" She sat up, nearly planting her knee in the family jewels as she scrambled to fish her phone out of her back pocket. She pulled it free, looked at the screen, and froze.

It buzzed again.

"You going to answer that?"

"What if they say no?"

"What if they don't?" He leaned up and kissed her. "Either way, you'll know."

That got her moving, because Abby loved knowing. In fact, she lived to be in the know on everything.

"Hello, this is Abigail," she said. "Hi, Perkins. What? No, no problem at all."

After several *Uh-huhs* and *Yes sirs* and a very professional, *Thank you*, she hung up the phone and just stared at him. Then smiled. Big and beautiful and hot damn, he knew that smile.

"You got the approval."

She knelt on the lounger in front of him, her eyes wide with excitement. And pride. An emotion he hadn't seen on her face in a long time. An emotion that looked damn good on her. Hell, she was practically vibrating with it.

"*We* got the approval." She brought her fingers up to her lips, as though that alone was the one thing stopping her from spilling the rest. Because, oh yeah, there was more. "And Perkins apologized for the delay, but finalists are notified last."

Now it was his turn to smile. "You finaled?"

"The Jackson Bottlery, once owned by the renowned olive farmer and winemaker Randal Jackson himself, is an official finalist of the Memory Lane Manor Walk. Do you have any idea what this could mean? Not just for the Pungent Barrel, but for my firm?"

He knew. And God he wanted her to win. It would take her from small-town closet organizer to industry-celebrated designer in one press release. "It means you did good. Better than good. You inspired them."

"We did good," she whispered and launched herself at him, wrapping those arms and gorgeous legs around him.

He nuzzled her neck, taking in the way she smelled, how she felt, every aspect of this moment. Because he wanted to savor it.

Remember it.

"Abby, you know the bottlery didn't final." She pulled back, an adorable crease in her brow. "Your plans finaled."

"Yeah," she whispered in awe. "They did, huh?"

"Yeah, they did." He kissed her. "And you can win this."

"I want to win this so badly. And with you on my team, I think we can. But," she dragged out the word, long and sweetly, locking her ankles behind his back and her arms around his neck. She was buttering him up. Not necessary since the "with you on my team" part pretty much sealed the deal. "The HPC announces the winner on August twenty-seventh."

Tanner choked a little. "Darling, that's a week and a half away."

"I know." She winced. "Trust me, I so know. And I know what I'd be asking of you and the crew, but we're talking *Architectural Digest* and Martha Stewart. Martha freaking Stewart." She smiled up at him and was literally beaming with excitement. Everything she was feeling was right there on her face for him to see. "Is it even a realistic goal to think we can do it in time?"

Tanner could do anything if it meant she'd keep looking at him like that. But a week and some change was going to be tough. It would require bringing on another crew to work the swing shift, his being at the shop around the clock—but yeah, he could do it. For her, he'd make it happen.

"I might need to hire an assistant," he said, eying her cleavage.

She snuggled closer. "What kind of assistance are we talking?"

"I don't know, why don't you start assisting and I'll let you know what I need."

By Friday afternoon, the warehouse was looking less like a bottlery and more like a high-end cheese shop. The conveyer belts had been retrofitted and the reclaimed limestone had been delivered that morning from an old mission Abby had found near San Luis Obispo.

And, the best part of her day? She'd found a glassblower in Sonoma who was able to take the thousand or so vintage wine bottles Gus had discovered in the old carriage house and turn them into lighting fixtures, including the two massive chandeliers that would hang on either side of the arch.

Wiping a bead of sweat off her brow and most likely smearing cobwebs into her hair, Abby stretched her arms as far as they would go around a case of bottles and, ignoring the way her shoulders and back protested, staggered to a stand. She used her foot to kick open the doors, a blast of summer heat causing her tank top to shrink-wrap to her body like a second skin, and the farther into the sun she walked, the sweatier her hands became.

Afraid of dropping the bottles, she waddled as fast as she could, wondering how much longer her arms would hold out. Not long enough to make it to the truck, she imagined, since each case weighed over thirty pounds and this was her fifteenth box of the day.

She was nearly to the shipping truck when her fingers started slipping. Not wanting to drop the box, she sped up and hobbled right into Tanner.

"Whoa, let me get that," he said, his arms coming around the box and lifting it effortlessly right out of her hands and placing it in the back of the truck in two strides—the big showoff. "What are you doing?"

"Getting the wine bottles on the truck," she said, her breath coming out in harsh little out-of-shape puffs.

"I can see that." He brushed something off the side of her face.

"Is it a spider?" She closed her eyes. "Don't let it be a spider."

"It's a harmless dust bunny." As far as she was concerned, nothing dwelling in that carriage house was harmless. "Why didn't you ask one of the guys to do it?"

"They're on lunch break." He frowned at that, so she patted his arm—his really muscular, really sexy arm. "I told them to go. It's stifling today, even hotter in the warehouse. So when it hit lunchtime I asked Lexi to make them a special treat to say thanks for pulling so many long hours."

"You didn't have to do that."

She shrugged. "No biggie. Plus the owner is sleeping with my brother, so I get a discount."

"Yeah." He moved closer, cupping her hips, running his hands down her sides, then back up. "I'm sleeping with you, so does that mean I get a special treat for lunch?"

"That kind of treat has to wait. It's not five o'clock," she said, but let her fingers do some running of their own—right over his chest and down every single one of his eight-pack. The man was built.

He flashed a grin that had her stomach flipping. "It's five somewhere."

Well, when put like that, who was she to object when he pulled her close and placed those very kissable lips right on hers? And he didn't stop there. No, Tanner squatted down, his arms tightening around her waist like a vise, and stood, taking her with him so they were more evenly matched—and every important part was lined up with perfect symmetry.

"Are you sure everyone is gone?" he asked as her legs dangled above the ground. Tanner had been tall back in college, but the NFL had filled him out quite a bit, taking him from hunky hardbody to total beefcake.

"Yes," she said against his mouth. "They're all gone."

"I'm giving them all a raise," he said, walking toward the carriage house. He backed through the door, the room suddenly dark in contrast to the bright sky outside.

Abby hesitated for all of half a second before wrapping her legs around his waist. If there were any scary creepy crawlers in there, they were no match for her gladiator.

"I'm glad I wore shorts today," she said.

His voice came out a low rumble of male appreciation. "Me too." To prove it, his hands went right to her butt, his thumbs sliding under the hem. "Shorts, that shirt you think passes for a tank top, and those cute pink sneakers," he growled. "They've been driving me crazy all day."

She laughed. "Pink sneakers drive you crazy?"

"Darling, anything on you drives me crazy because all I can think about is getting it off you."

"Funny, when I see you in those jeans and sweaty tee with the tool belt hanging temptingly low, all I can think about is getting you off."

Oh my God. Abby felt her face flush. Had she really just said that?

The heat in his eyes told her yes, yes she had. And he was more than on board. "Let's see what we can do about that."

He kissed her neck, pressing his lips down to the base of her throat—and lower. His thumbs, however, were working diligently at climbing higher until he met lace. She knew because she felt him smile against her skin.

"I thought I was going to get a show first," she said, tugging at his shirt.

"And here I thought this was a worksite," Colin said from the doorway of the carriage house.

"Loading the truck, huh?" Gus said from beside Colin, only he was smiling. Colin? Not so much. "Is that what you kids call it these days?"

With an apologetic smile that didn't quite meet his eyes, Tanner lowered Abby to the ground and, always the gentleman, positioned himself in front of her. Abby had to force herself to step out from behind his body. They were grown adults and she was tired of hiding.

"I thought you went with the rest of the crew to eat," Abby said to Gus, doing her best to avoid looking Colin directly in the eye.

"Nope, they were having tri-tip sandwiches and blue cheese fries. Plus I already had my lunch in the fridge." He held up a plate piled high with baked chicken, a nice helping of green vegetables, and—

"Gus, is that quinoa salad?"

He shrugged. "Thought it was rice. Tastes like rice."

Yesterday it was a healthy stir fry, that morning he'd had a bran muffin instead of a doughnut, and now quinoa? The dish also looked like the ones she'd seen at Babs's, but before Abby could comment, Colin stepped forward.

"Well, I just came to drop this off." He tossed the day's copy of the *Sentinel* on a stack of wine cases.

Abby picked it up and felt everything in her chest catch and tighten. There, covering half the front page, was a photo of the Jackson Bottlery, and next to it was a photo of Abby taken right after Richard had disappeared. But what had her blood rushing from her head was the headline that brought back every insecurity she'd worked so hard to overcome.

FINALIST CONTENDER OR CREATIVE FRAUD?

New findings have Jackson Bottlery on shaky ground with Historic Preservation Council. A walk down memory lane may provide answers.

And that wasn't the worst of it. The more she read, the more painful that feeling in her chest became until Abby was sure it would crush her whole.

"Abby," Tanner said quietly, resting a hand on her shoulder, and she realized she was shaking. "Are you okay?"

She swallowed past the lump in her throat. "It says here a source close to former Memory Lane Manor Walk recipient and HPC council member Nora Kincaid alleges Jackson Bottlery was never a residence and therefore does not qualify. It goes on to say that accounts of the building's history may have been embellished or even fabricated by a person close to the project." She looked up from the paper. "It doesn't say who made the false claims, but it's not difficult to connect the dots when my picture is right next to the article, huh?"

She handed him the paper. "Do you think Nora did this because of the statue?"

Tanner looked up from the article and cupped her face in support. "She's nosy and a stickler for the rules, but I've never known her to be mean or spiteful."

Abby wasn't so sure. There had been a lot of people in town who, before Richard left, she never would have imagined had a mean bone in their bodies. Then the money disappeared and Abby was left holding the bag, making her an easy target for their anger. Those who weren't looking at her with venom were talking about her behind her back, and oddly, their rejection had hurt worse than Richard's betrayal.

"I don't care who leaked it," Colin said. "I want to know why you lied and how you'll fix it."

"She didn't lie. Babs gave her the documentation," Tanner said, a low, menacing threat clear in his tone.

"Actually, Babs never showed me the documents," Abby said and wanted to cringe. "She told me the story over the phone."

"Maybe Ferris was right," Colin said, pinching the bridge of his nose. "Maybe this is the *Titanic* of cheese shops." He looked at Abby and shook his head. "Are you saying you based your entire case on a story someone told you over the phone?"

"It was a solid story, with lots of details, and if you look around at this place, this was the carriage house and . . ." Abby faded off because none of that mattered. She'd given in to the romance of the story, wanted it so badly to be true that she'd just believed it without ever questioning its validity.

After Richard left, Abby reminded herself regularly that blindly giving up trust only led to disappointment. The best solution was preventative—be open and friendly while remaining cautiously skeptical. Too late for that now.

"I'm sorry. I should have double-checked." Then she looked at Tanner and felt ill. "I'm so sorry."

"That's okay," Tanner said with a reassuring smile. "Just have Babs bring the paperwork down and we can get this cleared up. No harm done."

That was it. No blame, no judgment, no hesitation about her ability to fix things. Just complete faith—in her.

"No harm done?" Colin shouted. "Are you kidding me? What kind of professional neglects to verify information when submitting to a county-run council? If we did that, we'd lose our license—or worse." He threw his hands in the air and started pacing. "Jesus, man, I just spent twenty minutes listening to Ferris grill me, asking if I were him, with that much money on the line, would I consider partnering with a company who can't even manage to renovate a cheese shop. I had to say no, I wouldn't. I mean, at any point, did you even look over her paperwork?"

Tanner hadn't, it was written all over his face, and Abby felt awful. He hadn't looked over the package because he'd trusted her to do her job, and she'd messed up. Sure, she was the designer, but it was Tanner Construction's name attached to the build. Tanner Construction written on every permit and inspection certification. And it was Tanner Construction's reputation on the line with Ferris. And the HPC.

Colin stopped pacing, looked from Tanner to Abby and back to Tanner, and that's when the tension in the room became suffocating. "Was it that you didn't think to look it over, or you were too busy to look it over?"

"None of your fucking business," Tanner said with deadly intent. "And, none of your fucking business."

"Well now, hang on there," Gus said, pointing at them with his cane. "This isn't a boxing ring, it's a worksite, so unless you want me to bring out the hose on you boys, you'll just have to wait until the whistle blows before you two knock each other around."

"Which is ridiculous, since this was my fault and I can fix it," Abby said when Tanner took another step forward to defend her, because Abby realized she wasn't worthy of his defense. Not only had she been neglectful, she'd never once given any thought to what would happen to him if this project went sideways. "Gus, can you go call Babs and ask her to bring down everything she has?"

"Sure thing," Gus said, giving Abby a sweet smile, silently telling her everything would work out.

"And Colin." Abby swallowed. It was no secret he'd never liked her, which always made her work twice as hard to try to change his mind. "If you'd like, I can call Ferris and explain the situation."

"Don't worry about it," he said, waving a dismissive hand. Not dismissing the issue, but dismissing her. "Just get it cleared up so

Babs stops calling him and asking his advice on every damn problem that arises."

Abby wanted to point out that if Ferris gave his mother even an ounce of attention, she wouldn't call to gripe all the time, but since Tanner looked like he was reconsidering that impromptu boxing match, she just said, "Sure thing."

With a single nod, Colin stormed out of the carriage house, the door nearly slamming off its hinges behind him. She saw Tanner's body deflate.

"I'm sorry," she said again, and this time to her utter horror, her voice cracked. "I should have checked."

"And next time you will," he said, sliding an arm around her waist and pulling her into his embrace. "Nothing's wrong with believing in some sweet story an old lady told you."

"It was sweet," she whispered, as though by just saying the words, it would make her rookie move that much less sucky.

"Yeah, it was." His hand slid up her back and into her hair, not to pull her closer, but to let her know he was here—for her. "That you got wrapped up in it makes you who you are. And I know you're more upset about that article than Colin being an ass."

"That article made me sound like an awful, deceitful person. What if people believe I lied, that I tried to cheat the system?"

Her voice caught and Tanner was right. Sure, she was frustrated at herself that she didn't do her due diligence, upset she may have cost them all a really amazing opportunity, but she was terrified she'd taken a really huge step forward and the past was about to body slam her back to when Richard left. And she didn't want to go back. Not when going forward was turning out to be so much fun.

"So what if they do?" he challenged softly. "Your family knows the real you, so do your friends." She felt him shrug. "So do I."

She looked up and the sincerity in his expression warmed her heart. "You're going to make me cry."

"Have at it." He shrugged again, handling the threat of tears like he handled everything else, with confidence and ease. "You're standing in a dark storage room with no one to judge you or tell you what to do or how to feel."

"But you're here," she said, because what he was offering sounded amazing.

"And I'll still be here when you're done." His hand was on the move again, big and strong and so damn reassuring she felt herself start to give in. Felt all of the frustration and disappointment and sadness—*yeah*, even after all of the time that had passed, after all of the lies and heartache, there was still a deep ache of sadness that some days she was afraid might take her under. "If that still scares you, then pretend I'm a wall."

With a shuddered laugh, Abby dropped her forehead to his chest and tried to do just that. Not an easy task when the wall hugged back with a gentle yet controlled strength that made her want to hang on and stay for a while.

CHAPTER 15

It was well past ten on Saturday night by the time Tanner dragged his tired-ass body through his front door. The metalsmith had shown up, as promised, which meant Tanner had spent the past twelve hours hauling sheets of hammered steel from the loading dock into the main building, where it was secured to the old conveyor belts, only to haul the scraps back out to the Dumpster.

Except that, *whoops sorry*, they weren't all scraps, they were the backsplash for the prep area, which meant Tanner went Dumpster diving with a flashlight and general description of exactly which pieces needed to be recovered. Needless to say he was sweaty, sore as hell, and smelled.

Bad.

Bending over to untie his work boots, he dropped one by the door, then the other. Followed by his socks, hat, a stack of invoices he still had to file, and a cordless drill that some dumbass used instead of an impact driver when sinking anchors into a brick wall.

When he realized he'd been at the door for more than ten seconds and there wasn't a wet nose greeting to the goods, he remembered the wine cake on the counter. The last slice of wine cake he'd left on the counter.

Not bothering to turn on any lights, Tanner sprinted down the hallway toward the kitchen. He skidded around the corner, hit the switch, and nearly hit the roof.

Wreck stood on the center island, whiskers covered in crumbs, tail between his legs, looking guilty as sin. How a dog that had the coordination of a baby giraffe managed to lug himself up on the counter without breaking everything in a ten-foot radius, Tanner had no clue. All he knew was the dog was eating his cake.

"One more bite and I swear I will sell you on Craigslist. To a house with cats," Tanner said quietly, so as not to wake Gus, who he'd dropped off earlier that day when his dad started looking tired.

Only Gus wasn't in bed. He was by the back door in a button-up and a pair of light brown pants without any loops or extra pockets, looking as guilty as Wreck.

"I thought you were going to bed early," Tanner said to Gus.

"I was . . . I did. Took a nap. Then the guys called and I met them for a drink."

"Wearing your church clothes?"

Gus shrugged then deflected, something he did when he was hiding something. "You going to let him polish that off? Because sugar gives him gas and he's sleeping with you tonight."

Wreck was back to the cake. In fact, he was licking the plate clean. "Jesus, Wreck, I'm standing right here." Wreck panted happily. Tanner pointed at the dog, not so happily, then the floor. "Down."

The dog whimpered and lay down on the counter. Tanner threw his hands up. "What part of down does he not get?"

Gus opened the fridge, pulled out a hot dog, and gave a single whistle. Wreck leaped off the counter, skidded to a stop at Gus's feet, and sat unmoving, his eyes glued to the hot dog.

"Good boy." Gus ruffled the dog's ears and gave him the treat. Which Wreck inhaled in a single breath. Then looked up for more. When he realized there was no more coming, he plopped down on the tile, head on paws, one eye open—just in case.

"You just rewarded him for eating my cake. On the counter."

"He got down, didn't he?"

"He's not sleeping with me," Tanner said, even though he knew Wreck would end up in his bed. Had happened every night that week. "And you still didn't tell me where you were tonight."

Gus crossed his arms. "And here I thought I was moving in with my son, not my ex-wife."

Tanner looked up at the ceiling. "Just tell me you weren't driving."

Gus made a big deal of pulling his pockets inside out. No key. Thank God. "You done nagging? Good. I'm tired."

Tired didn't even touch what Tanner was. He was in desperate need of a cold beer, a hot shower, and an even hotter Abby—wearing nothing but his sheets. Since Abby was in her own sheets, most likely passed out from spending an entire day trying to locate those papers Babs couldn't seem to find, he'd have to settle on a beer and shower.

Gus headed toward the door, his cane tapping the tile angrily. Tanner opened the fridge to grab a beer he no longer wanted, then dropped his head against the top shelf. "You want a beer, Dad?"

Gus stopped in the threshold, looked at the beer, then at Tanner. For a brief moment, Tanner could have sworn his dad's eyes went a little misty. "Sure. But I don't want any of your micro-crap. There's some Bud on the bottom shelf I had Melvin bring me."

"If I knew you wanted Bud, I would have picked some up at the store," Tanner said, setting a Budweiser and a micro-crap on the counter.

"Been drinking Bud since before you were born," Gus said evenly. "It's all I drink."

Which Tanner should have remembered. A quick stab of guilt washed through him as he popped the can and slid it across the island, then pulled out a barstool. "Next time I go shopping I'll pick up a case for you."

"Make sure you tell me how much it is so I can reimburse you."

Tanner stopped midsip. "Dad, it's a case of beer. You don't—"

"How's our little designer doing? Did she find what she needed?"

Tanner allowed the deflection. "No. I called in a favor at the planning commission and they let Abby search their records. She was there all day and, as far as I know, found squat." Which was not good. "I can't believe Babs relayed some bullshit love story her husband told her as fact. Hell, for all we know he lied just to get her to agree to buy the property."

Gus froze, his face folding into a stern scowl. Tanner knew that scowl. Used to have nightmares about it. It was the one that said he'd disappointed his dad—yet again. "Son, don't you ever say that again. If Ms. Hampton heard you talk about her husband like that, it would break her heart."

Feeling all of twelve again, Tanner nodded. Which was ridiculous since he was a grown-ass man in his own grown-ass kitchen and that was his client he was talking about.

"Yeah, well, if Ferris walks, her broken heart will be the least of my concerns," Tanner mumbled, taking a pull from his beer. After swinging hammers in ninety-degree heat, the beer felt cool and refreshing and—Tanner took another sip and frowned—it also tasted like shit.

When the hell had he started drinking micro-crap?

"Why?" Gus asked, sipping on his Bud, and suddenly Tanner wanted to switch. "Because if the starched loafers walk, you'll have to actually put some real sweat into that property to make something of it?"

Here we go, Tanner thought, not even bothering to hide the fact his dad's words were like a solid one-two punch to the gut. "Are you saying you think I'm lazy?"

This was starting to sound like the same conversation they'd had a million times about every one of the million bad decisions Tanner had made in his lifetime. "Bad" decisions meaning they weren't the way Gus would have played it.

"No. I'm saying you work hard at things when they come easy to you."

"What the hell is that supposed to mean?" Tanner asked loudly enough to make Wreck whimper, fury and frustration lighting Tanner up. And fast. This was something he'd never heard, and it was complete bullshit.

Total and complete bullshit.

Playing ball and keeping solid grades in college was hard. The NFL was hard. Building a company from the ground up was hard. Almost as hard as hearing that his dad thought he lived his life by taking the easy way out.

"Is it?" Gus asked. "Name one thing that didn't fall into your lap that you went after?" When Tanner was quiet, thinking, Gus added, "Things come so naturally to you, you've never had to search far for the next thing. And if it doesn't seem easy, you just move on. You don't need Ferris to develop that land. You're just not interested in putting in the time to do it yourself."

Just like that, Tanner was done. Done with Colin's hissy fits, done with his dad's backhanded compliments, done working his ass off for a bunch of people who didn't seem to give a rat's ass about how hard he worked. Yup, he was done.

Done, done, done.

"You know what I'm not interested in?" Tanner said and pushed to his feet. "This conversation." And the headache starting behind his eyelids. "Thanks for the beer, Dad. Always a treat."

Sunday afternoon was hot and humid and yet there Abby stood, hunched over in the baking sun with grass stains on her cute pink sneakers and a thorn stuck in her little finger. A new shipment of rare orchids had been delivered to Petal Pushers earlier that morning, the equivalent of Christmas for the Garden Society, so Project Primrose was taking a holiday. Which gave Abby time to dispose of the ten dozen fresh-cut roses they'd placed around Richard's feet yesterday that were no match for the intense August heat.

Oddly enough, that wasn't even the worst part of her weekend. Abby had spent nearly every waking hour—and a few when she should have been sleeping—fantasizing and dreaming about finding the newspaper article that Babs had claimed to have seen. She'd also spent most of Friday and Saturday in the town's library and the basement of the planning department thumbing through old clippings and city records for proof that Randal Jackson Jr. and his secret lover had spent an entire summer in the carriage house. But many of the records dated before the turn of the century had been lost during the rebuilding of the west side of town hall after the 1906 earthquake. When she came up short, Abby had turned to the Internet for anything that could back up Babs's story and save Tanner's project with Ferris.

No such luck.

Which was how she found herself in the garden, once again trying to make sense of a situation that didn't make any sense at all.

"I've filed a complaint down at the sheriff's department." Nora crossed the lawn, gardening shears in one hand, cane in the other, and flowered apron and matching gardening gloves absolutely spotless even though Abby had heard her trimming the hedges over an hour ago. "I'm trying to get a court order that will require you to cover his man parts to protect his modesty and the virtues of women everywhere."

"Bring me the petition, I'll sign it," Abby mumbled around the thorn, which she'd finally managed to yank out with her teeth. She tossed it, and the bouquet of roses, in the garbage bag hanging from the man in question.

"Huh," Nora said, hand dug into her pudgy hips. "You aren't budging like I thought you would."

"No, Nora, I'm not budging." Abby picked up a lone potted orchid, a bead of perspiration trickling down her back, and tossed it in the bag. "I can't budge, seeing as my grandmother-in-law, who I never even knew I had, by the way, is coming from Italy to see her favorite grandson's final resting place. So I'm sorry if my embarrassing life mars your perfect view."

"Well, you don't need to get smart about it," Nora said, opening the garbage bag and digging out the orchid. "That's a perfectly good plant."

"The card says it's from Joyce Daniels. She worked for Richard," Abby said, feeling a little hysterical from lack of sleep and her rapidly depleting confidence. Everyone in town knew that "worked for Richard" meant "slept with Richard" when it came to young, pretty interns. "Where do you think I should put it? On my mantle?"

Nora looked at the flower and smoothed down her bun. "I've got a week's worth of doggie doo I've been meaning to return to that Stan O'Malley."

Stan O'Malley, the local mechanic and owner of Stan's Soup and Service Station, lived one street over and had a pack of bloodhounds who loved to welcome the morning on Nora's front lawn.

"I say you put the orchid in my collection and leave it on Joyce's porch." Nora slid Abby a rare smile. "I'll drive."

It was so unexpected, Abby couldn't keep a laugh from escaping. It was long and loud and didn't stop until her chest hurt and her eyes burned. "I'll think about it."

"You never told me his grandmother was coming," Nora said, picking up a handful of roses and tossing them in the bag.

"You never asked." The minute the words left her mouth, Abby realized what she'd said and paused. This one-sided thinking of hers was exactly what had landed Tanner into trouble with Ferris and Colin.

She took in Nora's sculpted shrubs, hand-painted eaves, and house-shaped mailbox that was a way-too-perfect replica of the real thing to be anything other than custom. Every house on the block had one—well, except Abby's. She'd torn down her mouse-occupied one when she'd moved in.

"I never asked why you wanted the statue moved so badly." She looked at Richard and sighed. "I mean besides the obvious."

Nora plucked a nonexistent speck of dirt from her apron. "When I was a girl I used to tinker with things—wood, metal, my dad's tractor. Built my own dollhouse and made my own dolls by hand. Thought I'd grow up and be something, leave my mark on the world, maybe be one of those Rosie the Riveters, but at that time women didn't travel the world unless they were a stewardesses, which are glorified housewives if you ask me, waiting on all those men in suits. I already had me a man in a suit, didn't need another one."

Nora waved a hand in disgust.

"Dalton Allan Reginald the Third, wasn't he a mistake? Married him when I was barely eighteen, and he moved me here to St.

Helena, a whole three thousand miles away from my family. Bought this big, dilapidated dump of a house because it had a library, instead of one of the cute family-ready bungalows closer to town. Said a man of stature needed a library." Nora made a sound that encompassed exactly what Abby thought of Richard's statue. "Said he married me to be a wife and a mother and run the kind of home worthy of the Reginald name, not tinker. So I became a wife and a mother, and I was damn good at both.

"Ten years it took me to get this house the way my husband wanted it, then less than a month later the son of a bitch up and died. Left me broke, with two kids to raise and this house to run."

When Nora turned to stand by Abby's side, she wasn't surprised to see a little moisture in the woman's eyes as she looked up at the three-story butter-yellow Victorian with lavender trim and a gleaming white door.

"So I ran it and I ran it well, and this house is my life's work. It's the one thing I can point to and say, 'That right there is sixty-one years of stubborn passion and love.' And next week, the Memory Lane Manor Walk will begin and thousands of people will come into my home and see what I built with these two hands. I may not have built a plane or a fancy villa in Italy, but I made this house into a home."

Something about the tone Nora's voice took on resonated with Abby. It was pride. Pride so deep it was difficult to talk about.

"Is it so bad I want it to look perfect?"

"No," Abby said quietly. "It's not." Then she cleared her throat and turned to face Nora. "Richard's grandmother arrives Friday. I promise you I will move the statue before Saturday's Memory Lane Manor Walk starts."

"Thank you." Nora gave Abby an awkward pat on the shoulder. "I'm not rescinding my complaint with the sheriff, though. In fact,

I hope he fines you, because then I can issue a GN fine as well. My eyes bleed every time I see him. It's like he's peeing on our beautiful street, marking his claim. And rules are rules, so if I make exceptions for you, people will start talking and the whole neighborhood will go to hell."

"Understood."

"Good, because I wanted to give you this, and I don't want any confusion about it being a bribe." Nora pulled an envelope out of her gardening apron. "This is because I'm a bigger person than you."

Not wanting to ruin this beautiful bonding moment with her neighbor, Abby opened the envelope. Inside was a newspaper clipping with the marriage announcement for Randal Jackson Jr. and Susette. Attached to it was an old, faded photo of them, standing in front of the carriage house—which was absolutely a residence. It had a little front porch and flower boxes filling the windows, and it was the evidence she needed to fix everything.

"I don't understand. Why would you sink me with the council then give me everything I need to prove your accusations wrong?"

"I'm giving you those because I know what it's like to lose everything and have to start over, and you've been working so hard on that cheese shop, I thought you had the right to know I didn't sink you."

"But the paper quoted you," Abby countered. "It was right there in black and white."

"I was merely repeating facts given to me from an extremely credible source."

"Credible?" Abby laughed and held up the envelope that was in direct conflict to that statement. "This says differently."

"I didn't discover the photos and article until after the interview. I went digging through the HPC archives when I began to wonder why the one person who had the most to lose would . . ." Nora dusted off her gardening gloves and stuck them in her apron before picking up a stuffed teddy bear someone had placed next to the statue. She plucked distractedly at the fur around its ear, and when she looked back up, her face of wrinkles was pursed with empathy. "Babs was my source. She told me that the carriage house being a residence was all hearsay."

"So you want to explain to me why you lied to Nora?" Tanner said to Babs the second he took a seat at his kitchen table, working hard to keep his anger in check.

"Oh dear," Babs said, her voice raw as she gripped the NINERS CAN SUCK IT coffee cup tighter. "I never meant for it to go this far. I never meant for anyone to get hurt."

"An hour ago I would have believed you," Tanner said, sitting back in his chair, because an hour ago he would have sworn his day couldn't get any shittier.

Not only was Colin still not talking to him, but Wreck had taken a dump in his work boots, then his dad had said Babs was in the kitchen and wanted to talk. Not to mention he hadn't seen Abby since Friday when she left to fix a problem that, turns out, wasn't her fault.

Not that it mattered anymore since Ferris called, which hadn't accomplished much more than cementing the fact Colin would never speak to him again. And, *ah, shit*, now Babs was crying. And Gus was glaring.

"She's trying to make this right, son," Gus said, resting his hand on Babs's frail one.

"I get that, and I appreciate that. But bottom line, people got hurt." He looked from Gus to Babs and, tears or not, he wasn't letting up. "This town thinks Tanner Construction participated in submitting falsified paperwork to a county-run board, Ferris is no longer considering Oakwood as a viable option, which means my partner is most likely going to quit, and Abby—"

God, Abby. His heart broke just thinking how she was going to take the news. "The most amazing woman I've ever known is going to face the same kind of ridicule she did when her husband walked out, and all because she was trying to make your shop amazing. So please, tell me where you saw this going."

Babs blanched, her tired and red-rimmed eyes going wide on her face. "I have messed everything up, haven't I?" She shook her head a little, and even her apricot halo seemed older, sadder. "I only meant to stall, to buy more time, so I told Nora that I didn't know if the documents existed, but Ferris might know and she should call him."

"Babs wanted to give Ferris a reason to come home," Gus interjected gently.

"That house is just so big, and at night when I sit down to dinner and I see all the empty seats . . ." she faded off and stirred her coffee for the fifth time in so many minutes.

"Ferris is a busy man. He would have made his father proud," Gus said, and Tanner wanted to ask him how a son did that, because obviously this prick who didn't visit his mom and wore loafers was doing something Tanner wasn't.

"I didn't want to call him and waste his time with nonsense," Babs said.

"Of course you didn't," Gus said in understanding, and Babs nodded. Suddenly, Tanner felt like the third wheel in his own kitchen.

"So I . . . I made reasons to call him. Found questions to ask him, and hoped if he heard enough little questions, easy things he could help me with, he'd come home and we could work on this together."

And then she wouldn't have to ask, Tanner thought sadly.

"I didn't want to be a burden," Babs whispered, and her tone just about did Tanner in.

He had been floored when Ferris called, saying he was going in a different direction—one that didn't involve two hundred acres in the hills above St. Helena. But when Babs had shown up, admitting to being Nora's big source, Tanner had lost it. He'd been so angry he'd had to take a walk to calm down, which only gave him time to think about how Colin was going to take the news—how Abby was going react—which only made him angrier.

Only now, listening to Babs talk about her screw-up of a son and watching her try not to cry, Tanner softened a little.

"But the little things weren't working," she went on. "He'd just send me e-mails with the answers, then when it became just the name of a contractor to call, I got desperate and did a lot of things I'm not proud of," she admitted. "But Ferris is just like his dad—impatient and hates waste. So I knew if the project went on long enough he would come back and take it over. Then Abby came on board with her sunny we-can attitude and got you, and then things started happening. Ferris stopped returning my calls and e-mails altogether. So I lied to Nora and she took it to the council."

"Ah, shit," Tanner said, gripping the back of his neck.

"Watch your Ps and Qs," Gus scolded, and Tanner resisted pointing out there wasn't a single P or Q in his statement, just like he didn't bother with the fact Gus swore like a sailor. Most of Tanner's four-letter vocabulary came straight from swinging hammers with his old man as a kid. His old man who—hold up? Did he just put his arm around Babs Hampton?

He did and Tanner couldn't believe it. His dad was actually courting their client. It was obvious from the way the two were acting that they were more than familiar. Just how familiar, Tanner had no desire to find out.

He did, however, shoot Gus a look, which Gus ignored because he was too busy whispering to Babs. Man, this project was turning out to be some awful nightmare that kept getting worse and worse.

Tanner cleared his throat. "Babs, do you realize lying to a county-regulated board not only made us all look bad, but also jeopardizes any future project that has Tanner Construction, Abby Designs, or Hampton Group on the paperwork? They could be up for additional scrutiny."

"I know," she said and the first tear fell, and didn't that make him feel like a class-A jerk. "I just don't know what to do anymore."

"Well, first you and I are going to the HPC and explaining everything."

"Everything?" Babs went completely pale, and Tanner felt for her. Standing in front of her peers and neighbors and explaining she lied because she was lonely was going to be hard—and awful. But not as awful as it would be if the project sank like the *Titanic*.

"It's the only way to get the bottlery reinstated as a finalist and have the newspaper retract their article," Gus said, then gave her hand a little squeeze. "And if you want, I will stand right by your side."

"Ferris is going to be so upset, and the last thing I want to be is a burden," she said to Gus, and Tanner was sensing a pattern. A pattern that hit him in the stomach like a fist when his dad said, "I know, honey. I know."

Because, holy shit! Is that what his dad felt like? A burden?

Sure, they'd had some growing pains being new roommates, and Tanner joked daily about burning his dad's chair and finding a new home for Wreck, but he'd never really do it. He kind of liked the chair. It reminded Tanner of being a kid sitting in his dad's lap while they watched the game. And Wreck wasn't so bad when he wasn't inhaling Tanner's underwear and messing in the house. Hell, Tanner was even starting to like eating on the couch.

And okay yeah, he was a little preachy about diet and physical therapy, but only because he wanted his dad to get better—

So he could move out, Tanner thought.

Jesus, he was as bad as Ferris. So what if his dad drove him nuts and gave him shit for his life choices? That's what dads did. They wanted their kids to grow up and make something of themselves and—Tanner looked at Gus, looked at his hunched shoulders and work-roughened hands, and how old he seemed, and felt his throat tighten.

His dad had swung hammers nearly every day for the past fifty years. And he was tired and lonely—and he wanted more for his son.

He pushed because he cared.

"My dad is right," Tanner said past the shame in his chest. "The best thing to do is get reinstated as a finalist so we don't lose any time off the schedule. We're still on course to get the shop ready in time for the Memory Lane Manor Walk inspection."

Babs looked shocked, then her face crumbled. "You're still going to help me?"

"Yes ma'am."

"Why?"

Because today I'm not going to let down another person in my life. Because for all the times it got hard and I should have been there for Abby, this is the time I'm going to follow through.

"Because that's the job you hired me to do. And because my father raised me to push through to the very end." He looked at Gus and smiled. "He didn't raise me to be the idiot I've been lately, but he did raise me to be a man of my word. Plus, I think we can win."

CHAPTER 16

Abby pulled the plastic covering off the barstool and ran her finger along the new leather.

It was perfect. The distressed dark wood of the legs and seat back were the perfect contrast to the rich, buttery seat cushion. They were elegant enough to catch the eye, make a statement, but comfortable enough to order a bottle of wine and a cheese platter and stay awhile. And they looked amazing next to the new steel countertops.

But even that didn't lighten her mood.

Abby took the envelope Nora had given her and poured the contents out on the counter and tried to figure out why Babs would lie. The only reason she could think of was to set Abby up.

A deep sense of sadness washed over her at the thought. It had taken two hours to come up with a plan and three seconds to realize she was stuck. If she went to the board with her proof, everyone would know Babs had lied. If she didn't, Abby would forever be Richard's dishonest wife. And until she had answers to why Babs had lied, Abby didn't feel comfortable ratting her out.

No one had bothered to ask Abby her side, and she'd had a good reason for waiting to report the missing money. She hadn't known it was missing. She was so busy trying to figure out what she'd done wrong in her marriage, the last thing she'd thought to do was check their bank account.

"Is this seat taken?"

Abby didn't have to turn around to see who was behind her. Her body was giving her clear signals of who that sexy voice belonged to.

"I only got one out," she said, looking at the mile-long bar, which was obviously lacking barstools. "The rest are still in the back room covered in shipping plastic."

"I don't mind sharing," he said and, before she could protest, slid his arms under to effortlessly pick her up and, after stealing her seat, plop her down on his lap.

Her legs dangled off to the side, and he wrapped his arms around her until she rested her cheek against his chest. He was so big, his body practically swallowed hers whole.

She smoothed down the skirt of her dress and he smiled. "Pretty."

He looked damn good too. Not pretty. Tanner could never look pretty. He was rugged, wearing a day's worth of stubble, and smelled too much like sawdust and sex to ever be considered pretty. Not that she had any complaints. Not a one. She didn't want pretty in a man. She wanted Tanner—big, scruffy, and incredibly sweet.

"What are you doing here?" she asked.

"Looking for you."

Abby had come here to be alone, to think. Now that she was here, she realized she was tired of being alone. She'd spent the past seven years alone and it felt really great to be a part of a "we" again.

"Babs was Nora's source," Abby admitted softly. "She lied to the council to—well, I don't know why, but I have proof the carriage house was a residence and that she," Abby swallowed, "lied."

Tanner searched her face and his concern was so genuine she busied herself with the contents of the envelope so she wouldn't cry.

"I see." His arms came around her as he moved the photo and news clippings to read them. "And yet you have the proof and not the council?"

She nodded and released a breath. Sinking back against his chest, she stared at the new countertops and decided Tanner had a really comfy chest—reassuring and warm. Just what she needed tonight.

"I wanted to talk to Babs before I did that. Ask her why she did it. Get her side of things first before I go pointing fingers." She tilted her head up. He was looking right at her. "Only, I don't know if I can face her yet without yelling or crying."

She would also rather leave the state than start a confrontation with someone who sounded like Mrs. Claus. But she would have to, and soon. Abby had to know why Babs had set her up to fail. She had to set things right for Tanner.

"How did it go with Ferris?" she asked. "Did you smooth things over?"

Tanner didn't say a word. He didn't have to. The frustration and disappointment was right there in his eyes. "Tanner. I am so sorry. How bad is it?"

"He's going with the Santa Barbara property."

"What?" She sat up. "Oh my God."

She didn't know what she expected him to say. Maybe that Ferris needed more time or he was going to micromanage the project, but not that Tanner had lost out. Totally and completely. And all because of her.

"Is there a way to change his mind? I mean, if it would help, I could call him, explain I messed up but now we have the information we need."

Tanner shook his head. "He signed on the other property this morning. It's a done deal. We're out of the running."

She cupped his face. "Sorry doesn't even begin to convey how badly I feel. But I am so sorry, Jack." He turned his head and kissed the inside of her wrist. "How did Colin take it?"

His whole frame fell a little. "Not good. He lost it, and like Colin does, got all dramatic. It didn't end with beer and watching ball. Not that I blame him. He worked his ass off for this project for over a year. It should have been a slam dunk."

Tanner froze as though surprised at what he'd said.

"Jesus." He choked out a bitter laugh, pressing his hand to his forehead. "Did you hear that? It should have been a slam dunk because Colin worked his ass off."

"You've worked hard on that property too."

One of his gorgeous but troubled blue eyes speared her through the slits of his fingers. "Unless you call dropping a wad of cash on the table and signing on the dotted line work, then nope, this whole project was Colin."

"A project that would have never happened if you didn't buy the land." When he didn't move, except to snort, she removed his hand, placed a kiss in the middle of it, then wrapped it around her. "All right, then what work would you have done?"

"Abby," he said on a tired breath.

"Humor me."

Tanner gave her a long-winded sigh but played along, making it clear it was solely for her benefit. "For starters, I could have at least shown up to more of the meetings with Ferris. Shown him how dedicated I was to the project. Taken a bigger interest in what he had planned for . . . what? Why are you giving me that look?"

"Because I don't care what Ferris wants," she explained. "I meant, what would you have done with the land? If there was no Ferris, what would you have done?"

He blinked as though no one had ever asked him that question. Actually, he looked so lost she wondered if he'd ever asked himself. And suddenly, Abby was starting to understand part of Tanner's problem.

"You said you'd put your house on the eighteenth hole, which I think is a perfect idea." She leaned up and snagged a little kiss when he smiled at her compliment. "So where would you put the eighteenth hole?"

"At the highest point on the bluff. I talked to one of my golf buddies about it a few years back." When he mentioned the golf buddy in question, it was a three-time Master's champion. "He said it would add a level of difficulty to the course that locals would have to go all the way to Pebble Beach to match. Plus, a little flag in the hole would flow with the land a hell of a lot better than some big Tuscan-style clubhouse."

She blinked up at him. "I thought you liked Tuscan style. Isn't that why you chose it for your house?"

"No," he said as though she'd asked him to hand over his man card. "When people move to the Napa Valley, they want Tuscan, so I chose Tuscan."

Abby tried really hard to hide her smile, but it was impossible since his answer made her beyond happy. "Tuscan bad, got it. Then what style would you choose? I mean if you were building a house for yourself and not taking into account resale value."

"I don't know. Craftsman, maybe." His fingers played absently with her hair, slid through the strands and down her spine, only to start over when they reached the small of her back. "I like indoor-outdoor living that works with the land, blends. Which is why I always thought it was crazy that Ferris wanted to drop three hundred homes on that land. That land is the highlight, not some cookie-cutter McMansion."

"I agree," she said, loving how excited he was getting. Tanner had thought a lot about this property. He knew exactly what he wanted it to look like, feel like. "When I saw the land, I pictured more of a Pebble Beach feel, with fewer homes on larger plots, meshing with the course and environment."

He looked down at her, and the smile he gave warmed her entire body.

"Have you ever considered Tanner Construction heading up the entire project?" she ventured cautiously. "No Ferris, no outside boss, just you and Colin developing the course the way you imagined."

He chuckled as though he thought she was cute. "I have money, darling, but not that kind of money."

"Then take out a loan, *darling*," she said, and his smile faded. "If you cut down the homes to fifty high-end ones, you're talking what, two hundred million, give or take?"

"Give or take," he said, but he was sitting straighter, no longer amused by her cuteness.

"Go out and talk to a few private equity people. I guarantee they will want in. Plus, with the kind of people you know, all it would take is a few of your football buddies or that golf friend you just mentioned to buy a parcel for you to build out, and before you know it you will have sold the houses even before they're built."

"Do you have any idea how many moving parts there are to this kind of project?" he asked, but she could tell he was thinking about it. He was thinking hard and he was getting excited. Not to mention a little scared, which made her want to hug him. "I have no idea how to even go about running a project like this."

She had no doubt it would be hard, but she also had no doubt Tanner could pull it off.

"Then do your research and find the best people for the jobs you aren't sure about. Ferris doesn't run the entire project. He hires people to do what he can't."

Tanner sat back and looked her dead in the eye. "You really think I can do this?"

"I have no doubt. As far as I'm concerned, there isn't much you can't do," she whispered, running her hands over his shoulders and down his chest. "I look around this shop and take in everything you've done, all the hard work, and God, Jack, just look at the beautiful brick walls and the counters. I don't know what to say . . . I am blown away and so in love with . . ." *You.* "It. I am so in love with it."

Abby's chest burned and her stomach clinched because she had almost ended that sentence with *you*. She wanted to end that sentence with *you*.

She looked into his eyes, saw a hint of vulnerability, as though her belief in him meant the world, and Abby felt everything inside of her shift. Reaching out toward him, desperate to be a part of him, to show him what an amazing and capable man he was, she knew she was in serious trouble. This wasn't some silly attraction or hormones talking. Her heart was involved and she wasn't sure how she felt about that.

Tanner had obliterated her heart, world, soul—take your pick. He'd broken her so badly she'd married a man she didn't love to stop the ache.

But the serious and vulnerable man who sat in front of her now was nowhere near the same cocky, see-where-it-falls guy he'd been back in school. Just like she wasn't the same desperate and lost girl.

None of that meant, though, that he was ready to give her what her heart needed. So she took a mental step back, shifting gears to something she could handle. Funny, charming Tanner didn't make her want to hand over her soul. Funny, charming Tanner they both knew how to deal with.

"I am so in love with it that I have been seriously considering promoting you from sidekick to bona fide superhero."

"Superhero, huh?" He ran a hand over his jaw, erasing every ounce of vulnerability and replacing it with swagger. Panty-melting swagger. "I don't know how I feel about wearing leggings. They make my butt look big."

Speaking of butts, that was where his hand was firmly planted. The other was on her thigh, moving right up and under her dress.

"Just your butt, huh?" Abby asked.

He never answered her question. He was too busy kissing her silly, too busy moving his hand higher and higher until she felt a tug on the zipper of her dress, then it was smooth sailing—exposing the entirety of her back.

"You know what I love about these counters?" he asked, taking her mouth in another searing kiss. When they came up for air, her dress was like a Hula-Hoop around her waist, his jeans were pressed against her inner thighs, including all the space in between, and the cool steel of the countertop was under her butt. "How sturdy they are."

Abby bounced, giving a little test of her own, and Tanner's hand went right to her chest. His smile said her decision to go braless received a solid two thumbs up.

"I can't wear a bra with this dress," she explained with a smile. "The straps show."

"Remind me to write to the designer personally and thank them from the bottom of my heart. Then order you one in every color they make."

She gave the counters a mischievous little pat. "Now, about this sturdiness you claim. Am I going to get the full demonstration?"

"Darling, you're going to get all the bells and whistles."

"How about we start with a kiss?" she said, running her hands through his hair. She loved his hair. Thick and soft and a little too long to be considered a style.

"Thought you'd never ask." His voice had a low rasp that ignited a hum of anticipation under her skin, because he wasn't looking at her mouth. Nope, Tanner was looking at the barely-there red thong he'd exposed by yanking her dress up and over and buh-bye.

Abby watched breathlessly as he lowered his head to brush his mouth along the inside of her thigh, sliding ever so slowly up to the lower edge of her panties, where he gave a sexy tug with his teeth that had her shaking with want.

But he didn't give in to her want. Tanner, the ultimate tease, made her wait, skipping right over the best part in the middle, to kiss down her other leg. And, because Tanner was never one to be rushed, he pulled up the barstool, settling in for the long haul on the return.

By his third pass Abby's body was on fire, so desperate for friction that when he came back up, she shifted her hips slightly, trying to line up his mouth with where she craved him most. He chuckled, instead placing an openmouthed kiss right below her belly button.

Then one lower.

And another even lower.

"Lay back," he ordered, scooting her forward until she was teetering on the edge of the counter and she could feel his breath against her core. His gaze met hers through his thick lashes and he smiled—with so much wicked promise her mouth went dry. "Or watch."

He gently took her ankle and lifted it to kiss the little freckle on the top of her foot. "Your call."

Another kiss. This time right below her knee. Then he placed her foot on the arm of the barstool, locking the heel of her shoe against the inner rim, and gave her a little squeeze, telling her to leave it there. As if she could even move when those intense blue eyes of his were locked on her like she was the sexiest thing he'd ever seen.

"Although I must admit, I've had a reoccurring fantasy about doing just this." He lifted her other foot, caressing and securing it the same way. "While you watch my every—move."

And moves he had. Starting at her calves, he trailed his fingers all the way up, caressing and touching every inch of skin with purpose until settling on her inner thigh. Slowly pressing them farther, he forced her to rest back on her palms to keep her balance. Then he dropped an oh-so-thorough kiss right to the center of her silk.

Abby gasped, but she didn't look away. And he let loose a smile that curled her toes.

"I take it my biggest fantasy is going to come true?" he said.

He didn't wait for her to answer, instead gently tugging her panties aside, watching her watch him, and Abby felt her stomach tremble with anticipation, and if the fate of the world depended on her looking away, she decided they'd all die. Because without breaking eye contact, Tanner slid his soft tongue all the way up her center.

Abby fought the urge to arch her back, fought the urge to scream, not wanting to miss a single second of what was about to happen. And she was rewarded, because the next pass he used his teeth, and finally his entire mouth, taking his time to drive her right to the edge and keep her there.

Then, well, she wasn't sure what happened, but she must have closed her eyes at some point because suddenly her panties were gone and she was flat on her back.

There was something incredibly erotic and empowering about being completely naked and laid out for his viewing pleasure. And he took a few moments to appreciate before he went back to her pleasure, keeping the pace slow, purposeful, taking her higher and higher without rushing her. But there was something genuine, reverent about the way he held her hip, the way his thumb slid back and forth over her stomach, offering her comfort and connection.

"Bells and whistles," she moaned, starting to understand. Because every bell and whistle she owned was ringing and sighing all at once. Then he pressed his tongue flat against her bundle of nerves and slid a finger in and she felt it. It started deep in her belly, pushing up and out until she flew apart.

When Abby was finally able to open her eyes, she found herself smiling up at Tanner, who leaned over her, a forearm on either side of her head. His biceps were taut and flexed as he held himself above her, and a condom sat on the counter within her peripheral view.

The way he looked at her, gently brushing her cheek with his lips, as though she were precious. Abby had never expected to fall again—ever—but the warm ache that had taken up residence in her heart told her that she had. Completely.

Without asking what he had in mind next, she slid his shirt up and off, and she couldn't help but give a little sigh of appreciation as she ran her hands down his chest to divest him of his belt.

He raised a brow and she matched the challenge with a flick of the fingers, unbuttoning his jeans. Then went the zipper. And right as her greedy fingers disappeared inside his briefs, he rose in one fluid motion with her in his arms and settled her on his lap. Only this time she was straddling him, the hard ridge of him pressing deliciously against her sensitive flesh. "Much more of that and we won't be able to test out the barstool."

"Oh?" She reached between them and gave a little stroke. He bucked into her hand.

"You want to test out the chair or not?" He leaned back, arms folded behind his head, content to let her keep going. "Because, darling, much more of that and it will be over before we even get to the touchdown dance."

Her hand slowed. "There's a dance?"

He cocked a single, sexy brow. "For what I have in mind? Oh yeah."

"Then have you decided yet?" She rose up and pulled his boxers down, freeing him. "Which half you want first?"

Tanner opened his mouth to say something light and flirty—she saw it in his eyes. Only nothing came out. He tried again but his smile faltered. He faltered. And all of the distance that was Jack Tanner disappeared, and with it that easygoing charm faded into something deeper—something real. Something that gave her hope.

"That's always been the problem, Abby," he finally whispered a good minute later. He was cradling her face in his hands and staring at her as though everything had changed for him. As though in that moment he finally allowed himself to feel the same intensity and connection she always had. "I can't choose, and that scares the shit out of me. Because with you, I want the whole fucking package."

"Then don't choose."

He whispered her name right as he took her mouth and never let go. Not as he rolled on the condom, not even as he lifted her up to gently slide home. And Abby's heart caught because that was what it truly felt like this time, finally coming home.

"You drive me . . ." he said.

"Crazy," she said between kisses. "I know."

He pulled free from her mouth. "But this thing between us. It's . . ."

"Crazy," she repeated, but he just stared, searching her gaze . . . for what, she didn't know. But she knew it was important, so she let him see everything he did to her, everything he meant to her.

"Abby," he said, sounding a little lost and whole lot off balance.

She couldn't help herself. She took his face in her hands, letting her fingers slide against the smooth warmth of his skin. "It's okay Jack, I feel it too."

She felt a lot of things. With him, she felt everything.

"Thank God." His arms came around her, tight and unyielding, plastering her to him, and he was kissing her. Hard and all-consuming and she felt him let go. Actually felt the moment Jack Tanner went all-in.

It was crazy. And it was incredible—how could it not be? The man was a Kissing Hall of Famer. But it was also breathtaking and raw and so beautifully different.

Tanner kissed her as though she was his, held her as though he would never let go, as though he would never *want* to let go. And Abby allowed herself to believe, believe in them.

Suddenly, all of their history disappeared, and the trust that had been torn from her came rushing back, leaving just her and Tanner. In the now. With a clean slate and a chance at a future.

And there was nothing for Abby left to do but fall.

She fell even further as he whispered her name over, sliding one palm up her side, covering her breast. His other hand pulled her toward him, until she felt so full, so complete, there was nowhere he wasn't touching.

"Every damn time, you turn me inside out," he said, moving inside of her, and the intensity behind his words, the sincerity in his expression was her undoing. She felt all the emotion spiral in her body and tighten, then a flash of intense heat gripped her.

"Every. Damn. Time," he said, lifting her up, and for several long seconds, time seemed to hang, frozen between them, then he pushed up into her as he guided her down, and the sensation was beyond anything she'd ever felt. The connection, the intensity, the way they fit so perfectly together washed over her.

All at once everything coiled and let go in one glorious rush and Abby screamed. Thank God it was just his name, because *I love you* was threatening to come, so she clenched her teeth, trapping it inside as he exploded into her until it triggered another wave.

And what seemed like an hour later, or at least enough time to realize there was no coming back from this—that Tanner owned every part of her—she heard him whisper, "Every fucking time, Abby."

And please, God please, let that be the truth. Because Abby knew that if he walked away, she'd never see her heart again.

CHAPTER 17

You busy?"

Tanner gave one last look through the pass-through of the prep area at Abby, who, wearing a pair of fantasy-inspiring cutoffs, was in the main warehouse on a ladder, showing Gus where she wanted the paintings hung. Tanner knew those shorts well. Had been staring at them all day while she flitted around and rearranged the tables. And every time she decided to bend over or rise up on her toes to point something out, the hem rose right with her and went that much further to ensuring a great day. Which, based on who was behind him, he'd need a few more bends to keep his mood up.

"According to your definition of busy, no, I'm not," Tanner said, turning to face Colin.

"I deserve that." Colin walked farther into the prep area and rested a hip against the prep island.

Tanner felt his body relax and he hopped up to sit on the counter. He gestured for Colin to do the same on the island. Hell, they hadn't spoken more than three words to each other since Tanner relayed Ferris's message, and those three words had been "Fucking knew it." So he didn't want this conversation to end in an argument.

"Nah, it's been a crappy few weeks," Tanner said, and Colin smiled. It was weak, but a smile all the same.

Colin scanned the prep area then peered through the pass-through window and let out a low whistle. "It looks like you're really going to get this done."

"By Thursday afternoon," Tanner said, and couldn't help but smile. If all went smoothly today, they were on course to finish a whole day early. The *Titanic* of foodie shops, the project everyone said would be an epic failure, was going to come in on time and under budget, thanks in large part to Abby.

"It looks—"

"Fantastic?"

Colin laughed. "Yeah. That."

"All Abby. Every inch of it." Tanner watched her through the pass-through window holding over her head a piece of art made out of old wine bottles that was big as she was—and he smiled. She was talented and dedicated and damn beautiful, and even though he knew he was staring, he couldn't seem to look away.

"Yeah, I know that too," Colin admitted. "And I know I really screwed up. And before you tell me it's okay, let me be clear that it's not."

Which worked for Tanner because, even though there were things Tanner wished he could have done differently, things he'd said he wished he could take back, there was no way in hell he'd ever say the way Colin treated Abby was okay.

"I thought about what you said, about my riding your coat-tails—"

"I was pissed. I didn't mean—"

Colin held up a hand. "Yeah, you did. But you're wrong. I came to terms a long time ago with the fact I wasn't Jack Tanner and I'd never have a Super Bowl ring. I even get that you own Oakwood, but *I* brought in Ferris." He placed his hand against his chest. "*I* brought in the initial seed money for the land surveys and got the planning commission on board when we didn't even have blueprints."

"I never, even once, thought you didn't work your ass off for this," Tanner admitted.

"We both did," Colin said, and maybe it was Gus messing with his head, but something about that comment felt off. "It would be great for the company and for both of us. But what I didn't realize until we'd lost it was just what it had represented for me. This was my Super Bowl, Tan. A game I have waited my whole life to play in, and I finally got my invitation. I was more than ready for the chance, and then it was gone, and it was like I was thrown back in the minors."

"I know, and I'm sorry it didn't work out." He was damn sorry. Colin was the kind of guy who worked behind the scenes making sure everything got handled, that everything ran smoothly, so Tanner could cruise in and do his job.

Problem was, Tanner was sorry his buddy lost out on something that could have been huge for him, but he couldn't seem to muster up any disappointment over losing Ferris. Abby was right—they didn't need Ferris to build out Oakwood.

The more Tanner thought about what she said, about developing it himself, the more excited he got about the idea. He wasn't talking about calling out the bulldozers tomorrow, but he was ready to start tossing some ideas around again, get back to the original concept of indoor-outdoor living and custom comfort, and maybe even see where Colin stood on the two of them making local history.

"That's what I wanted to talk to you about," Colin said, and Tanner didn't think his buddy was about to show him sketches of his thoughts. "Ferris called. He didn't pass because of the mix-up or even his mom."

That was good to know, and he couldn't wait to tell Abby. She'd been so distraught over her role in Ferris's decision. Not that it was her fault at all, but it was no use trying to tell her that.

"I guess another parcel came on the market," Colin went on, "giving the Santa Barbara property an unobstructed ocean view, and that was the deal-maker."

"Ferris was all about the view from the get-go."

"Yeah, but he wasn't impressed with the construction company the other guys used. So he offered us the build."

"What?"

Colin smiled. "He offered us the build, man. All of it. We get to do the homes, course, clubhouse, everything. And we get to watch what he does, learn firsthand how to take on a project that size. Plus, he handles all of the financial risk." Then to sweeten the deal, Colin threw out an outrageous figure Ferris was willing to pay.

Tanner let out a low whistle. "After deducting what I paid for the land, that's more than we would have made on Oakwood if we'd gone with him."

"I know," Colin said and released an audible breath. Tanner released one of his own. This was a lot to take in. It was exciting, challenging, and an ideal opportunity with nothing but the potential for upside. "Ferris suggested you running the build side of things and asked me to move over into creative and planning."

Which was exactly what Colin was amazing at. What he'd wanted to do since they were kids, but lacked the credentials because he'd never finished his civil engineering degree. But working under someone with Ferris's reputation would be all his friend would need to get under his belt. Then he could hire out the credentials to make his ideas sound.

Tanner hopped down and clapped Colin on the shoulder. "You did it."

Colin shook his head. "We both did. Ferris is still all bromanced out over the idea of working with the famous Hard Hammer Tanner."

"What kind of time frame is he looking at?" Tanner was already going through his mental lists of upcoming projects.

"He wants us down there as soon as possible to be involved in every step. I told him we have the DeLuca wine cave starting next week and we have to finish up that first, which by the way the slab was poured and the portable office will be up and running next week, just in time for you to come in and make it happen."

Colin kept going, but Tanner suddenly had a hard time keeping up. His heart lodged itself in his throat, somewhere between hearing the word DeLuca and the realization they'd be moving to Santa Barbara. This project offered everything he and his company needed.

Except for Abby.

Because like it or not—and he definitely liked it—Abby DeLuca was no longer a want of his . . . she was a need.

The sun was setting when Tanner strolled up Abby's front porch for his scheduled Thursday night piano lesson. Between the Pungent Barrel project and dealing with the drama at home, it had been all miss and no hit the last few weeks when it came to his lessons. Something he should be excited about rectifying.

Except, there he stood, finally . . . *finally*, with an open invitation to Abby's bedroom. And the screwed-up part was, he was considering canceling. He'd faced down some pretty scary scenarios in his life, but this one was in its own league, and he wanted to make sure he'd thought everything through.

But before he could go over his game plan, the door opened and, *holy hell*, he couldn't mess this up. But that ache in his chest, matched with a heavy dose of guilt, had him thinking that was exactly what he was bound to do.

Abby looked up at him with those big, brown bedroom eyes that had first caught his attention back in high school. Only instead of wearing tennies, cutoffs, and a bouncy ponytail, she had on strappy heels, a soft cotton dress, and a mass of chocolate curls tumbling down her back. And she looked so happy to see him. Like he was the highlight of her day. Like he wasn't about to drop a bomb so big on her it could ruin everything they'd started.

"Hey," she said shyly, and man, he had it bad. Abby was the perfect combination of sexy and girl next door, and if he looked hard enough, he could see the little spark of naughty twinkling in her eyes. But tonight there was something else—uncertainty. And out of nowhere he felt the weight of his earlier decision crush in on him. "I was starting to think you wouldn't make it."

He looked at his watch. *Shit.* He was an hour late for his lesson. "I was waiting for the guys to finish hanging the last chandelier and I lost track of time." He'd also been waiting on Ferris for two days to e-mail a deal memo to see if it was really as great a deal as Colin had sold it. Just his luck, it was better. "They weighed a ton."

"But it's done."

"It's done." He smiled, but even that hurt. "The guys will need to do some last-minute touch up in the morning, no more than an hour. Trey finished stocking the racks with enough Ryo and DeLuca wine to satisfy the entire NFL and . . ." What else could he possibly recap to stall? "Oh, Lexi wanted me to tell you the flowers for tomorrow night arrived and they are in her refrigerator. She'll bring them tomorrow when she helps set up."

"We're going to pull this off," she said, her voice giddy.

"Abs. We're going to win." And he had never wanted to kiss her so badly in his life. But if he did that, he'd peel her out of that dress and they wouldn't come up for air until next month. And he had things to say.

Her eyes went to his hand and she covered her mouth. "Oh my God, is that . . ." She snatched the sheet music in his hands and laughed. "The Imperial March?" She flipped it over and looked at the price tag on the back. "You must have bought this when you were a kid."

"I was ten and I bought it because Princess Leia looked hot on the cover." Abby laughed. "But after I got it, I wanted to learn how to play it." He'd tried teaching himself on the electric keyboard Colin's sister got for Christmas one year, but he couldn't figure out what note went with what key. "My mom used to play."

"I didn't know that."

"She was my first teacher. We never got to this piece, before"—*Jesus, did his throat just catch?*—"she left."

"Then this lesson is long past due," she said gently, and before he could shrug it off and pretend it didn't matter, she laced her fingers with his and led him inside. He had the strangest feeling that if he played things right, she wouldn't be opposed to leading him around forever.

Even stranger, that didn't completely freak him out.

Eyes on the sheet music, she sat down at the piano and crossed the finest pair of legs he'd ever seen. A pair of legs that, as of late, had spent a significant amount of time wrapped around his waist. And yeah, he was focusing on those because it was easier than acknowledging the big ball of emotions pressing on his chest like pissed-off linebackers.

"Have a seat." She patted the bench next to her. "It looks like we're going to be working on The Imperial March, a grade *four* piece."

He did as she asked, scooting much closer than appropriate. She didn't complain, so he stayed put. "What happened to my being a grade three?"

She placed her long, lean fingers on the keys and slid him a look that had that ball in his chest tightening. "I figure between the extra lessons and your practicing more," she waggled a brow, "we'll get you there in time for the next recital."

Her fingers flew over the keys, sexy and confident, as she played the song for him. His song. The song he'd wanted to learn and show his mom in case she ever decided to come back, and suddenly he couldn't do it. He couldn't sit there next to Abby on that too-small piano bench and pretend for another second everything wasn't about to change.

In about six months, he was going to load up his truck and head south. He had no idea what that meant for them, but he was determined to make this work.

"Abby, before we start the lesson, there is something I have to tell you." He took a deep breath. Then another. And, Jesus, this was hard. He would put himself out there, lay it on the line, and he had no idea how she'd respond.

She took his hand and he damn near embarrassed himself.

"I saw you talking to Colin the other day," she said, and because he needed a moment to gather his thoughts, he let her talk. "And based on the way you guys were glaring at each other, it didn't go well."

Wrong. It went fantastic. But she was back to talking, rambling, actually.

"I wasn't going to give you this until after tomorrow night, until after the Memory Lane Manor Walk winner was announced and we were alone, but," she looked behind her, gave an uncertain huff, then patted his hand, "stay here."

She disappeared into her office, which gave him a whole three seconds to get a fucking grip, but when she reemerged with a set of rolled-up designs tied with a big blue bow and a smile so wide, he didn't have the heart to interrupt her. Only she rolled out the designs on top of her baby grand and his whole chest crashed to the floor, taking his stomach with it.

It was Oakwood. Not Ferris's Oakwood, but Tanner's. She had taken everything he'd said, listened to every one of his ideas, and brought them to life. For him.

"Abby," he said, not sure what to say next, not sure he could even talk past the lump in his throat.

"They're just preliminary sketches. And there isn't anything that can't be changed or altered, or if you hate them we could even start over."

"I don't want to start over, which is why I need to—"

"And I didn't mean *we* as though I was expecting you to ask me to work with you on this." She waved a hand and he could see she was shaking. "I'm not expecting that at all, and I would never assume I'd be hired as the . . . all I'm trying to say is if you don't like it, that's okay because it's nothing fancy, just something I threw together."

Threw together his ass. He flipped the top sheet over and studied the designs. The pages and pages of designs. She had drawn sketches of the country club, of how to organically integrate the houses into the landscape, even a few samples of the kinds of homes he could build.

He got to the last page and looked up. "This is my lot."

She nodded stiffly and her smile looked so fragile he was afraid with one wrong word she would break. "And you don't have to tell me I'm not an architect and nowhere near qualified to say if this is even doable but—"

He would never say that, but someone obviously had. And he knew who.

"—I just wanted to give you a taste, let you see what your ideas looked like on paper. I went with a hunting lodge kind of feel, very masculine with some feminine curves to soften it, and easy flow of indoor to out." She reached over and pointed to the back elevation of the house. "Of course, a big porch that wraps around the entire back of the house so you can watch the storms blow in is a given. And if you look here—"

But he was too busy looking at her. "How long did this take you?"

Her face flushed and she shrugged as though it was no big deal. But it was a big deal. To him it was huge. "I've been working on it on and off since Sunday night." Based on the details and accuracy of the designs, she'd not only put in a good chunk of research at the planning department, but she'd spent some serious time putting this all together. Time he had no idea where she found, since she'd been pulling sixteen-hour days at the Pungent Barrel by his side, hauling tables, painting bathrooms, getting dirty when needed.

He watched her watching him and everything inside of him stilled. Abby wasn't hiding anything, she was looking at him with her heart in her eyes, every insecurity she owned right there for him to see. And what he saw made breathing impossible.

She was offering a sincere gesture of friendship and love. A gesture he wasn't sure he deserved. Because while he'd been keeping Ferris's offer close to his chest, waiting to figure out the best scenario that ended with Abby in his life, she'd been pouring everything into these sketches.

"Abby, about Oakwood, I uh—"

Her face fell, then went absolutely pale and she took a step back. "You hate them." She swallowed and forced a smile. "Which is okay, I mean, like I said, I was just throwing some ideas on paper to—"

He pulled her to him and kissed her because she was breaking his heart. Or maybe that was his heart breaking.

"I love them," he whispered against her lips.

She pulled back and damn, those eyes went straight through to his heart. "I love *you*, Jack."

And there it was. The one thing he'd been waiting forever to hear and was terrified of knowing. Out there between them, and Tanner felt his chest fill until it was too tight to breathe, let alone speak.

Abby loved him. The girl he'd been waiting most of his life to be seen by finally saw him. Not his money or his ring or the person he put out there for the world to notice. Nope, she saw him, flaws and all, and she loved him anyway. It was right there in her eyes. Maybe it always had been and he'd just been too stupid and scared to acknowledge it.

"I'm moving to Santa Barbara," he said.

She stepped back as though he'd just punched her right through the chest and ripped her heart out.

"Wait, that came out wrong, I'm just nervous because . . ." When her lower lip began to tremble he blurted out, "but I have a plan. To make this work."

Her face softened and her smile trembled, but it was the good kind of tremble. The kind that told him he got this right. "You want me to move to Santa Barbara with you?"

"What? No. I want to live here, in St. Helena." She looked as confused as he felt. "Ferris called and offered us the chance to build out the other property, which means I'll be living in Santa Barbara during the week. But I checked and it is only a six-hour drive, which means if I take off early on Fridays I could make it home in time to take you to dinner."

"So you're moving to Santa Barbara and you want to come back to St. Helena on the weekends?"

"Yeah." But she didn't seem to be as excited as he'd expected. In fact, she looked close to tears—and not the good kind. Maybe it was the bad delivery or that she'd shocked him with the whole *I love you* and he was reading this all wrong.

When she still wasn't smiling, he took her hands, wanting her to feel what she meant to him, to let her know he was committed to making this work. Committed to them. People did the long distance thing all the time. She was the reason he'd come back here.

"Colin and I were counting on this coming through, so as soon as we finish your brothers' wine cave, our calendar is clean." He intertwined their fingers, loving how delicate and elegant hers felt in his big, calloused ones. "I want this to work, Abs. I want to see where this goes. I want to be with you."

"But you won't," she said, pulling her hand away. "You'll be in Santa Barbara and I'll be here. How is that 'seeing where this goes'?"

"This is only for eighteen months, twenty-four tops." What part of this was she not getting? "Ferris shoulders all the risk, and Colin and I get to learn from the best. It's a win-win."

"A win-win," she said so quietly he barely heard her. "What about *your* win? What about Oakwood?"

"It will still be there when we're done." Even as he said it, he knew it wasn't true, and he had a sick feeling if he walked away, he was walking away from more than a development and it would never be the same. "It's a really big opportunity, Abs."

He watched her throat bob on a hard swallow. "Then I think you should take it. It's what you want."

Tanner's heart stopped. "Why does that sound like a good-bye?"

"Because it is," Abby said, and to her credit, she didn't look away once. She held his gaze as her eyes welled and tip of her nose turned pink and she shattered his heart. "Because I guess I thought the big opportunity was here," she touched his chest—right where it hurt the most, "between us. And to me it's worth more than rotating weekends and holidays."

CHAPTER 18

Abby sat on the bottom step of her front porch, knees pulled to her chest, and wiped her eyes with her shoulder. No matter how hard she tried to pull it together, the waterworks refused to stop, which made her mad because they were ruining her aim.

With a quick sniff, she lifted her slingshot, pulled back, and let it rip. The nail sailed through the air, hitting with enough force to shatter a baseball-sized chunk out of Richard's upper right thigh.

"Stupid tears," she mumbled, picking up another nail from the jar, angry she'd missed. She'd been aiming a little higher and to the left. Dead center, actually, trying to take out St. Helena's most infamous Dick.

She pulled back and—

"Ahhh!" She stomped her foot and her slippers let out a fierce growl.

It had been the perfect shot, but a tremor left over from sobbing shook her shoulders as she went to let go and it flew high, particles of his nose shattering and littering the grass. Undiscouraged, since she had another three hundred nails and bolts in her arsenal and a line of credit at the hardware store, she blinked back the tears and grabbed two bolts.

"You could knock it all off in one whack if you want." Nora stood on Abby's walkway dressed in a pair of bright yellow coveralls and a matching sun hat, wielding a sledgehammer fit for Thor. "I saw you talking to some overclassed lady this morning, could smell her perfume all the way through my closed windows."

"Yeah, that was Richard's grandmother."

Nora harrumphed. "Figured as much. No person with any sense would invade the neighborhood at such an ungodly hour, only to start harping and wailing for all the town to hear. It's un-American. Considered citing her for being a public pain in the ass but didn't know how international law would handle a GN violation."

"She came, she saw, she took his ashes, and when she learned the money was gone, she disappeared in a flash." And in true Moretti fashion, left all of the messy stuff behind for Abby to clean up—one piece at a time.

Nora held out the sledgehammer. "Again, one good whack and it will all be over."

That's what she'd thought about one good cry, and yet here she was out of tissues and looking like Rudolph.

"Every party needs a piñata. Even a pity party," Nora added.

Suddenly, Abby wanted to take that whack, because she wanted, more than anything, for it to all be over. She wanted the anger and sadness and that dark space that filled her chest until there was no room for anything else to go away so she could breathe again without feeling like it was her last breath.

Worse, she wanted it to be Tanner on her walkway with his sledgehammer, offering to help her get rid of her past once and for all and help her pick up the broken pieces so they could start their future. Together.

Only he didn't want together, he wanted weekends and holidays.

"And then what?" she asked, looking at her neighbor. And there went the waterworks again, because one final swing and Richard would be gone and Abby would finally be free.

And Tanner would be in Santa Barbara. Off living his next big opportunity, moving on to another chapter in his life without her. Something she should be used to by now. Her parents moved on, Richard moved on, and now Tanner was moving again. And for the life of her, she couldn't figure out why she was so easy to leave behind.

"Depends on what you want," Nora said, leaning the sledgehammer against the porch rail and taking a seat next to Abby.

She wanted to be important enough to keep. Important enough so that moving on without her was not an option. She wanted Tanner to finally step up and fight for her.

"I want to leave my mark," she finally said. Not on a vineyard or a cheese shop or even on Oakwood. She wanted to leave her mark on Tanner's heart—the same way he'd left one on hers. Not the gaping hole she felt now, but the warm, wonderful feeling that happened whenever he smiled at her or just held her hand.

"Well," Nora said, picking up the sledgehammer. "You want to sit there crying about it or be bold? That house didn't come from wallowing after my first husband died. No siree, the day he died, you know what I did?"

"Buried him with a bag of dog poop?"

"No, but I should have." Nora gave a rare smile. "I went down and bought this here sledgehammer and knocked down every wall in that library, then I built a workshop and started making these little mailboxes shaped like houses and selling them around town."

"You made those?" Abby gestured to the mailbox on Nora's front lawn then spread her hand to encompass the mailboxes on nearly every house on the block. All unique, but all by the same craftsman.

"Every single one. Including the one you tore down the first day you moved in." Nora gave her a stern look. "I sold it to Mr. Withers back in fifty-eight. He was my first customer."

"It was rotted and housing a family of mice," Abby started to explain, then caught herself. It didn't matter why—she had destroyed Nora's first mark on the world. "I'm sorry, Nora."

"No matter now, I already started building you a new one."

Abby felt her eyes well up again, this time from gratitude. "Thank you."

"You might want to wait until you see the bill before you go thanking me." Nora stood, handing her the sledge. "Now, you going to be bold and make your mark? Because my suggestion is to start with one right between his legs."

Abby wiped her eyes and grabbed the hammer. The heavy steel in her hand was cold and smooth and made her feel bold. Made her want to stand up to all the crap in her life and make her mark in one swing.

Remembering how Trey had taught her to hold a bat, she choked up on the handle, pulled back, and with a little hop to get going, she took off in a sprint. Battle cry in full effect, Abby used the momentum of her body as she took aim. Aiming higher than she'd originally planned, high enough to leave her mark on every last piece of his chest so he'd know what it felt like to have it shattered.

Hands shaking, heart in her throat, Abby swung that sledgehammer with everything she had left in her. Swung with enough force to push all the way through and come out the other side.

A crash sounded and her body rebounded from the impact, but she kept going, forced herself to hold on and finish.

"Direct hit," Nora hollered, pumping her fist in the air.

Another loud crack echoed through the cul-de-sac as the hammer crashed right through the back side of the marble, shards of rock splintering and shattering in every which direction. Pelting her hands, her face, scattering across the front lawn and down to the sidewalk.

Breathing heavily, tears streaming down her face, Abby stood there watching as the massive statue teetered back and forth, slowly picking up enough momentum to crash to the grass with a giant thud.

Sweat beading on her skin, blood pounding in her ears, Abby stood with the hammer hanging limply in her hand and looked down at the hundreds and hundreds of pieces of the worst mistake of her life.

"Well, would you look at that?" Nora said, coming up beside her. "The damn thing was hollow."

"I know," Abby said, laughing at the irony. She laughed so hard she started crying, then she was so tired she sat down. Right there on the lawn, surrounded by a million pieces of her marriage.

Piece by shattered piece, Abby would have to clean up the mess, just like she had after her parents died, after Tanner went to Buffalo, after Richard left her holding the empty vows of their marriage and an even emptier bank bag. And Abby was tired.

Tired of picking up all the pieces by herself. Tired of grinning and bearing it when her life was one big gigantic mess. Tired of being too scared to be bold. Tired of feeling empty and hollow, because she didn't want to be that person anymore. She wanted to be happy.

She wanted to be with Tanner.

Abby looked at the beautiful yellow Victorian next door with its picket fence and manicured lawn, then to the mailbox sitting charmingly at the curb. And she knew what she had to do.

Wiping her face on her shirt, Abby stood and handed the sledgehammer to Nora. Then she hugged her. Nora stood there taking it with as much dignity as she could muster until the older woman finally gave in and hugged Abby back.

"Thank you," Abby said, kissing the older woman on the cheek. Then with a lightness to her step she hadn't felt since the night of the accident, she walked toward her house.

"Where you going?" Nora hollered after her.

Abby hopped up the front steps, purpose in her strides. "Shopping."

"Shopping? For what? A bulldozer?" Nora sounded horrified. "What you need is to clean up this eyesore so you can get down to that cheese shop you been hemming and hawing about. The HPC will be coming through to make the announcement in just a few hours. You've made your first mark, Abigail DeLuca, it's time you made your next."

"Which is why I've got to get a dress first." Abby stopped on the top step and turned to smile at the most unlikely of allies. "I've knocked down the walls, Nora, now it's time to build my home."

CHAPTER 19

"Where's Abby?" Babs said, nerves wearing at her normally sunny smile.

She's not coming, Tanner thought, taking a sip of scotch and setting it back on the counter.

Beer wasn't going to cut it tonight.

Nope, tonight he stood at the back of the Pungent Barrel, watching Nora and the rest of the Historical Preservation Committee examine every inch of the room, pointing out the ingenuity behind the wine bottle chandeliers, admiring every little historical detail Abby had maintained, knowing by the way their eyes kept lighting up that they'd won. Yet all he could think about was the enormous knot in his chest.

It would almost be easier to give up breathing than face another minute there, in a place where every inch reminded him of what he'd lost. He knew she'd been by today—the flowers and last-minute decor had magically appeared when he'd taken a short break for lunch. But he hadn't seen her. And not wanting to take anything away from her on this special night, he had given her the space she obviously desired.

"She's not here," Tanner said, taking another sip, letting it burn down his throat. "Maybe give her a call."

"That's a good idea," Babs said, wringing her hands. "The committee has their decision, and they have a representative at each of the finalists' homes. Waiting. Nora asked me ten minutes ago where Abby was, said they need the designer present to announce the winner. Oh, look, Ferris is here."

Babs pointed to her son standing near Gus, who was stoically listening to every word Ferris said, which were likely about himself. If he was trying to win any points with Babs, it was working. The woman sighed and clasped her heart. Tanner rolled his eyes.

"I'll go call her," Babs said. "Tonight is going to be perfect. In fact, thanks to you and Abby, everything is perfect just like I dreamed. Thank you." With a kiss to his cheek—which felt damn good, if he were being honest—Babs disappeared into the crowd.

And it was a crowd. Most of the town had turned out. Partly to see the new cheese shop, but mainly to see if the rumors were true that Abigail DeLuca had really managed to raise the *Titanic*. The surprise was on them that she hadn't raised it—she had utterly transformed it.

Just like she'd transformed him. Only she wasn't here to witness either miracle.

Someone entered the shop and Tanner's gaze flew to the door. He held his breath as a beautiful brunette in a long black gown entered—a beautiful brunette who wasn't Abby.

"Fuck me," he mumbled, taking another sip.

"If we aren't getting any, then you sure as hell aren't," Marc said, walking up behind him, Nate and Trey in tow.

"Great." Just great, he thought as they sidled up to the bar, pressing in around him like one big DeLuca sandwich with a smear of pissed-off Italian. "After weeks of silence, you guys decide to start talking to me now?"

"Against our better judgment, yes," Nate said, flagging down the waiter and gesturing for another round of scotch.

"*I* want to take you outside and kick the shit out of you for making my sister cry, but Frankie will have my balls," Nate said, sending him a look that spoke volumes.

"She already has you by the balls," Trey laughed.

"Abby was crying?" Tanner asked, then shut up because he already knew. Tears had been right there in her eyes, ready to spill over the second she slammed the door in his face. He'd sat outside on her stoop, waiting to see if she'd change her mind and invite him back in, waiting with his ear pressed to the door, listening to make sure she was okay, telling himself at the first hint of a sniffle he'd break down the damn door. But he'd heard nothing.

Around four in the morning he was finished being that ten-year-old kid, sitting on the front porch waiting for his mom to come home and not knowing why she didn't. So he dragged his sorry ass home, where he lay in bed staring at the ceiling until morning trying to figure out what he'd done wrong.

And he'd come up short.

Sure, the game plan had changed, but he'd been honest from the start about working with Ferris, about how important this could be for Tanner Construction. It wasn't his fault Ferris decided to move the project to Santa Barbara. Or that she didn't see enough in him to think they could last through the distance.

Yet here he was, sitting on a barstool, waiting for her to come and tell him what he did wrong.

"Forget kicking his ass," Marc said with a laugh, and Tanner wanted to ask him what was so funny. "He looks even worse than anything we could ever inflict. Jesus, you look worse than Nate did when Frankie dropped on him they were having twins."

"You're having twins?" Tanner asked, surprised when he found himself wondering what that would feel like, knowing Abby was carrying his baby. Not that *that* was even a possibility now. "Congratulations."

"I'll relay your message to Mittens, since he's having twins," Nate said, referring to his wife's pet alpaca. "Seems that horse corral over off Silverado Trail added a few alpacas to the mix. Mittens made a run for it and spent two days in paradise before we found him. Frankie's already bought a box of cigars. So I guess this round's on me."

Nate dropped a bill on the countertop when the waiter delivered their drinks. Silently, they all toasted and took a sip.

Marc set his glass on the counter, then his forearms, and leaned in. "You want to tell me why my sister spent her day using that statue for target practice and why you look like you got caught in the crossfire?"

"She shot up Richard?"

"Or blew him up," Trey said with a laugh. "Took Rodney and me over two hours to find all of his parts."

"What does that even mean?" Tanner asked, resting his forehead on his hands.

"What do you want it to mean?" Nate asked quietly.

"Hell, I don't know," he admitted, not sure he even wanted to get into this with the three people who had been against him and Abby from the start. But they had more experience with women than anyone else he knew, most particularly Abby.

And yeah, he was that desperate.

"Everything was going fine, better than fine, perfect, then I told her about Ferris offering us the job and that was it. She was done. Didn't want to talk about how to make it work, just heard commute and out I went. But I didn't know she was crying." He looked up so the guys could see the truth in his eyes. "If I had heard her crying I never would have left."

The brothers exchanged a knowing look, then the bastards had the nerve to smile. "You know what?" Tanner stood. "Forget it."

"Slow down," Marc said, resting a hand on Tanner's shoulder. "I think I know what happened."

"Yeah?"

"Yeah, so take a seat." Tanner did. "In any part of your speech about the job—you guys, making the distance work—did you ever tell her you loved her?"

"No," Tanner said quickly, then stopped because his stomach started acting up, getting hot and pissed off—and this was why he never drank anything except beer. "We've only been seeing each other for a few weeks. Plus, she just got out of a divorce. The last thing she needs is some guy trying to push himself into her life."

And that was why he'd thought taking the job in Santa Barbara and seeing Abby on the weekends would work. Hell, it sounded like the perfect idea. They could explore where this was going and not rush into something that could hurt either one of them. But the more Tanner thought about it, the more he realized *he* was the one who had wanted distance, because he was afraid if he went all-in with Abby and lost her again, he wouldn't recover.

And he'd lost her anyway.

Marc grinned and Tanner wanted to punch him. "So is that a no you don't love her or no you didn't tell her?"

"What the hell difference does it make?" But suddenly it made all the difference in the world, because he did love her. Loved her with everything he was. Loved her more than Santa Barbara, more than Oakwood, more than his damn Super Bowl ring.

Holy shit. Abby was his Super Bowl. He'd passed and fumbled so many times with her he wasn't even sure what he was doing anymore. Except he didn't want to play in any game unless she was on his team. And he wanted to be on her team so badly it hurt to breathe.

"Yeah, that's what I thought," Marc said, picking up his scotch and draining it in one swallow.

"Go in the men's room and look yourself in the mirror and say, 'I love you, Abby, and I screwed up. Tell me how to fix it.' Then practice it a good hundred times before you see her," Trey said, clapping him on the back.

"You love Abby?"

Tanner looked up to find Colin on the other side of the bar. Face serious, everything they had shared over the past twenty years right there between them. And Tanner knew the next few moments could cost him the best friend he'd ever had.

Tanner nodded. "With everything I am, Col." And damn that felt good to say.

"I think I already knew that." A long, tense silence followed, filling the space. Colin looked over at Ferris then back to Tanner. "What about Santa Barbara?"

That was the question Tanner had been struggling with ever since Colin had brought it up earlier that week. And what Tanner kept coming back to was that Santa Barbara, while an opportunity of a lifetime, wasn't his opportunity.

Abby was his opportunity of a lifetime. An opportunity he had walked away from twice because figuring out how to mesh their worlds had seemed too hard. An opportunity he had one last shot at, and there was no way he was walking away this time.

"I'm not going," Tanner said.

"But we've worked for a year solid on this," Colin said. He didn't sound angry or betrayed, just hurt. Confused.

"*You* have worked toward this, Col. This is your thing, has been from the beginning, and I think you should go. I think we should set up a SoCal office, or if you want to start your own company, I would even be the first one to step up and invest." Tanner looked his friend in the eye, wanting him to know he had absolute faith in his abilities and talent. "Either way, you've got this, Col. You are more than ready and I'm always in your corner."

"But I don't get it. What will you do here you can't accomplish down there?" Colin asked, sounding lost, and Tanner wondered if that's what he'd looked like only moments ago.

"Going after what makes me happy. And that is Abby."

"'I love you, Abby, and I screwed up. Tell me how to fix it,'" Trey repeated from over his shoulder.

Tanner shot him a look because he got it. "Then after I finish up these assholes' cave, I'm going to start laying down the plans for Oakwood."

Colin started. "You're still going to build out Oakwood? On your own?"

"Yeah," Tanner said, thinking about Abby's designs. "I have a few ideas and the perfect designer in mind. I figure it will take about eighteen months to line up the permits, the investors, get all of the blueprints drawn up so that when you get back from your Super Bowl in Santa Barbara you can just roll in and we can start blowing shit up. That is, if you're still interested."

"Still interested?" Colin laughed and all of the tension between them drained away. "I've been waiting my whole career to build that land with you."

Tanner held out his hand and Colin took it, only he pulled him in for a bro hug. And for the first time since Ferris had approached them with an offer a year ago, Tanner felt like he'd made the right decision. And that he finally had his partner back.

"If you two are done hugging it out," Trey said, "it looks like they're about to announce the winner, so that gives you about thirty seconds to find a mirror, bro, because the designer just got here. And if you break her heart, I will kill you with my bare hands."

Tanner quickly scanned the room, his heart rolling over when he got to the big arch he'd helped Abby measure, because there she was. Abigail DeLuca. Standing at the head of the room, dressed in a slinky dress that hugged every single one of her luscious curves, complete with thigh-high slit.

And Tanner knew, without a doubt, this was his woman.

His future.

His everything.

Because not only was she the most important thing in his world—she was wearing Niners red.

"The Historical Preservation Council of St. Helena is proud to say the Jackson Bottlery is not only architectural preservation at its highest level, but quite possibly the most stunning and innovative residence we have seen in years. So it is with great honor I announce this year's Memory Lane Manor of the Year Award recipient, the Pungent Barrel, a bottlery turned cheese and wine destination that is sure to stun visitors and inspire restoration in generations to come."

Nora handed the gold nameplate to Babs, but Abby didn't miss the way her neighbor looked at her through the entire speech.

"It's beautiful," Babs said into the mic, running a weathered hand along the golden seal that would hang above the entryway, announcing to all who entered that this was an establishment of history and elegance. "Thank you to the council for this great honor, and to my late husband, Leroy, for being romantic enough to buy a whimsical old lady a piece of land because she heard a story that touched her heart."

Babs went on to list every person she'd ever met and every contractor who had ever heard of the project, but Abby wasn't listening. She was too busy scanning the crowd for the one person she wanted to see. The only person she wanted to share this moment with.

ChiChi and Lexi stood in the front row, wiggling their fingers in a wave. Gus was beaming with pride. She saw her brothers, their wives, her friends, her neighbors, but she couldn't see Jack.

She squinted harder, convincing herself she'd just missed him somehow in the swell of people, but then Babs was done and people were clapping, and Nora gave Abby a little shove forward and suddenly she was in front of the mic.

"Your turn," Nora whispered.

The room went silent. The mic buzzed with feedback. And Abby looked out at the three hundred sets of eyes on her and felt a wave of panic wash over her because she couldn't find the warm, gentle blue ones she loved in the crowd.

"Thank you for coming," she said, and despite the intense emotions swirling inside of her, she offered up a genuine smile. She'd grown up in this town, had known most of these people her entire life. And they were here to celebrate something she had been an important part of. "First, I need to thank Babette Hampton for falling in love with this beautiful piece of our town's history, then entrusting its care to me. She gave me a chance when—"

Abby stopped. Because there, in the back, near the bathroom door stood Jack Tanner, and everything she had rehearsed, the hours of practicing what she'd say if she won, died on her tongue. And all she could do was stare and watch him stare right back. And what she saw there had her chest aching.

He looked as nervous and unsure as she felt. Then his lips quirked up in a small smile and she could have sworn he mouthed, *Nice dress.*

"Thank you," she said, then realized she was still talking to the crowd. "Thank you everyone."

She stepped back from the mic because even though this moment was important, there was something more important she had to do.

"What are you doing?" Nora asked.

"Knocking down the last wall," she said over her shoulder as she threaded her way through the crowd.

She passed lots of smiling faces but for the life of her couldn't remember a one. She was too focused on Tanner, who was making his way toward her. They met in the middle of the room, next to the bar, and both of them spoke simultaneously.

"Congratulations, you deserve it."

"I couldn't find you."

She laughed and he gestured for her to go first.

"I couldn't have done any of this without you," she said softly, and now that she was closer she could see what he was wearing, and too-damn-handsome-for-his-own-good was putting it mildly. The man was a god. In his contractor getup, he was delicious. That body wrapped in a sophisticated dark suit was devastating.

"You look stunning." He swallowed—hard. "Better than stunning. Actually, you take my breath away," he said, looking her in the eyes. Which was fine with her because the deeper she fell into those baby blues, the more relaxed she became. The more she believed she was doing the right thing.

"You look beyond handsome," she said, and the tips of his ears went pink.

"Congratulations." He wiped his hand across his forehead. "I already said that, didn't I?"

Abby had never seen him so distraught. He was beyond nervous, like he was about to pass out.

"Abby, I know I screwed up, and I want to fix this."

"Wait." She placed a hand on his arm, because she didn't want to talk about last night. Not yet. "Before we talk about that, I need to ask you about something important. But first I need a quarter."

He didn't ask, didn't even blink at the odd request. Just fished through his pocket, mumbled something about never listening to Trey again, and handed her two dimes and a nickel. "Does this work?"

"Perfect." She took the nickel and then leaned over the bar to grab an empty glass. She took the nickel by its edges, closed one eye, and took the first swing.

Ping.

Clink.

"Why did you invest in Richard's vineyard?" she asked, because unless she could make sense of why he kept running, she'd never get him to stand still. "You hated him."

Tanner took a big breath and sat down sideways on the chair so he was facing her. "I didn't invest in a vineyard, Abby. I hate wine almost as much as I hated Richard." He shrugged, making no apology. "I invested in you and your dream. I decided if I couldn't be that guy standing next to you, maybe I could be the one who helped you find your happiness."

"Oh, Tanner." Her chest tightened painfully. For the both of them. "If you wanted to be—"

Ping.

Clink.

"My turn. Why did you marry Richard?"

God, what a question, with a humiliating answer. "Because he was supposed to be the sure thing."

"Bullshit."

"Because you broke my heart, Jack," she said with no hesitation, although her breath caught on his name. Just a little tremor of emotion, but enough to have him scooting closer. "You held me like I mattered and we talked about things I had never shared with another soul. And I fell in love with you, only this time it wasn't some high school girl's love, it was real. Then you pulled on your pants, kissed my cheek, told me you were going to Buffalo, and left."

And two months later she had met Richard. He'd been handsome and attentive and everything she'd needed to forget Tanner. Only she never forgot him. And now she was old enough to understand she never would.

"Abs, I didn't leave *you*. That's how the draft works." He moved even closer, their knees fighting to share the same space, craving the contact. "Knowing you were in California and I was going to be moving away killed me." He looked so earnest. "And I knew you still had a year left of school, so I ran before it got complicated. I ran before you could run."

She searched his eyes. "I gave up running the second you kissed me on your lounger. I realized then that when I'm with you, I don't feel lonely or smothered. I just feel . . . like everything is how it should be." She held out the nickel and pressed it into his hand. "So ask me to come with you."

She could tell he was surprised by her statement, surprised she wasn't asking him to give up Santa Barbara. Which she never would, because if that was part of his journey, she wanted him to follow it. All she hoped was that he loved her enough to want to share that part of his life with her, hoped he wanted her to be a real part of his life.

Tanner quietly gazed at her with those eyes that could look right through her as his hand closed around the nickel, and what she saw in his expression made her chest swell. Without looking away, he held the nickel over the tumbler and dropped it straight in with a *clink* that was final, so resolute it was as though the entire room heard it.

"I'll do you one better." Tanner reached out and took her hand, studying how perfectly hers fit into his. At least that's what she was doing. Then he looked her dead in the eye, his expression weary and hopeful and so full of love it made her breath catch. "I'm starting construction on this incredible hunting lodge that has a wraparound porch and a gorgeous view, but without you it will never be a home. Marry me, Abs, so I can finally come home."

"What about Santa Barbara?" she asked. "I thought that was your dream."

"You're my dream," he whispered, pulling her close. "I love you."

"I love you too, Jack Tanner," Abby said, her eyes filling, but she didn't care. "I love the way you hold me, the way you listen, the way you look at me when you want the last sip of beer but let me have it anyway. Every time you kiss me I fall more and more in love with you."

With a smile that spoke right to her heart, Tanner kissed her, soft and sweet, and he was right, it tasted like home.

"Every. Time," he whispered, and when he pulled back, Abby was sitting on his lap, her arms tight around his neck.

"Every time," she agreed.

"So, is that a yes?"

"Jack, it's been a yes from the moment we met."

READ ON FOR A SNEAK PEEK OF MARINA ADAIR'S NEXT HEARTWARMING ROMANCE

NEED YOU FOR KEEPS

Available 2015 on Amazon

Someone will come for me," Shay Michaels said, eyeballing her newest client—who looked as convinced by her statement as Shay felt. Maybe it was that she'd said the exact same thing over an hour ago, or that she'd been saying the same thing her entire life without any success.

But this time Shay had faith someone would come. Call it eternal optimism or romantic rebellion—one of these days karma would stop flipping her the bird and pay it forward.

And that day was today.

Please say that day is today, she thought, looking down at the client in question.

Domino sat stoically, tail wrapped around his massive feet, gazing up at her with his wet, brown doggie eyes that were so big they could persuade anyone, even the most heartless, to do something colossally stupid. Like crawl into a dog kennel that locked from the outside.

To be fair, when Shay was tired she made questionable decisions. And today she was exhausted.

As the resident saint at St. Paws Pet Rescue, not to mention top stylist to the town's most elite and furriest residents, she had been on her feet since the crack of dawn, scrubbing down all of her canine kids in preparation for St. Paws's monthly adoption day, and Domino had thrown a wrench into her schedule. So when he started whimpering as she steered him toward the kennel, which meant scooting all two hundred pounds of dog by his spotted Great Dane tush across the floor, she decided to climb in and show him that kennels weren't scary—in fact, with the right kennel mate, they could be fun.

Shay retracted *that* statement the minute the door slammed shut and locked behind her.

"You know, with your height and retrieval skills, you could grab me the keys off the counter over there," she said, pointing to the neon-green lanyard that was two inches out of reach.

Two inches!

"Woof." Tail wagging, tongue lolling, Domino meandered over to the table, right past the keys, and stuck his head in a fifty-pound bag of kibble.

"That's puppy chow. It will make your butt big, and no one wants to adopt a dog with a big butt," Shay warned, then remembered the box of chocolate mini doughnuts she'd inhaled for lunch and made a mental note to run at least five miles tomorrow morning.

Domino, however, seemed unconcerned about his figure and stuck his head in until it disappeared in the bag. At the sound of the crinkling paper all of the dogs ran to the front of their kennels, noses pressed through the bars, straining for a handout. When none came, they started barking—all dozen of them. Which did nothing for the headache she felt coming on.

Shay was just tired enough that she actually could sleep in a dog kennel, and since she was the only stylist on the schedule today, this could easily become an all-nighter. Luckily her superpower was the ability to fall asleep anytime, anywhere, no matter what—something she'd learned by her third foster home.

When the dogs' barks reached DEFCON 1, so did her headache. She closed her eyes and rested her forehead against her bent knees, needing a moment.

"If you ask me, small butts are overrated," a low and sexy voice said.

Her eyes snapped open just as a pair of rugged, manly steel-toed boots stopped at the edge of the kennel door. Shay lifted her head and looked up, way up, and—*gulp*—met the eyes of Jonah Baudouin.

He flashed her that department-issued smile and something low in her belly tightened. She'd like to blame it on a natural reaction to the weapon holstered at his hip or quite possibly the badge he carried, but she had a sinking feeling it had more to do with the way he filled out that uniform.

Six foot two of hard muscle on a body that was built to protect and serve, he was the perfect catch if one was into brooding hero types. But Shay didn't do brooding or heroes, and she most certainly did not do cops.

Ones who made her tingle or otherwise.

Not that it mattered. The only reactions she seemed to inspire within him were irritation or amusement. Today he was packing both. He was also sipping on a giant-sized coffee cup that made her mouth water.

"Sheriff," she said casually through the bars. This wasn't her first time in the pokey.

"Deputy," he corrected. "Still got a month before the election."

"If you're here soliciting for support, I have to be honest and say I'm voting for the other guy." It was clearly a lie. Deputy "Do-Nothing" Bryant could bring a snow machine into hell and still not win. He was lazy and shady, and only had a badge because his grandpa was the current sheriff. "But since you're here, could you hand me the keys off the grooming station behind you?"

"I'm investigating a stolen property claim," he said, not even glancing toward the keys. "Mr. Barnwell reported his Dalmatian missing about three hours ago." Jonah was cool and casual, not a feather ruffled in his perfectly pressed uniform. And that was a bad sign.

"How awful." Shay placed a horrified hand to her chest.

"Yeah, awful," he agreed mildly. "Have you seen him today?"

"Mr. Barnwell's Dalmatian?" She shook her head, hoping she looked more baffled than guilty. "Nope."

"You wouldn't lie to an officer of the law, would you?"

She smiled. "Not today."

"Huh." He took a leisurely sip of his coffee, which she'd bet the keys to the place was a plain old-fashioned drip—no frills. "That's odd, because a Caucasian female, wavy light brown hair, about five four and a buck twenty was seen shoving Domino into the back of a late nineties Honda Civic."

Domino, the *Great Dane*, lifted his head out from the kibble bag and cocked it at the sound of his name. Then he eyed Jonah, and Shay could almost see the dog vibrating with indecision.

Kibble or doggie high five to the crotch? So many choices.

Thank God the kibble won out.

"Lots of people drive Civics," Shay challenged, tucking a light brown wave of hair behind her ear.

"Yeah, well, only one five-foot-four Civic owner is on record claiming Mr. Barnwell to be"—eyes locked on hers, Jonah set the coffee right next to the keys and pulled a little official-looking notepad from his front shirt pocket and flipped to the middle—"cruel, criminal, and a bad neighbor with questionable hygiene."

She'd called him a lot more in private. "Sounds like Mr. Barnwell really should brush his teeth twice a day if he intends on making a habit out of yelling in his neighbors' faces."

"The getaway car had a St. Paws Animal Rescue sticker on the door—"

"*Getaway car?* Is that official cop jargon?"

"—And the shover in question was reported to be wearing a pair of faded jeans and an orange T-shirt that read 'I brake for squirrels.'"

He lifted his gaze and zeroed in on the squirrel on her orange shirt.

Shay crossed her arms over the cute squirrel and shrugged. "Sorry, Deputy, can't help you."

"Jesus, Shay," he said, sounding all put out, like he was the one behind bars. "I'm trying to help you here. My bet is that dog is worth a few grand, which means if you have him in your possession it's a felony. But if you hand Domino over, we will call it a day."

Either Domino had finished all fifty pounds of kibble in record time or hearing his name again was too tempting, but he lifted his head and barked. Twice. Loudly. Then bounded across the floor at NASCAR speed, skidding to a stop at Jonah's feet, his nose going straight to the crotch for a big, welcoming sniff.

"You want to change your statement?" he asked. "Or do I need to get out the cuffs and haul you in?"

Maybe she was more exhausted than she thought. Or maybe she'd just gone too long without a bedmate who didn't shed, but her entire body perked up at the thought of Deputy Serious and his seriously hot cuffs. Which was annoying because uptight, by-the-book men were not her type.

Then again, it had been so long she wasn't sure she even had a type.

An awkward silence hung between them while they glared at each other, and Domino stared between them, panting.

Breaking eye contact with Jonah, because he was better at it than her, damn it, Shay bent over to pet Domino's head through the bars.

Domino stopped, dropped, and rolled to assume the belly rub position. She obliged the best she could, her heart going heavy when his tail slapped the floor with excitement and he looked up at her adoringly.

Domino was a lover. He needed attention, affection, love—a family who wanted him, not one obligated to feed and house him.

The perfect family was out there—she just hadn't found it yet.

Determined, Shay stood to face down one very pissed deputy. Apparently hauling her butt in was not how he'd envisioned his afternoon going. Or more likely, it was all of the paperwork she'd just added to his plate.

"For the record, I didn't lie. Domino is a Great Dane, not a Dalmatian. A Great Dane, Jonah, who weighs two hundred pounds." She grabbed the bars and pressed her forehead against the cool metal. "Have you seen the size of the crate they have for him? It's built for a Chihuahua. He can't even stand up and he is locked in there all day long. Can you even imagine?"

"Shay," he sighed, looking up at the ceiling as though seeking divine intervention. She got that a lot.

"It's cruel and it's terrible and no one will help me," she whispered. Jonah stepped forward until she could smell the heat on his skin, and that normal cool and distant expression he wore like Kevlar softened, and so did Shay's resolve.

"Hard to do when you go breaking into other people's property and steal their pets."

"I called your office three times last week when the temperatures hit surface of the sun and I had to give him water through the bars." She didn't mention she'd spent most of yesterday sitting by his crate, rubbing his head, and that she'd only decided to take him when Mr. Barnwell threw out the pamphlet she'd put on his doorstep about crate cruelty.

But a felony? This situation was so beyond what she could handle. Mr. Barnwell wasn't mean, at least she didn't think so, he was just misinformed—and stubborn.

She looked up at one of the town's finest and admitted—silently, to herself—that she needed help. She needed his help.

And didn't that just piss her off.

"If you promise to do something so he isn't locked back in that crate ever again, then I promise to give him back."

"You're making a list of demands?" He laughed, and even though it was aimed at her, she had to admit he had a great laugh. "I have a gun and cuffs and you're locked in a cage."

And why did that image have her hormones short-circuiting? No wonder all the women in town pawed over him—the uniform and high-octane testosterone radiating from his every pore were a lethal combination.

"But do you have enough manpower to watch him twenty-four/seven? To make sure he doesn't 'run away' again?" she said.

He braced his hands overhead on the top of the kennel's door, his mighty fine arms bulging tight against the fabric of his shirt as his frame towered over her. He looked at her long and hard, then at the dog who was staring up at him like he would follow Jonah to the ends of the earth. Which just meant Domino thought Jonah had a stash of bacon stuffed in his pocket.

She knew the moment he gave in. His shoulders relaxed and those intense blue eyes narrowed.

"Fine," he sighed. "I'll talk to Mr. Barnwell, but I can't promise you anything."

"Thank you, thank you, thank you." With a smile, Shay stuck her arm through the bars to make their discussion official with a shake. "You can take Domino then."

When Jonah's big, rough hand engulfed hers, a zing of something hot raced up her arms and spread out to every happy spot she owned, and a few she'd thought she'd lost. And Shay had no business getting zings or tingles for any man, let alone this one.

Nope, Jonah Baudouin was stable, a straight shooter and, sexy or not, the soon-to-be sheriff—in a place she'd started to think of as more than a temporary stopover.

This wasn't their first tangle over the law, and she was pretty sure, based on her history, it wouldn't be their last. So finding out if he used those cuffs for business or pleasure wasn't in her best interest.

She shook once and waited for him to release her hand. When he just stared at her, she snatched it back. "And I'll try to stay out of your hair, but I can't promise anything."

His mouth twitched. "You do that." He clipped a leash on Domino and tipped his hat. "Have a good day, Shay."

"Wait," she hollered after him. "What about letting me out?"

"Call the other guy. You know, the one you're voting for."

ACKNOWLEDGMENTS

Thanks to my editors, Maria Gomez and Lindsay Guzzardo, and the rest of the Author Team at Montlake, for all of the amazing work and support throughout this series. And to my agent, Jill Marsal, for being my cheerleader and biggest critic, always pushing me to make each book as good as it can be.

As always, a special thanks to my family for living with my craziness when I am under deadline.

ABOUT THE AUTHOR

PHOTO BY TOSH TANAKA

Marina Adair is a #1 national bestselling author of romance novels. Along with the St. Helena Vineyard series, she is also the author of *Sugar's Twice as Sweet*, part of the Sugar, Georgia series. She lives with her husband, daughter, and two neurotic cats in Northern California.